Dead Man's Chest

Books by Kerry Greenwood

The Phryne Fisher Series
Cocaine Blues
Flying Too High
Murder on the Ballarat Train
Death at Victoria Dock
The Green Mill Murder
Blood and Circuses
Ruddy Gore
Urn Burial
Raisins and Almonds
Death Before Wicket
Away With the Fairies
Murder in Montparnasse
The Castlemaine Murders
Queen of the Flowers
Death by Water
Murder in the Dark
Murder on a Midsummer Night
Dead Man's Chest

The Corinna Chapman Series
Earthly Delights
Heavenly Pleasures
Devil's Food
Trick or Treat
Forbidden Fruit

Short Story Anthology
A Question of Death:
An Illustrated Phryne Fisher Anthology

Dead Man's Chest

A Phryne Fisher Mystery

Kerry Greenwood

Poisoned Pen Press

Poisoned
Pen
Press

Copyright © 2010 by Kerry Greenwood

First U.S. Edition 2010

10 9 8 7 6 5 4 3 2 1

Library of Congress Catalog Card Number: 2010923839

ISBN: 9781590587973 Hardcover
        9781590587997 Trade Paperback

Poisoned Pen Press
6962 E. First Ave., Ste. 103
Scottsdale, AZ 85251
www.poisonedpenpress.com
info@poisonedpenpress.com

Printed in the United States of America

Dedicated to that strangely inspiring person Tom Lane.

With thanks to my fearless researchers Jean Greenwood, David Greagg Michael Warby; Jenny Pausacker, Ika Willis, Tamzin, and Meredith Phillips.

And in loving memory of Dennis Pryor, a perfect scholar.

Fifteen men on a dead man's chest
Yo-ho-ho and a bottle of rum!
Drink and the devil had done for the rest
Yo-ho-ho and a bottle of rum!

—Robert Louis Stevenson
Treasure Island

Chapter One

When I was at home I was in a better place;
but travellers must be content.

William Shakespeare
As You Like It

Dot opened her eyes. Only because the Hispano-Suiza had, at last, stopped. It was a four-hour journey from Melbourne to Queenscliff, the holiday destination of the Hon. Miss Fisher, her maid and companion Dot, her two adoptive daughters Jane and Ruth, and their dog Molly. Miss Fisher wanted to make it a three-hour journey and she drove like a demon. Only Phryne, Molly and Jane had really enjoyed the flashing panorama of fields, trees, cows, little towns, fist-waving motorists and shouting traffic policemen—Phryne because she loved speed and Jane because she was calculating how fast the car was going by counting seconds between milestones. She had been given a wristwatch for Christmas. Sometimes the car's speed had exceeded eighty miles an hour. Jane was impressed. Ruth, who wanted to be a cook if she survived this trek, was feeling sick. She stared fixedly at the horizon and tried not to think of food. Dot had given up on courage and had just closed her eyes, crossed her maidenly breast and commended her soul to God. Molly had hung her head out the window and let the wind blow her ears inside out.

Dot saw that the car had arrived in the main street of a respectable little town. They were at the bottom of a steep hill. In the road three well-dressed youths were tormenting a dungaree-clad boy carrying a basket of fish for which some cook was undoubtedly waiting. Impatiently.

Phryne was getting out of the car. Dot closed her eyes. Miss Fisher was about to happen to someone again. She hoped that Phryne wouldn't get blood on her shoes. That glacé kid was a beast to clean. Ruth took a deep breath of relief as her sickness subsided and grabbed Molly. Jane wondered whether there would be any interesting injuries.

Phryne walked up to the group. Nice flannels, white shirts, blazers of a well-known and expensive public school. They had surrounded the young man and were pushing him from side to side, hoping that he would drop the basket so they could kick the fish all over the road and get the poor boy into trouble. Oafs, thought Phryne, disgusted. I just don't seem to be able to get away from oafs.

'Play time's over, chaps,' she said in a clear, authoritative voice. 'It's tea time, and Nanny's getting cross.'

'Who're you?' grunted an oaf with short blond hair, giving the fisherboy another shove.

'Phryne Fisher. Who are you?'

The curly-headed oaf was struck with an inconvenient memory when he heard that tone. He suddenly recalled a Maori storyteller from his childhood. One of their heroes had addressed an enemy: 'What name shall I put on the cup I shall make from your skull?' It had always made him shudder. He shuddered now, and began to back away.

'Kiwi, what's the matter with you?' snarled the blond.

'I never liked you, Fraser,' said Kiwi. 'Come on, Jolyon. This is a beastly sort of game.'

'Moral courage,' observed Phryne. 'How proud your school will be when I tell them how their alumni spend their holidays. Surfing? Good game of tennis? Torturing the peasantry?'

Fraser glared and retained his grip on the fisherboy's arm, twisting it behind his back. He winced but still did not speak.

'Let him go now,' said Phryne. 'Fun's over.'

'Oh, Lord,' whispered Jolyon, stout and red-faced. 'I know her.'

'Why, who is she then?' Fraser bared his teeth.

'She's the Hon. Miss Fisher,' muttered the boy. 'Like she said. My mother's been angling for an invitation to one of her parties. She's rich. And famous.'

'So? Your mater's a climber.'

'Kiwi's right,' said Jolyon with considerable dignity. 'I never liked you either. How about a game of billiards, Kiwi?'

'Let that boy go right now,' said Phryne, who had arrived somehow behind Fraser without him noticing that she had moved. 'Or you will be really, really sorry.'

He hesitated. Phryne, who was preparing to kick his feet out from under him and dance on his chest in her heavy driving shoes, observed the movement and caught his arm, putting him in the identical arm-lock but with a lot more skill.

'Not so fast. Those fish will have spoiled. Dig into those pockets, fellows, how much have you got?'

Such was her suasion that they assembled seven shillings and eight pence halfpenny and handed them over to Dot, who had left the car and was standing by to assist in any way, from yelling for the police to belting the nearest head with the tyre lever she held in her hand. She made Jolyon feel even worse. She was a plain young woman with a bun and a firmly fixed hat with orange geraniums in it. She looked so respectable!

Phryne released Fraser, shoving him away, and put a hand on the fisherboy's shoulder.

'Just a moment. We'll give you a lift to avoid any little recurrence of trouble. And boys, I'm going to be here for weeks, and if I see any of you so much as look sideways at an innocent man, woman, child or dog, expect retribution to set in with unusual accuracy and force. You hear me?'

They nodded, hangdog, beaten. Phryne took the victim by the shoulder and marched him to the car. Molly, excited by his delightful aroma of fish, licked his face. Ruth moved over to accommodate him. The big car moved off. Molly paused to bark scornfully at the three schoolboys standing amazed in the middle of the street.

The fisherboy, who was fairly sure that he was hallucinating, clutched his basket.

'I have to go to Mercer Street,' said the driver, an angel from heaven who had, doubtless for reasons of camouflage, appeared as a very well-dressed young woman. 'Turn left?'

'That would be right,' he said, finding his voice. All his aches suddenly made themselves felt. 'T'ank you, t'ank you, Missus! I thought I was gone and done for, so I did.'

'West of Ireland,' she commented. 'Gaeltacht?'

'Galway.' He was beyond amazement. Angels knew most things and, of course, they did go everywhere. 'Here's your house, Missus.' He pointed to a tall building a good height above the sea, unlit and shuttered.

'Thanks. If you have any more trouble with those louts, you come and tell me. What's your name?'

'Michael, Missus Fisher. Michael Callaghan. T'anks,' he repeated. As soon as the door was opened, he took his basket and alighted. He clawed off his flat cap and bowed. Phryne smiled at him. He was a wiry, red-headed boy with creamy Celtic skin much weathered at the wrists and neck. He gave her another clumsy bow and vanished, running, down the hill.

'Well,' said Phryne, 'that was stimulating. Is this the right house? It is. I have the key and the owner's note. No one appears to be at home,' she added, as the doorbell pealed in an empty space. 'Odd. What did Mr. Thomas say, Dot?'

Dot unfolded the note. 'He says that his married couple will look after the divine Miss Fisher…I'll leave out a bit…their name is Johnson and they seem very reliable.'

Phryne got the door open at last. She stepped into the hall.

'I think he was mistaken about that,' she commented.

The house was of a pleasant, if familiar, design. Two storeys: a long hallway into the main rooms, kitchen and bathroom at the back, up the stairs to bedrooms. The floor was unswept. Leaves and sand had blown in under the door. Ruth, who read a lot of Gothic romances, released Molly with shaking hands.

Molly ran barking down the hallway and into the kitchen, a place she could always find.

'Dot, keep the girls here while I go and see if there is any reason to worry,' said Phryne in a low voice. Dot nodded and herded the two young women into a search of the parlour and the withdrawing room.

Phryne, who sometimes hated the way her mind worked, walked down the unlit hall into the world beyond the green baize door, dreading what she might find. Corpses, perhaps? There was no smell except for the sea and an overlay of dust. Molly was barking hysterically—but that's dogs for you, she thought. Their solution to any problem was to give it a good barking.

The house was dusty, unloved and uncleaned, but not for very long. No trailing cobwebs caressed her face as she opened the door into the kitchen, the butler's pantry, the scullery. The house was making the usual creaks and groans of an old house but they were exaggerated by the still air. Phryne wished she had her little gun in her hand, though any peril must be long gone by now. She had left the gun in the car.

She was relieved to find nothing more frightful than an open back door. Beyond, the kitchen garden looked dry but not desiccated. A strong scent of herbs came to her. That mint bed could do with watering. Now, what had happened here?

The kitchen table was bare. The dishes from the last meal served here had been washed up and put away. The floor was damp because the ice in the ice chest had melted because the door had been left open. There was no betraying butter by which she could estimate anything by observing the depth to which the parsley had sunk. The sink was dry. The cupboards were void of anything, even salt, even tea. The kitchen had been looted. Cheap cutlery in the drawer, but the owner would not leave silver in a holiday house. There were plates, cups and glasses, and there was table linen in the linen press. The butler's cupboard, however, was empty of even a sniff of cooking sherry.

Molly came in from the garden grinning and panting. She had not found anything alarming.

Off the kitchen were the servants' quarters. These usually comprised a bedroom, a bathroom and a sitting room. They were quite empty except for a stripped bed, a wicker armchair which was unravelling quietly in the dusty sunlight, and some litter on the floor: a few crumpled papers, a bathing shoe, a scatter of coins and a broken shoelace. All the signs of a hasty—but thorough—departure. Phryne could see the man, sitting on the side of that bed, tugging angrily at a bootlace and swearing as it snapped in that charming way shoelaces have when one is in a hurry. No blood. No signs of violence.

She returned to the hall, where Dot was looking worried.

'There's a few things missing, Miss,' she said.

'And from the kitchen, which is quite empty. Mr. Thomas's married couple seem to have left abruptly, pausing only for a spot of pillage.'

'There's sheets and blankets and so on upstairs,' said Dot. 'But some ornaments and a painting are missing. You can tell from marks in the dust. What do you want to do, Miss?'

'I'm not having you housekeep while we loll around,' said Phryne. 'Oh, for my Mr. and Mrs. Butler! Tell you what. Let's bring the things in—I notice that our trunks are here—and settle in for the night, and tomorrow we can find some servants.'

'I don't reckon we'll find anyone free in the season,' said Dot. 'But I don't mind, Miss. Nice house like this.'

Phryne looked at Dot affectionately. She was mousy and quiet where Phryne was bold, devout where Phryne was outrageous, and good girl was written all the way through her, like Castlemaine through Castlemaine Rock. And Phryne relied on her as she relied on her own right hand.

'Good. Well, girls?'

'Nothing scary,' said Jane, who disliked Ruth's emotionalism and never read novels. 'Have they gone, Miss Phryne?'

'Yes, and taken a lot of little souvenirs to remember poor Mr. Thomas by.'

'Are we staying?' asked Ruth.

'What do you think?'

'I say yes,' said Ruth, her courage much restored by not being expected to drive in that frightful vehicle anymore. Leaving would mean getting back into the Hispano-Suiza and Ruth was presently contemplating walking home to St. Kilda rather than doing that.

'So do I,' agreed Jane. 'I wonder if the neighbours saw the truck?'

'The truck, Jane?' asked Phryne, who was getting peckish.

'They must have had a truck to take all the things they stole.'

'Good observation. Let's ask them. You two carry up your own things then make up beds, and Dot can come with me. You'll be all right on your own?' she asked, seeing a shadow on Ruth's plump cheek.

'Of course,' said Jane flatly, and led the way to the luggage.

'I might just close and lock the back door,' said Phryne. 'Come and have a look at the kitchen, Dot. And where's that note? Mr. Thomas said something about the neighbours.'

Assisted by Molly, the girls opened the first trunk and began to haul their own belongings up the stairs. Dot walked into the kitchen and stared.

'They've even taken the tea,' she said, shocked. 'And the condiments, and the flour—look, there's been a whole sack here. And if it wasn't them, Miss, who did?'

'Perhaps someone who needed the flour more than we do,' said Phryne absently. 'The back gate might be open, too.' She led the way into a rather bijou little herb garden.

'Only been a couple of days without water,' remarked Dot.

The back gate, a heavy wooden construction topped hospitably with broken glass, stood ajar. Phryne shut and latched it.

'Flour,' she said, noticing traces of white powder on the gravel.

'I don't like this,' said Dot quietly.

'No, on consideration, Dot dear, I don't like it either—but whatever has happened has already happened. Let's call on the... what's their name?'

Dot consulted the note.

'He says that the lady on the left is a Miss Rose Sélavy, she isn't here all the time and he doesn't know her, and the lady on the right is a nice Mrs. Mason, who will be delighted to introduce you to the worthies of Queenscliff.'

'Then let's go and call on nice Mrs. Mason, and see if she can spare someone to summon the constabulary.'

◇◇◇

Mrs. Mason, when they gained admittance to the spacious house next door, did not seem conspicuously nice. She was large, pink, suicidally blonde, bridling and suspicious, but it did not take Phryne long to divine the cause.

'And I suppose you know Mr. Thomas well?' she asked, keeping her visitors standing in the hall, which was not polite.

'Not at all,' said Phryne promptly. 'Only met him once, at a big party. He said he had a house to lend and I accepted.'

Mrs. Mason relaxed, smiled and ushered them into the parlour.

Dot exchanged a glance with Phryne. Nice Mrs. Mason, apparently, had hopes of a closer relationship with nice Mr. Thomas.

The sun parlour was spotless and comfortable, furnished with cane chairs and possibly just a thought too many wicker whatnots. A small maid came in with tea on a trolley, an innovation of which Phryne approved. The weight of the average tray of teapot, milk jug, hot-water jug, sugar basin, slop basin, strainer, and cups and saucers was far too much for any young woman. Not to mention what looked like a rather good pound cake, a succulent fruitcake and a mound of freshly made scones. Phryne was hungry.

She allowed Dot to explain the situation as she made a healthy attack on the cake and loaded a scone or two with plum jam and cream. Mrs. Mason, now relieved of her fears for her nice Mr. Thomas's affections, exclaimed in horror.

'The Johnsons not back! I can't believe it! No warning! No letter! That is not like them, really it isn't,' she said, raising her plump pink hands. Now that she was being nice Mrs. Mason, she had a pleasant, educated, alto voice. 'And the kitchen empty?'

'Not a crumb,' said Phryne, taking over the conversation so that Dot could have her turn at the cake. 'These scones are first rate, Mrs. Mason.'

'Thank you—my cook is very good,' said Mrs. Mason distractedly. 'I really can't imagine what might have happened! The Johnsons were on a week's leave—they should have been back yesterday! But first things first. We shall telephone that nice Constable Dawson. Then we shall telephone Miss Miller, who has the employment agency. She might have a few people on her books, but really, this far into the season, I fear all the good people will be taken. But there might have been a cancellation,' said Mrs. Mason bravely. 'Then of course you will dine with me tonight, and tomorrow the tradesmen will call as usual and you can order replacements. And you say that your daughters are still in the house and not a bite to eat? I shall order a hamper to be sent over immediately. And a bone for the doggie, of course.'

She bustled away. Phryne poured herself another cup of tea.

'I know what you are thinking,' she said to Dot, who was nibbling her second slice of cake.

'Yes, Miss?'

'You are thinking that I attract mysteries,' said Phryne, a little uneasily. She had promised everyone a nice holiday by the sea and absolutely no murders. Though the Johnsons might be alive and well and living on damper (made from Mr. Thomas's flour) on Swan Island, of course.

Dot swallowed and considered.

'Well, yes, Miss, you do. But I don't reckon this was anyways your fault,' she said generously, much restored by tea and pound cake, her favourite. 'We just walked straight into this one.'

'Thank you, Dot. Have a scone? They're very good.'

'Thanks,' said Dot. 'I will.'

They had made considerable inroads into the scones before Mrs. Mason came back. She escorted a stout, self-possessed woman in an apron, who brought with her an appetising smell of onions and cucumber and mixed fruits. Mrs. Mason introduced her with a small chuckle.

'This is Mrs. Cook, my cook.'

'Cook by name and cook by profession,' put in the round woman, inspecting the newcomers with interest. She had bright blue eyes, red cheeks, and the very clean hands of one who has been making pastry.

'It's fate,' said Phryne, smiling. 'My butler is called Mr. Butler.'

'Is he, dear? That's fate for you. You say the Johnsons have not come back?'

'They have not, leaving only a broken bootlace behind,' Phryne replied.

'I wouldn't have thought it of them,' said the cook slowly. 'Seemed perfectly devoted to that Mr. Thomas. Been with him a long time, too. And to steal the provisions—that I can't believe.'

'Nonetheless, a good-sized mouse would starve in that kitchen. Now, what are we to do?'

'You'll have to find someone else, dear, that's true. I can lend you my scullery maid to get the new things settled in but she can't cook for toffee.'

'I thought of calling Miss Miller,' suggested Mrs. Mason deferentially. It was clear where power lay in this household. A good cook at holiday time must be worth her weight in diamonds.

'She won't have no one suitable,' the cook assured her mistress. 'Not this far into the season. I'll ask around, Miss,' she said to Phryne. 'I've sent the boy over with a hamper which will feed you through breakfast tomorrow, then we shall see.'

'Thank you,' murmured Phryne.

'And I've told him to light the pilot light for the hot water,' said the cook. 'You'll be wanting a wash after all that travelling. You can hang on to the cheeky young monkey to do some of your lifting. If you can get any work out of him you'll be doing well. It's more than I can do.'

'Thank you, Mrs. Cook,' said Mrs. Mason. The cook smiled at Phryne and Dot and bobbed something which might pass for a curtsey.

'Can't leave my puff paste for long,' she said, and went with a whisk of her apron.

'She's a character,' said Mrs. Mason admiringly.

'She certainly is,' agreed Phryne.

◇◇◇

Returning to the house, Phryne found that the hamper had arrived and her household was gathered around the kitchen table watching Ruth make tea. She was managing it with a fine flourish. Mrs. Butler taught her pupils well.

Jane was calculating how much the water would need to cool before she could drink the tea, and whether it was better to put the milk in first or last in order to cool it most expeditiously.

A lanky boy lounged in the doorway. His cap was on the back of his head, a gasper was in his mouth, and he did not look like a representative of the great working class.

'Girls, you deserve tea, so you shall have it. George, you haven't done any work yet, so you will have to earn it,' Phryne announced briskly. 'Stub the smoke and start on the trunks, if you want anything to eat before these starving ladies scoff it all.'

'My name ain't George,' he scowled. 'It's Eddie.'

'George it will be until I see some progress. Come along! Policemen will be here any moment.'

'P'lice?' said George, awestruck. Phryne diagnosed an avid reader of shilling shockers.

'Off you go, Sexton Blake,' she told him. He gaped at her. No one had read his mind since that strange lady next door had got him in the street and told him he was destined to be a cop. He ground out the gasper and almost ran into the hall.

'You're very good,' said Dot admiringly. 'The cook said she couldn't get a hand's turn out of him.'

'Just a matter of knowing where to apply the lever,' said Phryne.

Chapter Two

From time to time a prince would try to force his way through the hedge to get to the castle, but no one ever succeeded.

Brothers Grimm
'Sleeping Beauty'

Mr. Thomas had been prepared for visitors. There was a trunk hoist for lifting the luggage to the top floor.

Phryne, deciding that the best thing she could do was get out of the way of the domestic preparations, climbed the stairs in a thoughtful frame of mind. It might be a good idea to have a look at the scene of the…crime, perhaps…before it was converted entirely to Phryne's household usages.

The layout of the house was simple and agreeable. The main staircase debouched onto a substantial landing, rather dark but provided with a skylight, and on Phryne's right, at the back of the house, was a formidable padlocked door. It was customary for one who often lent his house to strangers to keep one room inviolate, a place to store his precious glassware, vintage port and dubious etchings, and to keep them from prying eyes or serious thirsts by locking the room ostentatiously. This was a brass padlock weighing about a pound and Phryne could take a hint.

Beside the sanctum was a large linen press, a service table for trays of early morning tea, and the back stair. Phryne ventured down it a few steps and heard the girls in the kitchen. Dot was saying with approval, 'Now that was a very good cup of tea!' Phryne returned and found two small rooms were on the other side, evidently bedrooms as they were provided with iron bedsteads on which flock mattresses lay neatly rolled and tied. She searched them and found nothing but one dropped earring (silver, globular). To the front of the house she saw the main bedroom, which already contained a lot of Phryne's clothes laid out on a large bed dressed with Phryne's own dark green sheets. Dot had been at work. Nothing odd in this room, either, except a couple of collar studs and the odd pin. Out of a new shirt, perhaps.

The room had a cast-iron balcony which looked straight out to sea. The view was glorious. Phryne promised herself long hours of staring out to the horizon—or, at least, Portsea—and continued her search. Bathroom—spacious, very clean, no sign that a man had, for instance, shaved here. Recently renewed with a bath big enough to wallow in, gorgeous green tiles and a blue cork floor. She tried the hot tap. After an initial spray of cold, hot water gushed out. Phryne was pleased. She really craved a deep, scented, foamy bath after driving and after the swim she intended to take soon. The bathroom's balcony window was of an appropriately frosted glass, lest those outside in the street should be honoured with a more intimate view of Miss Fisher than she allowed her casual acquaintances.

The three little front bedrooms had been claimed by Dot, Jane and Ruth. The rooms were charmingly characteristic. Ruth, who had been a slavey and had never forgotten it, cherishing her new-found prosperity, had made her bed with hospital corners, hung and folded her clothes, and set her favourite bedside reading—Carême's *Cuisine*—with its accompanying dictionary on the square chest of drawers which served as a bedside table. Her shoes were paired and under her bed.

Jane, who had no interest in frivolities, had obviously allowed Ruth to make her bed and had then flung an armload of assorted garments to crumple nicely on the quilt. However, stacked meticulously on her bedside table, were a lot of books, a pad of paper and a bundle of pencils. In among the writing implements was a toothbrush, Phryne was glad to see. Jane was presently reading a volume on chess, presumably for light relief.

Dot's room was like Dot herself: neat, well designed, everything to hand, the only unusual note being the rosary hanging from her bedside light. To be handy for any late-night prayers, apparently. Dot was reading *The Sheik's Desert Lover*, shame on her. Nothing here—someone had swept the floor.

Phryne went downstairs as someone pounded on the front door. No Mr. Butler to sift the unwanted from the welcome visitors. How I suffer, reflected Phryne humorously, quoting her friend Mrs. Grossman. *Dah—ling, how I suffer!*

She hauled open the front door to find herself confronted with a uniformed policeman. He seemed to be taken aback.

'Er...Lady Fisher?' he stammered, blushing.

Phryne grinned to herself. Clearly her fame had preceded her. This rural cop was very young with blue eyes and had turned an unattractive shade of beetroot. It clashed with the red plush wallpaper of the hall.

'Just call me Miss Fisher, and do come in,' she said. 'It seems that we have a bit of a mystery.'

'Constable Dawson, Miss,' he said, sidling past her. 'They say that the Johnsons have flitted.'

'Leaving not a rack behind,' agreed Phryne. 'They cleaned out the kitchen, took all their goods and furniture, and I believe that a couple of artworks are missing.'

'You searched the house?' he asked briskly.

'Certainly. Just a few bits and bobs.'

'No...er...' He was wondering how to ask this of one of the delicately nurtured. Phryne might have allowed him to keep on stammering but she was not a cruel woman.

'No sign of a struggle, no bloodstains, no marks or scuffs such as one would find if bodies had been dragged,' she told him, leading the way to the servants' quarters. 'All the locks were intact. But when I arrived the kitchen door was open, and so was the garden gate. I have locked both of them since,' she added, to spare him the trouble of delivering the standard policeman's lecture on securing one's premises against the visitations of the ungodly. And to spare herself the tedium of listening to it.

The kitchen contained Ruth, sitting at the table and making notes for her shopping list. The tea tray had been tidied and prepared for further supply. Phryne gestured at Ruth not to get up.

'Don't forget ice,' she advised, leading Constable Dawson into the empty rooms beside the kitchen.

'No, Miss Phryne,' replied Ruth, scribbling.

'Nothing left, is there?' asked Constable Dawson helplessly, tipping back his helmet and scratching his curly brown hair.

'Not a lot. Tell me about the Johnsons,' commanded Phryne.

'Both about fifty. Getting on, as you might say. Supposed to be devoted to Mr. Thomas. Been with him all his life. Mrs. Johnson was his family's cook and Mr. Johnson the houseman. Never drunk, never chased girls—beg pardon, Miss Fisher—used to put a little bit on the gee-gees. Only a little bit. She was teetotal, a real good cook, and they both used to sing in the Presbyterian church choir.'

'Not the stuff of which villains are made,' commented Phryne.

'On the other hand, maybe the stuff of which victims are made,' returned the constable, rather neatly. 'Have you searched the cellar?'

'I didn't know we had one,' said Phryne, with a certain sinking in her well-tailored middle.

'Just down here,' said the constable, pushing aside a piece of drugget and lifting a previously unnoticed trapdoor which fitted flush with the scullery floor. 'You don't have to come down, Miss.'

'Oh, yes, I do,' said Phryne. 'You need me to hold the light.'

'Ought to be a switch here somewhere…' muttered Dawson, taking two steps down into the dark. He flailed around for the string for the light and failed to find it.

'Stay there,' said Phryne, and called out for the boy. He arrived panting, cap pushed back, eyes bright.

'Yes, guv'nor?'

'Go out to the car and get my electric torch, will you, Tinker?' The boy sprinted off.

'You're getting on with that workshy young blighter,' observed Constable Dawson, who was completely unable to place Miss Fisher. A fashionable young lady, with that black hair cut in a cap and those rose-red lips, her skirt so short he could almost see her knees. But she had known about blood and scuff marks and she was not turning a hair at the idea of going down into a cellar which might contain the horrible remains of the late lamented Johnsons.

'He's suffering from a bad attack of hero worship,' observed Miss Fisher. 'He just needed someone to emulate. And it's Sexton Blake, in his case.'

'Ah,' said Dawson, who himself subscribed to the monthly adventures of that ageless sleuth. 'Bit childish?'

'I don't find him so,' said this remarkable woman. 'You have noticed, I trust, that there is no smell coming from the cellar? Nothing except cold earth and a faint scent of wine. I do not believe that we will find our missing lambs down in the dark.'

'No, Miss?' asked Constable Dawson, who had not been looking forward to going down those stairs.

Tinker returned with the torch and was allowed to stay as Phryne and the constable stepped gingerly down into the cellar. It did, the policeman noticed, indeed smell of cold earth and wine. And nothing else. Not that dreadful unforgettable sweet reek of rotting flesh. When they had brought in that drowned fisherman, the station stank of him for days and Dawson had alarmed his mother by totally refusing to eat meat for a week. Missing out on his previous favourite, rabbit stew.

He never wanted to smell that smell again. It wasn't present and neither were the Johnsons. The cellar contained spiderwebs, a lot of bottles on racks, some corkscrews, decanters and what Miss Fisher informed him were tasting glasses. One painting, tipped so that it was facing the wall. It was of a pretty girl in a swing; very frothy petticoats, she had. Constable Dawson wished that he had not been born with a blush reflex.

'Boucher,' announced Miss Fisher. 'Isn't it fun?'

Constable Dawson thought it verged on obscene but did not venture an opinion. He knew he didn't know anything about Art. But if that gentleman in the picture couldn't see right up that lady's skirts, he was a Dutchman.

There was also a box which contained a set of china ornaments. They were nice, the constable thought. Four china ladies in hoop skirts and big hats. One of them had a sheep with her, for reasons known only to the porcelain designer.

'The seasons,' said Miss Fisher. 'Chelsea. Very valuable and not a chip. I'll put them back. Autumn with her lamb, Spring with her blossom, Winter with her bundle of holly, Summer with her roses. Well. No corpses, that is a nice surprise. Thank you, Tinker, you may replace the torch. Shall we ascend? I'll ask Ruth to make some tea while we are looking at the missing artworks—or, rather, where they had been. You know what I mean. Dot? All clear,' she said, as Dot's anxious face appeared above her.

'That's good news,' said Dot.

'This is Miss Williams, my companion. Dot, this is Constable Dawson,' Phryne said. 'No, leave the drugget, I'd like to inspect Mr. Thomas's wine. Now, some tea would be nice. Can you make some tea for us, Ruth?'

'I can,' said Ruth, glowing with pride.

Dot escorted Constable Dawson into the parlour, where a large unfaded patch in the plush wallpaper denoted the loss of a painting.

'And there are four marks in the dust on this mantelpiece,' she added.

'Nothing else missing, Miss?' asked Dawson. 'Only I reckon those marks were left when someone put them china ladies in the cellar.'

'And the painting is the Boucher,' agreed Phryne. 'What an observant young officer you are! I can tell that you will go far in your chosen profession. We can prove the hypothesis. Tinker, take your piece of string and measure that painting in the cellar, will you?'

'Right away, Guv'nor!' gasped the boy and dashed out.

'How did you know he would have a piece of string?' asked Jane, who had tucked herself into a corner of the couch after her preliminary survey of the bookshelves. She had a small stack of books on the little table next to her.

'He's a boy,' said Phryne. 'Boys always have string. And toffee and all manner of interesting stuff in their pockets. When my mother was washing I used to empty said pockets and I found fishhooks, BB pellets, pins, elastic bands, bottle caps, cigarette cards, fudge, corks, everything you can imagine—including, on one occasion, a live frog, and on another a couple of blue-tongue lizards.'

'Gosh! Alive?' asked Jane.

'And very disgruntled,' Phryne told her. 'Nothing ruins a well-conducted lizard's day like being stuffed into a boy's pocket with nothing but elderly fudge and fishhooks to eat and the prospect of being plunged into a boiling copper to look forward to.'

'What happened to the frog?' asked Jane.

'It got away,' Phryne replied.

Constable Dawson was confused. This Miss Phryne was a lady and her mother took in washing? There was a story there, he could tell. But he probably wasn't going to hear it. Now her companion, that Miss Williams, he could place her. Good girl, in bed every night by ten, read improving books, saving up for her own home, good plain cook, very competent about the house, probably had a bloke of her own. They almost always did, in Constable Dawson's sad experience. He sighed a small constabulary sigh and attended to Tinker, who came running back and, with obvious pride, climbed on a chair and demonstrated, by the knots in his long piece of string, that the saucy painting in the cellar was the same size as the patch on the wallpaper.

'Very neat, Tinker, you can get down now. How are we going with the trunks?' asked Phryne.

'All upstairs, Guv'nor,' he said.

'Good. I wonder if I can hire you from Mrs. Mason? Would you like that?'

Tinker shot her a look of the sort of intense devotion which St Catherine of Siena might consider overdrawn.

'Please, Miss! The old chook…I mean, Mrs. M don't like me above half,' he explained. 'I don't think she'd miss me. Plenty of boys around.'

'All right. Go and ask Ruth if there is anything you can do for her, and help her unpack my special box, will you? And be very careful with the port,' she added, as he poised on one toe at the door, like a shabby, tweed-capped Hermes on his way to take messages to lower-class maidens from Zeus, when slumming.

There was a faint 'Right you are, Guv'nor' as he vanished kitchenwards.

'Well, Constable Dawson, that's all we have to show you,' said Phryne. 'Come and have some tea and we shall discuss this further.'

Dot and Ruth entered the breakfast room, pushing a trolley on which reposed a good teapot, the usual accoutrements, a plate of ginger biscuits and one of plain thin-cut bread and butter. A meagre spread compared to Phryne's usual level of catering but perfectly adequate.

'You can be mother,' Phryne told Dot. 'Tomorrow we shall have better fare.'

'If you'll excuse me, Miss Phryne, I'd better go back to my list,' said Ruth.

'Can I help you?' asked Jane, who was deeply entrenched in her first detective story and disinclined to move. This Miss Sayers. How could Jane have missed her before?

'No, thanks, I've got Tinker for the heavy work,' said Ruth without irony.

'I found this cookbook,' said Jane, much relieved. 'It looks interesting.'

Ruth took it and her cup and went back to the kitchen. There Tinker was unpacking Miss Fisher's travelling comestibles. There were coffee beans and a coffee grinder, a sinister packet of that really strong Turkish coffee, bottles of liqueurs, bottles of olive oil and tarragon vinegar, garlic, essences like rosewater and orange flower water, an array of pickles and jams, the cocktail shaker, the port, the red and white wines. Phryne had travelled to the country before.

Tinker was talking excitedly.

'She's wonderful! What a bonzer sheila, the boss is! How long have you been with her?'

'A year,' said Ruth. 'Don't shake those bottles. That's the port, it goes all muddy if you shake it. You be careful, Tinker. Do as she says and she's a lovely lady. Disobey her and she's very scary.'

'Blind Freddy could see that,' said Tinker scornfully. 'What are you doing, Miss? Can I help?'

'Making a shopping list,' said Ruth. 'We need to telephone it to the tradesmen to bring the food tomorrow. Tell you what, it would be nice if you watered the herbs now the sun's off them. Miss Phryne said they are drying out.'

'Water's the problem around here,' he told her. 'But you got company's water, as well as that bl— I mean very big rainwater tank. The old chook only has rainwater and does she create if someone leaves a tap dripping!' He winced, as if the old scars ached even in this balmy weather. 'Right-o, I'll do the garden. You call me if she wants me?'

'Of course,' said Ruth. Inwardly she was both elated and very scared. This kitchen was hers. She had chafed under Mrs. Butler's tutelage, longing to reign alone. Now she could, and the idea was both intoxicating and terrifying. She sat down at the scrubbed table, raised her chin and also her resolution. She could do it. The list was complete. She had ordered greengrocery—everything from potatoes to pineapples; dry grocery—spices and sugar and flour and packet biscuits; dairy foods; such things as ice for the ice chest and replacements for the missing condiments; also toilet paper, kitchen paper, bicarbonate of soda, cream of tartar, salt and soap. Tonight they were dining with the next-door neighbour, Tinker's Old Chook. Tomorrow belongs to me, thought Ruth.

Then she opened *The Gentle Art of Cookery*, by Mrs. CF Leyel and Miss Olga Hartley, and was swept away.

◇◇◇

In the breakfast room a puzzled Constable Dawson was attempting to make sense of the vanishment of the Johnsons.

'They had a good reputation,' he repeated, onto his third cup of tea and sixth piece of bread and butter. Ruth had sliced the bread thinly with a knife dipped in hot water and buttered it with maître d'hôtel butter, and Constable Dawson had never tasted bread that good. 'No hint of trouble. This is a small place, Miss Fisher, and we pick up all the gossip. My brother runs the Esplanade Hotel and my sister cooks for the Queenscliff Hotel so we hear all the news. Sometimes before it's actually news,' he admitted. 'Not a peep.'

'Well, there are things which you might do,' suggested Phryne, very gently. 'You might check to see what mail they received. Also, I need the address of Mr. Thomas—we ought to tell him that his old servants have levanted. It might be that he has an explanation.'

'Don't you know where he is, Miss?'

Phryne shrugged, a move fascinating in itself.

'Arnhem Land is the best I can do. He lent me this house on the barest acquaintance. He's an anthropologist, you know. Studies the Aborigines.'

'Used to be some of them round here,' the constable told her. 'Long gone now. Yair. Mr. Thomas used to bring home bones and such. I stopped him once for speeding in that big black car of his, and he had a load of skulls and bones on the seat beside him. Fair turned me up. He said they were blackfeller skulls. They were all red with ochre, he said, and he was studying burial customs.' The constable was evidently quoting.

Dot crossed herself unobtrusively. Disturbing the dead was not a proper occupation, she considered, for a gentleman. And Mr. Thomas must be a gentleman. This was obviously a gentleman's house. Nice furniture, bit old-fashioned. Everything squared away neatly. Clean and swept. Still, gentlemen would have their hobbies.

'Indeed,' said Phryne. 'You might also enquire as to the vehicle which removed all the Johnsons' furniture. They must have had a bed and chairs and so on, and they are all gone. Someone might have noticed the truck or whatever.'

'Good notion, Miss Fisher,' said Constable Dawson, uncoupling his notebook.

'And the exchange might have noticed who called the house,' continued Phryne, prompting.

'Exchange, yes,' said the constable, making notes.

'Now, if you are quite finished, I would like to take my family for a swim,' said Phryne, getting up.

And despite his private regret for the remains of that excellent bread, Constable Dawson had to take his leave.

Dot caught him at the door and gave him the last slice in a paper napkin, and he walked away munching it.

'Excellent tea, Ruth dear.' Phryne entered the kitchen to the divine scent of wet herb beds, watered with skill by Tinker, who had an adroit thumb on the hosepipe. Mint, sage, thyme, basil, tarragon, all exhaled in gratitude as the drops descended. The scent was magical.

'Arabian Nights,' whispered Ruth. She lifted to Phryne a face transformed by joy. 'I've got this cookbook, Miss Phryne, and I would like to cook you a dinner from it,' she said.

'Go to it,' encouraged Phryne. 'Have you got that list? I'll phone it to the tradesmen and then we ought to go for a bathe.'

'Oh, yes,' said Ruth, and added, in her clear cursive, several extra ingredients which might give Jno Handlesman, Grocer, a bit of pause for thought. Where was he going to get Turkish delight and preserved quinces? And why would anyone suppose that he had preserved quinces, in a reasonable universe?

'I'll collect Jane and find our bathing dresses,' she promised and left the kitchen at some thirty mph, moving like a disgruntled blue-tongue lizard.

Phryne shrugged and took the list to the telephone, which like all telephones was in the hall, in the draughtiest and most inconvenient spot. After a certain wrangling with Exchange, who did not seem to be able to use even the available half of her wits, she managed to be connected with the right people, all of whom promised to deliver in the early morning. At which time Phryne was intending to be asleep. She would square Ruth and Tinker to receive the food. And until the ice arrived she was not going to get a cocktail, so she hoped they were prompt. Dinner tonight with Mrs. Mason might prove to be trying and Phryne liked a little alcoholic applause for her social efforts.

But she gathered the girls and Dot and conducted them easily on a short walk to the sea baths, when the tide was just on the turn, and the water was fine and clean, and Phryne's daring red costume—no back and hardly any front—attracted a satisfying number of stares.

Dot, in her respectable bathers with legs and a modesty skirt, attracted no stares at all, which was the way she wanted it. She was a little light-headed with relief that the missing Johnsons were not in the house, in any state, and swam further than she ordinarily did, in the cool clean ocean and the knowledge that the boy Tinker had lit the pilot light for a reliable supply of hot water.

The girls dog-paddled out a reasonable distance and allowed the tide to swish them back towards the shore.

'I'm cooking dinner!' murmured Ruth.

'I know,' said Jane kindly. She loved her adoptive sister and could recognise a fulfilled ambition when she saw it. 'I'll help you any way I can.'

'Will you do the carving?' asked Ruth. 'You're good at carving. I want to do the roast duck with cherry jelly.'

'Certainly,' said Jane. 'That is a nice house,' she added, as they idled in the cool water. 'Lots of books.'

'Oh, books,' said Ruth. 'Anything interesting?'

'I haven't had time to search through them yet,' said Jane with the happy complacency of someone who knew that, by the end of the holiday, she would have read them all. 'Did you like your cookbook?'

'Oh, yes,' said Ruth. She turned over in the water to embrace her sister. 'Thank you!'

'Delighted,' said Jane, hugging her. Pleasures, as Miss Phryne said, were always intensely personal.

They returned salty but happy for a sumptuous bath and a restoring but unfortunately warm gin squash (Phryne) or cup of coffee (the rest of the inhabitants) before walking next door for dinner with Mrs. Mason.

Chapter Three

I like children (except boys).

Lewis Carroll

Phryne surveyed her little family as they waited for the door to be opened. Jane and Ruth, clean and combed, in their holiday cotton frocks (one lavender, one rose, with matching hair ribbons). Dot in her standard beige dinner dress with terracotta-coloured jacket in case of draughts, and an orange geranium in her bandeau. Phryne in her loose purple silk shift with jazz-coloured scallop-shell appliques—silver, black and green. Her headdress was a silvery crown of wire with a soft black plume depending from it. She never took jewellery on holidays so wore none.

'Very chic,' murmured Dot, catching her glance.

'Indeed, we are a handsome group,' replied Phryne.

The door opened. They were conducted into a reception room by a thin butler who looked like he had just bitten an unripe persimmon. His whole face seemed to be contracted with disgust. Phryne awarded him a cool glance which at least averted his gaze. She had been stared out of countenance a few times, when much younger, and did not mean to have this happen ever again.

Mrs. Mason, on the other hand, was pleased. She bustled forward, took Phryne's hand, and conducted them into a parlour. Drinks, it seemed, were to be served. The butler enquired as to the ladies' pleasure as though requesting information on their choice of arsenic or cyanide. Phryne allowed him to construct a sidecar for her. The girls had half a glass of muscat each, and Dot took sherry with her usual thrill of the forbidden. She had, after all, signed The Pledge when she was twelve. Mrs. Mason had a sidecar also; by her giggle, not the first of the evening. Phryne tasted. Good. Strong on lemon juice, a fine brandy and icy cold.

'Well, now, what are you going to do on your holiday?' asked Mrs. Mason of the girls.

'Read,' replied Jane with perfect truth. 'Mr. Thomas has a very good library. I wonder if there are more books in that locked room?'

'Oh, I expect so,' said Mrs. Mason. 'He's a very learned man, you know. But of course if he locked the room it must stay locked. Even I don't have the key.'

'And you such an old friend,' murmured Phryne. Should she venture on another glass? Why, in fact, not?

'Yes, we've been close friends ever since my husband died,' said Mrs. Mason, affecting a sob and wiping with a miniscule handkerchief at a perfectly dry eye. 'Such a dear clever scholar and such a comfort to have a man nearby when one is all alone in the world.'

Phryne caught, just for a second, a flicker on the butler's contracted face. Unseen by Mrs. Mason, she winked at him. He maintained the perfect frozen expression of his tribe, but his eyes softened slightly and he filled this distinguished visitor's glass to the very top with the icy, lemony cocktail.

'You do make good cocktails,' she told him. He bowed and did not speak. 'So there's just you in the house?' asked Phryne of her hostess.

'During term,' Mrs. Mason answered. 'During the holidays I have my son and his friends staying—if he isn't staying with them, of course. They are such good chums. And such high spirits!'

The butler winced again and so did Mrs. Mason. Both of them, Phryne inferred, preferred the spirits to be found in expensive bottles to the ones which kicked sand all over the floor, ground mud into carpets and played cricket in the kitchen garden, to the merry tinkle of breaking windows.

'I've only passingly been to Queenscliff before,' Phryne told Mrs. Mason, wondering, inter alia, who had persuaded a woman with such a high complexion that cerise satin was her colour and texture. There ought to be some kind of law against dressmakers like that. Crimes against Couture.

'Oh, it used to be select, very select,' Mrs. Mason answered. She seemed to be listening for something. 'Mrs. Alfred Deakin always stays here, you know. And the dear Archbishop. Lots of church people and politicians. But since the railway went through we have lots of trippers. My dear! Pork-pie hats and trailing braces and eating ice cream in the street!'

'The working classes,' said Phryne, 'have their pleasures, too.'

'Working class! No, no, these are small shopkeepers. Trade.'

Phryne was selecting one of the three crushing rejoinders and was about to inflict it on her hostess when there was a rush of feet and three boys entered, shoving each other at the door and then standing as though emulating the fate of Lot's wife. Phryne was thus rescued from social ostracism in the select village of Queenscliff. But she wasn't a bit grateful.

For there, now shuffling a few feet and looking as though they had been struck repeatedly with a carpenter's mallet, were her three assailants from the street. Fraser, Jolyon and Kiwi, as she recalled. Fraser was the one with the scowl and the blond hair. Kiwi the taller, all skinned knees and elbows. And the scion of the house, Jolyon, blushing furiously, a well-built lad with brown hair like his mother's.

Jane looked at them as though they were a specimen she had in mind to dissect. Ruth gaped until Dot moved close to her and nudged. Phryne smiled sweetly.

At that smile the boys shuddered. A jellyfish might have managed more tremble per square inch, but only a jellyfish. They hung on her lips. What was she going to say? All she had to do was peach on them and the rest of the holiday would be close confinement and Good Works.

'My son, Jolyon,' said Mrs. Mason, who had not noticed anything wrong in the atmosphere. 'His friends Tony Fraser and John Patterson. This is the Hon. Miss Phryne Fisher and her companion Miss Williams. And her daughters Jane and Ruth. You are late, boys! Go and wash your hands, dinner is almost ready.'

The boys shook hands solemnly with Phryne and Dot, stared at Jane and Ruth, and barrelled out to do as they were told. But they were not relieved, not yet. There was still dinner to get through, and that Miss Fisher might yet decide to sneak.

'Your son takes after you,' Phryne observed.

'A little, perhaps, I like to think so,' Mrs. Mason agreed. 'But he's going to be as big as his father. It's as much as his female relatives can do to keep him in socks.'

Phryne, who had never knitted a sock in her life but was sure that if she needed socks she could find someone to knit them for her, smiled an assent. Mrs. Mason took another cocktail. Phryne didn't. Dot sipped her sherry. Ruth was astounded by the advent of the bad boys in a respectable house, and Jane was groping for a conversational topic. Dot had been training her in Suitable Topics for a Lady's Dinner Table, which did not include Rat Dissection for Beginners or Beastly Customs of the Heathen, which was a pity because Jane knew a lot about both of these.

'I noticed a cinema down in the town,' she observed. 'We haven't been to the pictures for a month.'

'Oh, yes, we have quite a good selection of films,' Mrs. Mason replied, a little blurrily. 'Only two days later than the Melbourne releases. Improving cinema, of course. *The Pioneers. For the Term of his Natural Life. The Birth of White Australia.* They're shown at the town hall. I always send the boys to see the Australian pictures, so good for them.'

'None of the Hollywood films, then?' asked Ruth, who had a passion for Ronald Coleman shared by Dot, who doted on that thin moustache he wore.

'Well, yes, the Vue Grand cinema further down the hill shows them. Some of them are quite unsuitable for the young,' said Mrs. Mason.

'I never censor, of course,' said Phryne, in such a bright tone that Mrs. Mason found herself nodding in agreement. 'Young people must form their own tastes. Here come the boys, I believe,' she added, as a thunder of footsteps came to her ear. It was either them or distant cattle stampeding.

'Madam, dinner is served,' announced the acidulated butler.

Dinner was, Phryne considered, sticky. The food was excellent of its kind. Conventional vegetable soup. A perfectly acceptable dish of fried fish with its accompaniment of chips. A slice or two of pleasantly cooked roast beef in its own gravy and the proper vegetables. A rice pudding. Anchovy toast.

The feast of reason and the flow of soul, however, lagged. Dot plugged along gamely on pictures she had seen, assisted by Ruth. Jane contemplated the boys with a cool, scientific eye. Mrs. Mason ate heavily, as did Phryne. It had been a long day. The boys ate like wharfies who had been unloading coal all night. Conversation languished again. Jolyon yelped as some-one—could it have been his mother?—kicked him in the shin.

'You want to watch out for your hair,' he told Ruth.

'Oh? Why?' she asked. It was an unusual conversational opening.

'The phantom snipper,' replied the boy in a deep radio-play tone.

'Who's he?' asked Ruth, as she was required to ask.

'You're just walking along,' elaborated Jolyon, 'hatless and taking the air, when you feel a sudden pull from behind, and—snip! You turn around and there's no one there. And when you feel around behind your neck,' he said, groping at his nape in demonstration, 'your plait's gone or hanging by a thread! No one's seen him, no one knows who he is…the phantom snipper!'

'Jolyon, what nonsense,' reproved Mrs. Mason.

'So there is no phantom snipper?' asked Ruth, relieved. She greatly valued her long, thick chestnut hair.

'Oh, there have been a couple of pranks, childish nonsense. Take no notice of it,' ordered Mrs. Mason. Ruth did not feel comforted.

Kiwi decided that it was his turn to carry the conversational burden.

'Are you at school?' he asked Jane, who was sitting nearest him.

'Why, yes,' she answered. 'Are you?'

''Course,' he said. And that appeared to exhaust his ability to chat.

'I am going to be a doctor,' Jane informed him.

'Me too,' said Kiwi, 'but I'm a bit of a duffer at maths.'

'I find chemistry difficult,' confessed Jane. 'The school doesn't treat it seriously.'

'I know.' Kiwi was interested—in a girl! He never thought such a thing would happen. A little girl, too, not a glamorous creature. She still had plaits, until the phantom snipper caught her. But, however, she was right. 'Stinks, they call it,' he said bitterly.

'And just as you get your solution hydrated someone comes in and makes you go and play hockey,' Jane rejoined.

'Too true! Or football,' sighed Kiwi.

'All right for you brainy chaps, I like football,' objected Jolyon. 'I'm going into my father's office so I have to learn languages, and after a few hours of those fiendish Chinese verb forms I'm ready for a good game of footer. Or cricket. Anything that means I don't have to think in tones.'

'At least you've got your own tutor,' said Kiwi. 'I've got to share the science lab with a gang of oafs who just want me to make stinks. Rotten-egg gas. For one of their beastly rags.'

'Hydrogen sulphide,' said Jane. Kiwi regarded her with approval.

'I say,' he said. 'I've got a lot of homework. Maths. Are you good at maths?'

'No,' said Jane, with perfect truth. 'I am a maths prodigy, my teacher Miss Jones says. I am superbly good at maths.'

'Wait a bit,' put in Fraser. He pulled Kiwi towards him and hissed, 'You don't want to spend the hols reading! What about the treasure?'

'No, but I need to do the homework,' said Kiwi. 'She can help me.'

'Beastly swot!' whispered Fraser.

'I can hear you, you know,' Jane informed him. 'And who says I want to spend my holidays helping some boy emerge from his ignorance? As it happens, I don't.'

She selected another piece of anchovy toast and ate it in a pointed manner. Ruth, almost bursting with laughter, smothered her face in her napkin. Dot smiled. The boys stared at each other, astounded. They had been willing to bestow the light of their countenances on this girl, even asking for her help, and she had firmly and haughtily rejected them. And she had eaten the last bit of anchovy toast.

Jane was rapidly gaining their respect.

Phryne, who had missed this byplay, was rising as her hostess did to retreat to the drawing room for coffee and an end, at last, to this uncomfortable dinner. She was surprised to find that her look of affectionate sympathy to the girls and Dot was being met by muffled giggles.

'Nice to see the young people getting on so well,' observed Mrs. Mason.

◇◇◇

The Phryne party fell over the front doorstep and into the house, shutting the door so they could snicker in comfort. Ruth sat down on the hallstand and almost cried with laughter. Dot chuckled. Jane was puzzled. So was Phryne.

'What was that all about?' she asked. 'Come into the kitchen for a nice cup of cocoa and tell me all.'

They explained. They laughed again. They fed biscuits to Molly, who was ecstatic at their return. They heated the milk and made the hot drinks. Phryne patted Jane on the shoulder.

'It's all right, Jane dear, you did just the right thing.'

'But what did they expect me to do?' asked Jane, accepting her cocoa.

'They expected you to be overwhelmed by the honour and spend your holidays doing this boy's maths for him,' said Dot. 'The lazy little toad.'

'But why should I do that?' Jane asked, genuinely puzzled.

'Because he's a boy to whom no one has ever refused anything,' explained Phryne. 'Because he is used to getting his own way and he probably has a doting mother and several doting sisters who jump to it at his lightest whim.'

'And aunties who knit him socks and nice woolly jumpers,' added Ruth, mopping her wet face.

'Oh,' said Jane. 'Very well then. I think I'll just take a few of Mr. Thomas's books and go to bed.'

'Me too. Tinker's coming over at seven and I have to be up early for the deliveries.' Ruth picked up her cup, then leaned over and kissed Miss Fisher on the cheek. 'Thank you for a lovely party,' she said, and giggled her way up the stairs. Yawning, Dot followed.

'I am very proud of my adoptive daughters,' said Phryne to Molly, who had taken up her usual station on Phryne's feet. 'I pity the doctor who tells Jane she can't do something because she's a girl. They'll have to scrape him off the lecture-theatre floor and post him home to Mother. Ah, well, now, I suppose you wouldn't want to stay here and guard the house, would you, Molly dear? No? Then come up with me,' said Phryne, carrying her fillet in one hand. 'It's definitely time for bed.'

Morning announced itself to Miss Fisher's displeased ear with the shouts and cries of those who labour for a living.

The first, from the sprightly conversation, was the ice man, who called Ruth 'sweetheart' and seemed to be smashing through doors rather than going to the bother of opening them. A brief pause, then it was a dray at the back gate loaded with a truly remarkable number of sacks, packets and boxes, some of which chinked. He called Ruth 'darling' and Tinker 'young feller-me-lad' and also seemed to have some prejudice about opening doors. But loved slamming them shut. The next was the butcher's boy, who whistled 'Lily of Laguna' a precise half-tone flat. Molly proved herself to be a dog of good socialist principles by barking at all without fear or favour.

In a quiet interval, Dot brought a cup of Hellenic coffee and a fresh hot roll to Phryne, who sat up in bed to receive the tray.

'Knew you'd be awake, Miss,' she said apologetically. 'Only one of the Seven Sleepers could have slept through that racket. Jane has, though,' she added, as Phryne sipped the inky beverage.

'Probably stayed awake half the night reading Mr. Thomas's books,' rejoined Phryne. 'Are there more tradesmen to come?'

'Oh, yes, Miss, there's the fruiterer and the ham-and-beef and the man from the pub,' Dot informed her.

'Then I shall rise and go for a refreshing morning dip,' Phryne decided. 'What's the weather like?'

'Fine and clear,' said Dot.

'Good. Are you coming, Dot dear?'

'No, Miss, too chilly for me yet. The girls don't want me in the kitchen so I'll put on my hat and go for a walk. They'll see this kitchen maid settled in and all the rest of the provisions delivered. That Tinker's still unpacking stuff. He's being a good boy,' said Dot with faint astonishment. Tinker was not living up to his reputation.

'Pip pip, then,' said Phryne. Houses were not her business. She would give this experiment a couple of days, and if it seemed that her household was working too hard, they would shift en masse to the Queenscliff Hotel, a most superior hostelry. Money, thought Phryne as she finished her coffee and found her bathing suit, was sometimes very useful in smoothing the rough patches in the path of life.

The town of Queenscliff was out and about when she walked from the house and into the cool morning air. Generally Phryne only saw this part of the day if she had approached it from the other end.

I shall be so robust if I do this every day, she thought to herself. Strong and hearty. What a ghastly thought. I wonder how long Mrs. Mason has been on the sauce? Her son didn't appear to be surprised at her consumption and her butler has clearly been through times that try butlers' souls. On the other hand, Jane squashed the upstart boy and the cocktails were first rate. Oh, Lord, and now we will have to ask Mrs. M and her brood to dinner—and only Ruth to cook it. That should be interesting. Must make sure that the gin supplies hold out…

The sea embraced her almost-naked skin. She dived.

◇◇◇

Ruth looked up from ticking supplies off her list at the appearance of a languid girl of about sixteen. She was thin and blonde and had watery blue eyes. From her crisp grey uniform, Ruth assumed that this was the kitchen maid which Mrs. Cook had offered to lend her to get her kitchen into order. The girl advanced to the step, tripped over it and said, 'H'lo.'

'Hello, I'm Ruth, what's your name?'

'Lily,' replied the girl, aiming for a drawl but not managing it.

'Come in, then. I'm just making sure we've got all the things Miss Phryne ordered.'

'How about a cup of tea first?' asked Lily. 'Your Miss Phryne's still out, she won't catch us.'

Ruth was shocked.

'She's out, but we're in, and we're going to do this right,' she told Lily very firmly. 'This is my first kitchen and I'm going to make sure that she gets as good a dinner as I can cook. Now you can help me, or you can go back to Mrs. Cook and I'll manage with Tinker.'

'So there, Miss La-di-dah!' sneered Tinker, laying down a load of boxes.

'He's helping you? Wouldn't scratch his own…I mean, he's a lazy beggar. And his name's Eddie,' snapped Lily.

'Really? Here we call him Tinker,' said Ruth.

'She's callin' me lazy! Always moonin' over movie stars, while poor ol' Amos the butcher's boy is breakin' his heart over 'er,' added Tinker.

'You little hound!' exclaimed Lily, blushing.

Ruth felt that she needed to assert some control over her minions.

'Well, shall we do some work? If we get it all done soon I'll make some banana cake. Those bananas are just about overripe. I need to find out how the oven works, too.'

'I can show you that,' said Tinker eagerly.

'And you can go on with the list,' said Lily, giving up on an easy day. If she went back, Mrs. Cook would find more and more things for her to do. 'I'll stack and put away.'

Ruth took up the list again, bit her pencil, and reflected that the gentle art of cookery might be the least of the challenges involved in running a tight kitchen.

◇◇◇

Lubricated by tea and nourished by Miss Phryne's additions to the list, which included a large paper bag of Swallow & Ariell's Best Assorted biscuits, Ruth had her kitchen and pantry arranged to her liking in four hours. She knew where all the stores were. She had overseen Tinker's cleaning of the empty bins and lockers. She had checked for signs of rats and cockroaches. Her table was scrubbed. Her floor was swept. She had allowed Tinker to sharpen the knives, which he greatly enjoyed. She had hardboiled the eggs. She had sliced ham and cheese. She had washed and polished a variety of summer fruits. She had cut several plates of ham and pickle sandwiches, cream cheese and chive sandwiches and tomato sandwiches, and her banana bread had come out of a nice efficient reliable oven just the right colour and cooked all the way through.

She sent Lily to set the luncheon table for a buffet and had Tinker wheel the food in, place it carefully on the side table and cover it with a muslin cloth to keep off flies. The lemonade was made and cooling in the icebox, orange slices and mint swimming in the tart, refreshing fluid, just waiting for the fizzy injection of soda water to make it perfect. Miss Phryne's gin was chilling beside it.

Then the kitchen staff sat down to their own preferred luncheon, which in Tinker's case was a doorstop of bread topped with a handful of pickled onions, as much ham and cheese as he could cram onto it, sealed with another doorstop.

'You're never going to get that in your mouth,' jeered Lily.

'Yah,' replied Tinker.

Ruth ate her own sandwich in silence. She was considering her menu with the calm, devoted contemplation of an enclosed nun reflecting on the sacrament. Not even watching Tinker engulf his sandwich as though he could unhinge his jaw was enough to distract her. She had Miss Leyel's book open on the table in front of her.

Lily was bored. No one to talk to in this hole, she thought. Still, one more try before she went back to Mrs. Cook. At least there she had other people around who weren't rude boys or real strange girls who were only half there.

'Going to the movies while you're here?' she asked Ruth.

'Yes, I expect so,' said Ruth. 'Tinker, can you go and find Miss Jane and ask her to come and help me? Sorry, Lily, I really don't want to talk about anything. I want to think about my menu. Thank you for your help. Can you come in tomorrow for breakfast?'

'Dunno,' said Lily, mentally vowing that hell would freeze over first. 'Missus might send the other girl. See you,' she said and made it out the kitchen door as fast as she could. That was a strange house and she didn't want to go back to it.

Fortunately thoughts of Gary Cooper came to comfort and distract her. Gary Cooper could always distract Lily. Amos the butcher's boy in his distasteful stained apron was too, too impossible, even though he dogged her footsteps and stared at her with his mouth open. One day, she dreamed, Gary Cooper would come to the kitchen door, rip off her apron and sweep her off her feet.

Jane came in, marking her place in her book with her finger until she found a more durable bookmark. Nothing seemed available except lettuce.

'Here I am,' she announced, as Ruth was staring into space. 'I say, Ruthie? Are you all right?'

'Oh, Jane, can you help me? There are too many recipes,' exclaimed Ruth. 'I want to cook them all!'

'Steady on,' said Jane. 'Give me a look.'

Ruth sipped a strengthening cup of mint tea as Jane skimmed the masterwork. But what would Jane know? She was a scientist! Cookery was an art!

'I see,' murmured Jane. 'Well, I've got an idea,' she told her sister. 'Pick one from each chapter and that makes a menu.'

'No, it doesn't,' said Ruth sharply. 'It has to be balanced. Not too much cream, not too much sweetness…'

'Let's give it a try,' suggested Jane, who preferred experiment to theory every time. 'Then if one thing doesn't work we just go back to the chapter and find one which does. Now, what sort of meat have you got?'

'A leg of lamb. And a duck, but the duck's got to hang to let the fat drain out of it, so it's for tomorrow,' explained Ruth.

'Lucky Ember isn't here. Just think how he'd feel about a hanging duck!'

Ruth chuckled, imagining the black cat batting the duck back and forth until it flew into his mouth and was thus lawful prey. Jane was continuing her research in Miss Leyel's book.

'All right, how are you going to cook your leg of lamb? Let's see. How about boned with a herb stuffing on page 189?'

'That sounds good.' Ruth was feeling better. The problem, once stated, had become manageable. 'Then what about the vegetables?'

'What did you order?'

'I've got green peas,' said Ruth, truffling about in the cool space under the sink. 'Green beans, a cauliflower and a lot of potatoes and onions.'

'Peas,' decided Jane. 'Mint sauce. Now for soup. And the finger alights on…potato.'

'Too heavy. We need something light.'

Jane grinned and tossed back her plaits.

'Then the moving finger writes and having writ comes up with…*potage bonne femme*, which is made of…carrots, mostly.'

'Sounds good,' agreed Ruth. 'I can send Tinker downtown for some. And for dessert, we can have that amazing *crème d'abricot*, 'cos I've lots of apricots. Thank you!' She embraced Jane suddenly. 'Now, as a special favour, you can bone the leg of lamb while I go and cut the herbs for the stuffing.'

'Jolly good,' said Jane, taking up the smallest and most flexible of the carving knives and trying to recall the anatomical diagram in Mrs. Beeton.

Tinker, constructing himself another sandwich of architectural complexity, thought that they were very nice sisters indeed, and not at all like his own, who quarrelled without ceasing over anything whatsoever. He sat on the back step, feeding scraps of ham to Molly, and felt that life was, for a change, treating him well.

Chapter Four

Work apace, apace, apace
Honest labour bears a lovely face.

Thomas Dekker
'Sweet Content'

Phryne and Dot returned to the house to find lunch all laid out on a buffet. At the sound of her entry, Ruth brought the lemonade out of the icebox, put it and the gin bottle onto a tray, and bore them into the parlour, where Jane was already nibbling and reading, Dot was selecting a ham and pickle sandwich and a bunch of grapes, and Phryne was taking off her straw hat.

'Lunch!' she said. 'Let me just go and wash the salt off. Won't be a tick. Two fingers of gin in the glass, Ruth dear, then fill it up with ice and lemonade. I must have swum for miles.'

'And I must have walked for miles,' groaned Dot, easing off her shoes. 'Put on the kettle, Ruth, I need tea.'

'All ready,' replied Ruth, whipping off another muslin cloth to reveal the tea urn simmering. Ruth made the tea with dispatch, not forgetting to warm the pot and slick the cup in boiling water. Dot smiled at her earnest expression.

'You're doing really well,' she told Ruth.

'I hope so,' Ruth replied. 'This is what I always wanted, and now it's very scary.'

'That's the way of it with wishes,' said Dot, after her first deep ambrosial sip. 'You have to be careful because you might get exactly what you want. But you make a heavenly cup of tea, my dear. For that alone you could get a job.'

'Try one of the cheese sandwiches,' offered Jane, not coming out of her book. 'They're really creamy. And sort of salty. And just a little bit oniony.'

'So they are,' agreed Dot, taking one more.

Phryne flew in a little later, her hair still wet, dressed in one of her long Chinese gowns. 'I'm starving,' she exclaimed, accepting the gin squash. 'What do we have here? Looks scrumptious.' She sampled. 'Is scrumptious. Well done, Ruth dear. Now do sit down and stop hovering. How does dinner look?'

'It looks good,' Jane said, still reading. 'We came up with a nice mathematical method of selecting dishes. I boned the leg of lamb.'

'You are so deft,' said Phryne affectionately. 'In the good old days you would have been very good at picking locks, embroidery, petit point, lacemaking.'

'I can't see the point of handicrafts,' said Jane.

'It's soothing to have something to occupy your hands while you are thinking,' said Dot.

'Not while there are books in the world,' said Jane flatly.

'Have you been for a walk today?' asked Dot. She was worried by Jane's habit of taking a supply of literature into her room and refusing to come out until she ran out of books. Young girls ought to take exercise or they risked green-sickness, Dot's grandmother had always said.

'I'm going for a swim with Ruth later,' said Jane, crossing her fingers.

Dot took another cup of tea. Phryne poured herself another drink. For the first time she felt that she was actually on holiday.

'How was the kitchen maid from the Mason household?'

'I don't think she liked me giving her orders, Miss Phryne,' said Ruth gravely. 'And she wanted to talk all the time and drink tea.'

'Not one of the world's workers, then.'

'No,' said Jane. 'And Tinker doesn't like her. Also, she trod on Molly's tail and didn't apologise.'

'That was discourteous,' agreed Phryne. 'One cannot avoid occasionally treading on Molly, she does spread herself rather, but one should say sorry when one does.'

'She says Mrs. Cook will send the other maid tomorrow. She didn't like us, either.' Jane seemed unconcerned.

Dot put down her empty cup and picked up her shoes.

'That was a nice lunch, and I'm going to lie down for a while. I walked a long way.'

'Where to?' asked Phryne.

'Just around the shops. Then I went down to the docks to look at the fishing boats. There's a whole fleet setting out from here, you know. Well, coming in, at this hour. Quite nice shops,' said Dot, who had not expected anywhere outside the city to resemble civilisation. She was already debating whether her intended, Hugh Collins, an amiable police constable (who had said he was coming down to see Dot and perhaps do a little fishing after he finished his fraud case), would like her in a soft shift of ivory cotton with sportive orange starfish dancing around the hem.

She mounted the stairs, shoes in hand, resolving to see if the dress was still there tomorrow. Phryne paid very well. Dot had money to spend on treats for herself, if she felt she needed a treat.

Ruth and Jane removed the remains of the feast to the kitchen. Phryne decided to survey Mr. Thomas's library. She felt like emulating Dot. A nice lie-down with a good detective story was indicated, especially after that second gin squash. Nice collection of detective stories, including a whole shelf of R Austin Freeman which she had not read. She picked up *The Famous Cases of Dr. Thorndyke* and her half-empty glass and prepared to ascend to softer and more luxurious regions.

Molly, however, rocketed up almost under her feet and sped into the back part of the house, whence emanated barking and yelling. Phryne put down the book and, carrying the glass, her gown swishing around her, headed for the centre of the disturbance.

The pantry contained, reading from left to right, Tinker hanging onto Molly, Jane looking perturbed, Ruth clasping a large raw bone to her aproned bosom and a small, shaggy, indescribably dirty creature, wagging a stump of a tail and carrying a very large, very dead rat in its mouth. Phryne took charge.

'Tinker, shut Molly in the scullery. Jane, could you close the baize door, Dot is trying to have a nap. Ruth, you could probably put down that bone, now. And you can come here,' she said, sinking onto her heels and holding out her hand.

The animal edged closer and deposited the rat, proudly.

'Yes, a very big rat, how clever of you, a real Sherlock Holmes Giant Rat of Sumatra,' soothed Phryne. 'You have definitely earned a reward. Tinker, can you dispose of the rat? And Ruth, can you find some scraps for the...er...'

'I suppose it is a dog,' said Jane dubiously.

''Course it's a dog,' said Tinker. 'It's the Johnsons' dog, Gaston. You remember me, Gaston?'

Gaston decided that he did remember Tinker, but was concentrating on the plate of scraps which Ruth was assembling. When they arrived he dived headlong into the plate, his miniature tail whirring. The effluvia arising from his coat was rank enough to make Jane sneeze. Even Phryne, with Great War battle experience, had seldom smelt worse.

'I dunno where he's been,' said Tinker.

'A rubbish heap,' said Phryne. 'I hope. Don't I remember an old hip bath hanging up in the scullery? That's your next task, Tinker dear. Disinter the dog from under the mud, or what I fervently hope is mud, identify him, and then manage to introduce him to Molly. I will not have dog fights. Were the Johnsons fond of Gaston?'

'Doted on him, Guv'nor,' replied Tinker promptly. 'Not a good sign, is it?'

'No,' said Phryne. 'Carry on,' she said, refilled her glass with lemonade and ice, and left them to it.

'Molly's in the scullery,' said Ruth, reasoning it out. 'Miss Phryne says we have to wash this dog in the hip bath. Which is in the scullery. Without causing a dog fight.'

There was a silence.

'Bit of a facer,' commented Tinker.

'You're not washing that thing in my nice clean sink,' said Ruth, anticipating him. 'I prepare food in here. That creature's been digging into a septic tank. It probably carries cholera.'

In the end they managed it by recourse to an old problem in logic which involved a river, a tiger, a cabbage and a goat, which Jane explained as they shuttled Molly and Gaston in and out of the scullery, finally managing to get the filthy mongrel, the tub and a good supply of soapy hot water on one side of a door and Molly on the other, who was both placated and gagged with the huge lamb bone.

Gaston was resigned to being washed and did not even yelp as Tinker ruthlessly scrubbed horrible debris from his coat. The hip bath was filled and emptied twice before Gaston emerged as a handsome (if thin) Jack Russell terrier, liver and white, a collar with his name tag on it still around his neck. Tinker rubbed him almost dry with a washed thin towel and Ruth allowed him another plate of scraps. She was now rapidly running out of scraps.

'Poor little blighter!' said Tinker. 'He's been doing a perish all right. He's thin as a lath.'

'Not for long, if he stays around here,' said Jane, as Ruth added some gravy-soaked bread to the plate.

'Who wants to peel potatoes?' asked Ruth brightly.

Jane and her book vanished with a whisking noise like the sound of a rapidly turned page. Tinker sat down on the step philosophically with the bucket of potatoes and began peeling. He knew a hint when it was applied, even with a soft oven glove. And it wasn't as if Miss Ruth wasn't working as hard as anyone.

Silence fell in the house. Gaston, exhausted by hygiene and his first good meal in a week, fell asleep in the mint bed. Molly, assured that her bone would remain her very own exclusive property, flopped down under the kitchen table and gnawed, resolving to ignore this intruder for now. Ruth peeled and chopped carrots for her *potage bonne femme*. Jane continued her anthropological research in the parlour.

Phryne, already making inroads into R Austin Freeman, listened to the seductive voice of the sea and closed her eyes. Peace reigned in Mercer Street, Queenscliff, at three in the afternoon of a warm January day.

It couldn't last, of course. But the household got in a solid hour's rest before the policeman hammered on the door.

Dot woke with a start and jumped to her feet. Jane dropped her book—but caught it before it hit the floor. Phryne rose in one motion and was at the door before she was quite awake. The speed of her reflexes had delivered her from many unpleasant encounters, such as a drunken Gascon with a switchblade and a fair number of high-explosive shells.

She admitted an unexploded police constable in a high state of excitement.

'Miss Fisher! They say you found the Johnsons' little dog?'

'Yes, he came to the door bringing me a very sizeable rat. You breed rats big by the seaside. Would you like to see him?' Phryne reflected that news moved fast in Queenscliff.

'If you please,' said the constable, clearly bung-full of news and anxious to impart it.

Phryne led him through the green baize door to the kitchen where Ruth was sucking a cut finger and Tinker was picking up fallen potatoes. He had tipped over his bucket. He scowled when he saw the visitor and identified him as a cop, then remembered that he was now on the side of the angels and tried a grin.

'Yes, that's Gaston all right,' said PC Dawson.

'Yair, well, he's still got his collar and all,' drawled Tinker.

Gaston wagged his tail uncertainly.

'You would have thought they'd take him with them,' said the constable.

'Yair, you would have. Mrs. Johnson used to carry him around like he was a baby.' Tinker was Helping the Police with Their Enquiries. Until the advent of Miss Fisher into his life, he would have put good money on that not ever happening.

'But we've found the furniture van. Ellis and Co, of Point Lonsdale. They packed up everything and left. Tuesday morning, very early.'

'Indeed. Did they also take the contents of the kitchen?' asked Phryne.

'The witness didn't say.'

'Because you didn't ask him, I expect.' Phryne was still sounding gentle.

Tinker pricked up his ears. He had taken his bucket of peeled potatoes into the kitchen and was rinsing them in the sink. Ruth knew that tone, too. Miss Fisher was losing patience. That cop had better adjust his views or she might adjust them for him, with painful results.

'Anyway, they skipped,' said the policeman, sealing his fate.

'Have you heard from Mr. Thomas?' asked Phryne sweetly.

'No, Miss, he's somewhere out on the never-never, we can't find him,' answered the young man, backing away a little.

'Fine,' said Phryne, escorting him to the door. 'So you won't be making any more enquiries about the fate of the Johnsons?'

'No, Miss, it's all solved.'

'God bless you,' said Phryne, shoving him gently out onto the porch. 'And give you better sense,' she added. 'Tinker?'

'Yes, Guv'nor?'

'Conference,' she said, and led him into the parlour. He stood awkwardly, cap dangling, aware suddenly of how grimy he was. He was not used to parlours, soft furnishings, or beautiful ladies with jade eyes.

'Ruth, can you manage tea?' called Phryne.

'Yes, Miss,' called Ruth, who had already laid out the afternoon tea before she had started peeling what seemed to be a world of carrots. Her domestic confidence was growing. This is what I will do for the rest of my life, she thought, and was suddenly so happy that she distributed the heel of the ham between Molly and Gaston.

Phryne considered Tinker. All arms and legs. Had outgrown those trousers two or three years ago. Boots, scant as to laces. Shirt, entirely missing. Washed thin grey jumper, unravelling at the elbows. Hands, large and dirty. Face, unwashed. Cap, filthy old tweed doubtless inherited from a father or uncle. He wriggled under her gaze. Bright blue eyes, probably blondish hair under the grime. Intelligent eyes, in fact, softened only with devotion. She made up her mind.

'Tinker, we are going to find out what happened to the Johnsons.'

'Yes, Guv'nor?'

'And to do that we need an operative who can go boldly but carefully down amongst the poor and oppressed and gather information. Can you do that?'

'Yes, Guv'nor,' he replied instantly.

'I will double your wages,' said Phryne. Not a big financial sacrifice, she thought. Twice a pittance was still a pittance. 'You can eat as much as you want of Ruth's cooking, and that includes a proper breakfast. Where do you live?'

'Fishermen's Flat, Guv'nor.'

'Where is that?'

'Down by the harbour, Guv'nor. There's me mum and seven of us. Dad's a sailor. He ain't home much,' said Tinker, and Phryne got the impression that this was all right with Tinker. 'We live in a house, but we rent it out to the trippers in summer.'

'So where do you live then?'

'In a tent, Guv'nor, in the backyard. It's all right in summer,' Tinker told Phryne. 'I could bring a blanket and stay here, Guv'nor, if you want to have a man in the house. I could stay in the Johnsons' old room. Not to mess up your nice house, like.'

'I think we could do better than that,' said Phryne. 'Move one of the iron beds from upstairs, get Dot to organise you some linen and so on, purchase a pair of pyjamas, which you will wear, and unfortunately that includes a bath every Saturday night and one immediately before you put your new shirt on. Is that fair?'

'Yes, Guv'nor! But I got no money, Guv'nor!' he told her, shamefaced.

'No matter, I have. Dot will take you down to the shops and buy some clothes. But hang onto your present garments. They will make a very good disguise. Where do you line up in the seven children, Tinker?'

'I'm the eldest, Guv'nor,' he said. 'Then there's sisters all the way down to little Albie and Tommy and…'

'I see. Can your mother spare you?'

'If I'm bringing in some cash, Guv'nor, she'll be jake. She was real cut when she thought I was going to get the sack. We got to stash the rent money, see, to last us through the winter. There ain't no trippers in the winter. And Mum can't work like she used to, since the last baby.'

'All right. Do you want to work for me, Tinker?'

'Yes, Guv'nor!' His eyes burned hot with adoration.

'You have to keep anything you find secret, you understand? No boasting to the other boys, no little hints about how much you know, no gossip about my household.'

Tinker stood to attention.

'Lips are sealed, Guv'nor!'

'All right then, it's a deal,' said Phryne, extending her hand to be shaken. 'Now we have to make a plan. Sit down—it's all right, the chair covers are washable. Ah, tea. Hello, Dot, did you finally get some rest?'

'Yes, Miss, until that cop turned up.' Dot sank down into one of the easy chairs. 'What did he want?'

'To tell us that the Johnsons had ordered a carrier to take their furniture away and that no further action was to be taken.'

'What, even though they left their little doggie they were so fond of?' demanded Dot, outraged.

'Even so. I ushered the lad out before I clipped his ears, as clipping the ears of the constabulary seldom profits an investigator.

I have taken Tinker into my household. This is Miss Dot, and you will do as she says,' Phryne introduced them.

'H'lo,' said Tinker, looking down.

'I'm sure you'll be a good boy and help Miss Phryne,' said Dot, despite inner misgivings. The boy was clearly a guttersnipe. On the other hand, Miss Phryne was very perceptive about people. He might have hidden depths. Well hidden. But Dot's not to reason why. Poor boy could do with some feeding up, that was plain.

'Oh, yes, Miss,' said Tinker.

Ruth brought in tea. They ate her banana bread. They drank. Tinker managed without spilling anything or dropping crumbs on the carpet.

'Right,' said Phryne, producing a sea-green notebook and unscrewing the top from her fountain pen. 'Here is what we know.'

In an hour, they had laid out a comprehensive document. Phryne read it over then put the lid back on her pen.

1. The Johnsons were quiet people with no known vices.

2. They seemed happy with their employer, Mr. Thomas, who as far as he knew lent me a house with devoted and stable staff.

3. They apparently ordered a van from Ellis and Co, Point Lonsdale, and put all of their worldly goods, and a lot of food, on board.

4. They left not a rack behind except a scatter of oddments and their beloved little dog, Gaston.

5. No one saw them leave? Check this, Tinker.

6. What was the destination of the van? Check this, Phryne.

7. They left the back door open.

8. They put the Boucher and the Chelsea figures in the wine cellar—for safekeeping, perhaps? And they didn't touch the wine when they were looting the house.

9. They gave no notice, as far as we know, to Mr. Thomas, who is out in the backblocks and cannot be contacted. And not due back for several months. Talk to his university colleagues? Phryne.

10. The house was not ransacked. There are a lot of nice things here, and no sign that the upper floor has even been entered.

11. Police have decided that no further action need be taken. Idiots.

'As nice a little puzzle as Dr. Thorndyke ever solved,' said Phryne with satisfaction.

'And no murders,' replied Dot, fervently hoping that this was so.

'So far,' said Ruth. Intercepting a stern glance from Phryne, she added hastily, 'My dinner's all ready to go in the oven, and now I've got to take Jane swimming,' and she collected her sister, despite her perennial protest that she'd come when she finished her chapter.

'It'll be here when we get back,' soothed Ruth as she led her towards the stairs to change into bathing suits.

'The sea would still be there when I finished my chapter…'

'What do you think's happened to the Johnsons?' asked Dot, really wanting an emollient answer. She did not get one.

'I can't imagine,' replied Phryne. 'Now, if you would, Dot, go down to those shops again and buy some respectable clothes for this ragamuffin. Shirts, you know, and underwear and so on. I've got an account at the draper's. Or I could go myself,' she suggested. 'If your feet are still sore.'

'No, no, my feet are fine, that nice lie-down was just the thing,' said Dot quickly. The Lord alone knew what Miss Phryne might buy if set loose in a draper's shop.

'Good, then I will possess myself of the telephone and see what I can find out amongst the intelligentsia.'

She was aware that Tinker was at her side, quivering slightly. 'Tinker?'

'Guv'nor, if you want me to go about finding out things, it would be good to have a bike.'

'Yes?' asked Phryne, wondering how far the young man would push his luck.

'Only Jack said he had an old one he could let me have for five shillings. Needs new tyres but it'll be bonzer once I scrape off the rust and give it a good polish. I could get about a lot quicker with a bike, Guv'nor.'

'So you could.' Phryne reached for her purse and counted out ten shillings into the grimy hand. 'Buy new tyres and a tin of polish, too. That's an advance, Tinker. You'll have to pay me back sixpence a week.'

'Right you are, Guv'nor!' Tinker went to the door with Dot, walking on air. A bike meant the difference between employment as any kind of messenger and penury and a monotonous diet of porridge, bread and tea in the winter. 'You beaut!' said Tinker, and Dot smiled at him. With a comprehensive bath and some new clothes, he might be quite personable. And with him sleeping in the Johnsons' rooms, there would be a guard on the back door. Besides, Dot loved shopping, and had now decided on the purchase of the ivory dress with the appliqué. This task took her back to the very shop, hopefully before someone else had had time to buy it.

In the distance they saw Jane, accompanied by Ruth, running down the hill towards the baths. No green-sickness for Miss Fisher's girls. Dot led the way into the draper's, feeling pleased with the world.

Chapter Five

Canst thou draw out Leviathan with an hook?

Job 41:1
The Holy Bible

Phryne pushed back her chair and lit a gasper.

'That,' she told Ruth, 'was a wonderful dinner. The soup was delicate, the roast lamb superb, the vegetables succulent and the apricot cream positively adorable. Well done, Ruth dear. Applause, please,' she requested, and the company, including a very clean Tinker in a blinding shirt, applauded. 'Now, we need to settle what we want to do,' Phryne continued. 'You are not going to cook every night, Ruth, unless you want to. What do you want?'

'I love cooking,' said Ruth. 'But I need a kitchen maid. It's not fair to drag Jane away from her books and Tinker is going to be working for you.'

'True. But if we find a kitchen maid, would you like to continue?'

'Yes, Miss Phryne, except maybe I could cook dinner for say five nights and then have two off? There are lots of good restaurants in Queenscliff, they say.'

'Every one of the big hotels boasts of their chef,' Phryne responded. 'That sounds fair. Make it four and three, eh? And if at any time you want to throw your copy of *The Gentle Art of Cookery* at the wall, we can go and buy fish and chips down at the harbour. Deal?'

'Deal,' said Ruth promptly.

'Now as to the Johnsons. I have been talking at wearisome and probably very expensive length to the grave and reverend signors of the university and it appears that no one knows where Mr. Thomas is. He has a favourite tribe, it seems, who tell him secret anthropological things, and he doesn't want to share them with anyone else. This sort of thing is common in universities, apparently. "Like a dog with a bone," one gentleman informed me. However, I have got a couple of telegraphic addresses, and I shall try sending messages tomorrow.'

'What about the locked room?' asked Jane eagerly. She was forbidden to read at dinner and had actually been listening.

'Ah, yes, the locked room. Not yet,' said Phryne affectionately. 'First we need to survey his own literary works, which means going through all these books, which means you and me, Jane. Ruth and Dot will be helping Tinker to set up his room. By the way, Tinker, you have sole charge of poor Gaston. He knows you. Keep him with you. If he gets out and comes back bemired, you know who is going to be washing him.'

'Yes, Guv'nor, it'll be me,' said Tinker, unfazed. He had washed Gaston once and he could do it again. Besides, the little dog would be company. Tinker had never slept solo in all of his sixteen years. Although he had hated the stuffy family tent packed with humanity, he didn't know about being alone. Still, he was now the proud possessor of a job, a lot of clothes, a very short haircut, and a bike which would be sparkling once he had scraped and sanded all the rust off it. Tomorrow he'd give Mum his first week's wages, which Phryne had advanced for that purpose. He could not, offhand, imagine that he could be any happier.

Phryne and Jane began at one corner of the library and scanned shelves.

'Here's biology,' remarked Phryne. 'Tulloch, MacKay. All the texts. Darwin—looks like a complete collection. Even *The Voyage of the Beagle.*'

'I've got chemistry here,' said Jane in reply. 'Your favourite Glaister, *The Power of Poison*. University textbooks. Botany. *Indigenous Dicotyledons of the Otways*. A rather good old *Herbal*. Gerard. And here are Culpeper's *Complete Herbal* and *English Physician*. Hmm. He says that mint is a refrigerant. We've just been eating refrigerant herbs. I don't feel any cooler, though.'

'But think how hot you might feel if you hadn't been eating mint,' Phryne told her. 'Stop reading and keep scanning, Jane, if you please. I've moved on to mathematics and chess. All Greek to me. Iris on auction bridge. *A Book of Games*. Music—opera plots, various analysts, life of Diagalev, *Ballet for Beginners*. Cultured sort of chap, our Mr. Thomas. What have you got?'

'Astronomy. Advanced, bound papers. How interesting!'

'Later,' said Phryne, cutting off a stream of information at its source. 'Here are classics—Roman plays, Juvenal, Lucan. And the Greeks—Aristotle, Socrates, Plato. Politics. We have Thomas Paine. We have *Das Kapital*. In German. We have Engels' *Condition of the Working Class in England*. Much more readable, by the way, than the master Marx. What have you got, fellow librarian?'

'Children's books,' said Jane. 'Fairy tales. *Mother Goose. The Wind in the Willows*. I like this one. *The House at Pooh Corner*, just published. I'll set that aside to read later. Lots of these are new.'

'How do you know?' asked Phryne.

'They smell new,' said Jane. 'Never been opened, I'd think. He must have laid them in for someone's children.'

'He does lend the house,' agreed Phryne. 'Up here I've got three-volume novels—*The Rosary* by Florence Barclay, *The Daisy Chain* by Charlotte M Yonge. I read them when I was your age, Jane. Reliable read and they did go on for ages.'

'Like those all-day suckers,' said Jane wisely. 'They don't taste all that good but they do last all day.'

'Precisely,' said Phryne.

There was a crash, a thud, and a lot of creaking from the luggage hoist.

'That will be the iron bed for Tinker,' said Jane, not taking her eyes off the shelves.

Molly began to bark hysterically.

'And that will be the escape of Gaston from the servants' quarters,' said Phryne, weighing *The Descent of Man* in one hand.

Something scuttled into the library and hid under the couch.

'Gaston,' said Jane, walking over to the door and shutting it. 'Poor little creature. I wonder how the Johnsons came to leave him behind?'

'He might have leapt out of the truck,' said Phryne. 'Here's anthropology, Jane, come and see. Dogs do tend to lose their heads when anything strange happens, you know.'

'I know,' said Jane. 'Ooh! Here's one by our own Mr. Thomas himself. *Journeys in Arnhem Land*. And here's another, *Fetish and Mystery in Arnhem Land*.'

'Fetish? Isn't that African? I seem to remember Mary Kingsley talking about fetish religions. Can you see a copy of *The Golden Bough*?'

'Here, all three volumes of it.' Jane hefted down the third, which had the index.

Phryne scanned rapidly. 'Fetish Kings in West Africa,' she read. 'Nothing about Australia. Never mind. No doubt Mr. Thomas will enlighten us. Gosh, listen to this from the much-respected Mr. Frazer: "Amongst the aborigines of Australia, the rudest savages as to whom we possess accurate information, magic is universally practised, whereas religion in the sense of a propitiation or conciliation of the higher powers seems to be nearly unknown. Roughly speaking, all men in Australia are magicians, and not one is a priest: everyone fancies he can influence his fellows or the course of nature by sympathetic magic, but no one dreams of propitiating the gods by prayer or sacrifice." Well, Mr. Frazer, that seems a little harsh.'

'Why?' asked Jane, reaching for the second volume.

'Assuming that if you don't sacrifice to the gods then you are a rude savage.'

'I'm a rude savage,' said Jane unhesitatingly.

'Me too. Though I would not advise rubbing ochre onto the person. I once got coated in red mud while caving, and it might have been easier just to apply another coat than get that muck out of my hair. It took hours. Almost caused Dot to swear.'

'No!' objected Jane.

'Well, she blessed me a lot of times in the name of various saints and was distinctly heard to say "drat" more than once. That's strong language for Dot. There's a whole shelf of works on the Phoenicians in England here. It's something of a fad at the moment, I believe.'

'Phoenicians? Like in Ancient Greece?' Jane climbed up onto a chair to reach the higher shelves.

'Yes, those Phoenicians. They would travel anywhere to sell something or buy something. The Afghans of the ancient world. They traded around Africa for gold and ivory. They might have got as far as Cuba. They certainly bought their tin from Cornwall. Tin being essential to the manufacture of…'

'Bronze,' said Jane quickly.

'Good! And since it was the Bronze Age, they'd feel silly without any bronze. They'd have to call it the Copper Age, and I don't believe copper is at all useful for weapons.'

'Too soft,' said Jane. 'Mind you, bronze is mostly copper with about ten percent tin thrown in to harden it.'

'And it is beautiful,' said Phryne, lifting down her armload of books and offering a hand to her daughter.

'Oh,' said Jane, who had never understood the term. 'I suppose so, Miss Phryne.'

The sofa and the table were piled with anthropological texts.

'Well, there's our research work,' said Phryne.

'What are we looking for, Miss Phryne?' asked Jane, taking up a weighty tome and wondering where she had left her notebook and pencil.

'Any clue as to the present or prospective whereabouts of Mr. Thomas, or his destination, or even his closest allies,' Phryne told her.

'Ah,' said Jane, who had found both notebook and pencil keeping her place in *The Mystery of the Gilded Bones*. Detective stories could wait. This was a real-life mystery. Jane sat down to read through Mr. Thomas's first book. Phryne took the second. Jane was supplied, by Ruth, with a night-time cup of cocoa, and Miss Fisher took another gin and lemonade.

Dot, Ruth, Tinker, Molly and Gaston (retrieved from under the couch and comforted with a biscuit) retired to the cosy confines of the kitchen and left them to it. Gaston was not happy. The kitchen was his kitchen, but the familiar furniture had gone and the human smells were different. He yearned for his people. He shivered, though the night was warm.

Then the boy called him. The boy had not been a close friend but he belonged to the part of Gaston's life which had contained affection and biscuits. He trotted into the bedroom, where the boy lay in a bed made up suitably with pillows, sheets and blankets. They, too, had the proper scent of the household.

Tinker was uncomfortable. The house was making creaking noises and something appeared to be breathing near the window. He had never slept alone in his life. The bed was clean and he was clean and this, too, was strange. He kept getting tangled in his sheets, never having lain in sheets before. His new pyjamas, which he was wearing as a condition of his employment, were scratchy starched cotton and they pulled at various points where he had been used to wearing only a shirt, when his shirt was clean enough to wear. Every time he closed his eyes he expected that whatever had happened to the Johnsons was about to happen to him, for Tinker was sure that they were dead, probably murdered. A snake? A deadly krait, the 'hundred steps' snake which was all the victim would ever walk before he died horribly? Some sort of spider? There had been a huntsman on the ceiling and it was gone now. What would Sexton Blake do?

Find an ally, of course.

'Come on, Gaston,' called Tinker, and heard the clatter of the little dog's claws on the hard stone floor.

Gaston leapt up into Tinker's arms, turned around three times to give himself room, gave the boy's face a passing lick, and settled down to sleep. Tinker closed his eyes and undid the top button of the pyjama jacket, letting in some welcome air and the smell of dog, to combat all this cleanliness.

Both of them sighed deeply.

Even though the huntsman descended the wall to find out if he was edible at all, and retired disappointed to catch moths, Tinker and Gaston did not wake again until daybreak.

◇◇◇

Morning was announced by the merry cries of the baker's boy, the butcher's boy (hoping to see his beloved Lily and retiring broken-hearted), the milkman, the grocery man and, oddly enough, the ham-and-beef's adorable fourteen-year-old daughter, whose little brother had been caught playing with the fisherboys and had been confined to barracks for spanking, scolding and disinfection. Warned by the previous day's experience, Phryne slept through this visitation. Jane also showed no signs of rising.

Dot, who had agreed to cook breakfast for the duration, fried tomatoes, mushrooms, bacon and eggs. Ruth sliced bread and laid the kitchen table for their breakfast. Molly ate rinds, as did Gaston. Tinker had fought his way into his new clothes and appeared, having voluntarily washed his own face and hands. This was easy, he explained, when you just had to turn on a tap and water came out. Hot water.

'A bloke doesn't even have to boil a billy,' he said, sitting down where indicated and picking up his eating implements.

'It is wonderful,' agreed Dot. 'I remember getting up in the freezing dawn to light the copper.'

'Me too,' said Ruth, shuddering slightly. 'Fingers so cold they wouldn't work. Dropping the matches. Praying that the little flame would catch.'

'Here, hang on,' objected Tinker. 'How do you know all that stuff? You're ladies.'

'Certainly we are ladies,' Dot told him. 'Where does it say that a woman who works for a living can't be a lady? Isn't your mother a lady?'

Tinker was astounded. His entire political and social world view had been knocked off its axis. Dot loaded his plate with provender, filled his cup with well-sugared tea, and bade him eat up and think about it later. Tinker could understand that, at least. And he had been told to do as Miss Dot ordered. Besides, he had never eaten tucker like this in his underfed life. Thinking, Tinker felt, could always wait.

Ruth, between bites, wrote out her tasks for the day. It was rather a daunting list. The only trouble with Miss Leyel's wonderful recipes was that they took a lot of peeling and chopping and mincing. Dot observed the fraught way in which she was chewing the end of her pencil and said, 'Never mind, we will get a kitchen maid for you,' and Ruth smiled and took the implement from between her teeth. Then she frowned afresh.

'Not if it's Lily again. What's wrong with her, anyway?'

'La-di-dah,' said Tinker through a gargantuan mouthful. He liked to taste all of the components of this wonderful breakfast at once. He swallowed and went on, 'All she thinks about is the movies. Thinks she's Theda Bara. Works all right if you yell at her. That's what Mrs. Cook does. That Lily's only got a job because it's the height of the season. Soon as Easter's over, she'll be goin' back to Mother.'

'And good riddance,' murmured Dot. No one had ever allowed her to behave like that.

'Still, any port in a storm, that's what the fishos say.' Tinker had cleared his plate and was now leaning back with the expression of a tiger shark who had ravened down a goodly portion of sperm whale and really couldn't eat another toothful of that nice nourishing blubber. 'Eh, Gaston?'

The little dog had absorbed a solid meal of dog biscuits and leftovers and seemed replete. He was lying with his head on Tinker's foot. Molly, still not too sure of Gaston, kept her distance and growled occasionally to remind him that he was unwelcome.

'All right,' said Ruth, getting up and handing him the kettle. 'Refill that, will you, Tinker, and then can you water the herb garden? After that there's a lot of peeling.'

Tinker took the kettle. It was work, but the company was very pleasant, and for a breakfast like that every day Miss Fisher had his entire devotion.

Phryne woke after a disturbed night in which she had been: 1) sacrificed to the Corn King, 2) shut in a dark hut and fed only on sago, and 3) thrown into a volcano. That's what comes of too much anthropology late at night, she thought, then brightened. These dreams could not be omens of trouble ahead. All of the said sacrifices had to be virgins, and it was far, far too late for Phryne Fisher to qualify.

She rose and bathed in the elegant bathroom. She wrapped herself in one of her flowing Chinese robes. There was no bell in the room so she went out in search of breakfast and met Dot on the landing. She was carrying a tray.

'Coffee, Miss Phryne, and a nice new roll. I've found that apricot jam you like, too, and the Queenscliff butter is first rate. Shall I take the tray onto your balcony? There's a nice little table and chair there.'

'Thanks, Dot dear, that is really kind of you. How fares the household this morning?'

Phryne seated herself at the iron table and Dot poured her a cup of the inky, dangerous Hellenic coffee which jolted Phryne into wakefulness.

'Jane isn't up yet,' said Dot disapprovingly. 'Ruth and Tinker are starting the peeling and so on.'

'Ah, yes, a kitchen maid. We shall have to do something about that today. Did you sleep well, Dot?'

'Yes, Miss, I could hear the sea. It's really hard to keep awake if you can hear the waves.'

'I stayed up reading those anthropology texts, Dot dear, and they were too, too dire. I strongly suspect the "naked savages" of having a little quiet fun at the expense of the enquirers.'

'Well, why shouldn't they?' asked Dot. 'Poor benighted heathens, why should they have to answer all them questions from a lot of white men? They're likely to think it's none of their business. You got all you want, Miss?'

'Yes, thank you, I shall be down soon,' Phryne assured her.

To beguile her very good bread with excellent butter and superlative apricot jam, she read a few more pages of Dr. Thorndyke. Phryne had been educated enough as to the beastly ways of the poor benighted heathens.

When Phryne had assumed some summer garments, omitted stockings and found her sandals, she descended to the kitchen, where the household now seemed to gather, and found that the staff had been augmented, once more, by Lily. She was peeling oranges with a discontented air and seemed pleased to see Miss Fisher, who might be interested in the amazing news she had to impart.

'There's a movie being made in Queenscliff!' she exclaimed, spraying orange juice into her immediate environs. Tinker, who was sitting next to her chopping dates, made a disgusted noise and moved his chopping board rather pointedly to the other end of the table. He had never had a clean shirt (and another to change into and one in the wash, making three shirts in all) before, and he objected to being stained so early in the morning.

'Really!' Phryne sounded gratifyingly interested. 'What are you making, Ruth?'

'It's an Arabian Night dessert, Miss Phryne,' said Ruth. 'So I need the oranges in cups, not in bits.'

'Like this,' said Phryne, taking the little knife away from Lily and sliding it into the halved orange. 'You just slip the knife around like this, and *voila*! An orange cup. You do the next one and tell me about this film.'

Lily made such a mess of the next orange that Phryne removed the knife for public safety reasons and gave her the potato peeler.

'Tcha!' remarked Ruth. Being a cook had not improved Ruth's temper.

'I'll do the oranges, you peel,' Phryne encouraged. 'You can't stay in the kitchen unless you work, you see.'

Lily looked at Miss Fisher. A lady, Mrs. Mason had said. She was dressed in a loose cotton shift printed with seaweed and scallop shells which seemed simple. Lily somehow knew that her entire monthly salary would not begin to pay for it. Dot dropped an apron over Miss Fisher's head, confirming Lily's view that this was haute couture. And she was real good with that knife.

'They just came in this morning,' Lily told Phryne. 'Staying at the Esplanade.'

'Oh, very high class,' said Tinker, chopping mint now in a cloud of scent. 'If they're so swanky, why ain't they staying at the Queenscliff?'

'You shut up,' snapped Lily.

'Tinker, do put a sock in it,' requested Phryne. The boy blushed and continued with the herbs, which smelt divine. 'If you don't like potatoes, we can give you the onions,' hinted Phryne. Lily hated chopping onions. The smell went into her hair and sank into her skin so that everyone would know she was a skivvy, fit mate for a butcher's boy.

'Mr. Applegate and Mr. Orphin,' said Lily sulkily, mutilating an innocent potato. 'They had a lot of gear, cameras and film and stuff. And they say that they're making a film about Queenscliff, and we're all going to be in it!'

'Ha!' said Tinker, remembered his orders, and turned it into a cough. 'I reckon that's all the mint, Miss Ruth. What's next?'

'Strain the orange juice into this jug,' requested Ruth. She was wondering what to have for her fish course. The fishmonger's boy had not yet come, which argued that there had not been a good catch, at least, not enough left over for the town when the fishermen had fulfilled their quota of fish for the city of Melbourne, whose tables and fish-and-chip shops all that bounty of barracouta were destined to furnish forth. Perhaps she could do as Miss Leytel daringly suggested and leave out the fish course, supplying more vegetables, simply but beautifully cooked. There were globe artichokes and those lovely carrots just cried out to be candied with ginger.

She would ask Miss Phryne when she had finished interrogating Lily. Ruth and Dot knew an interrogation when they heard it. Though most felons reported that it was a pleasure to tell Miss Fisher anything she wanted to know.

'So, what is the name of the film?' asked Phryne. She made very beautiful orange cups and Ruth marvelled. Never had she thought that Phryne would be able to turn her hand to anything in the kitchen. Greatly daring, and believing that Phryne might need an excuse to stay in the kitchen and talk to Lily, she presented Phryne with a platter of lemons to be sliced, deseeded and laid in sugar to be candied. Miss Leytel had a very good recipe for candied peel.

Phryne began slicing lemons expertly. Lily, emboldened, mangled another potato and gasped, '*Benito's Treasure*—it's a mystery!'

'You would think there were enough of them around here,' observed Dot, who was stoning cherries with a paperclip.

'But they're using the story of the pirates!' imparted Lily, putting down a potato peeled to the size of a walnut.

Dot hated waste. She took the peeling on herself, now that she had completed her cherries. Dot could peel potatoes in her sleep.

'Those boys were talking about treasure,' said Ruth, coming out of her text for a moment. Lily giggled.

'Ooh, yes, everyone knows about it. It was Benito's treasure. He came into the bay in his ship, landed the treasure from some cathedral, all golden saints and church cups, and when he came out again a navy ship was waiting and blew him out of the water. Everyone knows about the treasure, though no one knows where it is.'

'It sounds like it will make a good story,' prompted Phryne.

'They're already setting up in Swan Bay,' Lily told her. 'I'm going out there when…when…'

'When you have finished here. Which is now. Take off your apron, dear girl, and I hope to see you on the silver screen,' said Phryne, and Lily found herself free, and vanished out the back door. 'And good fortune to you,' said Phryne, handing over her lemon slices. 'We really must find you a kitchen maid, Ruth dear. That one is a wet slap and a dead loss.'

'But where?' wailed Ruth.

'Missus?' said a tentative voice outside the door. Tinker opened it.

'It's one of the fishos,' he told Phryne. 'A Mick.'

'You will not use that word again, Tinker, or you will be finding other employment,' Phryne told him. It was the fisherboy from the day before, looking frightened and bearing in his arms a huge fish. It had a disgruntled expression, for which it could hardly be blamed.

'Hello, Michael,' said Phryne. 'Is that for me?'

'Caught it meself, Missus,' said the boy, looking away. 'To say thank you, like. For saving my skin like you did.'

'That's a very good thankyou.' Phryne admired the fish. 'Can you cook this, Ruth?'

'Ooh, yes, baked with olive oil, lemon and herbs,' said Ruth, receiving the snapper into her arms and hugging it.

Michael Callaghan shifted from foot to foot.

'Was I after hearing that the lady needs a kitchen maid?' he asked.

'You were, yes,' said Phryne.

'Then there's me cousin, Missus, out of place through no fault of her own. Máire O'Malley is her name, and she could be starting right away. Could I be sending her up here so you could try her skills?'

'You could.' Phryne smiled at him and he stopped shuffling. 'Do that very thing and that right speedily.'

He bowed and then he was gone and the back gate swung shut behind him.

'Well,' said Ruth, 'she has to be an improvement on Lily.'

And then it was time for morning tea and the base preparations for dinner were almost done.

Phryne moved around to the other side of the table. The snapper seemed to be glaring at her.

Chapter Six

Sun-girt City, thou hast been
Ocean's child, and then his queen

Percy Bysshe Shelley
'Lines Written among the Euganean Hills'

Phryne betook herself and an iced orange juice cocktail to her balcony for a mid-morning consultation with Dr. Thorndyke but found herself distracted from the admirable prose of R Austin Freeman.

Treasure? Surely not. The story as given was absurd. What would a Royal Navy ship be doing down here, so far away from any settled colony? What, indeed, would a respectable pirate be doing down here, so far away from any achievable loot? But Ruth had said that the boys next door were hunting for it. Probably generations of holidaying boys had searched for it. Nothing like a really improbable quest to occupy a holiday. It prepared one for later life quests, like Justice and Truth, equally unattainable. For some reason her life, lately, had been haunted by pirates, of whom she could not approve. She had never found them romantic. On the other hand, perhaps she might see if there was any mention of this Benito in the encyclopedia downstairs. Later. The view was really engrossing. The sea was like a crumpled blue satin sheet, liberally embroidered with sails. The sky matched it, with clouds. Delightful.

◇◇◇

Tinker had completed his kitchen tasks, had sharpened the carving knife again, and was now engrossed in the enjoyable and very messy task of disinterring his new bike from under the detritus of years. Gaston was in attendance at a safe distance, supervising from his favourite place in the mint bed. Tinker had borrowed a paring knife and a trowel and a handful of sandpaper and Dot had insisted on him wearing the houseman's apron, made of thick, dark green canvas. Tinker was not used to the idea of having clothes which needed protecting.

He had taken off his good shirt, which freed his arms, and he was now arrayed in his apron, his new blue singlet and his proper working trousers.

Dot reflected that she had better arrange something about the washing soon. She should also call on Mrs. Cook and tell her that her kitchen maid had gone off to the film set and might not be expected back. Therefore, she put on her straw hat and went next door, cutting through the back gate and the lane and coming upon Mrs. Mason's house from the kitchen garden. This was the route adopted by all the tradesmen, and Dot heard Mrs. Cook's voice raised in wrath from as far away as the compost heap. The cook was denouncing the fishmonger's boy, whose fish apparently were both stale and late. Dot thought of the massive piscine feast which awaited the Fisher household that night. Dot adored fish in almost any form. She felt a little guilty, but only a little.

She almost collided with the boy, coming out, as she was at the door, going in. He accelerated towards his bike and set off in a cloud of dust. Mrs. Cook was not going to be in a good temper.

However, Dot had met incandescent cooks before. She knocked politely, and went in.

Another boy with a trike watched desolately from the shadows.

◇◇◇

Ruth was peacefully shelling peas when her sister Jane drifted into the kitchen, seeking tea. For once, Jane did not have a book with her. She was pale and mute.

'I say, Janey, are you all right?' Ruth asked, pouring hot water onto the leaves.

'Read too much anthropology,' faltered Jane. 'Too many feasts and taboos and horrible initiation rituals.'

'Buck up,' Ruth urged. 'That's all in the past and not here. How about some toast? Maybe an egg?'

'Just tea,' Jane replied. 'There isn't a thing to eat which isn't the subject of something too nasty.'

'Even bread?' asked Ruth.

'Especially bread. And apples. And corn. And meat.'

'Drink your tea, then, and let's talk about something else. That dreep Lily's been here. And she's gone. Someone is making a film in Queenscliff about Benito's treasure,' said Ruth, casting around for subjects which did not relate to food or religion, which rather limited her choice.

'Those boys talked about treasure,' said Jane, picking up a little and drinking her tea with three sugars.

'I asked Miss Phryne about it, but you know how she is about pirates. Ever since that Chinese lady pirate Mountain of Gold cut off Mr. Lin's ear.'

'Gosh, yes. Though he has got a nice rubber one and it did make him head of the family,' Jane responded.

Tinker, rubbing industriously at a spoke, pricked up his ears. This was something he did know about it. Benito was Queenscliff folklore.

'I can tell you about him,' he offered. Both girls turned to him. Miss Jane looked real sick and if she wanted a story to take her mind off things, Tinker was her man.

'Tell,' said Jane. Then she added, 'If you please, Tinker.'

'He was called Benito of the Red Sword, because he killed a lot of people,' said Tinker. 'He was sailing off Lima in 1842 when the revolution happened and they had to get the gold out of the city quick. He was a Royal Navy captain, then. They loaded all the gold and the church things, cups and candlesticks, and twelve statues of the apostles, and a statue of the Virgin Mary made all of gold.'

Ruth gently insinuated a bowl of fruit puree under Jane's gaze and put a spoon in her hand. Jane started to eat without noticing. Ruth hugged herself. That was a very good puree, of peaches and apples and nectarines. That ought to put some life back into her limp and depressed sister.

'Gold leaf, maybe,' said Jane. 'All gold would be too heavy to carry.'

Tinker shrugged. 'S'what they say,' he maintained. 'Anyway, this Benito killed the priests and the soldiers who were sent to guard the gold, and then he took off on the grand account. He was a pirate after that. Then he ended up here, in Australia, and the navy sent a ship to take him, and he hoisted the black flag, which means "no quarter", and—bugger!'

He stopped to shake a pricked finger. Someone had wired the old tyres onto the rims when they began to fall apart.

'Don't you dare put that finger in your mouth!' Ruth ordered, pouring water from the kettle into a bowl and adding carbolic. 'You come in here and soak your hand in this, and I'll make you some tea—and maybe some banana bread? And you could go on with the story,' she added, fascinated.

'What am I eating?' asked Jane, putting the spoon back into the bowl.

'Nectarines,' said Ruth cunningly. 'I bet there aren't any taboos about nectarines.'

'No, I didn't read of any,' conceded Jane, picking up the spoon again. 'It tastes very nice, Ruthie.'

'I always wanted to repay Miss Phryne,' said Ruth shyly. 'You know, for rescuing us. This way, I can do something for her that she couldn't do herself. Though she's a whiz with a knife, you should have seen her making orange cups.' Ruth became aware of an affronted boy staring at her and was glad to change the subject. 'Sorry, Tinker. What happened then?'

'Then there was a big fight, and Benito ran the rip. First ship to ever do it, they say.'

'What's the rip?' asked Jane.

'You ain't seen it? I'll take you there sometime. It's the mouth of the harbour, where it meets the sea. There's a wave. Anyway, Benito dived into harbour and the navy ship dursen't follow. They could wait for him to come out again. There weren't no people here then, just a few fishos and the odd escaped convict. So he hid the treasure in a cave in Swan Bay somewhere, left two people, a woman and a boy, then off through the rip again where the navy was waiting for him. First shot hit the magazine, they reckon, and the ship blew up and Benito and all his men and the rest of the treasure sank to the bottom.'

'Gosh,' said Jane, finishing the fruit.

'Ouch,' said Tinker as Ruth cleaned his hand, dried it, and applied iodine. 'Thanks,' he added. Tinker was not used to being tended.

'Tea,' said Ruth. 'And banana bread.'

'So no one has ever found the treasure?' asked Jane, distracted from horrible rituals as Ruth had meant her to be.

'Ah, there's stories,' said Tinker with his mouth full, tapping the side of his nose with his iodined finger. 'But no one knows anything.'

''Scuse me,' said a gentle voice from the door.

They looked up. A thin young woman dressed in a faded grey dress, barefoot, her head enveloped in a scarf, smiled tentatively at them.

'Hello, are you Máire?'

'Máire I am,' she answered.

'Come in,' said Ruth. 'I'm Miss Ruth, that is Miss Jane, and here is Tinker. So you are my new kitchen maid?'

'Yes, Missus,' said Máire.

'Then here is your apron,' said Ruth, presenting Lily's unused one. 'Come in, sit down, and start peeling apples. We are going to make a cake or two. But first you are going to have tea and the last of the banana bread,' added Ruth. This girl's skin was so white as to be translucent, and she was as thin as a moonbeam. Her hair, when the headscarf was removed, proved to be deep black.

Tinker returned to his bike. He would have to unravel all that wire before he could clean the rims and put on his new tyres. Molly awoke and came to greet the newcomer, putting her head into the girl's lap, hoping for a bite or crumb. Molly was partial to banana bread as well.

Máire sat as ordered, ate and drank, smuggled a crust of the cake to Molly, and won general approval by picking up a paring knife and beginning on the apples as soon as her cup was empty.

'We're going swimming after lunch,' said Ruth to Jane. 'Miss Phryne's on her balcony and Dot's gone to speak to Mrs. Cook about the washing. She'll be back directly.'

'Then I'll go and sit in the garden,' said Jane. 'And I'll read…' She intercepted Ruth's reproving glance. 'On second thought, why don't I sit here and read aloud to the workers? What shall we have? The fairy stories?'

'They aren't going to amuse Tinker,' said Ruth, who loved fairy stories.

'He has his work,' said Jane loftily.

Tinker bristled. Then he thought, Why not?

'I like them stories well enough, Miss,' he called to Jane. 'I c'n tell 'em to the littlies in the winter.'

'Good man,' approved Ruth.

Jane fetched the book, removed herself as far as was prudent from spurting juice or spraying flour, and began.

'"Le Maître Chat", or "Puss in Boots". *There were three sons of a miller who had just died, and his property was distributed as follows: first, the mill, to the eldest son, second, the donkey and cart, to the second son, and for the youngest son there was nothing but the mill's cat. "Woe is me," said the boy as he took hold of his legacy. "After I have eaten this cat and made a cap out of its skin, I will have nothing." "By no means," said the cat. "You do not want to eat me. I will make your fortune, if you will swear to do as I tell you." "Just as you say," said the boy, who had nothing to lose.'*

'I know what that's like,' said Tinker.

'So do I,' said Jane.

'So do I,' said Ruth.

'And me,' ventured Máire.

There was a silence where they all contemplated each other. Each young person in that kitchen, in their own way, had come to the extremity of hunger and despair. Yet there they were, peeling apples and listening to fairy stories, clean, warm, well-fed and safe. Then Jane adjusted her glasses and went on.

"'You must make me a pair of top-boots," said the cat.'

Phryne was just thinking that she ought to tear herself away from the view, dress and go down to lunch, thereafter finding the telegraph office and sending some telegrams, when she saw a boy approaching the front door, which argued that he was not one of the multitudinous tradesmen but a messenger. Phryne leaned over the balcony.

He knocked and the door was opened by Dot, who was still wearing her hat and seemed to have just returned from an interview with Mrs. Cook. She sounded a little sharp. The cook must have been in a temper, deduced Phryne. Cooks so often were.

The boy didn't speak. He bowed deeply and handed Dot a card. Then he turned and left, all without a word.

Phryne smiled at Dot's 'Well!' as she slapped the door shut, found some suitable garments and assumed them, and went downstairs.

'Funny thing just happened, Miss Phryne,' Dot began.

'I was an ear-witness throughout,' Phryne told her. 'What did he deliver?'

'This.' Dot handed over the card. 'I arranged about the washing, Miss; it's going to the Chinese, they'll collect it at the end of the week. Quite a civilised place, Miss, if they've got a Chinese laundry. And it's all peace and quiet in the kitchen. That Irish boy sent his cousin and they're ploughing through the work while Jane reads them fairy tales. I didn't disturb them. I just heard her say *"Sire, Sire, the Marquis of Carabbas is drowning!"* as I went past.'

'"Puss in Boots",' decided Phryne. 'I wonder how Tinker is liking them? Still, he has his bike to fix. In that case perhaps we should lunch out, Dot. How do you fancy a stroll to the town and a little refection?'

'That would be nice,' Dot replied, wondering if it was entirely right to just laze about while others did the work. Still, it *would* be nice…

Phryne saw her companion's stern resolve weakening.

'Come along, Dot dear, just go and tell the kitchen that we shall not be in for lunch, remind Jane that she ought to take some exercise, and I'll fetch my hat and read this missive,' said Phryne.

Dot, persuaded, hurried to the green baize door. She knew Phryne hated to be kept waiting.

Phryne found and donned her white straw hat with the wide brim, scrutinised herself in the mirror and nodded—very pretty, could pose for a British Rail advertisement—then opened the envelope.

When Dot came back she was still staring at it.

'What's in the letter, Miss?' she asked anxiously. 'Not one of them anonymous ones?'

'No, it's a perfectly ordinary invitation to watch an Art Film with the Surrealist Club, tomorrow night next door. At nine. Interesting. Surrealists? I don't know any surrealists.'

'Your fame has gone before you,' said Dot, and opened the door.

It was a lovely day. The sun shone. The waves bounced in a friendly, unthreatening way. The people of Queenscliff smiled at the visitors, who paraded along the broad and well-swept streets arm in arm. There was an air of holiday; an expansive, unbuttoned amity.

'What shall we have for lunch, Dot? Your choice. Simple at the teashop or elaborate at one of the restaurants?'

'Simple,' said Dot. 'I've got to save my appetite for Ruth's dinner.'

'Simple it is,' said Phryne, turning in at the door of the Queenscliff Tea Rooms.

An hour later, hunger satisfied if not sated by an excellent beef pie, a very serviceable apple crumble and a lot of strong tea—Phryne did not venture on coffee in watering-places, because she really liked coffee—they strolled out into the street again. Queenscliff appeared to be built for a gentle post-prandial amble. Well-dressed people, strolling; Phryne noticed that many of them were wearing some form of fish as decoration. Patterned on a dress, on a tie, in silver or gold on a bosom or securing a hat. Well, it was a seaport.

So Phryne and Dot ambled, gently, along Hesse Street and surveyed the shops. It had a full complement of the usual: baker's, butcher's, grocer's, ham-and-beef shop, three fish-and-chip shops, four teashops, draper's, mercer's, fishmonger's. Then there were odd little shops, tucked in beside what was surely the thinnest house in the world; a newsagent's, hairdresser's, a lolly shop, an ice-cream shop and a purveyor of toys and games. Dot paused at the window of her preferred dress shop, Henrick Modes.

'I'd like to go and collect my dress, if you don't mind, Miss. They had to do a few alterations.'

'By all means,' Phryne agreed. She was feeling as sleepy as a sunned-on cat and disinclined to do anything energetic. This looked like quite a nice little shop. Ready-made, of course, but that was the coming thing. Pretty loose shifts made of cotton in bright colours, perfect for a summer purchase. Espadrilles in beige and white. An array of really very good parasols. Phryne had forgotten hers. A choice of sunset orange, cerise, purple, azure and spring green confronted her.

She put aside the green, which threw an after-death glow onto the face (useful for sunburn), and the cerise, which gave the user the complexion of a boiled lolly. But the azure was charming, like carrying your own summer sky. She twirled it. It had a sensible shaft of steel, unlike the common flimsy cane constructions, so could be leaned on or used as a weapon and would not bend in a high wind. Altogether a thoroughly virtuous little parasol.

Phryne took it with her to look at Dot in her new dress. Dot had good taste. The dress was loose enough to be comfortable, and the line of dancing starfish was very well executed, if you liked starfish. It fitted very tidily.

'Lovely,' commented Phryne. 'Why not wear it home? You do nice alterations,' she told Miss Henrick, who with two other Misses Henrick constituted Henrick Modes.

'My sister Faith made the dress,' said Miss Henrick, a small and bouncy young woman with a cap of curly blonde hair. 'My other sister Charity did the embroidery. And I do the alterations.'

'Stout work, Miss Hope,' said Phryne. 'I may be throwing some business your way but for the moment I would like this parasol, please.'

'They're a bit expensive,' said Miss Henrick, uniquely of all dressmakers in Phryne's experience. She bit her lip. 'They're the English ones. I'm afraid they're three pounds each.'

'And Dot shall choose one for herself, so that makes two, and here is your six pounds, and thank you,' said Phryne, handing over the money. Dot, flushed with the excitement of a new dress and now a sunset orange parasol to go with it, kissed Phryne on the cheek.

'I like being on holiday,' she exclaimed.

◇◇◇

The kitchen staff, relieved of having to make a proper lunch for Miss Phryne, had lunched heartily on sandwiches made of various ingredients. Ruth never tired of ham and pickle, Jane loved tinned salmon and mayonnaise, Máire was introduced to the club sandwich by Tinker, who ate everything, as did the dogs, who prowled the floor begging for scraps. They accompanied this repast with lemon cordial and soda water.

Then, as Miss Dot required, they all rested for an hour. Dot, whose father had ulcers and believed that they were caused by exertion immediately after food, had made this a rule.

Therefore Máire found herself, for the first time in her life, sitting in a deckchair in the garden with nothing to do, accompanied by Tinker, who was still perfecting his bike and Gaston, who had retired to the mint bed for a snooze. Jane and

Ruth took Molly up to their rooms, where Ruth drowsed over a book and Jane fell asleep. Reading aloud was just as tiring as working, she thought.

'What sort of people are they?' asked Máire eventually, after she had recovered a little from her surprise. No one she had ever worked for had ever given her any time off.

'Good sort of people,' said Tinker, unwinding the last bit of wire so that the rags of the old tyre started to peel off. 'That's got it! The boss, she's a lady. A titled lady. And she has a maid called Dot. And the two girls are her daughters, adopted. And they all work hard, so we work hard, and then they rest so we rest. I never thought,' said Tinker, blowing scraps of rubber off the bare rims, 'I never thought in all me born that I'd be working for a private detective.'

'And she gave you the bike?' asked Máire, staring down into her cupped hands.

'She lent me the money to buy it,' corrected Tinker. 'She's no soft touch. I got to pay her back. It'll be a bonzer machine when I've got all the rust off and put on them new tyres. You one of the fishos down Fishermen's Flat?'

'Just come from Eire—what you call Ireland,' she confessed. 'Me and seven of us, to join our cousins. My dad's a fisherman, my brothers also. But it's been a bad season, they say. Not enough of the 'couta to make the quota some weeks.'

'So,' said Tinker, negotiating the last curly twist of wire without stabbing any more fingers. 'How d'you like Australia, then?'

'It's so strange,' said Máire, not wanting to offend any natives. 'So hot and bright. All the time the sun seems to shine.'

'It gets chilly enough in the winter,' Tinker warned her. 'And you want to get a hat. You'll burn in this weather. You want to help me?'

Máire was not used to doing nothing. She willingly knelt down to steady the bicycle as Tinker fitted his new tyres. Tinker decided that even though she was a Mick, she wasn't all that bad, really. It was dawning on Tinker that everything his harassed mum said about the Church being the Scarlet Woman might not be entirely right.

'What happened to the people who were here before?' asked Máire suddenly.

Tinker spun the back wheel, delighted with the way it ran.

'The Johnsons? Dunno. It's a mystery. Miss Fisher got here and they'd done a moonlight flit.'

'Fetched away?' asked Máire, taking better hold of the bicycle as Tinker shifted his attentions to the front wheel.

'Snatched, you mean?' asked Tinker. 'I dunno. All their stuff went. The boss is going to send some telegrams and make a few phone calls. Then we'll see,' he added with relish, as the front wheel came free of its accretions and moved under his hand. 'That's bonzer. Better let go now, Mary, you'll get oil on your clean apron.'

'That's what aprons are for, surely to God,' replied Máire. 'I need to steady it. There, look at that now!'

'You're one of them O'Malleys, ain't yer?' asked Tinker, who had just remembered something.

'O'Malley is my name, and that a fine one,' replied Máire with spirit.

'Nah, nah, don't get your Irish up. I mean, that Grainy, she's your sister, ain't she? The sailor girl?'

'She is,' said Máire. Her jaw set and her sea-blue eyes regarded the boy one candle watt short of a glare. 'My father Dubhdara forbade Gráinne my sister to go out upon the sea—unlucky, not fitting for a girl. But she stowed away, and when she was found she expected a beating. But my father embraced her and told her she was a true daughter of Black Oak and he would teach her all he knew about the sea, and so he did. Here they say things about her. But not to me, for she is my sister and a good girl and very dear to me.'

'True dinks?' asked Tinker. Máire did not know the idiom but divined the meaning.

'By Jesus, Mary and Joseph,' she swore, crossing her aproned bosom. 'And Patrick,' she added, lest the patron saint should feel left out.

'All right then,' replied Tinker. 'I'll know what to say to the cur who says she's...who says...' He faltered. Euphemism was new to Tinker.

Máire rewarded him with a beaming, radiant, sunrise smile.

'Let's see to this bike then, God love you,' she suggested. 'We must be back in the kitchen in ten minutes. Can I not be seeing the clock from here?'

They bent to their task, well pleased with their company.

◇◇◇

Phryne and Dot looked in at the post office, a most imposing building erected by someone with a strong inclination for turrets, and sent two telegrams which might or might not find Mr. Thomas, somewhere near the Roper River. They strolled further, past Simpson Family Butchers and Game, A House, Land and Commission Agent, and then paused at the door of Leonard's Hair and Perfumery, Wig-maker and Artificial Flowers, from whence issued a ferocious smell compounded of attar of roses, patchouli, chypre and singed hair. A woman with hennaed hair and over-liberal lipstick snarled at them as they stood in her light. Then she changed the scowl to an unconvincing smile.

'How can I serve you, ladies?' she asked.

'Oh, just wandering for the present,' said Phryne airily, and led Dot away.

'I do not feel that I will need a haircut while in Queenscliff,' she opined.

'Nor me,' said Dot. 'Smelt like she was burning rope.'

'It's those marcel irons,' said Phryne. 'If you want hair like corrugated iron, you need to discipline it very severely.'

'I like my hair as it is,' said Dot, feeling the weight of her French plait. 'And so does Hugh.'

'Never felt like cutting it all off? No more long afternoons waiting for it to dry? Much easier to manage in summer,' teased Phryne.

'No, Miss Phryne.'

'Well, stay out of the way of the phantom pigtail snipper,' advised Phryne. 'And now I think we should carry our burdens up the hill for a little afternoon rest. And I fancy another swim. Does the road wind uphill all the way?' she asked, with Christina Rossetti.

'Yes, to the very end,' said Dot, unconscious of poetry.

Phryne chuckled all the way to Mercer Street and, provokingly, would not explain.

Chapter Seven

It is not true that the English have only one sauce, but it is true that in England sauces are very often badly made, badly mixed, and not flavoured at all.

Mrs. CF Leyel and Miss Olga Hartley
The Gentle Art of Cookery

A rest, a swim, a tantalising scent of cooking fish, and it was dinnertime again. Ruth bore in the huge snapper, lavishly enfolded in butter and herbs which made a scented cloak to wrap the white, flaky, delicious flesh. There were groans of delight and satisfied desire from the table which gladdened Ruth's heart. Phryne picked and picked again, as did the rest of the diners, until the whole skeleton of the fish was revealed.

'I believe that this is all in one piece.' Phryne marvelled at its symmetry and beauty, stripped of scale and fin. 'What a beautiful object. Could you boil it clean for me, Ruth, and dry it?'

'Yes, Miss Phryne, but why?'

'Ah,' said Phryne, and Ruth knew that she was not going to get an immediate answer.

'You want it to stay in one piece?' asked Dot. 'Then you don't want to boil it, Ruth, that'll dissolve the gluey stuff that holds the bones together.'

'Cartilage?' hazarded Jane. 'How do you know that it will do that?'

'Because you can make fish glue out of boiling fish bones,' replied Dot, who never took offence at Jane's questions. They arose from a pure desire for knowledge.

'Lick of lysol will take the stink out of it,' advised Tinker. 'That's what the fishos do for their house signs.'

'Lysol it is, then,' said Phryne. Jane was pleased.

'Perhaps we could start a collection of bones,' she said.

'You and your bones,' sniffed Ruth. 'Anyone for dessert?'

'Perhaps just a teeny-weeny slice,' said Phryne, as Ruth supplied orange jellies in orange cups and mango and pineapple ice cream stuck with almond wafers. Tinker carried out the plates.

'Dessert goes into a different stomach, that's what my mum says,' offered Dot, slipping a spoon into the icy, creamy confection.

'Too right,' agreed Tinker, to whom frozen custard with fruit in it was a novelty to which he hoped to become accustomed.

'Very, very nice,' agreed Phryne. She accepted a cup of coffee, lit a gasper, put her elbows on the table and conspired. 'Now, to our investigation. I sent the telegrams but the Lord knows if they will ever reach Mr. Thomas. They've gone to Roper River and to Mount Marumba, wherever they are. And I rang Ellis and Co, the removalists, and found out something very odd.'

'What, Guv'nor?' demanded Tinker.

'They know nothing about a removal from this house.'

'What?' asked Jane. 'But a van came and took all their stuff, and it had Ellis and Co painted on the side. People saw it.'

'Nonetheless, the obliging young clerk went through the whole book for me and they have no record of it.'

'How odd!' observed Dot. She was full of excellent food and finding it hard to keep her eyes open.

'Sinister, eh, Guv'nor?' asked Tinker.

'Yes, perhaps. But there could be a few other explanations. Let me hear you give them. Jane?'

'The van could have been stolen,' said Jane. She knew she was weaker in exposition, which to her came perilously close to guessing. Which she instinctively felt was wrong, and possibly sinful.

'True. Ruth?'

'One of the carters might have been doing someone a favour. Had a load to bring to Queenscliff, and would have brought the van back empty. So he took the Johnsons' stuff back with him.'

'Dot?'

Dot yawned. 'Sorry, Miss Phryne, I'm that tired. Must be all this sea air. What if the person who said they saw the Ellis and Co van was mistaken?'

'Or lying?' put in Tinker.

'Good,' said Phryne, very satisfied with her class on detection. 'Make no assumptions. So we have three explanations: mistake or deceit, a borrowed van or a stolen van. What do we do next?'

'Find the witnesses,' said Jane.

'Oh, I know who one musta been,' said Tinker. 'Old Mother Alice—I mean, Mrs. McNaster. She's never been known to sleep, spends all her time at the window. Real cranky old chook. Sorry. Not a nice friendly lady. Kicks dogs, hates the kids, sticks a knife into any ball that goes into her garden. Even though it ain't her garden, really.'

'Oh? And where does Mrs. McNaster live?' asked Phryne repressively.

'Cross the way,' said Tinker, waving an expansive fork. 'First floor. See them lace curtains? She watches through 'em all the time. She lives with her son-in-law, Dr. Green, poor bas— er, man. Mrs. Green, she's not home a lot. They give Mrs. McNaster the first floor for her own and they pay for her companion. But she never sleeps and she always watches. That's who would have said it was Ellis's van.'

'Well, I suppose a neighbourly call is in order,' said Phryne.

'Guv'nor! You ain't going there!' said Tinker in fright.

'I don't think she'll bite me,' soothed Phryne. 'And if she does I can always bite back. It's not as though I live in Queenscliff and have to get on with the locals. If Mrs. McNaster confirms the name and seems to be in possession of her faculties, however uncharitable, then I shall send you, Tinker, down to Point Lonsdale to see what you can pick up from the removal yard. What is the state of your bike?'

'Real good,' he said. 'That Mick…I mean the Irish girl, Mary, helped me with it and I got the new tyres fitted and a lick of polish and it'll be good as.'

'Right, that's tomorrow,' said Dot firmly. 'Now we are all going to bed soon, so why not come down to the parlour and see what's on that gramophone?'

'Those of us who aren't doing the dishes,' said Ruth firmly, leading Tinker out after her, laden down with plates, with Jane walking behind carrying an unsteady tray of clinking glasses. Phryne listened for the crash, but when it came it was an unimportant and entirely superfluous gravy boat, of which the household already boasted three, so that was all right.

<><><>

They sweetened the evening with Mr. Thomas's rather good collection of popular light classics, and went to bed early. The sea made everyone sleepy except Tinker. It was one of the first sounds he had ever heard. It had been the background of his entire life. He had never slept in a place where he could not hear it.

He took himself and Gaston to the servants' quarters, with a slice of coconut cake, a glass of milk and a handful of dog biscuits for inner comfort and a new Sexton Blake to amuse the intellectual self. He washed and changed into his pyjamas and settled himself in his own bed with a pillow behind his back, a dog on his lap and his provisions on the table beside him.

It was a bloody good story. The cake and the milk vanished, the biscuits were gnawed to crumbs, and Gaston fell asleep, but Tinker was gripped by the narrative and read on.

Then Gaston woke up and barked, and Tinker was dragged bodily out of his absorption in the escape of Sexton Blake from handcuffs as he was being welded into a metal trunk destined to be sunk into the bottomless abyss. Passingly, he wondered why these villains didn't just shoot Sexton Blake several times at close range, instead of trying to kill him in such elaborate ways, but supposed that this was the nature of Masters of Evil.

'What's the matter, you silly mutt?' he asked a little roughly. Gaston looked up into his face, whined, then pointed his nose at the door and barked again.

'Someone at the door?'

Tinker was afraid, but he was now the Man of the House and required to be brave. He put on his boots and armed himself with the fire axe then took a deep breath before he allowed the door to slip open a trifle. He saw no one. Moonlight streamed in. It was getting late, he thought, time to shut the book and go to sleep.

But Gaston dashed out into the garden, barking wildly, and Tinker followed. Inside the house, he heard Molly wake and bark, then subside as though she saw no need to keep on announcing that something had happened when clearly it had stopped happening.

Gaston arrived at the back gate and scrabbled, yelping madly and leaping like a small liver-and-white projectile, so that Tinker had to catch him up under one arm to get the gate open.

And there was the peaceful night, unscathed by any noise, not even footsteps. He put Gaston down and the small dog ran in an anxious circle, whining, then returned to hide behind Tinker, peering out around his pyjama-clad legs.

'Whatever it was,' Tinker told him, 'it's gone now,' and he secured the gate with especial care and returned to the house, where he locked and bolted the door. Then Tinker went to the kitchen and got himself some more milk and another generous slice of coconut cake—plus a few gourmet bikkies from the Swallow & Ariell bag for his distressed canine friend.

Then they retreated to bed again. They applied Sexton Blake and a little supper as a remedy for their grated nerves. This worked well enough. After half an hour, Gaston drowsed on Tinker's lap. After ten minutes more, the book slid from Tinker's hand and they both slept until morning was announced by the shouts and cries of disappointed tradesmen who had found the back gate locked. As he hurried to unchain it, he resolved to tell Miss Fisher that someone had come to the back gate in the night.

◇◇◇

Phryne was awoken by Dot, who carried coffee, butter, jam, a freshly baked roll and a proposition from Ruth.

'She wants to invite Mrs. Mason and the boys to dinner tonight,' announced Dot.

'I'm going out,' said Phryne. 'To see an art film.'

'But not until nine, and only next door,' put in Dot. 'And we can get rid of them all by then if we dine at six thirty. As Ruth says, we owe them a dinner, and this way we don't have to put up with them for too long.'

'Mmm,' said Phryne, buttering a piece of crust. 'Cruel but adroit social placement. All right, send the invitation, Dot dear. Isn't this view just heavenly?'

'It is,' agreed Dot. 'Drat, that's the telegraph boy.'

She left Phryne to go and answer the door. Dot had never got over her dread of telegrams. In the Great War they had delivered nothing but news of loss and grief. Even though the Great War was over Dot still couldn't like the things. And the boys who delivered them were always cheeky.

This one was no exception. He gave her two telegrams, held out his hand, received his penny tip, whistled, promised Dot that he wouldn't spend it all in riotous living, and went off on his bike before she could reply.

She turned the telegraph office envelopes over in her hands. One of them, for a wonder, was addressed to her. She opened it quickly, so that Fate might not notice her rash action.

A moment later she was running up the stairs. Phryne was in the bath.

'Miss! Miss! Hugh's coming!' she called through the door.

'Goodo,' said Phryne, who liked Dot's large, calm, policeman. 'When?'

'He'll be here tomorrow night,' said Dot. 'Staying at a boarding house in Queen Street. Hopes to get in some fishing, he says.'

'Invite him to dinner on Friday,' said Phryne. 'He's a darling. I'll be down presently,' she hinted, and Dot recollected herself and chose some clothes for Phryne, laying them out on a bed which she made in four precise movements. Nice day again, blue skies and a light wind. Just a shift and sandals, no need for stockings. Then she descended to the kitchen to advise Ruth to lay an extra setting for Hugh tomorrow and supervise Tinker in cleaning all the cutlery, which had looked a bit dull at dinner the night before. And to find a corner to blush in unobserved, perhaps. She hadn't seen Hugh since his fraud case started, which was almost three weeks ago. Dot had missed him.

◇◇◇

Phryne Fisher, dressed in hat and gloves and even the despised stockings, a smart blue dress of moderate length and wearing only a recently bought fish brooch for ornament, rang the doorbell of the house opposite and stepped back a little so that any observer would be able to scan the visitor. She had made an effort and wanted Mrs. McNaster to appreciate it. And she had no doubt that Mrs. McNaster was watching her. Phryne had seen the telltale twitch of the heavy lace curtains.

The step had been scrubbed—this morning, Phryne judged; it was still a little damp. The door's mahogany folds gleamed. The brass numbers reflected like small numerical suns. This was a very clean house. Even through the door a faint scent of carbolic was leaking through.

When the maid answered the door, Phryne handed over her card and was conducted into a very clean, sparsely furnished sitting room to wait. She declined tea. The maid, who was Irish and about sixteen, probably called Bridget, gave her an admiring look and said, 'I'd take the tea now, Miss, you won't get none from Herself.'

'Then how can you offer it?' asked Phryne.

'I belong to the house, not the first floor,' the maid told her. 'The master, now, he's a hospitable kind of man, he tells me,

Bridget, you're to offer refreshments to callers. Herself, she's as mean as a…I mean, she's not likely to offer no tea to a visitor. Not that she doesn't relish tea for herself,' said the maid. Phryne could take a hint, especially when it was delivered in that buttery accent.

'Well, then, perhaps tea for both of us, if she can sit in this room?'

'Surely she can, Miss,' said the maid. 'That's why there's only a few sticks in here. So that poor oul' Lavvie can move her chair around. Back directly, Miss,' she said, and bounced out, a plump, comely armful of a young woman who would probably not be in domestic service for long, if there was any of the old buccaneering spirit remaining in the boys of Queenscliff.

Phryne sat for another ten minutes, quite unconcerned, until a bumping and a voice like a corncrake which has been insulted by another corncrake and is afflicted with a terminal case of diphtheria offended the bright morning. The advent into the room of a wheeled chair dragged by a thin elderly woman coincided with that of the maid escorting a trolley of tea, which meant that Phryne got over the difficulty of introducing herself in the resulting scrimmage.

Once the old lady had been placed so that her feet were in the sun from the French windows but her head was in the shade, the tea trolley had been set so that she could reach her plate and her cup, and the maid had poured the first cup of tea, Mrs. McNaster applied herself to the bread and butter for some minutes, while Phryne, the maid and the companion watched.

Mrs. McNaster had clearly outlived manners. Phryne smiled at Lavvie, who had not been invited to sit.

'Tea?' she asked her. 'Do have one of these cupcakes, they look delicious.'

As her employer did not so much as scowl in her direction, Lavvie ventured on a cake and had just taken her first sip of tea when Mrs. McNaster swallowed the last bite of bread and butter and shrieked, 'Lavvie! Get back to the window!'

'Yes, Mrs. McNaster,' quaked Lavvie. 'Right away, Mrs. McNaster.'

She had pale grey eyes and pale grey hair and was dressed, predictably enough, in pale grey, and she slid out of the room like an apologetic ghost. Phryne was pleased to see the maid slip her a plate heaped with goodies behind Mrs. McNaster's back. Phryne winked at the maid. The maid put a finger to her lips.

'I understand you saw the Johnsons leave my house,' she observed, as Mrs. McNaster's gnarled hand shot out towards the pound cake.

'Me? No,' snarled the old woman. 'I never saw the Johnsons leave. Not a sight of them.'

'Really?' said Phryne. 'How interesting. I was sure…'

'Saw their stuff leave.' Mrs. McNaster was clearly a truthful observer. 'In a pantechnicon. Loads of it. All their furniture went.' She bit into the soft cake and crumbs fountained onto her withered bosom.

'Ellis and Co,' the old lady continued when she could speak again. 'It was written on the side. But the Johnsons weren't there. Hadn't been for a week. Two men loaded it all up and went. What do you mean *your* house, Miss? That house belongs to Thomas.'

'He lent it to me,' Phryne told her. The old eyes gleamed with greed. This woman wanted both more food and more information than anyone else, Phryne thought.

'And who are you to him?'

'I met him at a party,' Phryne told her. 'About now my own retainers will be supervising the renovation of my bathroom and I decided we all needed a holiday.'

'Husband?'

'Not a one,' replied Phryne sunnily.

'Not right.' Mrs. McNaster muffled her opinion in more cake. 'Young woman should have a husband.'

'So naturally I was surprised that the Johnsons weren't here when I arrived,' Phryne went on, as though the old woman had not spoken.

'Flitted,' said Mrs. McNaster.

'Really? But everyone says they were so devoted to Mr. Thomas.'

'Only as long as they could sting him for every penny he possessed. Like all servants. All thieves, if they aren't watched like a hawk.'

The Irish maid raised both eyes to heaven and seemed to be thanking her guardian angel that she wasn't Mrs. McNaster's servant.

'Like Lavvie. My sister's girl. She'll have a pretty penny when I go. Until then I have to watch her. Extravagances! Ribbons! Novels! Chocolates!'

Poor Lavvie, niece to this old monster who would probably live forever, if she could disoblige someone by so doing. Phryne put down her empty cup. It had been good tea. Dr. Green the son-in-law kept a good table.

'Oh, yes.' Mrs. McNaster nodded. Her carefully dressed hair could not hide the bald spot. Phryne tried to drag her eyes away from it.

'Indeed,' Phryne sympathised, and rose to take her leave.

'Been someone at your door, too, Miss,' hissed the old woman, grabbing Phryne by the wrist. Her fingers were disagreeably cold and strong. It was like being detained by an importunate octopus. Phryne fought down an instinct to break away.

'Indeed?'

'Early this morning. Just before dawn. I saw the boy come out and the little dog. That's the Johnsons' dog, isn't it?'

'Yes,' said Phryne. 'Gaston.'

'They loved that dog,' Mrs. McNaster told her. 'Doted on it. Would never have left it behind. Mark my words, something's happened to them, and someone's stolen their furniture.'

'Who came to my gate?' asked Phryne, at last retrieving her hand. Mrs. McNaster smelt very strongly of something medicinal—Friar's balsam, perhaps? Something darker? Phryne's nose began to itch.

'Couldn't see,' confessed Mrs. McNaster. It was clearly a painful thing for her to confess. 'Too dark.'

'Well, if they come back again, we'll find out what it was about. Goodbye, Mrs. McNaster, thanks for the tea. No need to show me out, I can find the way,' said Phryne to the Irish maid. She walked out into the sun on the old parrot screech of 'Lavvie! What did you see? What did I miss?'

'Phew,' said Phryne, and walked across the road, conscious of the beady old eyes between her shoulder blades. She tore off her hat as she walked in the front door, sat down and removed the stockings, shoes and gloves, and ran barefoot upstairs for her sandals and some company.

Everyone, it appeared, was in the kitchen or the garden, and Phryne joined them there.

Ruth had ordered the ingredients and then sent Tinker down to the village for the extra ingredients, and had her menu laid out and her assistants chopping and mincing. Dot, from her garden chair, a throne of shelled peas, offered Phryne a choice of tea or cordial or a cocktail and was unsurprised when her employer cast herself down beside Gaston in the mint bed, caressed the little dog's ears, and opted for alcohol.

'Was she as awful as Tinker says?' asked Jane, who was always interested in people and felt she really knew far too little about them as a species.

'Fully,' said Phryne. Tinker beamed. 'In fact, he was very polite about her.' Tinker beamed again. That was a fault of which he had never previously been accused. 'She is a ghastly old bitch and I pity the poor companion who has to endure that parrot screech all day and every day. No matter what her expectations, no gold is worth that sort of a life.'

'That's what my mum says,' offered Tinker. 'But poor old Lavvie's been so ground down by that old…er…lady…that Mum reckons she couldn't survive on her own.'

'Possibly.' Phryne took a deep gulp of the orange cocktail, to which Ruth had added some extras. 'This tastes ambrosial, Ruth dear. Do I detect a little almond? Some noyau, in fact?'

'Yes, Miss Phryne.' Ruth was impressed.

'Lovely,' Phryne told her. 'Remember that I am always available to taste your experiments.'

'Mrs. McNaster…' suggested Dot.

'Could have been named by Dickens. The name just suits her. But I am afraid that she did see the van and it was emblazoned *Ellis and Co.* And she is a good observer. But she says she hadn't seen the Johnsons for some time before their furniture left, and they weren't there to load it.'

'Someone stole their furniture?' asked Dot.

'Seems unlikely, when they didn't take the whole houseful of really quite good furniture, not to mention artworks, books and ornaments,' said Phryne. 'Is there any more in that jug? I'd like to wash the taste of Mrs. M right out of my mouth.'

'Someone collected it and it wasn't the Johnsons dispatching it,' mused Jane, who was making quite a good job out of crumbling bread for a crumbled topping.

'So next we have to find out who and why,' said Phryne.

'I'll just get my old duds on,' said Tinker, dropping the last potato into the bucket.

'Hold on,' said Phryne. 'Not so fast. What about the person who came to the gate very early this morning?'

'How did you…? Oh, Mrs. McNaster saw it,' mumbled Tinker. 'I was going to tell you, Guv'nor. As soon as I saw you. See, Gaston barked, and when I went out, he barked more…'

'Which must have been when Molly woke up,' said Ruth. 'She just gave one bark then went back to sleep so I didn't think anything of it.'

'I went out to the gate, but there was no one there,' said Tinker, standing straight and reporting. 'I could see all the way down both ways and there was no one. So I chained the gate and came back and locked the door, and put the bolt up as well.'

'And you didn't hear anything else?' asked Phryne, trying to sound severe though considerably relaxed by her second cocktail.

'Nothing, Guv'nor, not so much as a mouse.'

'All right then. In future make sure that I know anything you need to tell me as soon as possible. You tell it to Dot. She won't forget.'

'Yessir,' said Tinker.

'Tomorrow, I think, would be a good time to investigate the Ellis operation. I need to find out more about it first. Today you can help Ruth and see if you can keep a straight face waiting at table tonight.'

'Me, Guv'nor?' Tinker gaped. Phryne grinned.

'You. I wouldn't make you sit down with those horrible boys. Just try not to spill gravy down their necks unless they really, really deserve it, and keep your ears peeled.'

'What for?' asked Tinker.

'Anything interesting,' said Phryne.

The assistants peeled and Jane swapped her crumbs for the fairy tale book. The household settled down to listen.

'Once upon a time there were two sisters, and they were as unlike as they could be, for one was dark and one was fair. The dark sister was called Rose Red and the fair sister was called Snow White.'

'I like this one,' said Ruth.

Gaston and Phryne drowsed companionably in the mint bed.

Chapter Eight

This film is so cryptic as to be almost meaningless. If there is any meaning, it is doubtless objectionable.

British censor's report on *Le Coquille*

Having lazily beguiled the day with a swim, a sandwich lunch, a close reading of Dr. Thorndyke and a conversation about Ellis and Co with the land agent who was also her banker in Queenscliff, Phryne bathed and dressed for dinner without much expectation of pleasure. The food would be good, she was sure. The kitchen had been emitting delicious smells all day. But the company could not inspire her. And she was trying to remember the surrealists, who had been flourishing, in a small strange way, at the time when she herself had been in Paris during and just after the Great War.

Mostly poets, she recalled, as she dried her skin on a bath sheet and smoothed Milk of Roses into her shoulders, slightly touched by the sun. Apollinaire, who had died so young. Yes. André Breton, who wrote the manifesto. Bad boys: André Gide, for example, who adored dangerous brutes as long as they were male and muscular and didn't hit him too hard. He hung around the surrealists because they resolutely refused to be shocked by anything and Gide made a good test for their level of tolerance. Yves Tanguy, who captured and then ate spiders to scare passers-by. Man Ray, the photographer, turning women into musical instruments. The slightly disconnected Marcel Duchamp, who gave up painting because he got good at it and started constructing things out of wire and string. Could beat anyone at chess with that absent-minded little smile on his face. Once, when Phryne had asked him what he was thinking about, he had answered, 'The passion of ducks.' When she had exclaimed, someone else had whispered, 'M'sieur est Belge.' But being Belgian could not alone explain Duchamp...Plastic enigmas, authentic falsehoods, and Père Ubu...

Phryne realised that she had been sitting naked on her bed for ten minutes, dreaming of Paris and the poetry of desire, shook herself, and dressed. Wondering as she pulled the silky dark red evening dress over her head where they all were now, the strange bad boys of the *quartier*. Most of them, probably, good bon bourgeois papas with six children and a job in a bank. Some of them, almost certainly, dead. Some of them, probably, still seeing the world at right angles to reality. For a moment she yearned for Europe, for the babble of French voices, the smoke of Gitanes, the taste of real coffee in a cafe where the whole world would saunter past during the course of the day. And draw up a chair, order a *blanc*, and talk about art.

But here she was, thousands of miles away, and that was her choice and dinner was already being announced. So she got up, found her shoes, flung a Spanish shawl around her sunburnt shoulders, and sailed down to greet her guests.

At least Ruth would not be cooking a surrealist dinner, which might present the diner with a nice soup bowl of nuts and bolts, or a drink composed of etching acid and ink...

After fighting down a natural desire to cook all of Mrs. Leyel's most extravagant dishes in order to show off her skill, Ruth had taken Dot's advice and considered what sort of food the Mason household usually ate. Conventional. Ordinary. Boring. So she had made a menu which was French and not unfamiliar, with a few touches which ought to make it memorable. In view of the sunny weather, it was all cold and had been chilling in the icebox for most of the afternoon. She wrote it out in her best handwriting, deciding against using her cooks' French. It tended to make Miss Phryne giggle.

Leek and potato soup, iced
Grey mullet in jelly with cucumbers
Salads: tomato and potato
Onion tart
Chicken in a white sauce
Mixed green salad with hard-boiled eggs, anchovies and olives
Turkish delight fruit salad with orange-soaked dates
  and rosewater
Cheese and biscuits
Coffee

And then, with any luck, they would all go home. But, Ruth resolved, they would all go home full.

Phryne flowed down the stairs in time to see the Mason contingent arrive. Best clothes and best behaviour. Someone had scrubbed the boys until they shone—with a rather sullen light, it was true. Perhaps they were not looking forward to seeing those little blossoms of education, Jane and Ruth, again.

Mrs. Mason had donned another satin gown, this time in a shade of dusty pink which was not so trying to her complexion. She wore a rose bandeau.

On entry, her eyes darted to all corners, hoping for something; clues to Mr. Thomas's regard, perhaps. Phryne had seen much the same greedy light in the eyes of the horrible old woman opposite. She hadn't liked it the first time.

'Cocktails,' she announced, and led the way into the pleasantly shabby parlour, where a tray awaited, the jug beaded with condensation and sloshing with the fine alcoholic fluid which might make this evening bearable.

Kiwi, Jolyon and Fraser took lemonade under firm maternal instructions. Jane and Ruth sipped their half glasses of sherry and tried to Make Conversation. The boys had obviously been threatened with a dreadful doom if they didn't behave, and they were trying to do the same thing. But the girls didn't know any of the chaps at school, understood nothing of the noble games of cricket or football, couldn't take a joke and were far too brainy. What was a chap to do? Fortunately, Fraser thought of something at the same time as Jane offered Kiwi her glass of sherry.

'Would you like this?' she asked. 'It makes me sleepy. I haven't touched it.'

'Wouldn't matter if you had,' he replied graciously, taking the glass and gulping and passing it to Fraser. 'Alcohol is a disinfectant.'

'And anti-bacterial,' agreed Jane. They smiled at each other. Jolyon claimed the rest of the glass and Jane filled it again. Dot and Phryne were talking to Mrs. Mason and no one was watching the young people.

'Been to the movies yet?' asked Fraser. 'We been down in Swan Bay all day watching them make *Benito's Treasure*. It was...' He searched for a suitable term which didn't sound childish. 'Int'resting.'

'Tell all!' invited Ruth, who adored films.

'They paint the actors' faces yellow,' said Kiwi. 'Yellow as Chinks! I swear!'

Jane and Ruth exchanged a glance. The Chinese of their acquaintance had all been of a light biscuit colour, not yellow at all. But these were boys, Ruth reflected. No brains at all at that age, Miss Phryne had said.

'Really?' she prompted.

'Crew of three,' Kiwi informed her. 'Cameraman Orphin, director Applegate and the other sheila with the papers.'

'Script, you idiot,' said Jolyon. 'The story of the movie. That's why she's always shouting things at the actors. So they do the right things. Actions.'

'And what was happening in the picture today?' prompted Jane patiently. Really, it was like shovelling sand to get them moving in the polite direction.

'The beautiful girl was being marooned on the desolate shore. Not that it's all that desolate, really—they had to move a couple of times so as not to show the houses. If you got marooned there today you could just knock on a door.'

'And who was the beautiful girl?'

'You'll laugh,' warned Kiwi.

'That will be a nice change,' Jane informed him solemnly.

'Of all people it was Lily—you know, that droopy slavey that the mater was about to fire?' chuckled Jolyon. Ruth disliked him afresh.

'I'm glad to know she succeeded in her quest,' she said. 'She really wanted to get into films.'

'There she was,' Jolyon went on, enjoying the joke, 'face painted yellow, dressed in an old-fashioned sort of big dress, waving her arms and wailing. We rolled on the sand laughing.'

'Quite,' said Ruth, who had heard Miss Phryne quash the doltish. It had no effect on the boys. They nudged and giggled.

Jane firmly refused to notice the pleading sherry glass which was held out for a refill and followed the party in to dinner.

The food had been laid out on a sideboard, which Ruth had converted to a buffet with the addition of a card table and a lot of spotless napery. One began at the left side of it and proceeded along to the right side, which was dessert. Tinker flicked back the muslin covering and the group of diners possessed themselves of bowls for soup.

'This is cold,' protested Jolyon at the top of his voice. His mother blushed.

'I'm so sorry,' she said to Phryne. 'We've never had cold soup. He doesn't know any better. You'd think that school would teach them table manners,' she added, as the boys dived into the food like starved swine. Fraser, whose father had a French cook, kicked Jolyon before he could demand that his soup be reheated.

'Tastes like library paste,' muttered Jolyon.

'Tastes good to me,' said Fraser. 'It's *vichyssoise*, you idiot. Just eat up and shut up. If you need to compare, compare this to that seaweed slop we get at school.'

'You can eat it hot,' observed Ruth. 'I could…'

'But you're not going to,' murmured Jane.

'No matter,' said Phryne. 'A glass of hock?'

'Thank you,' said Mrs. Mason. 'That was very good soup. And this jellied fish is superb. So you did manage to find a cook?' she asked, with increasing interest.

'Right under my nose,' said Phryne, smiling. 'The boys seem to be fascinated by this film that someone is making in Queenscliff.'

'It's about Benito's treasure. I remember looking for it with my brothers when I was a girl. We always came here for the holidays, you know, when my father the judge was alive. Thank you,' she said, as Tinker filled her glass again with a lemon-yellow plonk which he had tasted and found far too sour.

He was unfreezing. No one had even looked at him in his stout green apron. It was as though he had become invisible and that was all right with Tinker. Those boys had thrown enough rocks at him in his time. Though apparently the guv'nor had set them to the rightabouts. As one would have expected.

He moved over to supply the young persons with lemonade. They didn't notice him either, though Ruth gave him a furtive grin.

'Your father was a judge?' asked Phryne.

'Yes, a famous one. You have probably heard of him.' Phryne hadn't, but she smiled and nodded. 'He had this house built and we came here, as I said, every holidays. And no one has ever found Benito's hoard, so it remains to entertain the boys.'

'Nothing like pirate treasure,' said Phryne drily. Dot took over.

'We are thinking of going to the cinema on Friday,' she told Mrs. Mason. 'What would you recommend?'

'Go to the first house,' she said firmly, as she came back with a plateful of salad and cold chicken. 'After eight the streets become…rowdy. Fishermen and…so on. The only thing worth seeing at present is *For The Term of his Natural Life*. A worthy production and an Australian classic, on at the town hall. I sent the boys.'

'She did,' confirmed Jolyon gloomily.

'In the other cinema there is a dreadful thing called *Our Painted Daughters*. How they allow such filth onto the screen...'

Mrs. Mason accepted a glass of a rather young red wine to accompany her salad and continued her condemnation, with the result that the entire company resolved to see *Our Painted Daughters* at the earliest opportunity. Even Dot, who was a self-confessed Good Girl, found herself interested.

'Well, well, such are the times,' said Phryne. 'I have been wondering about what Queenscliff was like before the Great War.'

'Select, my dear.' Mrs. Mason elaborately did not notice Tinker refilling her glass with a wine which he thought was even more sour than the first bottle of plonk. Might as well drink lemon juice, he thought as he poured.

'Mrs. McNaster, my neighbour, is she an old resident?'

'Been here all her life, since her father—and there were rumours about him—came to establish his practice here. Her daughter married Dr. Green. Moved here due to bad health, they say. Weak lungs. This is a very good place for people with weak lungs. His mother-in-law is a sore trial to him. But his wife is a great comfort, I believe. Such a civic-minded woman. He is a great friend of Mr. Thomas.'

'And Miss Sélavy, next door?'

'She's a bit of a mystery,' said Mrs. Mason, lowering her voice. This had the effect of attracting the attention of the whole table. 'Always wears strange clothes. Has young men visiting her. But she's Hungarian,' she said bracingly. 'Titled.'

'Oh, indeed?' Phryne had known some very dubious titled people. Particularly Hungarians. Particularly titled ones.

'And she's an artist,' added Mrs. Mason, allowing Tinker to take her empty plate and tottering over to the buffet for the delectable fruit salad. Moral indignation had not affected her appetite.

'Indeed,' said Phryne again. The same went for artists, double. That made tonight's little excursion full of interest.

Dinner concluded with coffee and some passable cheddar, a glass of liqueur, and professions of fond neighbourly affection.

Jane had managed to signal to Tinker that the boys ought to have a Cointreau each, and they too were full of goodwill as they took their leave, even asking Jane and Ruth to come swimming with them the following morning. They had provisionally agreed, not knowing what Miss Phryne had planned.

Finally the door shut on them.

'Brilliant dinner, Ruth,' said Phryne.

'Pearls before swine,' grumbled Ruth.

'Even swine must be fed,' said Dot.

'I suppose so,' said Ruth.

'Look,' said Tinker. 'They ate almost all of it. That's good, isn't it?'

'They told us what they eat at school,' replied Ruth. 'They'd eat cordite pudding with blotting-paper sauce. But they did seem to like most of it,' she acknowledged, cheering up. 'And the leftovers, Tinker dear, are all yours.'

'You beaut,' said Tinker, gathering plates. He had eaten well before dinner, but this being invisible took it out of a bloke. And there was still quite a lot of that grouse fruit salad with the squashy dates and the orange pieces left. He had just the place for it.

◇◇◇

The first thing that Madame Sélavy noticed as her slim, dark-haired neighbour sauntered into the very surprising room was that she was not surprised at all.

Miss Fisher was wearing a loose purple and silver gown over a daring pair of beach pyjamas. Her head was bare—most unusual. Social distinction in women depended on who was wearing the hat. Hatless was for servants and workers. Hatted was for ladies. Intriguing. The guest wore long earrings made of seagull's feathers. And she was carrying, hanging negligently from her wrist like a fan, a bare, ivory-coloured fish skeleton.

Madame Sélavy considered that the evening might be less fatiguing than she had thought. Perhaps Miss Fisher played chess…

Phryne paused at the drinks tray. It was going to be an interesting evening. The room was startling. Even if you managed to ignore the stuffed elephant, which was a task in itself, there were the paintings; eye-afflicting abstracts which might turn into coherence seconds after the migraine set in. Strange rustic gatherings of part-human, part-animal. One superb Picasso of a cat stretching. A house of taste, in a way. She was strongly reminded of her own days as a model in Montparnasse. Where she had been cold, bare, hungry, and vastly appreciated.

The room rose to greet Phryne. First a straight-backed girl, possibly, in I Zingari cricket costume, with a stick of celery in his or her lapel instead of a daisy. His or her black hair, cut into a becoming cap, was as shiny and soft as a raven's feather. He or she was introduced as Pete. He or she growled 'Hello' in a deepish voice and ducked his or her head like a schoolboy. Pete's companion was dressed in a filmy gown with layers of black, pink and green tulle; a ladies' tea gown circa 1910. Looped around her neck and hanging to her knees was a necklace apparently composed of licorice allsorts, interspersed with mint leaves. This was definitely a female person, with a wise and mocking smile and unexpected dimples. She took the tips of Phryne's fingers in her own and announced herself as Sylvia.

Madame Sélavy said in her honeyed Hungarian voice, 'Wine, Miss Fisher?' and waved a hand at a young man who was entirely naked except, to Phryne's regret, a band of fur around his rather luscious loins. Described as Lucius Brazenose, the primitivist poet, he brought Phryne a glass and whispered, 'You're doing well, most newcomers don't get offered wine,' and Phryne sipped. A big full red.

'Bull's blood,' explained Madame. 'Conduct Miss Fisher to a chair, RM.'

Two identical persons rose. They were dressed in lounge suits, white shirts and red ties. They had the same scrubby haircut. They moved in perfect accord. Twins? Phryne scanned the faces. They were different, but each difference had been erased by greasepaint. RM 1, for instance, had broader cheekbones than

RM 2, so RM 2 had used theatrical pads to widen his. The telltale scent of stage makeup reached Phryne's sensitive nose. They led her to what looked like a perfectly ordinary armchair. She examined it narrowly for traps and springs and little surprises before she sat. Then she smiled, waved one of the RMs to sit down, and the arms of the chair folded around him. Phryne perched herself on his trapped knees. The audience laughed and clapped.

'Very good, Miss Fisher!' said Lucius Brazenose. 'I can see that you are going to enjoy our company. Up you get, RM.' He hauled the slightly crushed epicene figure to his feet.

'I have met surrealists before,' smiled Phryne.

An orange cat which looked as though it had been in every cat fight in Queenscliff since he had been a slip of a kitten strolled into the room. His ears had been deckle-edged and he had scars all over his big bruiser's face. He had great authority. No doubt that this was the local Master Cat. All he lacked were the top-boots.

He stalked to Phryne's feet and sat down, staring up at her and twitching the very end of his bitten tail. She allowed a suitable interval to pass, then offered him a closed hand to sniff. He did so, bit her gently on the knuckle, and passed on to shred a curtain.

'Perroquet,' said Madame, 'has his fancies.'

'He hates me,' said a young man, dressed in the soft shirt and black suit of a Paris bohemian. 'Thaddeus Trove. Can I refill your glass?'

'Only with wine,' temporised Phryne. One must always beware of unconditional offers from artists. A cat called Parrot? Well, why not? The cat didn't care what he was called as long as he was always called for dinner. Though that one would probably be out rolling sailors. And eating them.

There was, however, a real parrot, wakening from forty winks and shrilling, 'Chance! Canned chance!' Phryne guessed at the name.

'Hello, Pussycat,' she said, offering the cockatoo a grape from the fruit bowl on the table. It took the grape suspiciously, which was perhaps explicable in a surrealist house, then ate it with a snap of its strong beak. It was an old parrot, rather moth-eaten about the tail. It had originally been white with a yellow crest. Now its feathers were the colour of bread mould but the bird itself seemed alert and aggressive. 'Chaos!' it remarked.

'Pussykins,' corrected Thaddeus. 'Good guess, though.' Phryne selected a chair next to Sylvia, who was explaining to a gushing young woman that it wasn't hard to make the licorice allsorts necklace.

'You just string them on thread with a darning needle,' she said.

'But don't they go stale and fall off?' asked the girl. She was mostly wearing a red evening dress designed for an older and stouter relative. She needed, Phryne considered, a couple of safety pins or cleaner underwear.

'Then you can make another one,' said Sylvia earnestly. 'I like my jewellery to be always fresh, don't you?'

'Of course,' said the young woman.

'This is Magdalen Morse,' Sylvia introduced her. 'Poet and artist. Come and I'll introduce you to Cyril.'

'Why not?' asked Phryne, amused.

A middle-aged man sat rigidly in a straight chair, clutching a stuffed hyena.

'This is Miss Fisher,' said Sylvia, fluttering a few acres of tulle.

'Hello, Cyril,' said Phryne, holding out her free hand.

The man did not move or look at her.

'No, no,' chuckled Sylvia. 'Cyril is the hyena. This is Mr. Wellbeloved.'

'Ah,' said Phryne. She had turned away to speak to Magdalen Morse when a voice croaked behind her.

'Nice fish.'

'Was that you or Cyril?' she asked, and neither answered. The man was silent. So was the hyena. Phryne smiled.

'Come and see my latest collage,' urged Magdalen. Phryne went. There is no point in arguing with artists.

The collage stood in the centre of a dining room, where a table was laid with various covered dishes. Phryne was not in the least hungry, having eaten well, but was pleased to receive a refill of wine from a poet as she examined the artwork before her.

'*Objets trouvés*,' proclaimed Magdalen.

'So they are,' said Phryne.

The collage was a casting in bronze of a heap of seaside rubbish. It included a crushed packet of Woodbines and a tangle of fishing line. There was a hook or two, some shells, some pebbles, a flattened bully beef tin, four spruce cones and a wooden sandcastle spade lost by some child. Also, for some reason, a mouse.

'I like it,' said Phryne, who admired the skill with which the crushed fag packet had been rendered. 'But what about the mouse?'

'Perroquet brought it and left it there,' Magdalen told her. Phryne looked closer. Yes, that bronze mouse did have a rather battered, nibbled look. 'So I cast it.'

'Of course,' said Phryne. 'Canned chance.'

'Indeed!' Magdalen beamed. Despite the dress and the general impression of a nice girl who had been abandoned on a beach for a month without access to soap or a comb, she had a very innocent smile. Her occupation as a bronze caster did explain the small burns on her strong hands.

Someone was pulling at Phryne's sleeve. It was a conventional-looking young man dressed unconventionally in a tattered ballgown and tiara.

'Look at mine!' he urged.

'Julian Strange,' Magdalen told Phryne. 'Anarchist.'

Phryne contemplated the construction of string and bolts and paper flowers. All the anarchists she had known were more interested in bloody revolution than art. She said so. Julian grasped her arm.

'I call this *Collectivism*.'

'Well, of course you do,' smiled Phryne.

A dark, rotund, affable man in a blue silk smoking jacket brocaded with magnificent goldfish leaned forward to supply Phryne with a light for her gasper.

'T Superbus,' he said, introducing himself. Phryne was about to offer her hand but something in the dark, concentrated gaze made her wave lightly instead.

'Intuitive,' commented Madame. 'T Superbus does not touch. Humans, that is.'

T Superbus gave Phryne a comradely smile.

A small child dressed in a Greek tunic passed solemnly through the room, bearing a wooden lemon squeezer on a richly embroidered cushion.

'Manifesto,' said Madame Sélavy in her rich voice. 'Manifeste du surréalisme *par André Breton.* Poisson soluble.'

Phryne held up her wrist and exhibited her deceased snapper. '*Poisson insoluble,*' she said firmly.

There was a moment of complete silence. Then the fine maquillage cracked. Madame began to laugh. Relieved, so did the whole company. Magdalen was explaining to Thaddeus.

'*Poisson soluble* means soluble fish. Miss Fisher is saying that in the essence things are not soluble, in fact that the fish is real and cohesive. It is living and ceasing to live that are imaginary solutions. Existence is elsewhere.'

'How about another drink?' asked Thaddeus. In Phryne's opinion, this was the most sensible question of the evening.

'Reality is imaginary,' proclaimed Madame, in English. 'Existence is insignificant. But the imagination is ruthless. Surrealism is a drug. It is the fortuitous juxtaposition of two terms that shed a particular light to which we are infinitely sensitive. The strongest image is arbitrary.'

'The eye exists in a primitive state,' agreed Sylvia cosily. 'Let's do some automatic drawing tonight.'

'After the film,' said Madame amiably. Phryne suddenly felt comfortable. This was not a cult of personality. Madame was not an absolute ruler. And automatic drawing had to be better than the last surrealist game she had played, back in 1918, when three people had drawn random notes from cut-up musical scores out of a hat and assembled them. And then made Phryne listen as they played them. That was no way to treat Bach, even if it was inferior Bach.

The child with the lemon squeezer returned. Phryne raised an eyebrow at Pete.

'Every thirty-six minutes,' she informed the visitor.

'Why?'

'Why not?'

'Ah.'

Surrealism aimed to detach events from each other, so each occurred as a perfect thing to be examined and appreciated. Dreams. Nightmares. And that probably explained that horrific little box frame made like a window at which a monster coral-coloured lobster scratched. It was probably cross about being boiled...

The guests took their seats facing the opposite wall, and a cranking clicking was heard. The lights dimmed, the film's title was displayed. *Entr'acte*. Two men playing chess with great concentration. They played more chess. Someone in a corner of the room played nursery rhymes on a comb and tissue paper. The left-hand man made another move. The right-hand man considered it.

It might, Phryne thought, be time for a little more wine...

Chapter Nine

Surprise: non sequitur: revolution.

André Breton
Surrealist Manifesto

The washing-up was done. Every dish was clean, dry and in its right place. Dot supplied herself, Jane, Ruth and Tinker with cocoa and a few biscuits to guard against night starvation. Ruth was dropping asleep as she staggered up the stairs with Jane's arm around her waist. Molly plodded behind. Tinker yawned hugely, summoned Gaston and went to bed behind the baize door. Silence fell. In ten minutes the whole Mercer Street household was asleep, except Dot, who sat up for Phryne. She was not too sure of that strange collection of people next door. Artists. Poets. You never knew with people like that. Or with people altogether.

Dot sipped her cocoa. Now that the house was quiet, she could hear the sea again. It sighed. No noise came from the street and the night outside was wholly dark, moonless, velvety and soft. Dot nodded, drowsy with the soothing, shushing sound. Then she sat up firmly and reached for her knitting. She would not sleep until Phryne came home safe.

◇◇◇

Phryne had just regained her seat when a huge bucket of water was emptied over both players, splashing the camera, washing the chess game and the pieces away. It was cathartic. Phryne laughed aloud. So did the surrealists.

'I know that it's coming, but I never get used to it,' said the half-naked young poet. 'Well,' he added as the film whizzed and clocked its way back onto the reel and the lights came up again, 'time for supper. Can I get you a small *amuse-bouche*, Miss Fisher?'

'No,' said Phryne, who had presided over strange feasts before. 'I've eaten. And I have drunk, too. No more, thank you,' she added. 'That bull's blood is strong stuff.'

'Pity,' commented a middle-aged man wearing a Greek tunic. It looked rather good on him. He had nicely muscled legs. 'You might have enjoyed the string spaghetti.'

'I might,' Phryne told him. 'But I'm not going to. You can have my portion,' she added generously. He laughed. He had short curly hair and soft dark eyes.

'In this costume I am called Anteus,' he said, taking her hand. 'But if you see me in a suit please call me Dr. Green.'

'Certainly,' said Phryne. 'What brings you to the surrealists, Anteus?'

'Sheer boredom,' he said. 'I am quite successful as a doctor here. I treat all the fashionable invalids with sea bathing and fruit diets. And of course there are accidents and illnesses amongst the fisherfolk. But I am not born to be respectable.'

'Then there would be plenty of debauchery available if that was your bent.' Phryne observed. 'Or at least I assume so—this is a seaport, after all.'

'Oh, yes, there is, but I am not looking to be debauched,' said the doctor. 'Just diverted. And this is the most interesting company in Queenscliff. Poets, artists, lunatics. The bulk of the populace is aggravatingly sane.'

'Too bad,' sympathised Sylvia, who was holding a small dessert bowl half full of ball bearings. 'We probably do try too hard,' she said to Phryne, catching her thought in a slightly unnerving fashion. 'But just breaking away from normality takes a large amount of effort. Life has been so much more fun since Madame arrived.'

'When was that?' asked Phryne.

'Three years ago. Of course, she may not stay. This is not Europe. Bit of a cultural wasteland, Australia. In fact we all wonder why she came here. But we are so pleased she did that we don't like to enquire. Have a ball bearing?'

'Thanks,' said Phryne, took one, and put it in her sleeve. 'But Queenscliff isn't boring at present. You have a phantom hair snipper. And my housekeepers, the Johnsons, have vanished without a trace. Furniture and all.'

'Both tediously explicable,' said the doctor. He had a cool, clear voice which must have been a comfort to those invalids who needed companionship and attention as much as sea bathing. 'What is the common factor in all the snipper's victims?'

'They had plaits,' responded Phryne.

'Precisely.' The doctor pulled his Greek tunic over his knees. 'They are all young women under the age of sixteen. Over sixteen, young women either put up their hair or get a bob, like yours. And very charming it is, I might say. Only young girls, that is, pre-pubertal, manifestly not sexually available, wear pigtails. And there is the explanation.'

'He is a hair fetishist?' asked Sylvia. Pete had materialised at her side and was offering her a glass of fizzy wine. Pete himself had a glass of clear liquid which smelt of cucumbers.

'Krafft-Ebing has a chapter about it,' said the doctor. 'To possess the hair is to possess the girl. Tedious, very.'

'Lacks the skill, money or confidence to approach a real girl?' asked Phryne. She had read Krafft-Ebing and had even been able to translate the Latin, to which language the writer had resorted when he felt that the hoi polloi should not be privy to the depths of human depravity which he was describing. The book had not impressed her. Human sexuality, in which Phryne took a keen interest, had more convolutions than a sea shell, and she was only interested in a small number of them.

'No, not necessarily. He may be a paedophile, one who only becomes sexually aroused by children. Possibly he is so twisted that the hair doesn't just represent the girl, the hair is the girl.'

'In which case he is probably a surrealist,' said Phryne lightly. The doctor looked grave.

'Possibly,' he conceded. 'But not one of Us.'

'And the Johnsons?' asked Sylvia, thoughtfully biting a mint leaf off her necklace. 'That has caused a lot of talk, you know. They were such staid, careful people. To vanish like that—it was odd.'

'Crisis,' decided the doctor. 'They had been repressed for too long and one night they just broke out. Freud wrote about such cases. Not interesting.'

'Planning,' objected Phryne.

'I'm sorry?' asked the doctor, who was not used to being contradicted.

'Freud wrote about people who just threw down their tools and their lives and walked away. The irruption into the sane Ego of the unconscious Id. This wasn't the case. I spoke to your mother-in-law about it and she is a very good observer.'

The doctor winced slightly.

'Yes, she is, isn't she?'

'These people arranged to have their furniture removed. Ergo, they had somewhere else to be.'

'That is a point,' conceded the doctor. 'Has anyone told Thomas about it?'

'I sent telegrams, so far I have had no reply,' said Phryne.

'Had a letter from him only yesterday,' said the doctor. 'Didn't say anything about the Johnsons.'

'Perhaps you might come to dinner and tell me about him? Tomorrow night?'

'I should be honoured,' said Dr. Green.

'Bring the letter. It is a mystery,' said Phryne. 'One I mean to get to the bottom of,' she added.

'Why?' growled the schoolboy, Pete.

'Because,' said Phryne. This was such a surrealist answer that conversation halted for a moment in respect.

'Automatic drawing,' observed Sylvia, seeing two servants remove the feast and lay out a protective cloth, sheets of paper and handfuls of charcoal sticks. 'Come along!'

Phryne was seated next to Madame. This was the first good look at her hostess she had had.

Madame Sélavy was tall, thin and haggard. Her face was bony, her nose beaky, her eyes as bright as pins. She was heavily made-up, white paint and red lips and kohl around the eyes. She wore a draped gown which Princess Eugenie might have considered overdecorated, dripping with black and gold bugle beads, embroideries, tassels and fringes to the utmost tolerance of woven cloth. She smelt strongly of patchouli. Rings burdened every finger, her neck was wrapped in pearl-studded chains and a band of brilliants encircled her throat.

'Madame Sélavy, *enchanté*,' said Phryne, knowing that she was being inspected in return. She knew what Madame must be seeing. Slim, small, pale skin, green eyes, black hair cut in Lulu bob, no decoration except the seagull feather earrings which Dot had threaded for her. Madame gave Phryne her beringed hand. Phryne raised it and kissed it. The skin beneath her lips was old and papery.

'Mademoiselle, *enchanté*,' replied Madame, and kissed Phryne's hand in turn. They looked at each other. Both smiled.

'This is automatic drawing,' said Madame. 'You are familiar with it?'

'Yes,' said Phryne.

'Call me Rrose,' said Madame unexpectedly.

'And I am Phryne,' replied Phryne.

Madame took a sheet of paper, thought for a moment, then drew a quick scribble and folded it over. Phryne did likewise and passed the bundle on. At the opposite end of the table Magdalen Morse was doing the same. The papers passed rapidly along the ranks, each person drawing a few lines and then folding and passing the composition on. It actually was fun to be playing a Victorian parlour game in such eccentric company. Phryne, who could not draw, was not at a disadvantage.

The child with the lemon squeezer passed through the room unregarded. Perroquet drifted in and decided to sit on Phryne's lap. There was just enough room. He elevated his chin to be scratched and his deep bass purr added an odd counterpoint to the music of Erik Satie, which clunked and wheezed and chimed.

'Perroquet,' said Madame dotingly. 'He likes you.'

'I am sensible of the honour,' replied Phryne. She was finding the added burden of very heavy cat a little hard on the knees, and extremely cosy for the weather, but she knew cats had their fancies and soon a call from the kitchen or rubbish heap would summon Perroquet away. 'Rrose, this is an impertinent question, but what brings you to Queenscliff?'

'Europe,' said Madame. 'It was a cruel place. War, destruction, horror. My friend left me this house. So I came here. What does it matter where one is, if one's fondest wish is to be elsewhere?'

'And you found agreeable company,' said Phryne, looking at the table of people all busily scribbling and laughing.

'They try a little too hard,' said Madame, sotto voce. 'But they are witty and charming. And you, Phryne? What brings an urban sophisticate like you to this watering place?'

'Holiday,' said Phryne. 'One recent case was exigent and I nearly got assassinated. I am a private detective,' she told Madame. A momentary silence had fallen on the room. Phryne was used to this reaction. She smiled sunnily. 'And I am not investigating anyone here, I swear.'

There were a couple of sighs—of relief, perhaps? Madame ordered, 'The drawings,' and the papers were unfolded.

They were a strange and meaningless concoction, except for one. The first person had drawn a bull's head, and the subsequent artists, quite by chance, had added a man's torso, a horse's hind-quarters, and a fishy tail. Unless someone had peeked, it was a whole mythical animal derived entirely by chance. Not one that the Ancients would have recognised but perfectly convincing.

'That one goes on the wall,' announced Sylvia, and gave it to Pete to add to the others which were pinned to a high Victorian Gothic screen. 'Now for automatic writing.'

This was, as far as Phryne could tell, exactly the same as the old game of Consequences. More paper, pencils, more folding, one sentence per person. Liqueurs and chocolates and small salty cheese pastries were served. Phryne nibbled very circumspectly on a chocolate. It was a rich, creamy chocolate with an edgy hint of salt. It was, for some surrealist reason, one of the most satisfying savours she had ever experienced. Not, she understood, to be gorged on, when the salt might even become emetic. But so tasty that she allowed herself another small piece. Pete grinned at her. Perroquet purred. The company shuffled the completed essays and began unfolding poems and reading them. The only alteration allowed was to correct the gender of the speakers.

Some, by chance, were quite comprehensible. Sylvia Glass met Queen Elizabeth in a lift. She said, 'Off with her head!' She said, 'Don't be ridiculous!' And the result was a breach in the League of Nations.

Lucius Brazenose met Lorenzo di Medici in the Doge's Palace in Venice. He said, 'I adore you!' He said, 'I simply cannot understand a word you say.' And the result was a confusing poem about cabbages.

Magdalen Morse met the Lord Chief Justice in 79 Collins Street, Melbourne. He said, 'Down with all revolutionaries!' She said, 'Tomatoes are in season.' And the result was a small tin of baked beans.

T Superbus met Winnie-the-Pooh in Parliament House. He said, 'Only seagulls can really enjoy flying.' He said, 'Would you kiss me?' And the result was a bathing mat woven of human hair.

Thaddeus Trove met Theda Bara in a disused Chinese eating house. He said, 'I really cannot like sea bathing.' She said 'Come with me to my studio.' And the result was a small sickly child.

'That,' said Madame severely, 'verges perilously close to sense. Crumple it up.'

Julian Strange met both RMs in a fisherman's shelter. He said, 'I need a drink.' They said, 'Pumpkin shells can be hollowed out to make a lantern.' And the result was a stained-glass watering can.

'That one goes on the wall,' decided Anteus. 'I'll pin it up.'

Pete met Mr. Wellbeloved and Cyril in the Cafe Royale. He said, 'I cannot see the naked woman hidden in the forest.' He said, 'I hear the call of the wild.' And the result was a green snakeskin shoe.

Anteus met Sexton Blake in a shell hole. He said, 'What is the coefficient of friction of brass?' He said, 'Da da da da da.' And the result was a bald head with hair on it.

Madame Rrose met a very old drake with green wings in a dark savage forest. He said, 'We must prosecute the real world.' She said, 'Turn towards childhood for lucidity.' And the result was a clockwork eel-strangler.

'That, I like,' opined Madame. 'The last one is yours, Phryne.'

Phryne opened the last one: Phryne Fisher met Mussolini in a public convenience. She said, 'I will get to the bottom of this.' He said, 'If you gather thistles, expect prickles.' And the result was shorter hair. She could not help feeling that someone had cheated. Madame Rrose felt the same and was displeased.

'Crumple it up,' she ordered, and Phryne crushed the paper and, unobserved, stuffed it into her capacious sleeve. Sleeve pockets, she reflected, were essential for any conspiracy. No wonder the Ancient Chinese had so many of them.

'Now, coffee,' Madame Rrose ordered. 'Sweets. And more music!'

Servitors brought more coffee and pastries and the gramophone began to play nursery rhymes. A great improvement, Phryne felt, on the ear-crunching Satie.

Half a pound of tuppenny rice,
Half a pound of treacle,
Mix it up and make it nice,
Pop goes the weasel.

Phryne remarked that as far as she knew it was not the habit of weasels to go pop, they being slinky and silent hunters who preferred to avoid public notice, and Dr. Green explained.

'The original words were, "Up and down the city road, in and out the Eagle, that's the way the money goes, pop goes the weasel." Pop being the process of pawning something and a weasel being an essential tool of the trade if you are a tailor. Tailors get a bad press in street songs.'

'Nine tailors make a man,' said Sylvia.

'That's bells,' said Pete gruffly.

'So it is,' said the doctor admiringly. 'This really is the most educated of company!'

'Indeed,' said Phryne.

It was getting late and she had a sudden thought that Dot, despite orders, might have decided to wait up for her. That was Dot's own choice but Phryne, after almost a year of devoted attendance, was developing a conscience about Dot. Perroquet had leapt off her lap, leaving merely a few pinholes in her thighs to remember him by. And she felt that she had had enough absurdity for one night. She bade farewell to Madame, who was playing chess with both RMs, kissed Sylvia and patted the stuffed elephant's trunk as she walked past it. It did not feel like animal hide. She investigated further.

It was papier-mâché, which came as something of a relief. One would not like to think of a whole elephant being sacrificed for a surrealist joke.

Near the door was a big tank of water, in which a lot of goldfish were lying, evidently asleep or possibly bored. A small child—the lemon squeezer bearer—was sitting on the step under the tank, eating a toffee apple.

'Hello,' said Phryne. 'What do you do in this house?'

'I look after the fishies,' said the child in a strong Australian accent, uncorking his lips with some difficulty. 'I carry the stuff around.'

'Do you like it here?' asked Phryne, interested.

'Good job,' whispered the child. 'All I got to do is feed and clean the fishies, and take the dead ones to Miss Morse.'

'Because…?'

'She casts 'em. See?'

Phryne noticed a series of bronze fish hung on fishing line above the tank. Some must have been discovered late, for they were almost as skeletal as her snapper. She raised an eyebrow.

'But they're nice people,' hinted the child, holding out a sticky hand suggestively. Phryne dropped a shilling and a ball bearing into it. 'Gosh. Thanks, Miss. See, there's only my dad, and they were going to put us in an orphanage. But my mum came from Hungary and Madame heard about it and just said she'd employ us all so Dad could go back to sea. We live out the back. Lots of grub. We go to school and my sis Liz keeps the house and my sis Therese does the food. Madame's a bit ecc-en-tric—' the child brought out this long word with pride '—but she's all right.'

'So she is,' replied Phryne. 'I shall be seeing you again. What's your name?'

'Laszlo,' said the child, nodded affably, and replaced his toffee apple.

Phryne opened the front door and stepped out into a very dark night. As she paused in the street to allow her eyes to get used to the lack of light, someone grabbed her from behind by both shoulders and tried to drag her into a close embrace.

'You're gunna forget about them Johnsons,' growled a bass voice.

'Yair,' agreed a tenor.

Phryne was a little flown with wine, but not drunk. This might, she felt, allow her to fall into that trance state which was supposed to produce a perfect fighter. Or possibly not. She did not scream. She collapsed into the surprised arms behind her, then flung back her head. It impacted on a chin with a satisfying crunch. The man in front aimed a blow at her middle and received a slash from the snapper skeleton across his face. He howled and burbled. Phryne threw her weight back into the attacker's chest and allowed her loose gown to slip off her shoulders. He lost his grip.

She bounced away, bare to the waist, her white skin gleaming in the very faint light from the house, and both her attackers recoiled.

'Jeez!' someone grunted.

'My eyes! My eyes!' wailed the tenor.

'Come on,' said Phryne sweetly. 'That wasn't a very good fight! I've still got quite a few prongs left on this fishie!'

There was no answer. She heard the thudding footsteps as her assailants declined the challenge and took their road on their toes. Then she shook herself, reclaimed her gown, sandy from the ground, and went to her own house. She had a key, but Dot was opening the door as she reached the front verandah. She stepped inside quickly.

Above her, a window in the Sélavy house shut decisively.

Chapter Ten

Thus were they defiled with their own works...

Psalms 106:39
The Holy Bible

She contemplated her image in the hallstand mirror. Dishevelled, panting, bare-breasted. Attractive, though. Portrait of Liberty Leading the People.

'Yes, yes, I know,' said Phryne crisply to her worried companion. 'I have been in a fight. Drat, look at those bruises.' She surveyed the marks on her upper arms, rapidly darkening towards black. Dot took the gown and conducted Phryne to the kitchen, where she had last seen the arnica.

'Hot drink,' said Dot. 'I never heard of such a thing! Ladies assaulted in the street! Were they sailors, Miss?'

'I don't think so. They wanted to warn me not to continue investigating the disappearance of the Johnsons. But they were not expecting to be resisted.'

'Silly them,' commented Dot drily. 'Were they badly hurt?'

'One might have been. I slashed him with the fishie. Oh, dear, poor fishie,' said Phryne, inspecting the skeletal snapper. Several of the ribs, if fish had ribs, had been broken. 'I shall have to ask Dr. Green to look out for patients with fishbone-related injuries. Ouch.'

'You've lost a bit of skin here,' said Dot severely.

'You should have seen the other two,' said Phryne. She was pleased. She had fought off two strong men and emerged with hardly a hair out of place. 'Someone in the Sélavy house was watching. I heard the window close. Nasty, very, because I really liked those surrealists. Most interesting people. Never mind, Dot, nothing a good hot bath won't cure.'

'We're on a case again, aren't we?' asked Dot gloomily.

'Well, yes, but this time it really isn't my fault, Dot dear. I was dropped right into this one. And this time we have accomplices. Though I don't know if I should send Tinker along to Ellis and Co. Those men meant business and they were not delicate in their methods.'

'How about a nice cup of cocoa?' asked Dot.

'Good plan,' said Phryne. 'I'll just check all the locks while you make it and we can go up together.'

She reassumed the gown and trailed to the front door, which was rigidly locked and bolted. So were all the ground-floor windows. When she reached the back door a little voice whispered, 'Guv'nor?'

'Tinker?' asked Phryne.

'I heard what you said,' hissed the boy, trying not to attract Dot's attention as she waited for the milk to heat.

'And?'

'I met men like that before,' she heard from the small dark bedroom. 'I ain't afraid. I can run real fast and I'm small, they can't get a grip on me. You gotta send me, Guv'nor.'

'I believe that I do,' said Phryne. 'If you promise to be really careful.'

In the darkness Tinker crossed his pyjama top with a solemn forefinger. Then, realising that Phryne couldn't see him, he said, 'Promise.'

'All right. Goodnight, Tinker.'

'Goodnight, Guv'nor.' Tinker's voice was already blurring into sleep. Beside him Gaston gave a small, affirmative *wuff!* and laid his head down on his paws.

Phryne, in her own airy rooms, barred the French doors, drank her cocoa, soaked in a very hot bath with Epsom salts, and subsequently slept like a baby. This holiday was not, after all, to be one of unrivalled peace and quiet. And tedium. Phryne was content.

◇◇◇

Morning brought the usual tradespeople, at full volume, and Phryne woke stiff and cross. She particularly objected to the fruiterer, who was intoning, 'Oranges! Fine Mildura oranges, sweet and juicy!' as though he had the backing of a full Rhondda Valley male voice choir. Queenscliff clearly believed in the value of advertising.

Phryne stretched carefully. Bruises on upper arms, a little stiffness in the knees. Otherwise, fine. She donned her swimming costume and a cotton dress and ran downstairs.

'I'm going for a swim,' she called to the kitchen, from whence noises of eating and conversation told her that the rest of the household was at breakfast. She opened the gate and found the sack.

It was an ordinary hessian bag, intended to transport wheat. Phryne had no doubt that last night it was intended to transport Phryne Fisher to somewhere she did not wish to be. Either to contain her while she was beaten or to carry her away. A sobering thought.

She was not noticeably sobered.

She hung the sack neatly on the fence and ran down the street towards the sea. Whatever they had intended, today those attackers were inhabiting a small unpleasant world full of retribution.

Children were skipping as she passed onto the greensward in front of the public baths. Phryne remembered the chant from her own childhood.

> *Over the garden wall*
> *I let the baby fall*
> *Me ma came out and gave me a clout*
> *and sent me over the wall.*

Ah, the innocent fairyland of infancy, thought Phryne as she slid out of her dress and stepped down into the deep water.

Oh, cold, oh, lovely. It was too early for the families, who were still eating eggs and bacon in their guesthouses. Only the lone *mens sana in corpore sano* gentlemen were gravely bobbing up and down, bald heads shining in the morning sun. They made a pleasant audience for the red fish flash of Phryne's slim form traversing the pool, swimming as fast as she could. When she was blown, she turned over on her back and floated. The sea leached last night's remnants of pain and fear out of her skin.

What to do now, she pondered. Send Tinker to find out about Ellis and Co's unrecorded delivery. She knew a lot about the company from her interview with the land agent. And until Tinker came back or some answer came from her telegraphs, she didn't have a lot to go on.

It occurred to her that the argus-eyed, ever-observant Mrs. McNaster would have seen her fighting like an Amazon, bare-breasted, in the street, and she laughed so much that she sank, swallowed water, and decided that some coffee might make her feel less light-headed. She doused herself in the brief freshwater shower, pulled on her dress again, and set off uphill for home and breakfast.

On the way back she heard the children skipping to the tune of 'Red Wing'.

> *Oh the moon shines tonight on Charlie Chaplin*
> *His boots are cracking*
> *For want of blacking*
> *And his little baggy trousers will need mending*
> *Before they send him*
> *To the Dardanelles.*

And that was another sobering reflection. These street rhymes were as ruthless as the subconscious. Coffee. A roll and some of that apricot jam. Food was always a good way to placate a rampant Id.

◇◇◇

An hour later, Tinker was receiving his briefing. He was dressed in his old clothes and had grimed his face and hands and, apart from the shininess of his bike, looked as though he had spent his whole adolescence in a coal hole.

'Ellis and Co are a family company,' Phryne told him. 'Established by Old Mr. Ellis and carried on, now that he has left us for Higher Regions, by his sons Thomas and James. They are known as Tom and Jim. Big strong men with a short way with trespassers. The yard has vicious dogs in residence. It is rumoured that the brothers carry unlawful cargo—that is, overproof Queensland rum and tobacco which has not paid its sixpence to the Queen. This may prove useful. You might, for example, have come to try and buy a bottle. People always believe that other people have an ulterior motive. Here,' she handed over a poor excuse for a jacket, 'despite appearances, is a garment which has a number of advantages. Dot has sewn a couple of pounds into the left-hand pocket. I have contributed a handful of coins for various purposes. I want you to memorise the number of our house phone. Remember to run, hide, and be discreet. Queensberry rules are for equal contests. If you are grabbed, bite, scratch or kick your way free and head for the hills, as they say in the cowboy movies. Call for help if you need it. Any questions?'

Tinker shook his head. He was too excited to speak.

'Are you sure about taking Gaston?' asked Ruth. She had come to appreciate the small dog.

'I'll look after him,' said Tinker. 'He'll know if the Johnsons are around. He's a real bright little dog. He can sit in the basket.'

Gaston sat up on his hind legs and begged winsomely. Ruth gave him half her passionfruit biscuit. He crunched busily.

'Some mud on the bike,' suggested Jane. 'You have to match.'

'Yes, Miss Jane,' Tinker replied. It went to his heart to soil his beloved bike. But she was right.

'And make sure you make this dirty as well,' said Dot, handing over a bike chain and dropping the key, on a string, around

Tinker's unwashed neck. 'And you're for the bath when you get home!'

'Yes, Miss Dot.' Tinker was reconciled to baths. Actually it was quite nice not to itch.

'Good luck, Tinker,' said Phryne.

The boy tipped his horrible tweed cap to the ladies and went out the back way, stopping on the way to smear some mud on the only shiny items. The back gate slammed.

'Well,' said Phryne into the worried silence, 'what are your plans for the day, girls?'

'We thought we might go swimming with the boys next door,' said Jane. 'If you don't need us, Miss Phryne.'

'Enjoy yourselves,' said Phryne, and the two girls went out to don swimming costumes and find sunhats.

'What about you, Dot?'

'The Chinese are coming for the washing at ten,' Dot replied. 'Then I thought I might have a little swim. When the cold's off the water. Are you staying in, Miss?'

'Yes, until Tinker gets back.'

'Then we can make ourselves a few sandwiches for lunch. Ruth's got a ton of stuff in the kitchen. And she sorted out tonight's dinner yesterday. That girl's going to be a great cook.'

Phryne agreed. She made a phone call to Dr. Green to warn him to look out for her assailants. Then she drifted off to her balcony with a glass of lemon cordial and soda water and the fascinating company of Dr. Thorndyke. And the constant observation, she couldn't help noticing, of Mrs. McNaster. Why had Mrs. Green not joined her husband at Madame's? Mrs. Green was hardly ever home. There were usually reasons for that...

Dot made herself another cup of tea, nibbled a bit of Ruth's Impossible Pie, and read the local newspaper. She had time. After all, she was on holiday. Impossible Pie. One of Great-granny's favourite tricks. Mix all the ingredients together, pour the mixture into a pie dish, and—presto—in the oven it organised itself into a layered tart, coherent and delicious.

Dot had to hope that the present case would do the same...

◇◇◇

Tinker eluded the oncoming traffic with some difficulty. He was on the main road, following the railway line, and it was always busy. A van tried to sideswipe him and missed, going very fast even though the speed limit was twelve miles an hour on this road. On the outskirts of Point Lonsdale, he veered off into the tree line and dismounted.

He was terrified. Not of the task, but that he might let the guv'nor down. She had trusted him. No one had ever trusted Tinker before. Even when they had given him chores to do, they had stood behind him when he was, for example, scrubbing, and made comments like 'In my day boys were stronger than you' and 'You've missed that bit'.

However. He opened the satchel that Ruth had pressed upon him and found that he had a packet containing several big chunky sandwiches and fully half of what smelt like coconut cake. He also had a bottle of strong, milked and sugared, cold tea. Gaston whined and pressed close to his thigh, so he fed the dog as well.

They ate and drank. Tinker started to feel better. Ruth's sandwiches were solid and filling; egg and lettuce and mayonnaise, ham and pickle, tomato and cheese. Tinker's teeth were excellent and he bit and chewed with relish. Miss Phryne wouldn't have given this task to him if she hadn't thought he could do it. So therefore he could do it.

He wrapped up the rest of the packet for later, pulled his tweed cap down on his head, and remounted the bicycle. If he couldn't face up to his mission, then he didn't deserve the name Tinker.

Thus nerved and not at all hungry, he cycled to the yard of Ellis and Co. A truck was just coming in. A group of boys were waiting to unload it. He chained the bike and ran to the boss. He was tall and could barely sight Tinker over his stomach. He glared.

'Got a job, Mister?'

The man grunted, 'I don't know you. What's yer name?'

'Eddie,' said Tinker.

'Don't need anyone for this truck,' the man told him. 'Yer can wait for the next if yer like. Penny a load. And if I catch yer pinchin' anything, woe betide yer.' His gravelly voice promised really extensive woe and possibly broken bones. His eyes reminded Tinker of sharks he had met. They had the advantage of being mostly dead. This man was alive.

'Yair,' said Tinker, nodding his cap.

'Over there,' the man directed with a wave of a big meaty hand. 'Yer can wait there where I can keep an eye on yer.'

Tinker went where he was sent. He was inside the yard, and free to look around. So far, it was all going well. If only he didn't see anyone he knew!

'Eddie?' said one of the boys sitting on the wall next to the shed. 'What happened to Old Mother Mason?'

'Got fired,' muttered Tinker. Gaston barked once. Then, observing certain fanged shadows haunting the perimeter fence, he jumped into Tinker's lap. Tinker slumped down next to the speaker, an acquaintance, Harry the Fisho. Possibly the last person Tinker wanted to see. He was a thin boy with scrubby, almost-blond hair and he stank of the fish guts in which he worked. Harry knew Tinker's mother and might easily tell her he was scrumping for penny a load in Point Lonsdale. But Tinker was not without resource.

'What about you?' he demanded. 'They tossed you off the boats?'

'Yair,' agreed Harry the Fisho. 'Not enough work.'

'So here we are,' said Tinker affably.

'Yair. Wouldn't it rot yer socks!'

Tinker agreed that it would have rotted his socks, except he didn't have any in this costume. The boys watched the pantechnicon being unloaded with extreme efficiency and speed. Parcels, barrels, packages, furniture, all were removed with dispatch by boy-power alone. The boss never moved from his supervisory position, seated on an old cane chair and smoking a foul clay pipe. But his eyes were everywhere. Tinker dared not move.

'That's the top cocky,' Harry informed him. 'Bluey.'

Tinker saw a lanky redheaded kid directing operations. He had a peaked cap, which was the only part of his attire not torn or faded.

'He from Queenscliff?'

'Nah,' Harry spat. 'He's Point. Bit of a bastard. Hates us Queenscliff boys. But he's good at trucks,' he added reluctantly.

'That he is,' responded Tinker. The truck was emptying like magic.

'He'll have the hide off you if you don't do as he says,' Harry told him, spitting again. 'Or jump to it fast enough to suit his fancy. He's a slave driver, he is.'

'What happens to all the stuff?' asked Tinker.

'Into the cargo shed,' said Harry. 'Don't you think of wandering in there. It's off limits to us boys unless we're actually carryin'. And don't think of nickin' anything. They say that Jim Ellis killed a boy who took a penny he found on the floor of the shed.'

'Oh, yair?' asked Tinker with just the right amount of scorn. I'm good at this, he thought to himself.

'Yair!' declared Harry the Fisho.

'And when was that?' asked Tinker, taking off his tweed cap and scratching his scalp. He had got used to being clean in such a short time, he marvelled. The habits of a lifetime overturned in a moment.

'Sometime.' Harry waved off the question.

Tinker thought of his sisters' skipping rhyme: 'This week, next week, sometime, never.' He diagnosed this story as 'never' and hoped that was true. The glaucous eyes of the boss fell on him for a moment and he shivered. On the other hand…

'That's us,' said Harry as another big truck rumbled into the yard. 'Come on, Eddie.'

Tinker left Gaston sitting behind the brick wall, where he would be safe from the guard dogs, which appeared to be very similar to illustrations in his school book *Animals of the World* labelled 'timber wolves'. Then the boys were beside the truck. The redhead was selecting his team.

'Bates, Billy, Harry,' he said. 'You new?'

'Yair, I'm Eddie,' said Tinker. 'I need a job.'

'I'm short a man, so you'll have to do,' he told Tinker. 'Do just as I say and we'll be sweet. Cut any capers and you could be dead, even if the boss don't kill you. Trucks are dangerous and so is cargo, and I know how to unload it. See?'

'I see,' mumbled Tinker.

He saw. His name was written down on a list which was fixed to the back of the truck. Then the doors flew open and the world was full of boxes.

◇◇◇

Jane and Ruth knocked politely at the front door of the Mason house and enquired for the boys. The acidulated butler gave them a warning frown.

'You be careful of those young limbs of Satan,' he advised, before admitting them and sitting them down in the parlour. Ruth was still wondering about Impossible Pie.

'It's marvellous,' she said to Jane. 'How can it know that it's going to be a pie?'

'It doesn't,' Jane replied. 'It can't. No more than any chemical reaction knows that it is going to be an oxide.'

'Then why does it work? When I watched Dot mixing all those things together I thought it was going to be a mess.'

'It must be a matter of density,' Jane considered. 'Coconut is less dense than milk or sugar, flour is less dense than coconut. It settles like a pond when you stop mixing it. The eggs make it miscible. With the addition of heat to fix the reaction. And so you have pie.'

'I still think it's wonderful,' said Ruth.

'It is,' said Jane. 'Chemistry is wonderful. All of your cooking is chemistry. That's why you ought to pay more attention at school. Think about the physics of egg whites and meringue.'

'Not now,' said Ruth. 'I'm on holiday. We're agreed, though? If these boys turn nasty, we run away?'

'Very fast,' agreed Jane.

The boys shoved through the doorway and stood in a group, mute, panting a little. Jane was reminded of a pack of dogs. They always stayed within touching distance of each other, though they never touched without bruising; punching, thumping, pushing. She made a mental note.

'The mater's giving us a lift to Swan Island in the Bentley,' announced Jolyon. 'To see the filming. We've got a picnic. Come on! She gets into a frightful wax if anyone keeps her waiting.'

Jane and Ruth followed.

Mrs. Mason was sitting in a long, black saloon car. Ruth swallowed.

'She won't drive like Miss Phryne,' Jane whispered.

'No one can,' replied Ruth. 'Perhaps we could just walk and meet them there?'

'Courage,' said her sister.

They allowed themselves to be loaded in. It was a tight fit. Jane found herself faced with a choice of sitting on someone's knee or perching in the rumble seat with the picnic basket. As she was not sure of her balance she chose Kiwi as a suitable cushion. The boys hooted. Ruth blushed. Jane didn't.

'Boys,' reproved Mrs. Mason. She pulled out into Mercer Street and drove very carefully and circumspectly towards the sea.

They subsided a little. Kiwi tried in vain to find somewhere to put his hands which did not impact with Jane's body. As they passed the railway station he tried a conversational opening.

'This is where Benito is supposed to have hidden his treasure,' he informed Jane. 'Of course, no one really believes that it's here but it's fun to look for it.'

'Why look for something if you don't think it exists?' she asked in her clear voice, unembarrassed by the closeness of the boy.

'Because it might exist,' explained Kiwi.

'Then you should start off by believing that it does,' she informed him. 'And then devise experiments to test your hypothesis.'

'Yes, I suppose...'

Ruth smiled. Suddenly she felt much better.

Jolyon intervened to rescue his friend.

'This is where the phantom pigtail snipper haunts the shore,' he growled.

'Really?' asked Ruth, instinctively clutching at her long braid.

'Just along here,' agreed Fraser. He had not previously spoken. It appeared that he did not approve of adding a sweet feminine influence to this alfresco outing. 'He creeps along behind young girls and—slice! Their hair's hanging by a thread.'

Ruth squeaked in alarm.

'Here's a couple of hairpins,' said Jane, holding them out. 'Coil up your plait and pin it under your hat. Then no attacker, however silent, can get at it.'

'What about you, then?' asked Fraser, his eyes glinting.

'I don't care,' Jane told him. 'It's only hair. It'll grow again.'

'Boys,' said Mrs. Mason again.

The sweep of Swan Bay was before them. A few other cars were parked under the trees. There were several tables and benches, erected by the council, but Mrs. Mason firmly ignored the pleading glances that the boys directed to the picnic basket.

'You've only just had breakfast,' she told them. 'A nice little walk will give us an appetite.'

Jane looked at Ruth and shrugged. The boys were wearing boots. Mrs. Mason had walking shoes. They were wearing sandals. But perhaps it wouldn't be very far. Mrs. Mason did not strike them as a hiking sort of woman. And it was a very nice day. The sun was strong but not burning, the sky was blue, and little boats with ivory-coloured sails scudded across the sea. Jolyon and Fraser picked up the basket and blanket and followed Mrs. Mason along the sandy path.

'See the 'couta boats?' Kiwi asked Jane. 'That's the fishing fleet.'

'Why do some of them have advertising messages on them?' asked Jane. 'Look, there's Lifebouy Soap.'

'Cheap canvas—they call them poverty sails. The fishos live over there, behind us. Fishermen's Flat. They sell the stuff that isn't 'couta to us. Kingfish, whiting, salmon trout, crayfish. 'Couta goes to Melbourne to the fish-and-chip shops. I'm hoping for garfish. Mrs. Cook has a real good way of cooking them.'

'And you buy them off the pier?' asked Ruth. 'How does she cook them?'

Kiwi looked astonished at the question. 'I don't know,' he said in a faintly insulted tone. 'I don't know anything about cooking.'

Ruth turned her gaze out to sea. Boys, she thought.

'And that's Swan Island?' asked Jane.

'Yes. Because of the swans, see? There's always lots of swans.'

'What else is on the island?' asked Jane, labouring a little as Ruth had withdrawn from the conversation.

'Game,' said Fraser. 'Hunting. Ducks, rabbits, quail, pigeon—and swans, of course.'

'You eat swan?' asked Jane.

'Nah, they taste of fish. We just shoot them,' said Jolyon.

'Barbarian,' said Jane, losing patience with civilised discourse.

'Yair, that's us,' agreed Fraser, seemingly pleased.

However good the picnic, thought Jane, it was not going to be worth a moment longer in such company. She took Ruth's hand to suggest that they were leaving when the path led down onto a long narrow beach and the film company stood revealed.

There were only three. A young man was tending the tripod-perched camera. He was wearing overwrought plus-fours and a horrible checked cap. There was a tall muscular man in bathing costume and gown, who seemed to be directing, and a woman in a fuji dress, clutching a bundle of papers. Lily was sitting in a chair combing her long hair, now set into ringlets. They were surrounded by a fascinated collection of Queenscliff idlers, some of whom had other places to be, such as the butcher's boy Amos, staring at Lily with his mouth dropping open and a look of unbearable longing in his eyes. Such as the fishmonger's boy, complete with trike and basket.

'No wonder his fish are stale,' murmured Ruth to Jane.

'I wonder how that camera works?' murmured Jane.

Ruth knew that they were staying on that beach until her sister had an answer to her question, and resigned herself to a daydream about garfish.

Chapter Eleven

Hunger is the best sauce in all the world.

Miguel de Cervantes
Don Quixote

Phryne was idling on her balcony when she heard a knock at the back door and realised that the Irish maid Máire had come and there was no one to let her in. Dot had taken her costume and gone swimming on her own. Phryne suspected she had gone to find her affianced Hugh, and why not?

Cursing lightly, she ran down the stairs and admitted the young woman, struck afresh by how positively translucent she was.

'Come in, Máire, no work today, but you must let me give you breakfast—provided you cook it for yourself,' said Phryne. 'And since we are retaining you, here is the money for the next three days as well.'

'That's too much, Missus,' the girl exclaimed.

'Fair wage,' said Phryne. 'Now just take it, there's a good girl, and you could cook me a slice or two of toast while you are at it.'

'Of course,' murmured the girl. She undid her headscarf, put on her apron, and began slicing bread. She seemed to divine where everything was by some sort of housekeeping sorcery. Phryne settled down at the kitchen table. She liked kitchens, as long as no one expected her to do any work.

'What can I use in your fine kitchen, Missus?' asked the girl.

'Anything your heart desires,' replied Phryne. 'You ought to get a hat, though. That scarf isn't going to keep the sun off your skin.'

'I don't wear it for that,' said the girl, putting the big frying pan on the stove and melting a chunk of butter. 'Could you fancy a few eggs and some bacon, now, and a little soda bread?'

'If you want to cook it. I would really like a toasted sandwich with tomatoes and bacon.'

The girl took down the haunch of bacon which Ruth had purchased and began to slice it.

'Fine bacon, now, I'd love a taste of the bacon. Not that fish isn't good,' said Máire a little hastily. 'But when it's nothing but fish you begin to crave for flesh. Now I've got some pennies we can buy some bacon, butter and lard and some more flour.'

'What about potatoes?' asked Phryne. 'Oops. I mean, you need chips to go with the fish.'

Máire did not take offence at her assumption that the Irish needed perpetual potatoes.

'The dad and Gráinne have an agreement with one of the market gardeners. They let us take tatties, neaps and parsnips and carrots—and fine strong cabbages—and we leave him fish. His wife cooks this sort of fish soup. They're from Italy, to be sure. Take any trash fish, octopus and mussels and prawns—the dad picks 'em out of the bait basket. So we got bags of tatties and a fine meal they make. But I cannot take to them tomaties. New taste to me.'

'Never mind, you'll get used to them. And you may eat as much bacon as you wish.'

There was another tap on the back door.

'My cousin Michael, he's come to see it's all right with me,' apologised Máire. 'I'll send him away.'

'Call him in,' suggested Phryne. 'He looks like he could do with a bit of bacon, too.'

The boy with his basket peeped in at the door. Phryne sat back with a pang.

She had once been dragged along to a soup kitchen in London
by her Fabian Socialist sister Eliza, and she knew that look of
heart-wrenching hunger. Food enough to keep body and soul
together was provided. Treats, no. The expression made Phryne
abrupt. She gave orders.

'Come in, have some bacon, if you refuse my invitation I shall
be cross. Cook some more, Máire. What a nice lot of handsome
little fish! Are they for me?'

'For you, Missus,' husked the boy, salivating at the ambrosial
scent of frying. 'Garfish.'

'Put them in the sink,' said Phryne. 'Ruth shall deal with
them when she gets back.'

'I can be after filleting the little beauties for you, Missus,'
offered the boy. His cousin cuffed at his ears.

'Later,' she told him. 'Slice that cabbage for me, now, the
bacon's almost ready. Then you can wash your hands before you
sit down,' she added.

'I will,' promised the boy.

As the scent of bacon wafted through the house, the company was joined by Molly, who had been walking the grounds,
delighted at the removal of her rival. She sat down at Phryne's
feet. Molly knew where the power in that kitchen resided. Máire
produced Phryne's sandwich and dished up two huge plates
of bacon and cabbage for her cousin and herself. Then she sat
down with a blush and recited grace in Irish. It was a short grace
but heartfelt. Phryne nibbled her sandwich and watched them,
feeling benevolent.

◇◇◇

Tinker felt that he could not heave up another box and was
about to resign when he thought of Miss Fisher and stiffened
such sinews as he still had. The work was punishing and carried
out at top speed. This was the third load of wooden crates which
chinked suggestively and had been consigned, Tinker read, from
Bundaberg, Queensland.

Tinker's arms were aching, as was his back. His eyes were full of dust. As the third truck was emptied and reloaded with other cargo and roared off, a ten-minute break was decreed by the lanky redheaded slave master. Tinker and Harry the Fisho shared his remaining lunch, with assistance from Gaston, who was preserving his low profile behind the brick wall on which the boys were sitting. They drank deep from the bottle of cold sweet tea.

'They was slap-up sangers,' opined Harry. 'Your mum make 'em?'

'Nah,' replied Eddie, thinking fast. 'Got 'em give to me by a lady. Told her cook to make me some lunch. I did some yard work for her.'

'Which lady?' asked Harry. 'Come on, Eddie, ain't we pals?'

'Nah,' said Tinker, grinning.

'Us Cliff boys gotta hang together,' urged Harry. ''Gainst these Point bludgers.'

'Back to work,' said Bluey.

Jim Ellis had not moved from his rush-seated throne. The trucks rolled to a stop in front of him, received a nod and a wave, and then the driver got out, handed over his lading bills, and went off to the house for a cup of tea and a massive bun. The boys spoke enviously of these buns. Mrs. Jim made them and they were reputedly cooked in a baking dish. And full of unnumbered currants.

'You, you, Eddie, Harry, furniture into the shed,' ordered Bluey.

Harry groaned. 'Furniture's the worst,' he told Tinker. 'Remember what I said about picking any little thing up.'

'I remember,' said Tinker.

'Two to a table, one each for chairs, watch the bloody corners or I'll dock yer,' added Bluey.

Tinker was unimpressed. He was already being paid. He and Harry took up a large and very heavy mahogany table with great difficulty and staggered with it to the third shed.

This was the last shed, and Tinker needed to look around before he quit, which he meant to do with alacrity. Surely the storing of furniture was going to require more time than just lumping crates of illegal rum?

So it proved. Bluey stood inside the big, dusty shed and directed every movement. Tinker wondered if he was a relative of the Ellis family or, if not, why he worked so hard, as though every moment was being deducted in pennies from his money box.

'Left side,' he told Harry and Tinker. 'Against the wall, on its legs and wrap it up nice in a blanket. Scar the top and I'll skin youse both.'

There was no doubt in Tinker's mind that he meant it. They hefted the table into its corner and leaned on the wall, panting, while Bluey examined the glossy top, grunted, and swathed it in an old blue blanket evidently stolen from a naval hospital.

'Four chairs on top,' he ordered Tinker and Harry, and bustled away.

'I've had about enough,' wheezed Tinker.

'Hard work,' agreed Harry. 'But I can't go home without sixpence. That's for chips for tea. I already got the fish. Hauled in a boat this mornin'. Come on, he'll be going crook in a jiff.'

That was when Gaston made his move.

He had followed Tinker into each of the sheds as he entered them, slinking along next to the galvanised iron wall and escaping the notice of his large-fanged cousins, whom he suspected would not feel any family or even species loyalty to a fellow canine, but might consider him more in the nature of an entree. Like Rikki-Tikki-Tavi, his motto was 'run and find out'. The first two sheds contained only smells which made him sneeze and cartons which clinked. Below the notice of a nobly bred dog.

But in the third shed there was a scent, faint but familiar, and he dropped his small nose to the floor and tracked it. He knew this smell! It was the fragrance of his own people!

He pursued it to a large collection of furniture, faced with a big wardrobe, tied together with a rope and marked *Sale*. Their smell was there. But they weren't. Struck with sudden unbearable loss, he put up his muzzle and started to howl.

Tinker put down his chair and ran. Gaston was scrabbling at the back of a dresser and howling like a small banshee. Tinker grabbed for the dog, but Bluey was before him.

'No dogs,' he yelled, snatching at Gaston and lifting him into the air. 'Who owns this mutt?'

'Me,' said Tinker. 'Give him back!'

'I've a mind to break the mongrel's neck,' snarled Bluey, swinging Gaston out of reach. Tinker jumped for him and missed. Bluey laughed.

At this point Gaston made up his mind. Small dogs have their dignity and his was affronted. Those who would treat a terrier in this abandoned way must be snubbed, and, in Gaston's opinion, firmly bitten. He twisted, snapped, and Bluey dropped him to clutch at his hand.

'I quit,' yelled Tinker, grabbing Gaston and tucking him under his arm. He ran out of the shed and confronted Jim Ellis on his chair.

'You owe me threepence,' said Tinker.

The yard fell silent. The drivers, watching from the verandah, clapped ironically. The boys gave out a murmur of admiration. From the shed they could hear Bluey swearing in pain. Tinker held out his cupped hand.

'Here's your threepence,' said Jim Ellis after a nerve-shattering interval. 'If I see yer here again, I'll feed yer to the dogs. You and yer mutt.'

'Bye!' said Tinker. He walked to his bike, unchained it, put Gaston in the carrier, and rode nonchalantly away.

When he was out of sight he rode for Queenscliff as though wolves were after him.

◇◇◇

'What is the cameraman humming?' asked Jane. They had insinuated themselves to the front of the audience.

'Miss Phryne has a record of it,' said Ruth, who liked music. 'From an opera. It's "The Anvil Chorus". You remember, the anvils all sounding? Clang, clang, ca-clang, ca-clang, ca-clang…'

'Oh, yes,' agreed Jane, who considered music to be interesting only in a mathematical sense. 'He must be using it to pace the turns of the reel. Four-four time, of course.'

'Quite,' said Ruth, who had no idea what her sister was talking about.

'Well, you couldn't turn a wheel—it looks like twice a second or so—to a waltz or a polka. I wonder why he doesn't just use a metronome, like we have on the piano back home?'

'Because it's boring,' said the cameraman, who had finished a scene and was now waiting for the director to arrange and instruct the large crowd of people who had turned up, dressed as pirates. 'I'm not a machine, so I like to sing.'

'Oh,' said Jane. 'I see.'

'It is two turns a second, by the way,' the young man told her. 'That's sixteen frames a second or one foot of film. And in case you are interested in facts, a reel of film is one thousand feet long and that will play for about thirty minutes.'

'Correct,' said Jane, to whom calculations were second nature.

'This is a Bell and Howell 2709, best camera on the market,' added the camera operator, pushing back his horrible checked cap. 'Pity about the film, but there you are. You local?'

'No, we're visitors,' said Ruth.

'Thought you must be. This is a bit of a backwater. No one's been interested in the machine before,' he added, somewhat hurt. 'Just the charmless dressed up to please the brainless.'

'This isn't the sort of film you want to make, is it?' divined Ruth.

'It buys shoes for the baby,' admitted the cameraman. 'Until I can form my own company and do the sort of films I want. Horror. Dark doings. This'd make a bonzer spot for some blood-sucking ghosts. But there it is.'

'Ruth.' Ruth put out her hand. The cameraman took it.

'Ginger, they call me. Drop in again tomorrow and I'll let you try the camera,' he offered. Jane beamed.

'We'll be here,' said Ruth resignedly. 'We must go. Mrs. Mason is calling us.'

Mrs. Mason was suggesting a bathe in the sea beyond the crowd of pirates. The boys had not been able to get close to the camera but were convulsed with merriment at the acting.

'There she was, standing in the sea, one arm stretched out, mouthing, "Come back!",' giggled Jolyon.

There she was indeed, Ruth observed. Lily was sitting in a canvas chair, dressed in a crinoline and bonnet, and a woman was painting her face afresh. She waved a hand at Jane and Ruth and smiled. Lily was in Paradise. She glowed with joy.

'Where shall we swim?' Ruth asked. It seemed very unkind to mock a girl who had attained her heart's delight.

'Boys, carry the picnic,' ordered Mrs. Mason.

They obeyed, muttering. Mrs. Mason forged ahead, the young persons followed, and came onto a sandy beach with no one else in sight.

'Here,' she decided.

The boys stripped to their one-pieces and ran shouting into the water. Jane and Ruth, who had their bathing costumes on under their clothes, removed their dresses and followed. The water was refreshingly cool. Jane, not a confident swimmer, stuck to the edge, where the sand was firm underfoot. Ruth stayed with her.

Then the boys pounced on them, shoving and splashing. Jane went under and struggled and could hear their laughter above her. They were strong and there were three of them. Fraser grabbed her by her plait and ducked her. She had not taken a breath and when she struggled to the surface he ducked her again, holding her under by her hair.

Ruth dived into the middle of the fray, seized her sister and hauled her up into her arms. Jane wheezed and choked, red-faced and furious.

'Beasts!' yelled Ruth. 'Leave her alone!'

'Girls,' said Fraser disgustedly. 'Can't take a joke!'

'Get out of here,' threatened Ruth with such venom that two swam away. Kiwi remained, anxious that the joke had gone too far. Fraser really was a bit of an animal.

'Is she all right?' he faltered.

'Bugger off,' growled Ruth.

Kiwi buggered off. Ruth carried Jane to the shallows and sat by her as she vomited seawater and shook with outrage.

'He tried to kill me!' she exclaimed.

'I don't reckon we want to play with boys anymore,' said Ruth. 'Come on, can you walk? Lean on me. We're leaving.'

Chapter Twelve

To be weak is miserable
Doing or suffering

John Milton
Paradise Lost

Jane and Ruth plodded home up the hill, salty and disgusted. Mrs. Mason had offered to drive them home if they stayed for the picnic to which the boys were so looking forward, but they had fairly politely declined.

They were met by Phryne, who sent them upstairs for a bath in her own bathroom, with the special soap. Before they sank into the hot, foaming water, Jane borrowed Dot's embroidery shears and snipped off the long plait of her hair at the nape.

'No one,' she said to Ruth, 'is going to do that to me again.'

Ruth did not say a word. Jane had been badly treated as a child. When she was hurt, her face looked like it had back in the boarding house. Pale and set, as if carved out of wax. Ruth would do anything to take that look off. Therefore, instead of going downstairs to investigate who was cooking bacon and cabbage in her very own kitchen, she slid into the bath and started massaging Miss Phryne's coconut shampoo into her sister's outraged scalp.

They emerged clean and scented. They drained the bath and cleared the sand out of the bottom of the tub. They dressed in clean clothes and went down to the kitchen without a word.

Phryne was listening to Máire talk about the phantom snipper.

'He's a ghost,' she declared, crossing the bib of her white apron. 'I've worn my scarf ever since he cut the hair off Mary Nicholls, and she cried for days. And Alice Chestnut. She's got a bob now. But he's never seen. The girls say they just felt a tug, as though someone had pulled their hair, and felt around and it was gone. Oh, Jesus, Mary and Joseph protect us, he's got another, so he has!'

'I cut it off myself,' declared Jane.

'And very fetching it will look,' said Phryne. 'When trimmed a little. Are you hungry, girls?'

'Starved,' declared Ruth. 'We never got a bite of that picnic.'

'Boys played rough?' asked Phryne gently. Ruth nodded. 'I see.'

'I'll cook you up some more bacon and cabbage, will I now?' asked Máire.

'Do so,' invited Phryne. 'Then Michael can show Ruth how to fillet garfish.'

'I've just been thinking about garfish,' said Ruth.

'We need a rolling pin,' he said. 'Or a bottle.'

'I'm not fishifying my pastry pin,' said Ruth. 'After lunch, we can use an empty wine bottle. We've got plenty of them.'

Máire sliced more bacon. For the first time in her life she had actually eaten enough of that smoked treat. She felt positively virtuous.

After a record-breaking bicycle ride, Tinker fell through the back door with Gaston drooping in his wake.

'You found it?' asked Phryne.

'Yes, Guv'nor,' he replied. 'All tied up and marked for sale. Gaston smelt the stuff out and howled and howled and we had to quit before we got sacked.'

'Well done!' she congratulated him and he beamed, teeth white in his grubby face. 'Now you get into the bath, use pumice on those hands, and you'd better take poor Gaston with you. When you come back there will be bacon and cabbage.'

'Bacon and eggs,' Máire told her. 'It's that I have no more cabbage.'

'That will suit just as well,' Phryne replied.

'Yair, bonzer,' agreed Tinker, who was terribly, terribly hungry.

However, he took Gaston into the servants' bathroom, ran himself a hot bath with carbolic, and washed himself and the little dog with care. He was elated. He had been sent out on an undercover mission, and he had succeeded. Him and Gaston. The guv'nor was pleased with him. He deserved his bacon and eggs. And he had earned threepence, and threepence was three-pence. The water swirled black and he refilled it and soaked himself again. How had he got so dirty in only one day?

Gaston, who was used to baths, resigned himself to the absence of his people. These substitutes were at least affable and free with their scraps and biscuits. And he was beginning to be fond of Tinker. He sat on the bath mat and dripped, wrinkling his sensitive nose at the stink of the disinfectant.

When he saw Jane's hair, Tinker blinked but did not com-ment. His attention was drawn to a large plate containing not only bacon and eggs but mushrooms and onions and tomatoes. Gaston, at his feet, was treated to leftover chicken and dog bis-cuits in gravy. Both dined lavishly.

Then everyone decided that they could do with a little rest, it being one o'clock. Phryne declared a siesta and they scattered to their own lodgings. Michael and Máire took their leave, carrying the leftover bacon. The O'Malley family was going to dine well tonight. On something other than fish. And Ruth had learned the enchanting skill of bending a slit garfish around a bottle, whereupon the skeleton obligingly popped free and the fish was boned. They reposed in the sink in a little salty water, waiting for the triumphs of dinner.

Phryne had dosed Jane with a cup of valerian tea. She knew that sort of helpless, violated rage very well. Jane was white and shocked. And she urgently needed to see a hairdresser. Her hair, abruptly released from the weight of her plait, fluffed around her head like a dandelion. But Jane was greatly cheered by a short conversation she had had on the stairs.

'Do you want them punished, Jane?' asked Phryne lightly, hand on the banister.

'Only Fraser. The others didn't join in,' said Jane. 'And Kiwi came back to ask if I was all right.'

'Then Fraser shall be sorry,' said Phryne.

Jane looked at the cold light that glinted in her adoptive mother's green eyes. Then she fetched a short, deep, satisfied sigh.

'All right,' she said, and they climbed upwards towards rest.

◇◇◇

Dot arrived home with Hugh and the startling news that old Mrs. McNaster had died suddenly. Her son-in-law could not properly certify her death, and had called in another practitioner from Geelong. Local excitement was muted. There was a certain air, Dot said, of restrained celebration. Constable Dawson had visited the scene and found nothing awry.

'That bloke wouldn't notice if a tram was...' began Hugh, a large, charming policeman, looking even larger in shirtsleeves and flannels. He staunched his metaphor before it offended Dot. 'Not a zealous officer,' he explained. 'Wouldn't want to offend the nobs, if there was anything wrong with the death.'

'No reason to expect that there would be,' said Dot briskly. 'She was an old lady in frail health. You're not being a policeman here, Hugh.' Dot blushed as she called her affianced by his first name.

'And so she passed on, regretted by few,' said Phryne piously. 'A poisonous old party, now facing a searching examination by the recording angel. But, dammit, there goes my witness.'

'Witness?' asked Hugh, pricking up his ears.

'We'll explain over a drink,' said Phryne. She took his arm and led him inside. If Hugh arrived, could Lin Chung be far behind? All this exercise and good food had restored Phryne's weakened frame and she could just do, she thought, with a little, or perhaps a lot, of amorous exercise.

Drinks were served by Dot in the parlour. The junior members of the household were asleep, exhausted by emotion and daring.

Molly gave Hugh an affectionate lick and sat down on his feet. She liked him; he was a reliable supplier of titbits and was a deft hand with ear scratching.

'This is nice,' said Hugh, after a deep draught of the beer which his devoted fiancée had laid in for him. 'I went round to your house, Miss Fisher. You wouldn't want to be there at the moment. Only quiet place was the kitchen. There were workmen all over putting up your new crimson wallpaper, tiling the floor and, while I was there, they were hauling your malachite bath up the stairs.'

'Oh, dear, and I meant Mr. and Mrs. B to have a rest!' said Phryne.

Hugh grinned, rumpling his short fair hair.

'They're all right. Nice little dinners in their part of the house and of course it's all quiet at night. They reckon another two weeks and it will be right-ho. Mrs. B wanted me to tell you that Ember is well. He had another two goldfish out of the pond.'

'Ah, well, I have been eating a lot of fish myself,' said Phryne. She had resisted the designer Camellia's suggestion that she buy expensive Japanese carp for this very reason. If Ember was going to eat them—and he was—then he could snack on Woolworth's goldfish at sixpence each, not the Emperor's koi.

'And the fraud case is finished?' asked Dot, refilling the beer glass. She was drinking a daring sherry and Phryne had her usual gin and orange.

'All tied up with packing tape and consigned to the public prosecutor,' said Hugh easily. Since being concussed in an early investigation, he reckoned that finishing a case without being belted over the head meant that he was winning, at least on points. 'And they gave me my stripes,' he added.

'So, you're Detective Sergeant Collins now?' asked Dot. 'You deserve it!'

'Thanks. You've been having trouble, Miss Fisher?' asked Hugh, a little uncomfortable about being praised.

'It's been an interesting few days,' agreed Phryne. 'Dot will tell you all about them when she awakes. I'm taking Jane to the hairdresser, if you'll excuse me.'

◇◇◇

Jane did not like the hairdresser, and neither did Phryne. The shop was crowded with miscellaneous lotions, potions and liquids designed to produce a fine glossy chevalure from anything short of old hemp rope. The prevailing scent was chypre, overlaid with a strong suggestion of burnt horsehair. This was not a good combination. Jane sneezed.

'Oh, no, another victim of that madman!' exclaimed Miss Leonard, a woman with iron discipline, to judge by the perfect galvanised-iron waves of her coiffure. 'And such a lovely, lovely colour! A tragedy!'

Jane was about to inform her that it was merely hair, and she had done execution on it herself, but Phryne pressed a hand on her shoulder and she subsided into the chair. Miss Leonard did seem to know what she was doing, at least. Jane's world was suddenly full of shampoo.

'Just a bobby cut, Mrs…er…?' asked the hairdresser, sluicing off the suds and rubbing the hair dry.

'Fisher,' said Phryne. 'A bobby cut. Like mine.'

'I can't understand it,' said the hairdresser, applying some sort of unguent to Jane's scalp and rubbing industriously. 'How someone could want to hurt young girls like this.'

'People,' agreed Phryne, 'are strange. Are you all right, Jane?'

'Yes,' said Jane, after some consideration. 'Is this going to take long?'

'Never hurry an artist,' advised Phryne. 'I'll just take a tour of the shelves.'

'Everything to preserve, nourish and condition your hair,' said Miss Leonard. 'Now, Miss, if you would sit up, we'll just tidy up a few ends…'

Jane watched in some amazement as her face appeared again between two wings of hair. This was going to be easier to manage than that long plait. She should have disposed of it long ago. Less time on the care of hair was more time for reading books, she thought. No wonder scholars don't mind going bald. More face to wash, less hair to comb. Her face looked different, too. Thinner. More grown-up.

'There,' exclaimed Miss Leonard, flicking hair off the back of Jane's neck. 'What do you think?'

'Very nice,' said Jane.

'Indeed.' Phryne dragged her gaze away from fascinated contemplation of an array of wigs which looked as though their original owners had been scalped. They belonged in an ethnographical museum. There were, however, no shrunken heads that she could see. 'A very neat haircut. Thank you, Miss Leonard.'

Phryne parted with a small sum and followed Jane out of the shop, evading the hairdresser's cry of 'Anything for yourself, some Indian root tonic, perhaps? Some hair nourisher, some follicle food…?'

'I just have to order some more beer,' said Phryne. 'Now that we have Hugh with us. How are you feeling?'

'Good,' decided Jane, patting her new coiffure. 'Lighter.'

'I thought the same when I had mine cut. But it wouldn't do for Ruth, or for Dot.'

'No,' said Jane.

Beer ordered—and another bottle of gin in case Mrs. Mason dropped in—and they walked up the hill to the house, where, to the strains of the gramophone playing 'It Ain't Gonna Rain No More, No More', Dot was dancing with Hugh and Tinker was dancing with Ruth and Molly was giving her opinion of this frivolity by running between the dancers' legs whenever she could spy an opening.

She had just upset Dot, who was swept off her feet and into Hugh's arms, when Phryne and Jane came home.

Dot blushed and tried to release herself. Hugh hung onto her. She was a lovely armful, his affianced bride, and they weren't doing anything wrong. Phryne chuckled and swung Jane into the dance. Soon they had forgotten why they were dancing, and just danced.

The gramophone hissed to a halt. Phryne laughed.

'That was fun,' she said. 'What do we think of Jane's new style?'

'Fetching,' said Hugh.

'Nice,' said Ruth.

'Very pretty,' said Dot.

Jane smiled. She had never worried about being pretty. But it might be useful.

'Now,' said Phryne, 'a council of war, if you please. More drinks?'

'I'll get 'em,' volunteered Tinker.

He returned with a tray. Dot sipped decorously at another sherry. Hugh opened another bottle of beer. Tinker, very carefully, mixed another iced gin and orange for Miss Fisher, and the younger members of the household had lemonade. They all sat down in the parlour on the shabby chairs and looked attentive.

'Well, Detective Sergeant Collins, what do you think?' asked Phryne.

Tinker's eyes lit up.

'You're really a homicide cop?' he asked.

'I really am,' responded Hugh solemnly.

'Gosh,' said Tinker.

Phryne sipped cautiously. Tinker had been very generous with the gin. And although it was fitting and proper that he should find another hero, she felt a momentary pang.

'I don't know a thing about the phantom snipper,' said Hugh. 'I never heard of such a thing. Bloke must be a few sandwiches short of the full picnic, I reckon. He won't be caught until he makes a mistake and some sheila belts him with her handbag.'

'One thing,' offered Jane. 'How does he cut the hair? I had to make seven chops to cut mine, and that was with Miss Dot's sharp embroidery shears. Ordinary scissors wouldn't do it that fast.'

'Hedge cutters?' hazarded Dot. 'That's a big sharp snip.'

'Bit conspicuous,' said Phryne. 'You feel a tug on your hair, you turn round, and behind you is a man with a pair of hedge cutters. At which point you shriek and point him out to the attentive constabulary.'

'What about a knife?' asked Tinker.

'Have to be very sharp,' said Hugh.

'A razor,' Tinker elaborated. 'One of them cut-throat ones like my dad uses.' He gulped. The razor strop was not a good memory for Tinker.

'Good man,' said Hugh. Tinker glowed. 'Lend me your hair for a moment, Ruthie.'

Ruth turned her back, letting down her plait. Hugh walked up behind her, grabbed the braid, and performed a fast, upward slashing move with a pencil.

'No, that won't do,' he said. 'Not enough resistance to the blade. Must be like this, downwards.'

'Running a terrible risk of cutting the victim,' said Dot.

'Perhaps he doesn't care about that,' said Hugh. 'Who knows how madmen think?'

'All right,' said Phryne. 'How about the Johnsons?'

'The Johnsons?' asked Hugh.

'Gone and left not a rack behind,' said Phryne. 'Due to the bold and daring Tinker, we know that their stuff is in Ellis's cargo shed ready to be sold. They also left Gaston, who was their pride and joy. No doubt of his being abandoned. When we first met, he had been truffling for a living in the cesspits. Tinker had to scour and rinse him twice before we could tell that he was a dog.'

'He was filthy all right,' agreed Tinker. 'Poor little mutt.'

Gaston, who had been reposing on the sofa, woke at the sound of his name and wuffed.

'Sounds bad,' said Hugh. 'What clues did you find, Miss Fisher?'

'I have them here,' said Phryne, opening a box on the sideboard. 'Not much. A collar stud or two, a pin, an earring, a bit of telegram…'

'Have you asked the post office for a list of the telegrams sent to this address?' asked Hugh seriously. Phryne laughed.

'Well, no, Hugh dear, I'm not official. And that dolt in uniform declined to take any action.'

'I could do it,' he said. There was something about Hugh Collins which was very comforting, thought Dot proudly. He was so strong, solid, respectable and intelligent. A wonderful combination. She considered herself a lucky woman.

'Could you? You belong to Melbourne CIB, do you have jurisdiction?'

'I'm sure I could convince them,' responded Hugh. Phryne began to smell a rat of some sort.

'And it was just coincidence that you happened to finish your fraud case and wander down to Queenscliff in search of amusement?' she asked, arching an exquisite eyebrow.

'Well,' said Hugh. He wriggled. 'It's like this,' said Hugh. He poured some more beer. 'You see…'

'Spit it out,' advised Phryne inelegantly. 'You've been sent on one of those undercover tasks; those on which Jack Robinson sends you when he has a bee in his bonnet.'

'Steady on,' protested Hugh, unwilling to countenance the suggestion that his superior had insects in his headgear. 'He did just ask me to look around.'

'As it happens,' prompted Phryne.

'You want to join the police force, don't you, young feller?' Hugh asked of Tinker. 'Well, if you need a method of interrogation for your prisoners, you could learn a lot from Miss Fisher.'

'Yessir,' said Tinker. He was impressed. The victim had meant to keep the secret, and it had been wormed out of him by a mixture of…what was it? Force of character? The steady stare of those green eyes? He must observe further.

'Well, all right, Miss Fisher, there's a smuggling operation around here, bringing uncustomed rum from...'

'Bundaberg,' put in Tinker.

'How do you know that?' demanded Hugh, astonished.

'I near bust me...er...stays unloading it,' Tinker told him. 'Crates and crates of bottles from Bundaberg in Queensland. You're talking about Ellis and Co, ain't you?'

'Ellis and Co it is,' affirmed Hugh. 'I think you've got a lot to tell me, Tinker.'

'Yessir,' agreed Tinker.

'But what about the Johnsons?' asked Dot.

'There you have me, my girl,' said Hugh. 'Maybe if we get the text of that telegram it might tell us something. You don't think that the Johnsons are actually with their furniture, do you? I mean—sorry, Dot—that their bodies...'

An avid reader of Sexton Blake could not afford to be squeamish. Tinker answered promptly.

'No, sir—no smell. And Gaston howled because he misses his people.'

'And they weren't killed here,' said Phryne. 'No blood, no signs of dragging, no feeling of death. Nothing stolen but food. Not even the containers, mostly. The flour was gone but the flour bin was still there. The salt and pepper pots empty. Crockery untouched. Cutlery unlooted. And *objects d'art* carefully hidden in the cellar.'

'It's a puzzle,' said Hugh. They thought quietly for a while. No one had any new ideas. Phryne broke the silence.

'Now, it's four in the afternoon, I am going up for a rest. Can any of us help with dinner, Ruth?'

Ruth was recalled to duty.

'No, it's simple tonight. I've made the *vichyssoise*, and I just have to fry the garfish *á la meunière*. Jane did the veggies for the *salade russe* and there's sorbet and a surprise for dessert. How many for dinner? Weren't we expecting the doctor?'

'I doubt he'll come, what with a death in his house,' Phryne responded, suppressing her wince at Ruth's French pronunciation. Stratford Atte Bowe was Parisian compared to Ruth's Australian vowels. 'However much he hated his mother-in-law, he'll have to observe the niceties.'

'To be sure,' agreed Dot. 'Hugh and I might go for a walk and see about those telegrams, then.'

'Good idea,' said Phryne. 'Dinner at seven.'

'You want to come fishing with me tomorrow, young feller?' Hugh asked Tinker. Tinker nodded, too overcome to speak.

Phryne took herself to her room to read Dr. Thorndyke, pleasantly aware that no eyes were now fixed on her from the house opposite. Ruth and Tinker went to the kitchen. Jane, after examining her new look in the big bathroom mirror, had a handful of hairpins which would be of no further service.

She had a use for one of them, though. She was going to get into that closed room, and Uncle Bert had taught her basic lock-picking as part of a young woman's education. All you needed, he had explained, was patience and a hairpin. Jane had both.

Molly at her side, she sat down on her heels and examined the padlock. Large and simple. It was the work of only ten minutes and the ruination of three hairpins before she persuaded it to unlatch.

The door creaked as it opened.

And there before her enchanted eyes was a chamber full of bones straight out of a fairy story. Jane took a breath to calm herself, and then dived in.

Chapter Thirteen

Me this unchartered freedom tires;
I feel the weight of chance desires

William Wordsworth
'Ode to Duty'

Six o'clock and Phryne was just telling herself firmly that drink-ing gin at lunch was a good way of ensuring that she did nothing useful in the afternoon, when someone came hammering at the door, ringing the bell, and calling, 'Miss Fisher!'

A triple summons was not to be denied so she yawned her way downstairs and found a distraught Dr. Green on the front step, holding up a woman, grey-clad and grey-faced, who sagged in his arms.

'Come in,' she invited. The doctor deposited the lady on the hall seat. She was, Phryne realised, Lavinia, Mrs. McNaster's companion.

'Miss Fisher, may I ask you for a great favour?' the doctor gasped.

'You may,' said Phryne. Dr. Green was rather good-looking even without his Greek tunic. His curly hair was rumpled, his fish-patterned tie was nestling near his shoulder and he seemed to have been through some emotional ordeal which was far too trying for such a rationalist.

'My wife…' he started, choked, and tried again. 'Miss Lavinia…'

Bring the lady into the parlour,' instructed Phryne. 'I will get you a drink, and you shall tell me what you want me to do.'

The doctor did as he was bid. Miss Lavinia slid down on the sofa and Phryne put a pillow under her head. The doctor reached for the whisky bottle and poured himself a large glass. He drank it as Phryne arranged Miss Lavinia and wished Dot was with them. This looked like a faint. Sal volatile? Cold water on the brow?

Perhaps it would be better to leave the poor woman alone to enjoy her unconsciousness. As Phryne remembered it, Miss Lavinia had enjoyed few luxuries.

'Well?' Phryne asked Dr. Green.

'My wife…did you know that her mother passed away? Suddenly?'

'Yes, the grapevine is very efficient around here.' Phryne poured herself a small drink.

'Well, I can't give a certificate, of course, being a relative it wouldn't be proper, so I had to call my colleague, and my wife got the idea that there was something wrong about the death, and she is sure that Miss Lavinia murdered Mrs. McNaster.'

'I see. And did she?'

'No, of course not, she had a heart attack; she had all the signs, it was a completely natural death. But my wife is quite irrational about this. She won't have poor Lavvie in the house, and I can't send her to an hotel, all of Queenscliff will start gossiping and my practice will be ruined. And she hadn't any relative except the old lady.'

'I see. Very well. As you know, my house is without servants. If you would like me to care for Miss Lavinia, you'll have to lend me one of your parlour maids. The Irish one, for preference.'

The doctor blenched.

'Oh, Miss Fisher, I don't know what my wife will say…' he protested.

'Then I'll keep Lavinia tonight, and tomorrow she can move in with Madame Sélavy,' continued Phryne, determined not to be saddled with the care of another person. 'She knows how to keep secrets, if I'm any judge.'

'Very well, Miss Fisher, I'll call tomorrow and convey her to Madame. She's not at home on Fridays, to anyone. That's a good idea. I don't know why I didn't think of it,' he said, faintly aggrieved.

'You're tired and shocked,' suggested Phryne. 'Now off you go and mix some chloral for your wife.'

'Here's that letter you wanted to see,' said the doctor as the door was closing on him. Phryne took it and ushered him firmly out of the house. Then she returned to the parlour, moderately cross. What am I running, she reflected, the Queenscliff Home for Lost Causes?

Lavinia was still in her stupor so Phryne walked to the kitchen and asked Ruth to make some tea for herself and her guest. Ruth relayed the order to Tinker, found the smelling salts and followed Phryne back to tend the stricken. Phryne heard the woman sneeze and croak, 'I killed her...I killed her!' on a note of rising hysteria. Ruth recoiled. Phryne forced Miss Lavinia to swallow a measure of brandy and water, waited while she choked, and supplied more.

'Now, you must be quiet,' Phryne ordered. 'Do not say anything until you have had a nice cup of tea and some of Ruth's excellent date scones. Do you hear me?'

Miss Lavinia nodded, not daring to speak.

'Good.'

Tinker, who had been listening, wheeled in the tea tray. He did not have a light hand with the tea, either. The cup which Ruth sugared and milked contained tea which was sepia in colour and as strong as a thunderstorm.

'Could trot a moudiwarp on that,' observed Tinker proudly. Phryne shuddered slightly, but she was willing to admit that a mole of moderate size could certainly have waltzed on the surface without peril.

Lavinia drank it hot, with a gasp, then ate two scones. She was now more pink and less grey and Phryne decided it was safe to allow her to talk.

'Now, what can we do for you?' she asked firmly.

'Oh, Miss Fisher, I fell asleep,' confessed Miss Lavinia. 'She wanted me to watch for her and it was four in the morning and I was so tired, and I fell asleep!'

'Understandably,' said Phryne.

'But when I woke she was dead!'

'She was an old lady in frail health,' Phryne told her distraught guest. 'This is not your fault, Miss Lavinia.'

'And Mrs. Green said…she said…'

'Mrs. Green was not herself. She was probably feeling guilty at not liking her mother, and she needed a scapegoat, and you were so convenient.'

'But I inherit all that money…' wailed Miss Lavinia.

'Good, you will not want to stay in the doctor's house. You must now go up to my bathroom and wash your face and tidy your hair and then you may either lie down for a little rest on the spare bed or you may come down for dinner, which will be at seven. Ruth will help you,' said Phryne.

Ruth put out a hand and the elderly woman rose and stood steadily enough. Now that she looked at Miss Lavinia, Phryne could see that she was not old. She was perhaps forty, a dyed-in-the-wool spinster, but her skin was unlined and she did not seem to be conspicuously withered. With a reasonable diet, a few good nights' sleep and some fashionable clothes, Miss Lavinia would be a presentable figure of a woman.

'Did she do in the old bi—besom?' asked Tinker, gathering up the tea things.

'She had reason,' Phryne told him. 'But I don't think so. What do you think?'

'If she hadn't up to now, she wouldn't,' said Tinker. He was not used to people asking for his opinion. 'Mrs. McNaster's been ballyragging her for all my life. And she wasn't alone. The old bi—lady nagged her son-in-law, she screamed at her own daughter, she kept firing the maids and she hated everyone. Never a good word to say.'

'Not short of enemies, then,' murmured Phryne.

'Yair, Guv'nor, but she was in her own room in the middle of the night, even if the other old lady was asleep. It'd have to be one of the family,' protested Tinker.

'Contrary to Sexton Blake, Tinker dear, most murders *are* family affairs. Mrs. Green might be accusing Miss Lavinia in order to divert suspicion from herself. The doctor may have poisoned his mother-in-law with some…'

'Colourless, odourless, undetectable South American poison?' breathed Tinker.

'One of those, yes,' agreed Phryne. 'Now, if that is the end of the excitement for the day, you get the trolley back to the kitchen and I'll go and see how Ruth is managing with the poor lady.'

Tinker rattled off. Phryne climbed stairs. Ruth met her on the landing.

'She did as you said, Miss Phryne, and then I showed her the spare bed and she just collapsed into it. But it's funny.'

'What's funny?'

'I can't find Jane,' said Ruth. 'I thought she was in her room reading and she's been there but she's not there now and she isn't in the loo and…'

'Here she is now,' said Phryne. 'Don't lose your nerve, Ruth dear. It's been a nasty day and now we are going to have a nice dinner with Hugh and Dot.'

With a yelp, Ruth recollected that she still had to assemble the salad and she departed for the kitchen at some speed. Molly, who was a sympathetic dog, was curled at the side of Miss Lavinia's bed. She raised her head and thumped her tail as Phryne came in but did not otherwise move. Miss Lavinia's thin hand was on her head.

'Nice doggie,' murmured Miss Lavinia, very sleepily. 'Used to have a doggie like you when I was a girl…'

Phryne left Molly to work her healing magic and caught Jane just as she was about to slip into her own room.

'Jane?' she asked gently. 'There's nowhere to hide up here. What did you find in the locked room?'

Jane had never got the hang of lying. And with Miss Phryne there was little point.

'Bones,' she replied. 'Come and look.'

A few minutes later Phryne appreciated how accurate an answer that had been. There was a row of twenty ochre-stained skulls on top of the bookcase. There were boxes of ribs and long bones bound up like walking sticks with pink tape. On the room's one chair was a sack containing handfuls of finger bones. There were several complete and articulated skeletons at artistic intervals. It looked like a clean, modern, scientific *danse macabre*.

'Bones,' agreed Phryne. 'Switch on that desk lamp, will you, I've got a letter from the collector himself.'

Phryne laid the letter out flat and read:

Dear Anteus, having difficult time. Country is flooded. Had to get across the Roper by making a boat out of my cart. Even then got washed downstream considerably. My native boys didn't yabber the lingo and ran away. I set out with a surveyor, a cinematographer, a horse man, a camp manager and myself and two black boys. We left on the SS Marella from Sydney for Darwin—a ten-day trip on a tub which rolled villainously. Then we took a cattle train for Katherine thirteen hours, and when you get there there's only Katherine. Thence to Roper Bar 240 miles SE. Twenty-six horses and six mules. Crossed Roper River at Bar, washed down to Mount Marumba nine days later, following along the course of the Wilton River N 60 E towards the Goyder. Plentiful game here, low scrubby forest, quail, kangaroos, wild turkey, wallabies and buffalo. At least we are eating well. Tried to smoke some buffalo meat but must have the wrong kind of smoke. There's plentiful rock paintings that Morgensen would give his right hand to see. Found strange grave customs here, trying to secure some of the bones. The local natives are distrustful; they're not the ones I know. I keep losing horses to snakes. They grow some

*fearsome reptiles here. Hope that all is well with you and
that the divine Miss Fisher is enjoying my house. I know the
Johnsons will look after her well. Pip pip, Thomas.*

'He doesn't know anything about the fate of the Johnsons,'
observed Jane.

'No, and the question which remains with me is, why hasn't
some irritated native hit him over the head with a nullah-nullah?
You can't just barrel in and steal ancestral bones without so much
as a by-your-leave,' said Phryne. 'I'd be cross if someone hauled
the Fisher relatives out of their comfy cemetery in England and
I don't even like the Fishers.'

'But he's a scientist,' argued Jane. 'He needs the remains for
his research.'

There was a pause in the room of bones while humanist and
scientist stared at each other. Then Phryne shrugged.

'What did you find out from this room?' she asked.

'Haven't had time to really look,' replied Jane. 'You caught
me early.'

'Then truffle on by all means,' Phryne told her. 'But don't
let Ruth know. She's sensitive.'

Jane assented. They went out, shutting the door and hanging
the padlock back in its hasp. A clanging on the gong in the hall
announced that it was dinnertime. Hugh and Dot had returned
with a carefully copied bunch of telegrams, and Ruth had already
laid out the buffet. Miss Lavinia was sleeping peacefully when
Dot went up to her and Phryne decided to leave her alone.
Tinker, who was starving, was vibrating at the door of the dining
room. He had, Phryne observed, even washed his hands and
face despite the fact that the day had contained a bath. Gaston
bounced at his side. Phryne decided not to delay proceedings
by changing her dress. She, also, was distinctly peckish.

Dinner started well with the potato and leek soup and continued well with a huge platter of hot, delicate garfish, accompanied by the *salades composées* and a sprightly white wine from
the Barossa.

'Poor Miss Lavinia, I wonder what she is going to do now?' asked Dot.

'She has money,' Phryne pointed out. 'With money she can buy a little house, purchase a doggie of her very own, get some good clothes and hire a cook-maid. Money can't buy happiness but it can vastly improve the quality of your misery.'

'Miss Phryne!' exclaimed Dot.

'Well, it's true,' responded Phryne. 'If you're poor and your heart is broken you have few options but to remain where you are, where every person and every stick of furniture reminds you of the one who is lost. If you're rich, you can call up your yacht and embark on a four-week cruise of the Greek Islands for distraction. Unless, of course, Miss Lavinia did kill that disagreeable old woman. What do you think, Dot?'

'How can I tell? I never met either of them. But probably not. Can someone pass me some more of that green salad with the anchovies? Thanks.'

'Mrs. McNaster did say that Lavinia was her heir,' mused Phryne. 'And that seemed odd, you know, because she was so unpleasant that you wouldn't think she would leave anyone her money.'

'More likely to give it to the dogs' home,' said Tinker. 'Not that she liked dogs, either. Can you pass me the bread? Grouse bread, this.'

'Soda bread,' explained Ruth. 'Máire taught me how to make it. It uses bicarbonate of soda instead of yeast as a raising agent, like scones and cakes.'

'Really?' asked Hugh, who was deeply interested in food. 'That'd be good in an emergency.'

'Yes, like the bread all getting eaten up and no one thinking of ordering more,' observed Ruth tartly.

'How's the food at your boarding house?' asked Dot hastily.

'Not too flash,' responded her beloved. 'Mind you, I've only had dinner once and lunch, but it's real overcooked and ordinary. Shepherd's pie with sloppy potatoes. Careless.'

'Then why don't we invite Hugh to breakfast? Due to the lack of Johnsons, Dot has been making breakfast, and I'm told by trustworthy appetites that she fries a very crispy bit of bacon,' suggested Phryne. Lust was a reliable emotion, but greed was altogether simpler to satisfy and you got to keep your clothes on. She refrained from saying this in deference to her family's sensibilities.

Dessert was a lot of fruit and Ruth's surprise, a huge, gaily decorated gateau, with Chantilly cream and a plethora of fresh strawberries.

'God may have made a better berry, but so far he hasn't,' said Hugh, surreptitiously loosening his belt.

'Wonderful,' said Phryne, glad that she was wearing a shift dress.

Ruth cut and distributed the cake. It was superb. The table was drowned in cream and berries for some time.

Then, as Tinker brought in the coffee pot, Phryne was about to slip the last sliver of cake to Molly when she realised that the faithful hound was still attending on Miss Lavinia. What a good dog, she thought. Gaston, however, improvised while she was thinking this and whipped it swiftly out of her hand. Gaston liked cake. Mrs. Johnson had often let him lick the remains of the mixture. So far Ruth had not been sufficiently trained to offer it.

'Now, let's have a look at your telegrams,' she suggested, and Hugh Collins brought out his bundle of flimsies. Phryne scanned it rapidly, handing them along the table as she read.

'Nice handwriting, Dot,' she complimented. 'As easy to read as print. You are sure that these are all of the telegrams in that week?'

'Yessir,' said Hugh. He managed not to salute. Dot giggled.

'Here we have…arrangements about the sea voyage, train tickets, hiring a camera, buying horses. And—aha!'

'That's what I thought,' affirmed Dot, smug in the knowledge that she had personally written out the salient document.

'What?' demanded the other diners.

'Sent from—aha again—Point Leonard post office. IMPORTANT GET OUT OF THE HOUSE CAR WILL PICK UP SEVEN AM ON

SUNDAY AT BACK TAKE STUFF FOR A FEW DAYS WILL EXPLAIN URGENT VITAL THOMAS. Well!'

'Decoyed out of the house with their bits and pieces,' murmured Dot.

'Picked up by a car with darkened windows and carried away...' added Tinker, bouncing in his seat.

'Before they went they hid the belongings in the cellar,' pointed out Ruth.

'No struggles even for Mrs. McNaster to see because they went willingly,' said Phryne. 'How very unpleasant. Seven in the morning on Sunday, no one about but the odd fisherman.'

'Boarding houses serve breakfast from seven to eight,' Hugh informed them. 'All the trippers would be inside stuffing their faces.'

'So they are whisked off...where?' asked Dot.

'To be killed somewhere else,' suggested Tinker.

Ruth gave a small cry of fear and Jane took her hand.

'Do pipe down,' Phryne told him. 'You're frightening the innocent. They might have been further decoyed—sent to Katherine, for example. They wouldn't have got there yet. They might be being held captive. But that is very useful, Hugh, Dot. Now we know that they were taken away. All we have to find out is where they now are.'

'Oh, indeed,' said Hugh ironically. 'Simple.'

'You must have faith,' Phryne instructed him. 'Simple faith is more than Norman blood, or so we are informed. Now, how about some music? After we all do the dishes.'

'Miss Phryne, I'm still...' Jane fluttered a hand. Upstairs were a wealth of bones waiting to be explored.

'Of course, you have reading to do. But first,' Phryne picked up the cake plate, 'the dishes.'

The dishes washed and dried and put away to Ruth's satisfaction, the company adjourned to play the gramophone and, when they had recovered from dinner, dance. The evening ended with Hugh singing 'The Yeomen of England' in a rich, hearty bass, to Dot's rather shaky piano accompaniment. As an encore he did

'Simon the Cellarer' and retired pleased with his performance and his company.

Dot saw him to the door and went up to bed, first calling on Miss Lavinia. She was still fast asleep. Dot left her a nightlight and brought a handful of biscuits for Molly, who was still doing Noble Dog, though she had managed to edge the patient into the wall and was progressively occupying more and more of the narrow bed. She accepted the biscuits and crunched them noisily. Even this did not wake the sleeper.

Dot knew that Phryne would check all the locks and put herself to bed. It might be nice, she reflected, being married. To Hugh, of course. But she wasn't going to leave Miss Phryne yet.

A small niggle itched at the edge of her mind as she got into her bed and pulled the sheets up over her maiden breast. Something about the Johnsons and locks. She was too tired to remember.

Commending her soul to God until the morning, as was her invariable practice, she fell asleep. Tomorrow she would remember it. Whatever it was.

◇◇◇

When Hugh arrived for breakfast on Saturday he found the whole household in the kitchen, slavering as Dot cooked bacon, Ruth sliced bread, Jane read 'Bluebeard' aloud, Tinker found plates, Miss Lavinia sorted cutlery and Gaston and Molly got underfoot.

Miss Lavinia dropped a spoon with a squeak of alarm as Hugh came in. Dot introduced him as her fiancé and Miss Lavinia ducked her head and retrieved the spoon.

'So silly of me,' she whispered.

'Time to get the table laid, Tinker,' ordered Ruth. The young persons had not decided about Miss Lavinia yet. It was a point in her favour that Molly liked her. But, as Tinker had pointed out, dogs can be fooled. He was unwilling to leave the kitchen in case Miss Lavinia dropped a suspicious white powder into the kedgeree, but when Ruth scowled at him, he went. His father had always told him never to offend the galley man.

'"These are the keys to the two large storerooms where I keep my gold and silver,"' read Jane. *"Here are the ones for the caskets in which I keep my jewels. And here is the master key. Open anything you want. Go anywhere you please. But I forbid you to enter the small room at the end of the long gallery. If you open it I shall know and nothing will save you from my wrath."'*

'That was a trap,' remarked Hugh, taking up the large dish of kedgeree and carrying it into the dining room. Dot followed with the scrambled eggs. Jane put down the book and brought in the toast.

'What was a trap?' she asked, after Hugh had put down his cutlery for the first time.

'Telling her not to open one door of all the doors. No one could resist that. He was setting her up for...something nasty,' said Hugh.

Jane actually blushed. Ruth gave her a sharp look. Tinker, oblivious of this byplay, reached for the eggs.

'Don't stretch, dear, ask,' murmured Miss Lavinia.

'How are you feeling this morning, Miss Lavinia?' asked Dot, pushing the dish over to within the ambit of Tinker's eager spoon.

'Much better, thank you. I believe I slept all through the night in the company of your darling doggie. And the bathroom, really most luxurious. Also, such a lavish spread—these are very good scrambled eggs.'

'Too right,' agreed Hugh. 'Best I ever tasted.'

Now it was Dot's turn to blush.

'Miss Fisher...?' Miss Lavinia allowed the sentence to trail away.

'Always has breakfast in her room,' said Dot firmly.

'Ah. I wanted to thank her. I really do feel as though you have all rescued me. That was kind,' whispered Miss Lavinia.

'Our pleasure,' replied Dot. 'Do have some of this marmalade with your toast. Or there's plum jam in the little dish. More tea?'

Breakfast proceeded. Máire arrived to do the washing-up. She noticed the rods and reels and the wicker tackle basket which Hugh had left in the kitchen and asked, 'Would the gentleman be going fishing?'

'He would,' said Hugh. 'After a breakfast like that I ought to be able to hook a whale.'

'If he would like a boat, my father is at leisure this morning, so he is,' she said, running hot water into the sink.

'I know it,' said Tinker. 'The *Black Oak*. Nice little 'couta boat.'

'The 'couta aren't running, but there are a lot more fishes in the sea whose names I do not know that you could be after catching,' Máire suggested.

Hugh puzzled out the sentence.

'Good idea,' he told her. 'We'll go down presently. You coming, Tink?'

'Yessir.' Tinker wiped his mouth and fed the last bacon rind to Gaston.

'Put on your jersey, it can be cold out on the water,' scolded Dot. 'What's wrong, Máire?' The maid was looking stricken.

'Maybe it is that the sea will be too rough today,' temporised Máire, biting her lip. 'Perhaps another day might be better.'

'Nonsense,' said Hugh. 'Looked out this morning on the way over here. Flat as a plate. Come on, young feller. Let's go sort out the fish from the water.'

Tinker fell in behind like a mongrel who has at last found a home.

And Hugh kissed Dot goodbye and promised to be back before tea. Just like a husband. Ruth sighed and clasped her hands. A romance, under her very own roof!

Jane was plotting how quickly she could get down to the filming. The photographer had promised to let her operate the machine. She took up the fairytale book and slipped away as the last dish was put in its place and Máire began to teach Ruth how to make potato scones. Dot was undertaking a little mending while she waited for the washing to be returned. Dot liked mending.

◇◇◇

Phryne rose on a fair windless morning that promised to be hot. She had eaten her freshly baked soda bread roll. She had drunk her coffee. She had dressed in another loose shift and was determined to sit down and think about the Johnsons' abduction. In pursuance of which she took herself out to the garden, picked a leaf of mint and chewed it, and surveyed the layout of the house.

The back gate gave onto a broad alley down which the nightmen had once valiantly brought their cart and where the tradesmen now came with all the goodies that the household required. In fact, a Chinese man was presently opening the back gate and manoeuvering in a big laundry basket. He saw Phryne sitting on the kitchen step and paused.

She smiled and waved him in. He stepped past her, hefting the huge basket effortlessly, treading back on the heels of his soft cloth shoes. The Chinese did not have pigtails anymore, of course, except very old ones like Lin Chung's great-grand-uncle. But hadn't she heard of a pigtail-cutting panic in somewhere like—was it Macao? It had been in that book by that strange American, Charles Fort. And there was a copy of it on the shelves in the library.

But meanwhile, she was supposed to be thinking about the Johnsons. They had locked up the house, ensured that the valuables were safe, taken their overnight bags and walked out to a car to be whisked off into eternity…wait. Mrs. McNaster could have seen them. She was dead. But Miss Lavinia wasn't. And a condition of her servitude had been that she sat beside the loathsome but eagle-eyed Mrs. McNaster in her endless survey of the area.

Phryne smiled at the Chinese as he carried the empty washing basket out and went inside to find Miss Lavinia.

She found her in the parlour with Dot. Dot was mending a stocking, an eye-straining task which needed concentration. Miss Lavinia had no task at all for the first time in many years and was trying to talk.

Phryne sat down and patted the sofa beside her.

'How do you feel this morning, then, Miss Lavinia?' she asked. 'Up to a cup of tea and some gossip?'

'Certainly, dear, if that's what you want,' she said, a little stiffly.

'Only about the Johnsons,' said Phryne. 'They're missing. I want to find them.'

'It was very strange,' said Miss Lavinia. 'They were such respectable people. I used to see them every day. Their day ran like clockwork. I used to say to Mrs. McNaster, "It must be ten o'clock, the Johnsons are going to their own quarters." Every night at ten. Up at six every day except Sunday, and then it was seven. Mrs. Johnson used to sing in the choir, Mr. Johnson was a nice man who did, I gather, have a little flutter on the horses, but never more than five shillings. Our gardener used to take them for him. They seemed to be devoted to each other. If Mr. Johnson went out he would always bring Mrs. J a small gift when he came back. Went to the movies every Saturday night at the town hall.'

'What about Mr. Thomas? Was he a rackety man?'

'No, dear, not at all. I used to talk to Mrs. J sometimes when I could. Mrs. McNaster liked jam made out of a certain fig—one grows in your garden, Miss Fisher—and only Mrs. Johnson could make it to her satisfaction, so when she had fig jam made she would bring us a few pots. Mr. Thomas was vague. If an idea struck him he would dive upstairs and shout down that he wanted dinner the day after, and not to disturb him. Then he would wander down in the middle of the night and raid the larder. She used to make sandwiches and leave them for him and she told me they always got eaten. When he took off to travel they had a great bustle to get all of his kit ready; he goes into wild places, you know, dear, where there are no civilised conveniences. Otherwise he had few friends, except Madame Sélavy. She has some sort of club and he always went to their meetings. Travelled into Melbourne to the university once a week to give his lectures. A nice, peaceable sort of man.'

'And Mrs. Mason?'

'Oh, dear, she's got a little bit of a problem. Mrs. McNaster was very gleeful about it. Caught her every time smuggling bottles out to put into other people's rubbish bins. And her son is probably a good boy but his friend Fraser is not. She hasn't any control over those boys.'

'I noticed,' said Phryne grimly.

'When I was in the scholastic profession, I should have got them a strong-minded tutor and told him to use his cane freely,' stated Miss Lavinia. 'I saw them throw a stone at Gaston once. They used to go hunting and come back positively festooned with corpses.' Miss Lavinia shuddered. 'And they slip out at night, climbing down into that cypress tree, and come back at two or three in the morning. Heaven knows what they have been up to!'

'Hell knows, more probably,' said Phryne. 'Now, cast your mind back a couple of weeks. Do you remember the Johnsons leaving?'

'Seven am, yes, they both came out the back gate, carrying bags. There was a car there and they got in.'

'What sort of car?'

'One of those big ones,' said Miss Lavinia, to whom cars were clearly a closed book. 'Dark blue or black. Rather like the doctor's car, with those platforms on the sides.'

'Running boards.'

'Ah, thank you. And they had Gaston with them, I am sure. Mrs. Johnson had him under her arm. And you've got Gaston here! He came back to his home, the clever little doggie. What, then, has become of the Johnsons?'

'A good question. Now, what are your plans, Miss Lavinia?'

'I really don't know,' confessed the older lady. 'I was Mrs. McNaster's niece, you see, and I am the only remaining heir to the Holystone fortune. She had it for life. After she died it will be mine—is mine, I suppose, now. She had me so busy night and day I didn't really think about it. I never thought I'd outlive her, dear. I was perfectly happy as a teacher, and then she called me and said it was my duty to look after her, so I came here. I have been very unhappy. I thought I might die from lack of sleep at first. I haven't slept a night through for eleven years.'

Miss Lavinia's face bore a wistful look which softened her lines and made her look like the young, self-confident woman she had been before she had been ground down by domestic slavery.

'But you coped,' said Dot, finishing with the stocking and folding it up.

'One does, does one not?' asked Miss Lavinia mildly. 'My young man, the one I would have married, was killed at Passchendaele. So I had no one to miss me, and nothing to do, though I did like being a teacher. Perhaps I can still be useful in some small way.'

'Let me introduce you to my sister, who does social work in St Kilda,' Phryne offered. 'Anyone who can teach will be heartily welcome. And greatly needed. Or perhaps you might like to join the Lady Mayoress's Auxiliary? Do not think that you have nothing to offer the world. Do you want to stay in Queenscliff?'

Miss Lavinia suddenly sounded decisive.

'No, dear. I would like to go back to the city. I used to live in Hawthorn. I would like a nice little house in Hawthorn, the leafy part where the trees grow high in the street and meet overhead. And I would like a garden. Here the salt kills all my favourite flowers. Roses. Pansies, petunias, gillyflowers—all the cottage flowers. That would be so nice. And a kitchen garden, of course. Mrs. McNaster would not let me grow flowers. I used to sneak out sometimes and help the gardener. Oh,' said Miss Lavinia, with a shocked gasp, 'I am free, aren't I?'

'You certainly are,' said Phryne.

Miss Lavinia burst into tears.

Phryne left her with the sympathetic Dot and a clean hankie and wandered out into the kitchen. The potato scones were apparently coming along well. They smelt gorgeous. Ruth and Máire, who still looked worried, were consulting the cookbook, even though tonight the Fisher ménage was dining at the Esplanade Hotel. Phryne went out and inspected the fig tree which made the excellent jam. It seemed happy. Its leaves would have clothed the whole family of Adam and Eve...

Well, well, something had happened to the Johnsons after they got into that car, otherwise Gaston would not have escaped. And the event had happened not a great way away, because Gaston was a small dog and could not have travelled far. Then the Ellis brothers had taken away the furniture, keeping that job off the books. Why? The furniture would be of little value. But, of course, if it was removed, the investigating authorities would assume that the housekeepers had indeed performed a moonlight flit and stop looking for them. In fact they would not be discovered missing until Mr. Thomas came home, which argued that the kidnappers did not know that Miss Fisher was to occupy the house. Or perhaps they did not care…and with Constable Dolt in charge, crime must be positively waving in Queenscliff.

Phryne decided to leave Jane with her bones, Dot with Miss Lavinia and the washing, and Ruth with her cookery and take herself off for a swim. So she did.

Chapter Fourteen

See how love and murder will out.

William Congreve
The Double Dealer

Tinker was walking with Hugh down Hesse Street towards the sea when he was catcalled by three boys lounging outside the ice-cream shop.

'Yah! Pantry boy!' yelled Jolyon. 'Found a friend, then?'

They huddled together directly Hugh crossed the road and stood in front of them. He was huge. He was authoritative. Fraser, however, stuck out his jaw.

'Who're you, then?'

'As it happens, I'm Detective Sergeant Collins from CIB,' said Hugh evenly. 'And you must be Kiwi, Fraser and Mason.'

'What's it to you?' demanded Fraser hotly.

'I've met a lot of boys like you,' said Hugh tolerantly. They relaxed. 'Running wild, no fathers to clip their ears.' They stiffened. 'Well, boys, I'm here to tell you that if you so much as look squiggly-eyed at any of Miss Fisher's family again, if you lay a hand on them, I'll make you wish you'd never been born. I'm going to kick you up the bum now,' he added, suiting the action to the word. There were three yelps. 'And if you are ever drawn to my attention again, I'll break your bloody necks. Understood?'

A small crowd had gathered. They approved of this condign action. They were laughing. Several voices urged the detective sergeant to provide an encore. Fraser, Kiwi and Jolyon had not made themselves popular in Queenscliff. They were staggered, astonished and in pain. They ran away without another word.

'Come on, Tink,' said Hugh, and Tinker, aglow with hero worship, fell in behind, hefting his burdens with pride.

Máire had not mentioned that her father was a gnome. There was Mr. O'Malley, sitting on the pier, mending nets, and there was no other word for him, except, perhaps, leprechaun. He had a long straggly beard and hair which stuck out at equal lengths on every side of his woolly cap. He was wearing a neatly darned ancient fisherman's jersey which might once have been blue, sea boots, and oilskin trousers. At the other end of the net, spindle in hand, was a young woman in almost identical gear with the addition of a wide straw hat. Gráinne's mother might have bent to her husband's wishes about her daughter wearing trousers, but she was not going to allow her to ruin her fine milky complexion in all that sun and that was her last word on the subject, so it was.

'Mr. O'Malley?' said Hugh easily.

'And who would be doing the askin'?' The old man squinted up the height of Hugh. He had cornflower blue eyes, like his daughter. Then he switched his blowlamp gaze to Tinker. 'And you I know, young devil of an Edward, pinchin' fish for yer mam. Not that I ever grudged it to the poor woman, her havin' her man at sea and all them childer and all, God love her.'

Tinker wriggled in extreme discomfort at these personal observations.

'It's me, I got a job with a lady, and this is Miss Fisher's visitor, and we'd like to go fishing,' said Tinker. 'H'lo, Grainy.'

'Hello.' The girl regarded Tinker coolly. 'You'll be the gentleman that my sister Máire was tellin' me of?'

'That's me,' said Hugh. 'Well, what do you say?'

'It's gettin' late for the garfish,' said the old man. 'Would you fancy a little rock fishin', now? Perhaps come along while I pick up me cray pots?'

'That sounds good,' said Hugh.

'Then let me stow me net and we'll be off. Gráinne, my heart, you'll go back to your mother now.'

'I will not,' said Gráinne. 'You promised me, and you need me to pick up the pots. I know where they all are.'

'Well, well, what can I do with you?' cried her father. 'Step in then, sir, and my daughter can cast us off.'

Gráinne was still eyeing her father very narrowly. Tinker was not surprised that the boat shot off from its mooring. Neither was Gráinne, who leapt like a cat into the thwarts and settled down by the steering oar with a smile which was not quite smug. The smile said, 'You're not going to leave me behind, Daddy dear.'

The old man, unexpectedly, chuckled.

'You're a true daughter of mine, so you are,' he said to her. 'So be it, then, Swan Island it is and perhaps there might be a lot of the creatures in the pots, if God is good.'

'If God is good,' agreed Gráinne.

The sea was as flat as a silver platter and the sun was strong. The little boat crept across to the bulk of Swan Island, which was surrounded by reefs, apparently, and very dangerous. Also, as far as Tinker knew, uninhabited. A ragged fusillade of shots sounded across the water.

'That will be the young gentlemen hunting,' said Gráinne. 'Shoot at anything, they will. Seagulls. Swans. Still, they are such bad shots that rabbits run there safe as babes in arms.'

'Young men will be young men,' said her father. 'Some more than others, God knows. There's the ferry setting out,' he added. A huge brightly lit ship sailed majestically out in front of the small *Black Oak*. 'And she's pinched our wind, so she has.'

'Can you swim, Tink?' asked Hugh. 'I forgot to ask.'

''Course I can,' said Tinker with scorn. 'All the kids can swim around here. Except some of the girls. Look, we can see the filming.'

Hugh looked back. There was a crowd on the shore. In among them he was sure that he recognised Jane in her new bobby cut. She was standing next to the cinematographer, listening intently with her head on one side, like a bird picking up knowledge instead of worms. Hugh waved. But Jane was otherwise occupied.

In the crowd were the three Mason boys. Subdued for the present. And there was a butcher's trike, a string of sausages trailing sadly from the basket. The local dogs appreciated the position and were exploiting this golden opportunity by tugging the string and wolfing the sausages as they appeared.

'There's Amos,' commented Tinker, also enjoying the spectacle. 'He's going to get the sack if he don't stop mooning about after that la-di-dah Lily.'

But Amos had no eyes to spare for his own business. He was staring at Lily standing on the shore, waving her arms, then bending to embrace a small boy who had been forcibly dressed in a Bubbles costume and seemed mutinous.

'Lily?' asked Hugh.

'Her,' said Tinker. 'Miss Movie Star. Thinks she's so beautiful! I s'pose it's good though. She was a rotten cook. Mrs. C was about to sack her.'

'I see,' Hugh replied, a little nettled at this plain speaking. 'Didn't Mrs. Cook sack you, too?'

Tinker looked a little abashed.

'Well, yair, she was gonna, but then I met the guv'nor and I resigned.'

Tinker was pleased with his long word.

'When you fall in love, Tink, you will regret those unkind words,' Hugh told him. Amos's expression of dog-like devotion made Hugh uncomfortable. He had seen that look before. Gráinne giggled.

'Me, fall in lurve? Nah,' said Tinker. 'I don't have nothin' to do with the sheilas. I gotta make a livin'. Look at Amos—used to be a good bloke, now he's moonin' about, no thought about his job or his mum or nothin' as long as he can see Lily. Bloke'd be cracked to…' Aware suddenly of Hugh's affianced state and Gráinne glaring at him, he backtracked hurriedly. 'I mean, Miss

Dot is a fine woman and you're a good girl, Grainy, don't get me wrong…'

'Down sails and let's get the curragh overboard,' said the old man. 'Me first pot's about here.'

Gráinne jumped up and slackened lines. Then she heaved over a strange round object, like a big basket made of rushes with a tarred overcoat of—canvas, perhaps? Hugh had never seen such a thing before and said so.

''Tis a curragh,' Mr. O'Malley told him. 'Other boats use a dinghy but they have to haul it and that's a drag on a boat. Good sticks they've got here, they call them manuka, for making of a true Irish boat. Me and my daughter made it ourselves; it's just the same as a very big cray pot, so it is. Good manila line here and there's me corks. Over you go now, my girl, and God be between you and harm.'

Gráinne lowered herself down into the little boat, which bobbed like a duck, and began paddling towards a buoy. When she reached it, she hooked the marker onto a line which the old man began hauling. Despite his leprechaun size he was very strong.

'Heave-ho, up we go,' said Tinker as he grabbed the end. The pot came up, dripping seaweed. It was a basket with an inwoven funnel down which the crayfish could crawl, and out of which they could not retreat. Mr. O'Malley counted ten small crayfish, most of which he threw back.

'Go and grow up into fine big fish, with a blessing,' he told them. Three he placed into another basket, a long, wide, shallow tray, which he dropped into the water.

'They keep fresh better like that,' he said. Then he rebaited the pot with a piece of very aged meat—Hugh had been wondering where the smell came from—and passed it back to Gráinne waiting in the curragh below.

Hugh baited his line, dropped it in the water, and sat back to enjoy fishing. Dot had teasingly accused him of going fishing because he needed to rest and this was an acceptable way of sitting in the sun all day and doing nothing. In that she had been correct. Hugh was tired. The fraud and murder case had been trying and difficult and his boss, Jack Robinson, had been very anxious to get a conviction, meaning sleepless nights and long days for Detective Sergeant Collins.

Swan Island lay tangled and green on one quarter. The *Black Oak* rocked in the gentle offshore breeze. The line trailed into the blue water under the blue sky. Seagulls called. Hugh closed his eyes against the glare. Just for a moment.

◇◇◇

Phryne swam hard up and down for ten minutes, then she hauled herself ashore and rested. The Johnsons were probably still in the vicinity of Queenscliff or Point Lonsdale. If she had been official, she could have ordered a meticulous search. As she was extremely unofficial, she had to come up with an alternative method. How to find the Johnsons?

An idea occurred to her which was so outrageous that she gasped. Then she began to laugh. She rolled over and over on the greensward, giving rise to varied emotions in the hearts of the gentlemen who watched her. Finally, covered in grass, she sat up, hugging herself. Brilliant. She could make it work. It would work, human nature being what it was.

She would need to make a phone call to an acquaintance in Melbourne. But not today, curses. Tomorrow, he would be answering the phone. She dislodged a small cypress cone from her hair, shook herself, and went back into the sea to calm herself down. Even so, she giggled at intervals.

The elderly gentlemen sighed.

◇◇◇

Dot was warming to Miss Lavinia. They had had a cosy chat about drawn threadwork. They had shared a cup of tea. The doctor had sent the gardener over with Miss Lavinia's possessions—a small trunk, a smaller toiletries bag and a tiny handbag—and Dot had helped her to retrieve the dropped stitches in her fisherman's jersey, caused by some careless packing.

'I knit them for the fishers,' said Miss Lavinia. 'Little enough we can do for the brave fellows, going out on that dangerous sea to fetch us our dinners. "*Buy my caller herrin'/ They're not brought here without much darin'*,"' she sang in a small, true soprano.

'"*Wives and mothers, maist despairin'/ call them lives of men,*"' Dot joined in. '"*Buy my caller herrin'/New drawn frae the firth.*"'

'I like that song,' said Máire, who had come in to report sandwiches made for lunch.

'I'll teach it to you,' promised Miss Lavinia.

Máire made a little curtsey.

'T'ank you, Missus. Now lunch is on the table and potato scones have to be eaten hot, or they'll be spoiled completely,' she said, ushering Dot and Miss Lavinia into the parlour.

Ruth, the visitor, Dot and Máire, despite protestations that her place was in the kitchen, sat down to strong tea and potato scones loaded with butter. Jane was still with the film people, Phryne was swimming, Tinker and Hugh were fishing. The conversation turned to the proper recipe for Anzac biscuits, and proved engrossing.

No dinner had to be cooked tonight and Ruth was rather relieved, even though Mrs. Leyel's excellent treasure trove of a book still had many things to try which sounded delicious. Cooking was a full-time task and very hard work. After lunch, the washing-up done and Máire dismissed for the day, Ruth decided to retire to her own room and catch up on the fate of the stolen bride. There were sandwiches for anyone who came home hungry.

Miss Lavinia and Dot sat in the bay window, in good strong sunlight, mending the holes in Tinker's socks, which he had managed to wear or possibly tear through in a very short time. They listened to the radio as they sewed. Music from the Palm Court lounge. Very acceptable.

When Phryne came home she did not disturb them. She tiptoed past and raided the kitchen for the plate of sandwiches which she knew would be there. She took some up with her. She needed to perfect her scheme. This time her orangeade had no gin in it. Phryne required a clear mind.

She had finished her notes and was staring idly out the window when Jane came running. She rushed into the house and called, 'Miss! Miss Phryne! A terrible thing has happened!'

'What?' asked Phryne, appearing at the head of the stairs. 'Calm, Jane, take a deep breath. And another. There,' she said, coming down the stairs and putting a hand on the girl's shoulder. 'Now, tell me.'

'Lily!' gasped Jane.

'The movie star? What's wrong with her?'

'The pigtail snipper got her,' said Jane. 'And she's terribly wounded. He cut her throat.'

'Dear Lord,' murmured Miss Lavinia. 'It's those boys.'

Phryne felt that too much emotion was being expended for a front hall.

'Look, everyone come into the parlour, we shall all sit down, and calm down. Are you hurt, Jane?'

'Just winded from running up the hill,' responded Jane. 'And I suppose I'm in shock.' She examined herself. Blue fingernails. Faint. Short of breath. Dizzy. Yes, they were all the hallmarks of shock. She put her fingers to her pulse. Light and fast.

'Then we shall treat you for shock,' said Phryne briskly. 'Have a nice long sniff at Miss Lavinia's salts. Lean back. Dot, put her feet up.'

'Hot sweet tea,' said Ruth, and went to make it.

'Don't do anything for the present,' Phryne advised her adoptive daughter. 'Close your eyes and centre your energies, as Lin Chung would say. Now, Miss Lavinia, what did you say?'

Miss Lavinia was reluctant to repeat it, but Phryne insisted.

'I always suspected those boys of being the pigtail snipper. So did Mrs. McNaster. We used to see them go out down the tree—and we noticed that they were always out when the outrages occurred.'

'Any more evidence than Mrs. McNaster's feelings?'

'No,' confessed Miss Lavinia. 'But they are very bad boys.'

'Certainly, but that does not make them snippers. Jane, what do you say?'

'I was down at the filming, the cinematographer was letting me look through the viewfinder, it was really interesting,'
responded Jane, her voice becoming firmer as she spoke. 'Then
the director said, "Pack up, boys, that'll be all for the day, the
light's wrong now." So the people began to drift away. The
next-door boys were there all right. I saw them. Lily had her
hair combed and plaited into a long plait like I used to have
and she was talking to the people beside her, then she just went
down. I didn't see anything at first, but then I crept to the front.
Her throat was cut, her pigtail hanging by a few hairs. She was
bleeding like a fountain. So I came home to tell you. That cop's
on the way, they said.'

'Ah, Constable Moron,' said Phryne. 'That'll be a help. Now,
we need to make you feel better, Jane. What would you like?'

'I think I'll go and lie down,' said Jane. 'Perhaps Molly would
come with me?'

The faithful hound, delighted at being awarded another
suffering human to comfort, fell in behind as Jane was helped
up the stairs.

'She'll be all right,' said Dot.

'As long as she has that darling doggie with her,' agreed Miss
Lavinia. 'What a terrible thing to happen! And in Queenscliff,
too!'

'Yes,' replied Dot, who was glad that Hugh had chosen to go
fishing. 'Tell me, Miss Lavinia, what sort of dog will you buy
when you have your own house?'

'Well,' said Miss Lavinia, happy to be distracted, 'they say
that terriers are very faithful, but I would really like a dog which
would enjoy walking with me. I like walking.'

'So do I,' said Dot, sitting up in her chair. 'What about taking
a little walk now? Get out into the fresh air, do us good. That
looks like a nice forest, up behind the town.'

'Lovely,' said Miss Lavinia. 'I'll just get my hat. We might
see a dear little bunny, or even a fox.'

Phryne left them to it.

◇◇◇

Hugh returned with Tinker and a basket of fish, which he had cleaned at the pier, thus reducing weight and gaining merit with the local stray cats. Reminded that they were dining out at the Queenscliff Hotel on this night, he gave the basket to Tinker.

'Go round and give them to your mother, lad,' he said. Tinker beamed. He liked being a Provider. He stood, poised on one foot. He did not want to take Hugh anywhere near his poverty-stricken household in its shameful tent.

'Off you go, I'll see you at Miss Fisher's house,' said Hugh, understanding instantly. Tinker sped off, stopping only to greet an acquaintance. It was Harry, whom he had last seen at the Ellis's yard.

'You got another job, Eddie?' asked Harry.

'Yair,' said Tinker. 'Good job, too. Gent gave me all these fish.'

'You're well out of Ellis's,' said the boy. 'Been real narked since you stood him up for his threepence. Even belted Bluey. But you missed all the excitement on the foreshore.'

'Yair?' asked Tinker. He wanted to move on. His mum would be real pleased with this free dinner, and he had sixpence to give her from his wages. That meant she could buy potatoes, flour and lard, and there would be fried fish and chips for tea for all his siblings.

'Lily got her throat cut,' said the boy with relish. 'Right there!'

'Yah,' said Tinker, expressing scorn and disbelief.

'True dinks! See it wet, see it dry, cut my throat if I tell a lie!' the boy assured him.

'Who done it?' demanded Tinker.

'Dunno. She was in a crowd and she just dropped. Phantom pigtail snipper got her. Doctor's sent her to Geelong. Gotta go,' said Harry. 'C'n y' spare a mate a few measly fish?'

Tinker handed over some of the smaller fish. Then he went on to the tent at the back of his mother's house, whistling thoughtfully through his teeth. The guv'nor would have to know about this. And he could gather some statements from witnesses, as well. The boys of Queenscliff had all been watching the filming.

◇◇◇

The company assembled for the short walk to the Queenscliff Hotel, looking scrubbed and pleased with themselves. Hugh had slept for an hour, caught eleven mullet, an eel and a feral boot, which had put up an heroic struggle. He was slightly sunburnt and felt agreeably tired. Dot and Miss Lavinia had seen several bunnies, a fox, and a plethora of possums, one of whom had come down to ground level to demand his share of the apple which Dot had been eating. Dot had given him the core, and he had taken it from her hand. She doted on his cute little nose. Jane was pale but composed, Ruth rosy and rested. Tinker was intensely uncomfortable in his starched collar. He was sweating a little and delighted to find that it was fast losing its iron grip on his neck. He had lived in Queenscliff all his life, but had never gone into the Queenscliff Hotel—not through the front entrance.

It was imposing. Phryne had once landed in Queenscliff from an impromptu aeroplane adventure and had been impressed by this hotel's comfort, its unobtrusive good taste and the quality of its breakfasts, which were legendary. She had not had time to really look at the opulent sitting rooms, the stained-glass panels, the newspapers all ironed for easy reading and the huge crystal bowls of fresh flowers which lent the air a charming fragrance, mixed with the aroma of roasting meat and red wine.

Phryne smiled at the head waiter and they were ushered into the grand dining room. Candles, epergnes, heavy silver cutlery, spotless starched napery. Tinker suppressed a 'Bloody hell!' out of deference to his hostess. Phryne, in her purple, silver and black gown, took the head of the table, and the others seated themselves. The sommelier approached for a conference and Hugh whispered to Dot, 'I never been in a place like this before, Dot. Can I ask for a beer?'

'Beer for the gentleman,' ordered Phryne. 'One glass of champagne each for the young persons, a sherry for Miss Dorothy and I will have a *kir royale* to begin with.'

The young persons tasted their drinks and watched Phryne drink the glass of sparking purple liquid. What it was, thought Tinker, to be one of the ruling class. He would have run a mile before confronting that tall, snooty, frightening bloke in the tail coat. Miss Fisher just smiled at him and he rolled over—so to speak—and put his paws in the air. The guv'nor, he concluded as the delicate soup appeared, was a top-notch lady. Tinker was glad that he had joined the Fisher household. He proceeded to deliver his report. Phryne was pleased with him!

Chapter Fifteen

Stabat mater dolorosa
Juxta crucem lacrimosa
There stood the weeping mother at the cross

Jacopone da Todi
Stabat Mater

Sunday and a bright clear hot day. Morning broke with Mrs. Mason banging at the door and screaming. Phryne woke, dragged on a dressing gown and went down, intending to deliver a blistering, mustard-plaster snub. There had been altogether far too many people banging at her door lately and she meant to see the end of it. Also, the medicine cabinet was running out of sal volatile.

Mrs. Mason, however, was not alone. Accompanying her were a very embarrassed Constable Dawson and three hangdog boys. Muttering something quite actionable between her teeth, Phryne opened the door and admitted them.

'Good morning,' she said frostily.

'Oh, Miss Fisher, I forgot you had no Johnsons! I'm so sorry! But the boys…'

'Come in to the parlour,' said Phryne, beginning again what was seeming like a weary litany. 'Sit down and tell me all about it.'

The one who did not obey her instruction was the policeman. He stood stiffly at the door, a true guardian of the King's peace, and blocked the avenue by which the miserable felons might escape the full weight of the law.

'He wants to arrest them!' shrieked Mrs. Mason.

'Does he?' Phryne was intrigued. 'Why?'

'Because he says we slit up that silly tart,' snarled Fraser.

'Lily?' asked Phryne.

'We never,' sobbed Kiwi.

'And what,' said Phryne with a tinge of asperity, 'do you think I can do about it?'

'You must help me!' screamed Mrs. Mason.

'Must I?' asked Phryne, interested. 'Why?'

Mrs. Mason was silenced.

Kiwi said, 'We didn't do it,' again.

'Did you see who did?' asked Phryne.

'No. There were all these people, it was a crowd. She just made this gurgling noise and down she went. Then everyone yelled and milled about and I couldn't even tell who was next to me.'

'So you don't know if Jolyon or Fraser did it, either?'

'No,' said Kiwi, looking green. 'It was horrible.'

'All you can say is "I didn't do it,"' Phryne told him.

'I didn't!' he protested.

'And I didn't either,' said Fraser.

'Nor me,' echoed Jolyon.

'Then why, of all the people in the crowd, has this gallant constable arrested you?' she enquired.

'We had blood on us,' mumbled Kiwi.

'Yes, but throat wounds are very generous, they spatter blood on all and sundry,' Phryne told him. 'Why you three?'

The boys wriggled. The constable said, 'Is Detective Sergeant Collins at home, Miss?'

'He isn't staying here,' said Phryne. 'He's at the Home by the Sea boarding house on the Esplanade. I can, however, send for him. Why do you want him?'

'I believe he might be a witness, Miss.'

'I doubt it,' said Phryne. 'We dined together last night and I think he would have mentioned witnessing an attempted murder on the foreshore. Just as a matter of interest. But you stay here and I shall have him fetched and we shall see what we can make of this business.' Phryne swept out into the hall and found her entire household, agog.

'We have a problem,' she told them. 'Ruth, Jane, can you go and start breakfast? There may be a lot of extra mouths. I would kill, at present, for a cup of coffee—just a hint. Tinker, get dressed and go and get Hugh Collins, on the request of Constable Dawson—tell him Dot will give him breakfast. On your bike, Tinker, this is urgent. Dot, can you hold the fort for me in the parlour while I go and get dressed? I feel that this robe, though charming, is somehow not quite the thing for boys and investigations. Thanks,' she said, and ran up the stairs in a cloud of billowing silk figured with dragons.

Tinker ran for his own room. Jane and Ruth retreated to the kitchen. Dot, in her candlewick dressing gown, hair firmly in a plait, found the sal volatile, sighed, and went into the parlour. Half an hour later and Hugh Collins was in the parlour, relieving Constable Dawson's mind. He almost dared not arrest three such highly connected young malefactors—that had always preserved them before—but now he had proof that they were concerned in a serious assault. He couldn't ignore that. He had telephoned for the duty sergeant at Geelong and he was on his way. What else could he do? The young felons might run away. He had to secure them somehow.

Detective Sergeant Collins was a large presence, even in flannels. He had the three boys seated on the sofa, side by side, and had banished their hysterical mother in Dot's custody to the dining room. He believed that tea was being supplied to them and wished he had managed to get his hands on a cup before he had to go and be a policeman. But that was often the case.

'Now then,' he said to Constable Dawson. 'We've established that I didn't see anything unusual on that foreshore yesterday.

What evidence do you have that these three are involved in an attempted murder?'

'They are bad boys,' said the constable solemnly.

'Granted,' replied Hugh. 'What else?'

'They've got a plait of hair,' said the constable. 'They showed it to some boys down the pier last night.'

'Did they?' asked Hugh. 'And where is said plait of hair?' he asked Jolyon, Kiwi and Fraser.

'It was just a joke,' Kiwi began.

'Shut up, you nong!' snarled Fraser.

'Shut up yourself,' retorted Kiwi with spirit. 'You got us into this, Animal. I'll say what I like, so there!'

'Sucks to you,' muttered Fraser.

'We took the hair,' explained Kiwi. 'We thought it'd be a joke to scare the fishos with a tale. So that's what we did,' he ended lamely.

'Where's the hair now? And where did you get it?' demanded Hugh Collins.

'It's in the cypress tree, I can get it for you,' offered Jolyon. Released with a nod, he sped out of the house. Hugh persisted with the rest of his question.

'Where did you get it? Did you cut it off the victim?'

'Lily? No, no, that wasn't us!' wailed Kiwi. 'It was just a joke!'

Hugh changed his wish from a cup of tea to a pint or so of strong beer. He closed his eyes and began again. The litany grew more and more confused.

Phryne Fisher, at the end of her patience and fortified with coffee, stalked into the room and pinned Fraser with her gaze. He glared back at her. The gaze held until he blinked and looked away. Phryne could outstare a cat.

'You used a razor,' she said, and he nodded, as fascinated as a bird before a cobra. 'You cut off the plait and enjoyed the screams.' Another nod. 'No one noticed you because you were boys and you had a football with you.' Nod. 'You hid the hair? No, you did something with it. You sold the hair to Miss Leonard, to make wigs.' Nod. 'But the plait you were showing the fishos wasn't Lily's hair.' Nod again. Phryne turned to Hugh. 'They've been terrorising the girls of Queenscliff for a rag, the little beasts,' she said in a quiet voice which had the scathing quality of hydrochloric acid poured into the ear. 'They relished the screams and the panic and the girls wrapping their heads to preserve their hair. The horrible little public-school oafs. Payment from Miss Leonard financed other nasty, puerile pursuits, I am sure. Of them we will not enquire.'

Kiwi breathed a sigh of relief. Fraser was still mute and entranced. Hugh nodded. Constable Dawson blinked. He had never met anyone like Miss Fisher before.

Jolyon returned with the plait. The hair was not as blonde as Lily's hair. Phryne examined it briefly. Then she called into the kitchen, 'Jane!'

Jane arrived, drying her hands on a tea towel.

'What did you do with your hair when you cut it off, Jane dear?' asked Phryne.

'I don't recall,' said Jane. 'I didn't want it anymore. I might have dropped it out the window.'

'You did,' Phryne told her. 'Hugh, you can see it is the same shade.'

Both policemen rose to match the plait to the original. Both agreed that it was the same.

'These benighted morons improved the shining hour by pinching Jane's discarded hair to big-note themselves before the fisherboys,' said Phryne. 'Apart from assault, theft and other things relating to the phantom pigtail snipper, they are innocent. They didn't injure Lily.'

'Your reasoning, Miss Fisher?' asked Hugh Collins.

'Only one of them is tall enough to cut Lily's throat from behind,' she told him. 'It was cut in a straight line, so they say. And the other two would have told on him before now. Also, they had blood on them. The would-be murderer, standing behind the victim, would be shielded by her body. Now give them back to Mrs. Mason and get them all out of my house,' she added. 'This audience is over.'

Constable Dawson, the boys and Mrs. Mason were ushered out. Phryne stamped through the kitchen and out into the garden to greet Gaston and smoke a calming gasper. After ten minutes Dot sought her out, carrying a pacifying pot of coffee and a new-baked roll.

'You could go back to bed,' she suggested. 'It's still real early. No tradesmen today, it's Sunday. I'm off to mass soon, is there anything else I can get you before I go?'

'No, thank you, Dot. It's going to be hot, I shall go for a swim as soon as I have calmed down. Boys. I cannot imagine why they were invented.'

'Me neither,' agreed Dot, who assumed that they were created to render difficult the lives of women, as her grandma had always said.

Dot left to adopt suitable garments and primp a bit, as Hugh was escorting her to mass, to return to a gargantuan breakfast. She hoped the bacon would hold out with such appetites as Tinker and Hugh at the one table.

Phryne sat in the soothing vapours of various herbs and smoked another gasper and drank another cup of coffee and, after some consideration, ate her roll with raspberry jam and good Queenscliff butter. That was one horror removed for her girls, anyway. Ruth had been seriously concerned about the phantom pigtail sniper. Had those little bastards told her the whole truth, however? Phryne went inside and up the stairs at a run.

She met Miss Lavinia descending for breakfast, told her that one mystery had been solved, and began to ascertain how anyone could have got into the Thomas house. Jane was not clear on what she had done with her hair. Had she really dropped it out the window? Or had those fiendish boys found a way into the next-door mansion?

If so, she was going to make them even sorrier than they were at present. She began at the side of the house facing the Masons. Little guest rooms, almost identical. One window each, latched and locked. All the latches worked so far. Her own room, on the balcony. French windows locked and with the added security of hooks on each one. The bathroom, ditto. The other guest rooms, ditto, ditto, ditto. The room of bones, closed and locked. Good. The house was sealed up as snug as a bug in a rug, ergo, no boys, and Jane had indeed flung her tresses out the window, like a flapper Rapunzel. Phryne went into the bathroom to wash her grimy hands with rose geranium soap. The idea which had been floating around in the Antarctic Sea of her mind crystallised into an iceberg.

Locks! Mr. and Mrs. Johnson had left the house secured, even hiding the valuables in the cellar.

So why had they left the back door open?

She lathered her hands and rinsed them slowly, dried them carefully, and went down to examine the back door with her magnifying glass, which was where Tinker caught her.

'Guv'nor, the way you got the truth out of them oafs was…' He didn't have a word for his entire admiration. 'What's afoot?'

'Have a look, Tinker, and tell me if you can see any scratches.' Phryne passed him the glass. Tinker was thrilled. He was helping with another investigation. He looked. He peered. No scratches.

He said so and handed the implement back. It was a lovely thing, rimmed in flourishes of Benares brass, a perfect shining disc.

'Why do you want to see scratches?' he asked.

'That would mean that the lock was picked. There are no scratches, ergo…'

'The lock wasn't picked,' concluded Tinker.

'Right. And when we arrived the back door was open. Which means?'

'The Johnsons left it open,' reasoned Tinker. 'Not bloody likely,' he added. 'They was real careful!'

'Right; I agree with you. And therefore…'

'I dunno, Guv'nor,' confessed Tinker.

'Yes you do—someone opened it with a key. How many keys to this door?'

Tinker was alight with excitement.

'Three, there's only three. Mr. Johnson used to complain about it because he had one key, the people who came to stay had one key—he kept that in Melbourne—and Mr. Thomas had the other, and he couldn't leave one for the plumber when they was havin' trouble with the pipes and he and Mrs. Johnson were going to be out…'

'Someone has Mr. Johnson's keys,' said Phryne. 'Perhaps that same person has Mr. Johnson as well.'

'Guv,' said Tinker. 'That old biddy over the road used to watch all the time, and poor Miss Lavvie used to be with her. You could hear her screeching for Lavvie all the time, even in the middle of the night. Miss Lavvie might know something.'

'And she will tell me all about it after she has had breakfast, when we are moving her and her goods and chattels to Madame Sélavy's house. Has anyone seen the doctor lately?'

'He's been in the house, Guv'nor, you know, they're in mournin'. By the number of bottles bein' delivered, I reckon there's a lot of rejoicin' goin' on, now Mrs. Green has taken ill and all and can't take offence.'

'Mrs. Green has been taken ill?'

'Took to her bed in the high strikes, they say, and that doctor from Geelong come out to see 'er. Funeral's on Monday. That maid Bridget was over this morning borrowin' tea and sugar from Mrs. Cook, they're expecting so many for the viewin'. Which is today,' added Tinker hopefully. 'Mrs. Cook's making a cake, maybe Miss Ruth would like to…'

'She shall,' said Phryne. 'And we shall attend. You and me, Tinker dear. Suddenly I feel much better,' Phryne told him. 'Let's wander along to the kitchen, suggest that Miss Ruth makes a cake for the funeral baked meats, and get poor Miss Lavinia on the road.'

Ruth felt that she had still not fathomed the mysteries of Impossible Pie, so they left her compounding another and met Miss Lavinia in the hall, her miniscule luggage around her feet.

'Oh, Miss Fisher, I thought I'd just slip away,' she said, bending down to give Gaston a final pat on his shiny brown head. 'You've been so kind and I didn't want to disarrange your household any longer. I've left the sheets all folded at the foot of the bed, with my towel.'

'Just a moment more,' said Phryne. 'Let Tinker carry your baggage. I suppose Madame knows that you are coming?'

'Oh, dear, I don't know, I assumed that the doctor arranged it, I...' Miss Lavinia quite lost heart and sat down on the hallstand.

'I shall call on Madame in a moment,' Phryne told her. 'While you, if you would be so kind, give Gaston his breakfast? If we don't find the Johnsons,' she suppressed the term 'alive', 'perhaps you might give him a home? He's a good little dog,' she said.

Miss Lavinia picked up Gaston and buried her face for a moment in his glossy coat. Her small stock of courage, gathered so tightly to the sticking place, momentarily deserted her. Gaston licked her face encouragingly. He had heard the word 'breakfast'. Tinker had already fed him but Gaston was happy to profit from Phryne's ploy, as long as it included biscuits.

Phryne went next door and the small child Laszlo answered the door. This morning he was sucking a lollipop of massive dimensions and such bright colours that one could wonder what chemical marvels had gone into its manufacture. It seemed, however, to be giving satisfaction.

'Miss?' asked the boy.

'Is Madame expecting Miss Lavinia as a house guest?' asked Phryne.

'Yes, Miss. Bridget came and told us about it. Madame'll be down when she comes. 'Bout half an hour?'

'What a well-informed infant you are,' said Phryne, bestowing a penny.

She found Miss Lavinia in the garden, watching Gaston eat biscuits. His stub of a tail wagged happily.

'It's all right, they're expecting you. There's just one thing, Miss Lavinia. After the Johnsons left, the larder was looted by some persons who came in through the back door. Did you by any chance see who they were?'

'No, dear, they only came after dark. All we could see was shapes. Boys, I thought. They walked as though they were young.

They came every night for almost a week. Were they stealing food? How very unpleasant for you.'

'Oh, no, it was all old, anyway, someone might as well have taken it. Since then the door has been locked and guarded. Now, pat Gaston goodbye and we'll see you settled next door. Do you know Madame Sélavy well?'

'No, dear. Mrs. McNaster used to receive her occasionally. Madame took a little shine to me because I can play chess. I used to play all the time with my father. He was a vicar, and liked quiet pastimes. When he was in his final illness I played chess every day, and he died before we finished the last game. I have often wondered how it would have come out. He probably would have won. He usually did. Yes, let us get on, I can't keep you from your occupations all day, most discourteous.'

Phryne and Miss Lavinia, preceded by a staggering Tinker, were admitted to the Sélavy household and escorted upstairs. There were several guest rooms, not extravagantly surreal, with fresh linen and sea air from the open windows. Miss Lavinia took off her hat, tidied her hair, and drew a deep breath.

'Thank you,' she said to Phryne. 'I hope we shall meet again.'

'So do I,' said Phryne, and took her leave, collecting Tinker from an impromptu game of two-up in the front hall. Through the parlour door she could see Madame Sélavy. She was attired like an Eastern potentate, in silken garments and a rose-red turban. She was serving tea from a huge silver samovar. The chess board was laid out on a small baroque table before her. She gave Phryne a grave nod. Miss Lavinia seemed to fit, oddly enough, into the ménage. The air was heavy with frankincense.

Tinker, safely in the street, expressed his feelings in a long whistle.

'Quite, but she's better off there than in a house where the mistress is accusing her of murder,' Phryne told him. 'Exotic does not mean evil, keep that in mind.'

'Yes, Guv,' said Tinker. 'What're we doing today?'

'We are lazing away the morning, then we lunch here, and then we go to see Mrs. McNaster for the last time. And you dress nicely and keep your eyes and ears open, my boy. Dinner will be bought or out, I haven't decided which one yet. But first, I have to make a phone call.'

'Who to?' asked Tinker.

'Tinker,' reproved Phryne. 'If you need to know, I will tell you. And since I will need your help in this enterprise, I will soon tell you all.'

'When?' he asked, pushing his luck.

'Monday, depending on the courier,' said Phryne, waved him away and picked up the phone.

Tinker mooched along to the kitchen to see what was doing there. Always something doing in a kitchen. As it happened, it was the after-breakfast washing-up, but he was getting quite good at washing up, and Jane was reading.

Those fairy tales were not the pretty things Tinker had been expecting. Things happened in fairy tales which wouldn't happen in Sexton Blake.

'At first she could not see anything, because the windows were shuttered. Gradually she became aware that the floor was sticky with clotted blood. Even worse, the corpses of the previous wives were hanging on the wall. There were six of them. She knew suddenly that having broken the ban on opening the door, she would be the seventh.'

'See, you should do as your husband says,' said Tinker. Ruth threw a dishcloth at him.

'You should investigate husbands before you marry them,' she retorted. 'And you can dry the frying pan.'

'Women,' muttered Tinker, and dried the frying pan, because he didn't want to miss what was going to happen next.

◇◇◇

Phryne swam, bathed to remove the salt, ate a sandwich for lunch, and donned good clothes to visit the deceased Mrs. McNaster.

She was laid out in a rather nice coffin, swathed in satin. She looked dead, of course, but resting comfortably.

The coffin was standing on trestles in the breakfast parlour, directly next to the staircase which led to the first floor, where the deceased had held shrewish sway for so long. There had been a satisfactory turnout for the viewing. Many of the people Phryne did not quite know in their present incarnations, but she began to recognise a pattern after a while.

The large gentleman in the plum brocade waistcoat with the fish motif was T Superbus. The large lady in flowing violet was Sylvia, wearing a goldfish brooch on her black-plumed hat. Her attendant was Pete, in a dark suit and a discreet cravat with a trout tie-pin. There were two ladies in identical black garments who might, possibly, be one or both of the RMs. This thesis was supported by the fact that they both wore identical silver bracelets seemingly made of fish bones. Magdalen Morse was there in a dragged-down black dress and a cloche pinned, apparently to her skull, with a lobster brooch. Lucius Brazenose and Thaddeus Trove, well dressed, looked like they were longing for a drink.

Phryne had loosed Tinker to wander around and forage. He looked quite spruce in his good clothes. Jane and Ruth stood together and examined the people. Comments had been made on how like herself Mrs. McNaster looked. The weather was receiving its usual close conversational scrutiny. The doctor came in and greeted his guests in a distracted fashion.

At that moment Bridget the maid came down the stairs into the midst of the throng with an armload of sheets. She had obviously been remaking Mrs. McNaster's bed, possibly for another occupant. Seeing all the people, she checked and dropped a pillowcase. Phryne picked it up. It had a stiff patch, and there were little dents in the linen. Phryne said nothing but folded the case with the patch on the surface and held it out to the maid.

'Bridget, you're sacked!' roared the doctor, crimson with embarrassment.

'I just done what you told me to do!' objected Bridget, hugging the sheets to her generous bosom. 'Sacked, am I? I quit! I leave this house today!'

She stormed out and Tinker, at a nod from Phryne, went after her.

'I'm so sorry,' the doctor apologised to the company. 'It's so hard to get good servants these days…'

Which was an effective conversation starter, Phryne thought, as she turned aside and stowed the folded pillowcase in her bag. Just in—so to speak—case.

'Bit *bouleversé*, our comrade,' muttered Madgalen.

'Yes, what is the matter with him?' asked someone who might have been half of RM. 'Not as though he adored his mother-in-law. You'd think he'd be relieved.'

'Hush,' said the other RM.

'Got to do the civil,' murmured Lucius Brazenose to Phryne. 'But it's a bit hot to wear the full catastrophe, you know.'

Phryne, steaming lightly in stockings, shoes and her good suit and blouse, agreed. Drinks, however, were not forthcoming. Something seemed to have held up the kitchen and even tea was now in short supply. Ruth's Impossible Pie had vanished down to the last shred of coconut. Phryne suspected that Bridget had taken her grievances to the cook and was now packing her trunk and crying, and the cook had come out in sympathy with her oppressed Irish sister. Why had the doctor reacted so savagely? It could not just be the awkwardness of someone carrying the deceased's bedsheets, not noticeably soiled, through the funeral company in the parlour. That was a faux pas, not a hanging offence. Jolly bouncing competent maids didn't grow on any trees that Phryne knew. The doctor's wife would be very cross when she emerged from her swoon and found her maid gone and a mutiny taking place in the kitchen…

Mr. Wellbeloved, without his constant companion, the hyena Cyril, looked lonely. Julian Strange offered Phryne a nip from his flask. She took it, and regretted it. It was some vile aniseed raki or ouzo, which in its most debased form dissolved teeth. She obtained a cup of the pale imitation of tea which was all that was left, and rinsed her mouth.

Mrs. Mason was just telling Sylvia Glass that her own cook was a jewel, a real jewel, when there was a stir and Miss Lavinia was escorted in by a tall, gaunt man who hovered over her protectively.

There was a gasp and a cluck from the matrons of Queenscliff, but the surrealists to a man or woman or whatever surged to her support. Phryne joined them to offer Miss Lavinia her condolences on her release from slavery and her coming into a large fortune. The tall man offered a hard hand and she shook it. Then she looked up into the face. Beaky nose, strong jaw, pendulous earlobes, eyes as bright as a pin, twinkling with recognition.

'Monsieur,' she said rapidly in French. 'I believe that we have met before.'

'Madame,' he replied, ambiguously. 'I could not have forgotten if we had.'

Madame Sélavy—male or female? She was equally convincing as both. And in any case it was none of Phryne's business. She shook hands with the doctor, who seemed ready to expire with heat and irritation, murmured her best wishes to be conveyed to his prostrate wife, and looked around for her dependents.

Tinker was out of sight, probably in the kitchen. That boy had an affinity with any place which harboured food, Phryne thought. Well, he knew where he lived. Jane and Ruth rose obediently at her signal and they left in a convoy, out of the rustle of skirts and the fog of lavender water and respectability.

'Not a word until we get home,' Phryne warned as they crossed the road. Both heads nodded, the dark plait and the golden crop.

When the door had safely closed behind them, she asked, 'Observations?'

'They were a club or something, weren't they?' asked Jane. 'All the people wearing fish.'

'Yes, the surrealists,' said Phryne. 'Very good.'

'And they made the nice ladies accept Miss Lavinia,' continued Ruth. 'Even though they hadn't meant to.'

'Good,' said Phryne, taking off her hat.

'And there was something wrong with that pillowcase,' said Jane.

'Why do you think that?' asked Phryne.

'Because you pinched it, Miss Phryne,' they said in chorus.

'You,' said Phryne to her wards, 'are so sharp you will cut yourself. I'll have to think about it, then I'll tell you. If we had the foresight to buy clever-girl chocolates, you may have one each. Now, I'm going to change my clothes, then I'm going for a walk. What about you?'

'Not me,' said Ruth, who had chapters of the *Stolen Bride* to read.

'Nor me,' said Jane, who was exploring metacarpals in the Room of Bones.

'Then I'll take Molly,' said Phryne.

'What about Tinker?' asked Ruth.

'Leave him alone and he'll come home, wagging his tail behind him. I'll be a few hours. If he isn't back when I return we shall search—but he's a clever boy,' said Phryne airily. She went upstairs with the girls. Tinker was in the house before she set out.

Phryne walked Molly briskly up into the forest and the long way around the town, ending at the stretch of sand which lined Swan Bay. Molly arrived home so exhausted that she almost slept through dinner, which was very good fish and chips and pickled onions. Phryne arrived home hungry, tired, sandy and scratched but with a good knowledge of the local geography.

As soon as the parcel arrived from town, she would put her plan into place. Lin Chung had telegraphed that he would be in Queenscliff soon, and she wanted him all to herself with no interruptions from domestic problems, loss, kidnapping and attempted murder.

Chapter Sixteen

Shut, shut the door…! fatigued I said,
Tie up the knocker, say I'm sick, I'm dead.

Alexander Pope
Epistle to Dr. Arbuthnot

It was ten o'clock on Monday. Mrs. McNaster's funeral cortège had departed. Tinker, at the gate, coincided with the arrival of the motorcycle rider and stood staring in stunned admiration at the machine. It was black and huge and inscribed with *Harley-Davidson* on its sleek side. It sounded like a plane landing.

'Blimey,' Tinker greeted the rider.

'This Mercer Street? Miss Fisher in?' asked the rider, shedding his leather flying helmet. He had curly hair and bright brown eyes.

'She's waiting for yer,' said Tinker graciously, conducting this Hermes to the door and yelling, 'The courier's here, Guv!' into the parlour, where Phryne was writing notes to herself.

'Come in,' she invited. 'A cup of coffee, perhaps?'

'Got to get home,' said the young man. 'Mum worries when I'm out on the bike. Here's your stuff, with Grandad's compliments. He wants me to ask if you would be so kind as to call on him and let him know if it worked,' he added, evidently quoting the courtly Mr. Rosenberg.

'Done,' said Phryne, taking the leather bag which the young man removed from his jacket. It was warm from his skin, and so were the contents. The courier gave Phryne a nod, asked, 'Want a ride to the bottom of the street, young 'un?', and took an ecstatic Tinker out of the room.

Phryne sat down again at the parlour table, pushed aside Dot's drawn thread work, and opened the bag. Inside, carefully packed in cardboard and cotton wool, was a heap of coins. She gloated briefly. Then she dropped the local newspaper over them as Dot came in.

'Hugh's been dragged into seeing that policeman from Geelong,' she said discontentedly. 'And he's supposed to be on holiday!'

'You'll have to get used to it, Dot dear, if you want to marry a policeman. The trouble with crime is that criminals tend not to retire,' said Phryne sympathetically. 'Still, you did cook him breakfast and you did dine with him and you did miss out on a fairly dire viewing of the remains.'

Dot sat down and took up her embroidery.

'Oh, yes, of course, Mrs. McNaster. How was it, Miss? I forgot to ask about it yesterday, I didn't get back till ten!'

Dot was living the high life, and liking it. Last evening she had dined with Hugh at the Esplanade Hotel, watched *The Black Pirate*, starring Douglas Fairbanks, at the town hall, and had been walked home the long way with additional kisses and cuddles. Even though she had, indeed, prepared an heroic breakfast for Hugh, she had felt a wrench as she waved him off at the gate. Dot suspected that this, also, was part of being in love. She wasn't at all sure that she liked it. How did Miss Phryne manage, bidding farewell to all those lovers apparently without a care? It was a puzzle.

'All the surrealists were there, looking very respectable, which was a stretch for some of them,' Phryne was continuing. 'Mrs. Green, however, is still prostrate, or so we are informed by Dr. Green.' She went on to tell Dot about the incident with Bridget.

'Mrs. Green'll be real mad with her husband when she finds out that he's sacked a good maid,' Dot observed. 'What's happened to Bridget, then?'

'Tinker, who was an ear-witness throughout, was carrying her bundle when she presented herself at Madame Sélavy's door yesterday afternoon and was taken in,' Phryne replied.

'She's better off there,' Dot decided. 'Something not right about that Green household. I wouldn't want to work there.'

'I agree,' said Phryne.

Phryne was debating as to whether to show the pillowcase to Dot when Tinker rushed in, hair on end.

'I'm gonna get one of them Harleys,' he declared. 'When I can. Went down to the bottom of the street like lightning.'

'Later, Tinker, later,' said Phryne. 'Stick to a pushbike for the present.'

'What did the bloke on the bike bring yer, Guv?' asked Tinker.

'Later.' Phryne waved him away. 'The breakfast washing-up waits.'

'Nah, Máire's doing it.'

'Then go and help her,' instructed Phryne.

The penny finally dropped and Tinker went obediently to the kitchen.

'Now, Dot, something odd,' Phryne began. 'I'd like your opinion on it. When Bridget was carrying the linen, she dropped...'

The doorbell rang. Phryne shelved the subject. The pillowcase was too serious a thing to be gossiped about in a parlour on a bright warm day by the seaside, anyway. She decided to keep it to herself for the present, and await developments.

Phryne did not know the three who were shown in by Dot. A tall man, a frazzled-looking woman with flyaway red hair and a complexion to match, and a sullen young man.

'Miss Fisher?' asked the tall man. He was haunted by some secret sorrow, Phryne saw, which he was sure he was about to unload on her. This was becoming tedious.

'I am Miss Fisher,' she said, graciously enough. 'To what do I owe the honour of —'

'She lives here, doesn't she, the girl with the yen for cameras?' interrupted the sullen youth. 'I been asking up and down this blighted street, and—'

'You are referring to my daughter Jane?' asked Phryne in glacial tones. The tall man sloshed at the young man with a careless, fly-swatting motion.

'Give over, Ginger! I beg your pardon, Miss Fisher. I am Andrew Applegate, and this is my cameraman, Paul Orphin, known as Ginger, and my assistant and producer, Miss George. You have heard of the tragedy that befell our little enterprise?'

'Yes, your leading lady was almost murdered,' said Phryne bluntly. Miss George winced.

'Yes, poor Lily. The medical authorities say that she will certainly live and might not even be scarred. In any case we can shoot around a scar. She will go on! Destined for stardom, cut down in the first blush of her career, which will undoubtedly be a dazzling one, and we have her contract, but...'

'You are short one leading lady,' finished Phryne.

'As you say,' Applegate coughed. 'We have only the ship scenes to film, and the star is only seen from a distance in them, so since your daughter was so kind as to be interested in the workings of the camera, and since she has, like poor lost Lily, a fascination for the films...'

Jane and Ruth entered the parlour.

There was a dead silence as the film crew surveyed Jane's new coiffure.

'There must be plenty of Queenscliff girls who can stand in for poor Lily,' Phryne said in consolation.

'No, the silly young minxes have got it into their feather heads that there's a murderer stalking the film, and they won't sign up,' rasped Miss George, in a voice which suggested too many cigars in a day. 'We thought that your girl might not be so superstitious.'

'Oh, she's not,' said Phryne, beginning to enjoy herself. 'And I happen to know that there is a very good wig-maker in Queenscliff. Probably make you a good price, too—if you act now, before she's arrested for receiving stolen goods.'

'What do you say?' Applegate spoke directly to Jane. 'Five quid for a day's work, in your hand. No mention in the credits, though, no residuals, no royalties.'

'Miss Phryne?' asked Jane.

Phryne waved a hand. 'As you like, my dear girl.'

'Ten,' bargained Jane. 'There are some books I want to buy.'

'Ten it is,' said Applegate, making Jane wish she'd held out for twelve and got the full Britannica.

Miss George produced a contract, which Phryne read very carefully before she found and unscrewed her fountain pen. Jane took it and signed.

'One day's work, and that is today,' said Phryne. 'And one copy of the film when it is finished. Also, I would like to view what has been filmed thus far.'

'Deal,' said the cameraman promptly. 'I'll set up the gear. We need to do some editing, anyway. Miss Jane can help me. That wall all right?'

A large amount of gear was dragged in by Jane, Paul and Tinker. Dot drew the curtains. Máire came in from the kitchen to ask about lunch and was told to take a seat. There were three reels of film, and they were, Ruth decided, not anything like as interesting as they should have been. Lots of shots of the sea, lots of shots of Lily standing on the shore, hugging a sulky-looking infant. Lily talking to the male lead, Lily weeping. Lots of pirates—really Queenscliff fisherman, some of whom looked definitely frightening and might well have been pirates in a former life. Old Mr. O'Malley looked positively dangerous with a bandanna on and that knife between his few remaining teeth.

But Lily, thought Phryne, oh, poor Lily had had something very rare. The camera loved her. The cinema makeup had evened out her skin, the stringy hair had been shampooed and hung in ringlets, the light caressed the smooth planes of her cheek and throat. She was authentically beautiful, haunting in her abandoned cinematic sorrow, a model for Ariadne on Naxos. Dot thought the same.

'Who would have thought it?' she asked. 'That Lily. She might be a star, after all.'

'Yes.' Miss George was in tears. 'We actually have a real find in Lilias—we are going to change her name. She'll be the making of us, and of herself as well. And someone went and mutilated her!'

'Cruel,' said Phryne. She had seen all that she needed. She excused herself and went to the kitchen for a strong brandy and soda. Poor Lily. But even that dolt Constable Dawson would have put his hands on the assailant by now. It was obvious.

◇◇◇

Ruth delegated the luncheon sandwiches to Máire and followed Jane and the film crew to the foreshore, where a pirate ship had been hanging about for hours, waiting for the signal to land and filling in the time with a little hand-line fishing. Dot had just settled to her drawn threadwork again when Mrs. Mason came calling, and had to be admitted.

This time Phryne offered her a drink right away, as she had one herself. Molly came and sat companionably on her feet. Mrs. Mason was flurried and pink in the face and gulped down a sustaining gin and orange as though it was water.

'The boys, Miss Fisher…' she began, holding out her glass for more.

'What has happened to them?' asked Phryne, hoping for dengue fever.

'They've run away!' Mrs. Mason burst into tears. Dot offered her a handkerchief.

'How do you know? Did they leave you a note?' asked Phryne. In answer a piece of notepaper was stuffed into her hand. It was creased and had evidently come from someone's algebra homework. In a boyish hand was written: *ABC is an isosceles triangle. Angle a is 30 degrees. Got to get away from here Mum gone walking be back love Jol.*

'I wouldn't worry,' Phryne said calmly. 'They're ashamed and horrified and they've gone away to get nice and cold and wet and hungry. Then they'll be home demanding baths and food and first aid and sympathy. Give them three days, unless they're tougher than they look. Have they got any money?'

'A few pennies,' sobbed Mrs. Mason. 'But I don't know how much they got from…'

'Selling hair? Can't have been more than a few pounds. They can't get anywhere with that. They're nice civilised brats, not used to working, don't know how to approach country people except as the Young Master and I bet that won't go down well in Queenscliff and environs. More like two days, come to think of it. Finish your drink, go home and put your feet up and get your maid to read a nice book to you. If your son ran away to punish you, you must not comply and punish yourself. If he didn't, then it is foolish. Can we lend you a romance? Dot, find the lady an engrossing novel.'

'Don't you have any motherly feelings?' demanded Mrs. Mason, finishing her drink and getting to her feet.

'No, I seem to have missed out on them,' replied Phryne sunnily. 'Ah, here we are. *Bride of Midnight*. Sounds Gothic. Good morning, Mrs. Mason.'

Dot saw Mrs. Mason to her door, where the acidulated butler let her in. He gave Dot a conspiratorial look as Mrs. Mason staggered in, carrying her book and calling for her maid.

Dot returned to find Phryne adding ice to her second drink.

'You can't say I didn't try to avoid notice,' she complained to Dot as she belted the ice block with the pick. Shards flew. Dot fielded several large bits and dropped them into the jug of orange juice.

'I know, Miss, sometimes it's just like that. And Hugh not back yet; he said he'd be back for lunch.'

Máire, who had retreated behind the kitchen door out of the reach of shrapnel, suggested timidly that she could be getting on with making the sandwiches now, and Miss Ruth had left an egg and bacon pie, if that would suit? Implication being, if she had the kitchen to herself. And Phryne, relinquishing her weapon, carried the jug into the parlour.

Tinker, who had been in the garden with Gaston, watering the herbs, returned.

'Jeez,' he said. 'She's got a temper, the guv'nor.'

'She has that,' agreed Máire. 'And we'd better get the lunch all laid out proper, or she might take it out on us.'

Tinker didn't think this likely, but carried the cloths into the dining room and began to dress the table, in case.

'One more caller,' Phryne vowed, 'and I might commit an indictable offence.'

'Cheer up,' advised Dot. 'It might be someone nice.'

'Hah!' Phryne drank her drink and opened the volume of fairy tales. They might, she thought, sweeten her mood.

She was halfway through 'The Little Mermaid' and mentally cursing the name of Hans Christian Andersen, who, though undoubtedly a nice man, had convinced thousands of little girls that suffering the pain of dancing on knives was a good exchange for marrying the prince, and thus condemned them to lives of disappointment, when the bell rang again and she heard Tinker scurrying to answer it.

Dot got up and went out into the hall, shutting the door behind her. Phryne shut Hans Christian with a snap as Constable Dawson and Hugh came in and slumped down into the wicker chairs. Hugh's chair groaned and wheezed under his weight, but held up manfully.

'Oh dear, gentlemen, what is wrong?' she asked, surveying their downcast expressions.

'This attempted murder,' said Hugh. 'You can speak freely in front of Miss Fisher, Tom. She's a good friend of my boss, Detective Inspector Robinson. Sharpest mind outside the force, he says.'

'Have a drink,' said Phryne, and Dot flew off in search of the beer she had stowed in the bottom of the icebox. 'And light a smoke, and tell me all about it.'

Hugh Collins didn't smoke, the smell made him sick, but he wished he had a pipe at moments like this. His boss smoked Capstan, a strong tobacco apparently compounded of tar and horsehair, and it seemed to comfort Jack Robinson in times of trouble. Such as now. Possibly by restricting blood flow to his head, as Miss Jane had said when she reproved old Bert for smoking.

Dot opened the beer with an adroit flip of the opener and Hugh engulfed the bottle in his huge hand and emptied it at a draught. It was a good morning for fraught drinkers in Miss Fisher's parlour. Constable Dawson also grabbed and glugged. Dot leaned on the back of Hugh's chair and he put up his free hand to pat hers.

'You see, it's like this,' Constable Dawson began. 'It would be a real feather in my cap if I could find the pigtail snipper soon. Geelong's sending down a man tomorrow and he'll get the credit. I want to get out of Queenscliff and into town—there's no scope for a policeman in Queenscliff—and this is a real good opportunity for me.'

'Understood,' murmured Phryne. Her personal view, that Constable Dawson was several sandwiches short of the full picnic and would vanish in the flames of a tough station like burnt paper, need not be expressed. The boy had his dreams.

'We thought we had 'em when those boys confessed,' said Hugh. 'But you were right, Miss Fisher, it ain't them, the young hounds. Now I heard that you let Miss Jane and Miss Ruth go down to the filming. Them film people are buying a wig off Miss Leonard this moment. And this is happening when all of Queenscliff is sure that any girl that's in that film is in danger of getting her throat cut. And I'm sure as I can be that you wouldn't let Miss Jane do anything dangerous. Therefore,' said Hugh, approaching his point with slow majesty, 'I thought, Miss Fisher knows who the snipper is, and she don't think he's a danger anymore. So I says to Tom, we'll go ask Miss Fisher, and maybe she'll tell us, and maybe we can clear the case up and get you your promotion.'

'Dot, your young man does you credit,' exclaimed Phryne. 'He is a stalwart and valuable member of his proud force. You only had to ask, Hugh dear. Go get Tinker, Dot, and we'll clear this up before lunch.'

'Why do you need Tinker?' asked Hugh, lumbering to his feet.

'You'll see,' said Phryne. She collected her hat and her bag, her minion and her escort, and directed the constable to drive to Hesse Street, without the use of that big bell which was mounted on the roof of the car.

Stopped several yards from her target, Phryne briefed Tinker and sent him into the shop. He came out in a few minutes and waved them to an alley at the side of the establishment.

'He's got a shed in the back of the yard,' Tinker told Phryne very quietly. 'The boss says he's been locked in there ever since Lily got sent to hospital. P'raps I'd better go first, Guv?'

'Let's locate him and see how he is,' said Phryne, equally quietly. 'In silence, gentlemen, please. Hugh, you go to the right, Dawson to the left, Tinker will call him outside. No noise, no sudden moves, please. He'll be in a perilous state. We want him alive.'

'To hang,' muttered Constable Dawson. Phryne disliked him. She sent a warning look to Hugh to keep a hand on his excitable colleague.

Hugh nodded. He was something of a veteran of what Robinson called the 'Red Indian stuff' and preferred his victim to walk quietly into a trap, rather than scream and fight. Especially in view of the number of edged weapons at this one's disposal. This yard stank of blood and death. The ground was greasy with tallow.

Tinker knocked at the door of a wretched shed and called, 'You there? Only the boss is askin',' in just the right dispassionate tone. Phryne could have kissed him.

There was a mumble from inside. Tinker spoke a little louder.

'Come on, come on! Front and centre! Boss is creatin' out here!'

The shabby door sagged open on its hinges and Amos the butcher's boy crept out. He was holding a long skinning knife. Its edge was so sharp that it seemed to bend light. It was stained. He saw Phryne standing behind Tinker and moaned.

'Oh, no,' said Amos.

Grief had not treated him well. His eyes were like coals, his hair like straw, his skin blotched with tears. His loose mouth gaped. Phryne was sorry for him, then remembered Lily transformed by film into a goddess, all her dreams wasted and gone, and hardened her heart.

'Give me the knife,' she said firmly. 'Come along, we haven't got all day.'

Constable Dawson twitched and was suppressed by a look from Hugh. Tinker had frozen in position. Phryne nodded at him.

'Is that the knife you did it with?' he enthused, taking it gently from Amos's grasp. 'Jeez!'

'Was it just her hair?' asked Phryne. 'Did you mean to kill her?'

'She turned her head!' sobbed Amos, crumpling down into the crouch of a tortured animal. 'I thought if I cut her hair she'd…'

'Stay with you?' asked Phryne.

'She was going away!' wailed Amos the butcher's boy, wringing his blue and white striped apron. 'The film people told her she would be a star and she'd never look at me and she'd never come back to me…'

'Come along,' said Phryne, taking his arm and handing him to Hugh, who flanked him as they walked down the filthy alley and into the street. Tinker handed the skinning knife to Hugh, who wrapped it in his handkerchief. 'Better get the doctor to have a look at Amos, Constable Dawson, and keep a close watch. He'll kill himself now, if he can. Now, Hugh, Tinker and I will walk back, and you will, I trust, come to lunch, after you have assisted the constable in securing his…prize.'

And she stalked away with Tinker at her side.

'That wasn't nice, Guv'nor,' he said, almost running to keep pace with her swift stride.

'No, it wasn't.'

'It isn't like that in Sexton Blake,' he complained, and Phryne laughed and slowed down.

'So many things aren't, you know, Tinker.'

'How did you know, Guv?' he demanded.

'I watched the films. You saw them, too. In every shot there was Amos, staring at Lily. He's probably always stared at Lily.'

'Yair, ever since I knew him. Few kangaroos loose in the top paddock, Amos. Few pennies short of the full shilling, you know? And everyone knew that he was mad about Lily. She couldn't stand him. She was always tryin' to send him away and laughin' at him.'

'And he was always there, so no one saw him. And if he had blood on him, it was part of his trade. And those appalling louts gave him the idea of cutting Lily's hair to ruin her career. Which wouldn't have worked while there are wigs in the world…'

'At least he didn't mean it,' said Tinker, who was feeling battle-scarred. He had talked Amos out of his knife! He was good at this! Equally, his hitherto reliable stomach was making odd gurgling noises and he didn't feel very well. Imagine living in that hut in that stinking yard. The butcher had done all right out of Amos.

'That's what he says now,' said Phryne.

'Guv…' Tinker touched Phryne's hand. 'Will he…will Amos…'

'Hang? No,' she assured him. 'He's not even fit to plead. They'll lock him up in a nice safe mental home for the rest of his life. Amos will be all right,' she added.

Tinker cheered up. It was lunch time, and suddenly he felt that he might just be able to manage a slice of Ruth's egg and bacon pie. Or maybe two. And then Miss Fisher had a scheme, and he didn't want to miss that.

Phryne shelved all philosophical speculations on horror, pain and tragedy, washed her hands of Amos the butcher's boy and Lily with rose-petal soap, and went into luncheon. It might not have been well done, but at least it was done.

Chapter Seventeen

Bell, book and candle shall not drive me back
When gold and silver becks me to come on.

William Shakespeare
King John

Dot was so proud of her fiancé and her employer that she was almost bursting with goodwill, which made lunch a much cheerier event than Phryne had expected.

Tinker and Máire had elected to eat in the kitchen, where both Molly and Gaston were valiantly guarding the remains of the roast leg of lamb which Ruth had provided for sandwiches. Both dogs had their hearts set on the bone. Fortunately there were two bones which, after the meat had been largely removed, would provide a big bone for Molly and a smaller bone for Gaston and ought to prevent any domestic discord. Tinker adored roast lamb. In between bites he regaled the horrified Máire with the tale of Amos the butcher's boy, to gratifying gasps and cries of 'Holy Blessed Virgin Mary, protect us!' The lurid tale, however, did not seem to affect their appetites.

'I'll just make a few bites for the young ladies,' Máire observed. 'Miss told me to pack them a picnic basket. This very afternoon you're to go to Miss Jackson's and buy three army knapsacks and three thermos bottles, so milady says, and the money's on the table in that purse, so it is.'

'What does she want all that gear for?' asked Tinker with his mouth full.

'That she didn't tell me. Would you be coming with me to the filming to deliver this basket? I'd not like to go there by my lone.'

'Yair. Delighted,' said Tinker. No one had ever wanted his company before. No one had ever glimpsed in his grubby bosom the soul of a true knight. He grinned around his doorstop sandwich. Sir Edward the Brave. He liked that idea.

◇◇◇

Phryne sighed and pushed away her fruit salad.

'I couldn't eat another bite,' she confessed. 'I've never had fruit salad with coconut milk—wonderful. That Mrs. Leyel was a discovery.'

'Not just coconut milk,' said Dot primly. 'I'm sure that was rum I could taste.'

'Very Queensland,' said Hugh. 'Bundaberg rum.'

'Now, Hugh dear, I need your confidence,' Phryne said, putting one spoonful of amusingly coloured coffee crystals into her cup.

'Miss Fisher?' he asked, suddenly not as comfortable as he had been.

'I am planning a caper of sorts in Queenscliff,' she said. 'And I need to know if you are also planning an action against, as it might be, the Ellis brothers and their smuggling operation. Everyone knows about it, by the way. Rum and, I suspect from various evidence, tobacco from those extensive Queensland fields. What I am planning might cause a stir, and I don't want to upset anything you might be doing. Do you trust me?'

'Indeed,' said Hugh, running a finger around a collar which was suddenly too tight.

Dot looked from one face to another. She was disappointed in her betrothed.

'Hugh!' she reproved. 'Miss Phryne found you your slasher. That idiot constable is headed for his promotion and it won't do your career any harm, either. If she hadn't helped you there might have been a fight and someone could have been hurt.'

'Yes,' agreed Hugh, breaking out into a sweat. 'But, Dot, I can't...'

'You can,' she said sharply. 'I never heard of such...ingratitude!'

'Calm, Dot dear, calm, no need to differ with your fiancé,' said Phryne. 'I don't need to know the whole plan, Hugh, I'm sure you have been sworn to secrecy. I just need to know when.'

'I can't tell you...' Hugh began. Dot stood up abruptly. He took her hand and she snatched it back. 'No, no, Dot, don't be cross. I can't tell you what is happening, Miss Fisher, but I can tell you when, provided the news doesn't leave this room. Promise?'

'We promise,' agreed Phryne.

'Thursday,' said Hugh. 'At dawn or before.'

'That should give me ample time,' said Phryne, and smiled.

'Are you going to tell me what you are planning?' asked Hugh humbly.

'No, I don't think so,' said Phryne. 'You would be required to disapprove. I really cannot do with any disapproval at the moment. Nothing illegal, I assure you. Well, not very illegal. I expect. Have some more fruit salad.'

Dot had allowed him to reclaim her hand, so Hugh sighed and had some more fruit salad. It was very good fruit salad, with pineapple and mango. Miss Fisher would do what she felt was best, and there was nothing to be done about it. Queenscliff would just have to cope.

◇◇◇

Tinker had escorted Máire to the filming, which was in Swan Bay, and found the girls at the centre of a large crowd. Mr. Cutts the Family Butcher was a gossipy man, as butchers so often were, and the news that the phantom pigtail snipper and slasher of Lily had been marched off to the station by Constable Dawson—who would have thought? I believed he was a fool, just goes to show, still waters—had spread like lard on the griddle on which he was cooking sausages ('Best Pork!') for the delectation of the crowd. Penny each, on thick slices of bakery's bread, tomato sauce and onions halfpenny extra. Sensational news free. He was mobbed.

Queenscliff was not a foolish town, and deductions were made quickly. Who had Mr. Cutts seen walking down his side alley, emerging a moment later with poor Amos? That Miss Fisher, that's who, the titled lady who had taken Mr. Thomas's house, rich, beautiful, private detective from Melbourne, very well-connected, knew all the best people, but had only so far visited the Masons, who were next door after all, and Miss Sélavy, the mystery woman. Seen respectably clad at Mrs. McNaster's viewing. Bathed every day and swam like a fish in a very shocking costume. No scandal about her private life so far but her maid and companion had been seen walking out with that visiting policeman. One of her two adopted daughters was brave enough to take on Lily's role in the film. Altogether it was clear that Miss Fisher had solved the attempted murder. Queenscliff approved. This fact also confirmed the general opinion about the intelligence of Constable Dawson, as well. He would never have been able to find Amos on his own as he would be hard put to locate his own backside with both hands.

Tinker noted and listened as he and Máire wriggled their way through the crowd and arrived at the space in which Ruth was sitting on the sand and Jane was being dressed in Lily's costume. It was suspiciously damp around the bodice, where it had evidently been recently washed. Jane could not suppress a slight shiver, though she reminded herself she was not at all superstitious.

The mob in the pirate ship were growing obstreperous. The cameraman yelled, 'Get on with it!', echoed by the crowd. Mr. Applegate instructed Jane, 'All you need to do is stand by that rock and look out to sea. Don't move, don't wave. Just stand and stare and remember that you are being abandoned at the edge of the world.'

Jane thought that she could do that. The dress was voluminous and uncomfortable. The wig was heavy and itchy. She had got used to having short hair. But completing this task would buy her the *Encyclopedia Britannica*, with the two pounds she already had saved. For those twenty-four volumes she could dare anything.

She hefted her garments and found her position and stared out to sea.

There was a fight going on between two ships, the *Revenge* (pirates, a disguised *Black Oak*) and the *Consolation* (Royal Navy, or close imitation thereof, a disguised *Mary Duke*). Conflict was part of the plot but the sailors, tired of fishing with lines and stoked on Mr. O'Malley's cache of Bundaberg rum, were in no mood to accept direction. Before the signal came, Johnnie Taylor, ordinarily a patient crayman, fired the small cannon, and the wad of the blank hit the *Revenge* and knocked Mr. O'Malley down.

Roaring, 'Erin Go Bragh!', he ordered Gráinne to hoist the black flag which meant No Quarter and flung out grappling lines.

'Oh, that's not in the script!' mourned Miss George.

'It's fantastic,' whispered the cameraman, grinding gleefully. 'Magnificent! Go on, boys!'

The crowd on the foreshore, munching their sausages, had never seen such a wonderful show. They cheered. Jane stood like a pillar of salt, watching the clouds of smoke from the blanks and calculating the trajectory of the cannon balls, had there been any. This was difficult and required her to concentrate, and she was as still as a rock in the corner of the frame as the ships banged and flashed and men screamed Gaelic war cries and swarmed onto the deck of the *Consolation*.

'No, no, the pirates can't be winning!' cried Miss George. 'They have to lose!'

'Change the story,' suggested Ruth. 'Both ships can go down. You're going to have to make that bit up, anyway.'

'More, more!' screamed Queenscliff. 'Look out, Johnnie, here comes the boarders!'

'Must have been the porridge at breakfast!' yelled a wit. The gathering laughed. This was jolly, and amusing, and free.

Finally, just before the camera ran out of film, Johnnie Taylor put a match to the firework which was to mark the end of the encounter. He threw it up and it exploded in a huge cloud of black, stinking fog, which covered both ships and reduced the pirates to coughing and groping.

'Terrific,' said the cameraman, and let the film run through and wind clicking onto its reel. 'That's it, Mr. Applegate. You, girl, go and bring your sister back, she was wonderful, didn't move an inch; I've got her in the edge of every shot. What a film this will make!'

Ruth went and brought back Jane by the hand. She was thinking about something, Ruth knew. Ruth herself was starving and hoped that the basket brought by Máire and Tinker contained a lot of food. This film business was interesting, but these people seemed to have forgotten poor mutilated Lily.

Tinker laid out the cloth and the two girls sat down on the sand. Jane was divested of her dress and wig and shook her head with pleasure. She sank her teeth into a roast lamb and chutney sandwich. Then she looked out into the bay.

The ships had not disengaged and come in for their wages. They were still fighting. Máire saw her sister Gráinne, scarfed and laughing, swing from one ship to the other and kick Johnnie Taylor overboard with the force of her momentum, hitting him in the chest with both feet. Her father was grinning and bellowing in Irish. The *Consolation* was about to be taken. Most of her men were in the water.

Máire hoped that her father would then remember himself and not slaughter the captives and sail off for the South Seas. Saint Patrick preserve us, she wouldn't put it past him, the old reprobate…

Tinker poured tea from the thermos and seized an orange as his lawful booty. He loved a good fight.

The film people were signalling the ships to come ashore, and finally the fight was over. Dinghies darted about fetching the partly drowned and extremely drunk. Costumes were removed in the fishermen's shelter and a long line formed on the pier, hands out for their shilling apiece.

'How was it, being in a film?' asked Ruth.

'Uninteresting,' said Jane. 'Is there any more of your egg and bacon pie?'

After that, they trailed home for a wash and a rest. Tinker and Máire carried the picnic basket, now much lighter, between them. Jane held in her hand the rolled banknote which would purchase her limitless oceans of knowledge. Ruth was still feeling shaken. She had looked into Amos's avid, loose-lipped face several times when she had been at the filming with Jane. He had seemed both stupid and harmless. He had been stupid, but very far from harmless. Ruth wanted to tuck herself up in that big soft chair in her room, preferably with Molly, and read her romance and eat humbugs until she felt better.

She mentioned this to Jane and they detoured to obtain barley sugar for Jane, humbugs for Ruth, marshmallows for Máire and a packet of peppermints for Tinker from the lolly shop. The girl behind the counter threw in a free surprise packet and some licorice bootlaces in thanks, she said, to their Miss Fisher for discovering the assailant. Ruth and Jane nodded and accepted graciously.

'How does everyone know?' asked Jane. 'That arrest only happened this morning.'

'This is Queenscliff,' said Tinker smugly. 'We know things before they happen. Sometimes long before they happen,' he added.

'Don't be silly, there is no such thing as prophecy, no scientist would…'

Jane and Tinker wrangled. Ruth felt comforted. Máire ate her marshmallows and reflected that it had been a strange day, and it wasn't over yet, Lord have mercy.

◇◇◇

Dot went out, smiling, to dine with Hugh. Máire went back to Fishermen's Flat to listen to tales of derring-do on the fairly high seas. Tinker had carried home the fish and chips, which had been consumed down to the last little burnt crispy scrap chased along the inner wrapping paper with an enquiring forefinger. Drinks had been distributed. After dinner Phryne produced her leather bag and emptied the contents onto the dining table. The company stared.

'Coins,' said Jane. 'Old coins.'

'Absolutely. Now, we are going to borrow a few of Mr. Thomas's bones—Jane can sort out the ones which he doesn't need for his wretched thesis—and we are going to persuade Queenscliff that we have found the pirates' treasure.'

'Yes, Miss Phryne, but why?' asked Ruth, who was uncomfortable with bones of human origin. In fact, except in her work as a cook, she didn't like to contemplate bones at all.

'Because we need to find the Johnsons.'

They looked at her. Phryne grinned.

'I'm up for it, Guv'nor,' declared Tinker, who was getting an inkling of what his eccentric patron meant.

'Us, too, of course,' said Jane slowly. 'But...'

'Simple, it's simple. All you need to do is follow my little plan, and we shall see what we shall see,' explained Phryne hardly at all.

'All right, Guv,' said Tinker. 'What're the coins?'

'These gorgeous gold ones are doubloons,' said Phryne. 'See the pillar on the back? Eight escudos, minted at Lima.'

'Gosh, doubloons?' said Jane. She fingered the fine milled edge. 'Lovely. Gold has a shine to it, doesn't it?'

'It does. And these are American silver dollars.'

'And what are them ugly pewter ones?' asked Tinker. 'They look broken.'

'That, my boy, is a piece of eight. This is the full silver coin—a real *de a ocho*, eight reals. A spanish dollar. You can cut it into eight pieces, each worth...'

'One real, whatever a real is,' said Jane. 'I see. And all these coins date to before 1842, when the mythical Benito allegedly stole the cathedral's treasure?'

'Precisely. You are getting the idea,' responded Phryne.

'And I'll fetch a few bones. What sort do you want, Miss Phryne?'

'Small bones, but unmistakably human. Not skulls.'

'Oh, no, Mr. Thomas needs all his skulls.'

Jane ran upstairs. Tinker surveyed the handful of coins, and the full scandalous ambit of Miss Fisher's plan bloomed in his adolescent mind. Now this was something that Sexton Blake might have plotted. And it was going to be fun.

Ruth was puzzled but compliant.

'What do you need us to do, Miss Phryne?'

'I want you,' said Phryne, sipping her gin and orange, 'to salt the mine.'

Jane came back and scattered small bones across the white tablecloth.

'Metacarpals,' she said. 'No animal has them like this. Anyone with a basic knowledge of anatomy will identify them at once.'

'Good,' said Phryne. She found her notes. 'Now, tomorrow, with the pirate fever from the film still seething in town, this is what we are going to do…'

◇◇◇

No one could quite pinpoint the moment when the Great Queenscliff Treasure Hunt began. Was it when a grubby boy, one of the legion of grubby boys who infested Queenscliff, asked Mr. Jones the land agent and banker to give him a shilling for an old bent silver coin he had found in the alley behind Hesse Street? (Mr. Jones had beaten him down to sixpence, for which Tinker vowed retribution). Was it when a sandy girl who had clearly been beachcombing came into the lolly shop requesting help because she had found what was later identified as several human fingerbones and a gold coin in one of the multiple caves along Swan Bay? Was it when an anonymous well-wisher had sent Mr. Thames, editor of the local newspaper, an American silver dollar found in the shallows off Swan Island? When an Irish girl had given her father a twisted bit of silver coin, and he had woken the whole of Fishermen's Flat with his rendition of 'Fifteen men on a dead man's chest, Yo-ho-ho and a bottle of rum' (in which he had freely indulged by virtue of bartering the coin to the publican of the Esplanade Hotel for several bottles)? Or possibly when the neighbours had noticed Miss Fisher, clad in outrageous canvas trousers, with soldier's knapsack and her three attendants in tow, prospecting with an entrenching tool along that same shoreline?

Whenever it was, gold fever took hold of the respectable watering place. Dot, emerging from the movies on Monday night, where she had seen some of *Pirate Tales* and bent the rest of her attention on romancing Hugh, heard people murmuring 'treasure' and 'Benito' and 'gold coins'.

'What's happened?' asked Hugh, moulding Dot closer to his side as the people rushed past.

'Miss Phryne,' said Dot complacently. 'She said her plan might cause a stir.'

'Stir?' said Hugh, shoved to one side by people storming the draper's for tools and stout garments. 'More like a riot. Remind me, Dot,' he said, picking her up and swinging her into an alley as the mob throbbed and murmured, 'never to offend your Miss Fisher.'

'I'll remind you,' said Dot, and kissed him again.

◇◇◇

On Tuesday three people fell overboard from boats, eight reported to the doctor's clinic with heatstroke and one case of sunburn so severe that the doctor popped the patient into a bath of very dilute boracic acid. One of Miss Fisher's children brought another three fingerbones which the doctor identified as human.

'What's that red mark on the bone, sir?' asked the golden-haired girl respectfully. 'Could it be paint or dye?'

'No, it's probably an iron mark,' he said crossly. It was a very hot day. His clinic was full of patients, all casualties of the treasure hunt except the fisherman's baby with croup. It was crying and crowing and vomiting at intervals, which did not improve the already overheated atmosphere in the parlour. 'The body was buried next to an iron bolt or possibly sword, which rusted and left ferric oxide, which stained the bone. See?'

'I see,' said the golden-haired girl, and she went away, which is what the doctor had wanted her to do.

The mark on the bone had been Arnhem Land ochre, applied after the bone was bare. Jane had been given an object lesson in the failings of pure deduction. She was sobered.

◇◇◇

On Wednesday morning Phryne got up unaccustomedly early, as she had on Tuesday, and dressed in her canvas trousers and long jacket. Her boots were strong and laced up to the ankle. Her sola topee had been soaked in water overnight, her skin was slicked with Milk of Roses, and her scarf, which also acted as a fly net, was doused in citronella, which made her sneeze but was better, she judged, than coming home covered with itchy bites from the multitudinous mosquitos and sandflies and midges which haunted the salt marsh, hungering for human blood. She also had her English parasol for additional protection. Ruth had already made and packed three picnic lunches.

'Today,' Phryne instructed, 'we split up.'

'Miss Phryne, I don't like all this,' complained Ruth. 'I'm bitten and sunburnt and I just want to stay home in the cool and read my book.'

'Me too,' said Jane. 'But we're at your orders, Miss Phryne.'

Phryne looked at them and relented. They were city children, after all.

'You are very good girls and I am proud of you,' Phryne told them. 'You don't actually need to hunt for treasure, darlings, you just need to be seen to be hunting. I suggest that you set out, in all your gear, and make sure people see you. Then you can stop at the ice-cream shop—here's some money. Eat your ice cream in the street. Then exclaim, "We forgot the trowel!", stage a small quarrel about who should have remembered the trowel, and then come back. Remove the gear, have a nice cup of tea and spend the rest of the day quietly in the house. Eat your picnic in the parlour. What about that?'

'Goodo!' exclaimed Ruth. She really didn't like the outside all that much. It was hot and scratchy and there was nothing to cook except the occasional startled wallaby. 'Máire's not here today. Her mum's sick. So me and Jane will cook you a really good dinner, Miss Phryne. For when you come home.'

'Thank you! Dot will be up in a moment,' said Phryne. 'She'll be here, too, unless she's going treasure hunting with Hugh.'

'He's going fishing,' said Tinker. 'He said. With Mr. O'Malley. Half the fishos have left their boats and are digging up cellars. Grainy's all the crew he has left but he reckons she's enough. Miss Dot is going fishing with the detective sergeant, Guv.'

'The course of true love should not include seasickness,' said Phryne. 'All right, it's you and me, Tinker, unless you want to go fishing too?'

'I c'n always go fishing,' said Tinker. 'I'm with you, Guv.'

'Stout man. Got your pack? Your water bottle?'

Tinker stood to attention. He had certainly grown in a week. His hair was curlier. His expression was confident. It hadn't taken long to convert Tinker from Eddie the Bone-Idle Layabout to Tinker the Attentive.

'Come along, then,' said Phryne, smiled at the girls, put a leash on Molly, and went out.

'Better do as she says,' said Ruth to Jane. 'Then we can take the day off. There's this fascinating crayfish recipe in Mrs. Leyel. I wonder if we can pick up a few crayfish on the way home? Or maybe some clams for chowder?'

'Possibly,' said Jane. 'If anyone's gone fishing today.'

Chapter Eighteen

Latet anguis in herba
A snake lurks in the grass

Virgil
Aeneid

'Where're we goin', Guv?' asked Tinker.

'Good question,' said Phryne, surveying the burrowing populace. Men with braces dangling, women with their skirts tucked into their knickers and on shameless public display, children running unwatched into the creamy sea and being dragged out screaming. 'Most of the foreshore is covered with lunatics. How about going along the very edge of the cliff, on the sand I mean, where there was that big rockfall. That'll be too uncomfortable for those in bathing dresses, but we are well equipped and Molly is a strong dog, aren't you?' Molly wagged. She approved of getting out and about. 'How are you with heights, Tinker?'

'Never bothered me, Guv,' said Tinker. 'I fall soft.'

'A valuable skill for a detective.'

They climbed and scrambled to the edge of the big rockfall. The cliff had given way under the battering of a high tide and had slipped rather than fallen. Large boulders had rolled into the sea. No one was attempting to climb them. The sand was full of dried vegetation which cut the uncovered hand and seeded with frightful balls of thorns which looked, as Phryne picked one up to inspect it, like something invented by a fiendish armaments technician for the Great War. Probably to vent poisonous gas or explode with dreadful slaughter in the trench in which it landed.

'Bindi-eyes,' identified Tinker. 'Nasty.'

Phryne agreed. What this landscape really needed, she considered, was a flamethrower.

'There's *Black Oak* going out to Swan Island,' commented Tinker, stamping a burr vengefully underfoot. 'Guv, what are you goin' to do with me?'

'With you?' Phryne had been considering a strange little dent in the side of the collapsed cliff. 'I'm not going to do anything with you.'

Tinker climbed up beside Phryne and put a hand on her khaki-clad arm.

'I mean, yer picked me up, Guv, and what's goin' to happen to me when you go home to yer nice house in St Kilda what Miss Ruth was tellin' me about?'

'Depends on what you want,' said Phryne, who had been thinking about this very situation. 'Do you want to leave Queenscliff and come to the city? You'll have to go to school and it won't be nice. They will torment you for being a stranger. But when you are eighteen you can become a police cadet, if that's what you want to do.'

'That's all I ever wanted to do,' said Tinker, his grip tightening.

'What about your mother and the children?'

'I can get a job deliverin' things, I got a bike now. And them boys won't pick on me more'n once or twice. I c'n send money home. Me mum'd rather have me room than me company. One less mouth to feed.'   .

'All right. We'll try it. Six months. If it doesn't work, you can go home with no hard feelings,' said Phryne.

'You beaut!' yelled Tinker, and fell off the rocks.

When Tinker had been picked up—he had, indeed, fallen soft into the sand rather than hard onto the boulders—his bindi-eyes plucked off and Molly had licked him better, he and Phryne continued their examination of the fallen cliff.

'I reckon there might be cave there,' said Tinker. Phryne used her parasol to prod the affected area, where the sand was darker and there seemed to be perhaps a bush or two of the indestructible manuka behind it. The parasol went in to the hilt. Phryne poked harder and some sand fell away.

'Another couple of hours of this and we can go home,' said Phryne. 'Oh, I say!'

'What?' Tinker crawled to her side.

There was a real, palpable cave. And in it, visible through the manuka bushes which had hidden its opening, were several age-bitten shards of wood, a brass hinge, and a large terracotta pot. Molly began to bark wildly.

'Grouse!' Tinker dived ahead with both hands into the pit and then froze as massed hissing echoed from the little cave.

'Stay perfectly still,' Phryne ordered. 'Hush, Molly. Sit. Now let me see if I can remember the snake charmer's trick I saw in India. Aha.'

'How many joe blakes do y' reckon, Miss?' asked Tinker through teeth so tightly shut that he sounded drunk.

'Ten at the least, I can't see very far. What have you got in your hands?'

'Beads, I reckon. Not coins. And sand.'

The hissing rose in volume. Molly, bidden to be silent, writhed in protest, kicking up sand. Phryne could see that the cave was a mass of snakes. They must have been new hatched when the cave was sealed and presumably lived on rabbits and mice which were unwise enough to burrow into the dune. The warm weather had sent them into a very disagreeable state of wriggle and she could hear scales sliding over each other. They had not taken this intrusion well.

'I'm going to use the parasol to tip that terracotta pot towards us,' said Phryne. 'And I'm going to sing. No criticism, please.'

'Been good to know yer, Guv,' said Tinker valiantly.

'And it will continue to be so, if you shut up and stay still.'

Tinker stayed still. He had not mentioned to the fearless Miss Phryne that he loathed snakes. He could feel betraying shudders starting in his shoulders. He was as cold as if he had been dipped into the Irish Sea. Pretty soon, beyond his control, he would jerk or quiver, and then he could see those long curved fangs striking, sinking into his hands, into his unprotected face…

Miss Fisher began to sing a strange Oriental melody, which slid up and down the scales, and her parasol tip described a rhythmical arc. It waved to and fro as it approached the pot, caught at the lip, and tipped it, very gradually, towards the mouth of the cave. Tinker gasped.

The snakes were listening. Each scaly head was turning to the movement of the parasol and beginning, yes, to move along with it, while the strange tune wove and dipped. The pot moved on its base, and the snakes coiled and hissed again. Undaunted, Phryne persisted with her tune, waved the parasol tip, and the heads began to move in unison.

Finally, just before Tinker's arms fell off, the pot shifted so that its red side was between him and the snakes. Phryne said 'Now!' and Tinker pulled out his closed hands and rolled, again, down the slope onto the sand.

'There,' said Phryne composedly, stepping down to join him and opening her knapsack. 'Now, let's see what you've got, Tinker.'

'It's yours, you saved my life,' gasped Tinker, dropping the sand and beads into the knapsack and throwing himself into a throttling hug, in which Molly joined. She licked the tears off his face as they ran down. 'All yours!'

'No, no, fifty-fifty, at most,' she said, hugging him cordially.

'Where did you learn to do that, Guv?' asked Tinker, shaking himself down. Sand in every interstice. He was hot now, flushed, and short of breath from relief. With any luck the guv'nor would not have noticed his unmanly tears. Molly had disposed of the evidence.

'Oh, I saw them in India, and in Egypt. Snake charming is one of those tourist shows that they put on for the people off cruise ships. They say that it's the movement of the pipe, not the tune, and that snakes are deaf, but I suspect it's both, and the concentrated mind of the charmer, and I didn't dare leave anything out.'

'In case that was the important bit,' panted Tinker. 'I understand. I agree with the detective sergeant, Guv.'

'And what did the respected Hugh say?' asked Phryne, inspecting the spoil which had almost cost Tinker his life.

'He said you're the most remarkable woman in the world,' said Tinker. 'And he's right.'

'Thank you,' said Phryne, adjusting her sola topee. 'Look at this, my young associate!'

'Just a lot of old stones,' grumbled Tinker a little later.

Phryne laughed a little light-headedly. Snake charming was not as easy as it looked. Phryne, also, did not like poisonous snakes very much.

'Actually, my boy, those greenish ones are uncut emeralds and the blue ones like pebbles are sapphires, and this red knob of Queenscliff rock is a ruby—quite a big one. That ought to pay for your schooling.'

They sat a moment in silence, staring at a fortune.

'There's probably a lot more in that cave,' said Tinker questioningly.

'And it can stay there,' Phryne told him. 'Never press your luck unless you have to. That's always been my rule. Greed in this case could be fatal. There, now,' she said, as the sand, disturbed by being walked on, rustled down to cover the cave again. 'Fate agrees with me. Pick up your gear, Tinker. We are going back to the foreshore for a bathe and a wash and a nice picnic. I believe,' she added, hefting the pack with the precious stones inside, 'that Ruth has included my flask. I could do,' said Phryne, leading the way along the beach, 'with a drink.'

Molly and Tinker thought that they could, too.

◇◇◇

Phryne's words had proved prophetic. Dot's stomach, reliable in cars, buses and trains, proved not to be seaworthy, even though the water was only kicking up a 'wee chop low enough to wet a leprechaun's eyebrows', as Mr. O'Malley said. He was unusually Irish today, Hugh thought. It must have been that sea battle. As the *Black Oak* had fish to catch in the absence of other boats, and Dot was really queasy, Hugh negotiated that they should be set down on Swan Island, whence they could easily get home, and which might provide a few nooks suitable for either a little canoodling or rock fishing, whichever came first. The *Black Oak* set off. Hugh noticed that Mr. O'Malley had souvenired the black flag, and was still flying it.

There were salt marshes, swarming with insects. Although citronella was keeping off the hordes, enough hardy midges were getting through to make walking that way uncomfortable. Slapping with a suitable myrtle sprig, Hugh found a path littered with fish scales and followed it inland.

'Feeling better?' he asked, as Dot drank deeply from the water bottle.

'Oh, yes, thanks. I felt that queer. All that water going up and down, up and down...'

Dot was looking green again, so Hugh suggested, 'What about this little path? Might go somewhere nice.'

'All right,' gasped Dot.

They traversed the low, salt-scoured forest for some time. The wind had dropped. It was hot and, as in all Australian forests, there was nowhere to sit down which might not harbour a snake. Hugh held up a hand.

'I can smell smoke,' he commented.

'Might be a fisherman's camp. Oh, Hugh, and me not fit to be seen!'

'I'll just go on ahead,' said Hugh. 'You stay here. Won't be long,' he assured her.

Which was how Hugh Collins, coming in very quietly from the east, found the bivouac.

It was a tidy little camp, he considered. Little tin shed reroofed with manuka basketwork. Few rabbit skins hanging up on a bush. Sacks and boxes of food. Barrel of water. Nice latrine concealed behind a convenient bush. Garments hung out to dry. Very basic fishing gear; a many-hooked line wound around a beer bottle. Small fire, almost smokeless, and the kettle just beginning to sing. A rough bench had been constructed out of driftwood and would at least give poor Dot a chance to sit down.

Then a spear was poked into his side and a voice demanded, 'Who are you?'

The bell-like tones advised Hugh that this was not your average bushranger.

'I'm Detective Sergeant Hugh Collins,' he announced.

'Thank heavens,' said the voice. ' Are you alone?'

'Just my fiancée,' he told the voice. 'She's been really seasick and she could do with a cup of tea.'

'Poor child,' said a female voice. 'Do put down that silly spear now, Johnson, and let's get the young lady a cuppa. Nasty thing, seasickness.'

'Thanks,' said Hugh.

When Dot staggered into the clearing a tin mug of tea was ready for her.

'Allow me to introduce Mrs. Johnson,' said Hugh with pardonable pride. 'And Mr. Johnson.'

'Nice to meet you,' said Dot, accepting the tea.

'I'm afraid we've only got honey left now,' said Mrs. Johnson. 'And the milk's powdered.'

'I've got a bottle of beer here,' said Hugh. 'Would you care...?'

'Not for me,' said Mr. Johnson firmly. 'We're teetotal except in cases of swooning or sickness. But sit down, officer, and drink it yourself, and we'll see what we have for a little snack.'

'No need,' said Dot, holding out her cup for more tea. 'We've got a picnic.'

'Oh,' said Mrs. Johnson, sinking down onto the bench. 'Proper bread!'

'Roast beef sandwiches today,' said Hugh. 'And chicken legs and some of that potato salad. Better than fish and rabbits, eh?' he asked, distributing the feast liberally to the marooned. After the breakfasts which Dot had been cooking for him, he was feeling comfortably able to miss lunch.

Mrs. Johnson nibbled a chicken leg as though it had been cooked by Carême himself. Mr. Johnson helped himself to Ruth's divine potato salad. Dot ate a sandwich so as to seem companionable. Her stomach was still a little wobbly.

'It has been rather fun, actually,' said Mr. Johnson. His aldermanic figure might have been reduced by a week's privation. He had a bright shining bald head to go with his bright shining blue eyes. A thin fringe of white hair remained to define his face.

'Mr. Johnson was one of those farm boys who can do anything with a length of bailing wire and a little ingenuity,' put in Mrs. Johnson. Apart from her hair, which was dishevelled—she must not have brought a comb with her when they were decoyed away from the Thomas house into that mysterious black car— she looked just like the respectable housekeeper she was. She resupplied Dot's cup. 'And I was the daughter of a poor man, so I know how to contrive. We reroofed the tin hut, evicted the wildlife—several snakes, my Lord!—and we had our luggage, and later other things.'

'But you could have gone home,' said Dot, much refreshed. Nothing like tea, after all, she thought. For all Miss Phryne's cocktails, it was the cup that cheered but did not inebriate. 'You didn't have to stay here.'

'Yes, we did,' said Mr. Johnson. He looked grave. 'Can I suppose that the officer is here to do something about the smuggling business which has made Queenscliff a byword for drunkenness and all uncleanness?'

His voice had developed a faint parsonic twang.

'Yes, the officer is,' replied Hugh. 'We expect to round up the whole gang soon.'

'We had to wait until Mr. Thomas came home. We are staying here until you complete your arrests,' said Mr. Johnson. 'You see, we were kidnapped because I was fool enough to say that I would denounce them to the authorities. They tried to convince me otherwise. But I was firm. Alcohol is a mocker, I said, strong drink is raging, your rum is too cheap, half of the town is out on a toot and drunk from daybreak to midnight, and then they go home to beat their wives and children and start fights and fall in the sea and drown in their sottishness.'

'He's very principled,' explained Mrs. Johnson.

'Yes, but I could have suppressed my feelings and confided in the proper authorities. Pride, my dear, my sinful pride is what has reduced us to this. They tricked us into a car and drove us to the foreshore, and then we were muffled in sacks and dropped into a boat, and our baggage with us.'

'I was just commending my soul to my Maker when we were unwrapped and a nice Irish voice told us that he was going to put us ashore "just so to be out of the troubles", and so he did. He put us ashore just over there and dropped our bags down to us and told us that we had better stay out of sight for a while and if we would give him the key, he would arrange stores to be brought to us from our own house. I knew Mr. Thomas wouldn't mind, so I asked for some pots and so on—but forgot soap, which was so silly of me...' said Mrs. Johnson.

'And he faithfully came and brought us flour and sugar and everything I had asked for, even my favourite teapot. And threw in some fishing gear, as well. I've wires out for rabbits, fine fat ones here, and we found a patch of herbs and onions someone planted and forgot about. And the fishing is good around the rocks. We've been eating well and hiding during the day. And until the Ellis brothers are in custody, Detective Sergeant, me and the missus are staying put.'

'Good plan,' said Hugh, after some consideration. 'Who was this helpful fisherman?'

'I didn't see him,' said Mr. Johnson with a butler's wilful and professional blindness. 'It was dark.'

'And you didn't see him when he delivered the larder?'

'No, he cached the food and we picked it up after nightfall.'

Hugh recognised a will of adamant when he encountered it. Mr. Johnson was not going to betray his Irish rescuer, even though he had marooned them. Hugh had a sneaking suspicion as to who the boatman was. And it was a nice little camp. He could understand why it had been amusing for the Johnsons, with their background, to get away from running a big house for a while and eat fish straight out of the sea, cooked on that flat metal sheet, using a tin fork and no table manners.

'Anything I can bring you?' he asked, giving up on identification from these witnesses.

'Some soap would be nice,' said Mrs. Johnson hopefully. 'And a comb? We've really got quite enough food. In this weather it is no penalty to cook outdoors. And it isn't cold at night, not really,' she said bravely.

Dot reached into her capacious handbag, without which she never travelled an inch out of the house, and produced a small cake of hyacinth-scented soap, a comb and brush, a bottle of eau de cologne and another of citronella. Then she took off her woolly cardigan and held it out.

'Take it,' she said. 'You can give it back when this is all over. We're living in your house, you know. I'm Miss Fisher's companion, Dot Williams.'

'Oh, Lord, oh, what will Mr. Thomas say? Poor Miss Fisher arriving and nothing prepared for her and no one to look after her!' wailed Mrs. Johnson.

'We've managed,' Dot told her, patting her arm. 'Really. It's been fun for us, too. And this was hardly your fault. Don't be concerned. Are we going, Hugh?'

'I'll come back for you when it's all over,' Hugh told Mr. Johnson. 'Soon.'

'The Lord go with you and strengthen your arm,' said Mr. Johnson.

Dot turned back at the edge of the small clearing.

'I forgot,' she said. 'You'll be glad to know he's safe.'

'Not Gaston?' asked Mrs. Johnson, and broke into tears of relief. 'How is he?'

'He's healthy,' said Dot. 'He misses you, though. When he turned up at the house he was filthy. We had to wash him twice before we could identify him. But he's eating well and he'll be delighted to see you again.'

'I have been trying not to think about him,' confessed Mrs. Johnson, accepting Hugh's handkerchief. 'I was so sorrowful, and Mr. Johnson said I was being ungrateful to the Lord who had preserved our lives, and Gaston was only a dog, and he was right, but…'

Mr. Johnson was looking very uneasy. Being right in order to suppress someone's grief was not an attractive trait, Dot thought. He patted his wife awkwardly on the shoulder.

'How did he get lost?' asked Hugh.

Mrs. Johnson stopped crying.

'I had him in my arms when they put bags over our heads, and he jumped down and started attacking the men, and someone kicked him because I heard him yelp, and then there was a splash and they'd thrown him into the sea! My poor little darling Gaston…'

'He's fine,' Hugh told her. 'And they'll be sorry.'

When they looked back at the little camp Mrs. Johnson was chopping onions for a rabbit stew and Mr. Johnson was reading to her from his pocket Bible.

'*Woe to the crown of pride, to the drunkards of Ephraim, whose glorious destiny is a fading flower, which are upon the head of the fat valleys of them that are overcome with wine! Behold, the Lord hath a mighty and strong arm, which is as a tempest and a destroying storm, as a flood of mighty waters overflowing, shall cast down to the earth with His hand.*'

'And so say all of me,' said Hugh.

'Amen,' responded Dot.

Chapter Nineteen

Naturam expellas furca, tamen usque recurret
You may drive out nature with a pitchfork, but
she will return.

Horace
Epistles

Dinner that night was superlative. Hugh had informed the household that the Johnsons would be back, so Ruth had put her heart and soul into a magnificent feast before she had to hand over her kitchen. It might be a bit of a relief, at that, to surrender her responsibilities, but at least now she knew she could do it. She could run a household in trying circumstances; she could stock a kitchen from scratch, make her own bread, construct her own menus, cook her favourite recipes. She was proud of her own skill and her good teaching. And Mrs. Leyel. Mrs. Leyel was going home with Ruth. She would buy the book from Mr. Thomas. Or, if necessary, steal it. When it came to Mrs. Leyel, Ruth had no conscience.

So the dinner included all the Oriental recipes which looked so delicious: fish cooked in many forms; delicate vegetables in strange sauces; crayfish chowder, really piquant; roasted quinces as pink as an houri's lips; a dessert of fresh dates, tropical fruit and berries in pomegranate syrup; and rosewater Turkish delight to eat with coffee.

Everyone was pleased, everyone was talking, the gramophone was playing. Joy, in fact, was unconfined until ten in the Fisher household, when Hugh had to leave to carry out his operation against the Ellis brothers.

Dot hugged him goodbye at the door.

'You will be careful, Hugh, won't you?' she pleaded, and Hugh kissed her and promised that he would. And he meant to be. His planning had been meticulous, he had allowed for several contingencies, and it ought to go, he thought as he strode towards his lodging to put on his uniform, like clockwork.

The best-laid plans of mice and men gang aft a-gley, as the tender-hearted poet said to the dormouse, mourning over its ruined nest. The factor which would fling a wrench into the well-oiled machinery of Hugh Collins's plan was Ian Fraser.

After a night in the wilderness, the boys were fed up. They had tried to make a fire in the wet forest on Swan Island and had not been able to make it flame. It had, however, smoked villainously and begrimed all faces and made them cough while giving out no useful heat. They had not been able to break into the locked gun-cabinet, so they could not shoot anything. The fish they had at last caught proved impossible to cook on this fire but they had been so hungry that they had choked down the raw flesh, which tasted vile. They were muddy to the knees. They were wet with seawater which was drying into crusts which scored delicate skin across wrists and thighs. Kiwi had been bitten by a bull ant and they had seen several snakes.

They had also sighted Mr. Johnson, fishing with irritating skill off the rocks. He had caught three fish in the time that the boys had caught one measly little grey mullet, which Fraser had killed by beating it to death on the stones. It had then proved inedible because the flesh was full of shards of razor-sharp bone. The other one they caught was executed by Kiwi, who had been fishing with his father. It did not comfort their stomachs. It was cold in the dark and noisy; things hopped and creaked and bounced and called in the wet manuka. Something totally frightful groaned a long, triumphant croak which sent shivers down the spine. The fact that this was probably a bird of some kind did not console them at all.

'I'm going home,' announced Jolyon. He had considered his position. He would be in trouble. But, then, he usually was. His mother would scream at him. She usually did. He would be punished. What could be worse than this cold, wet, foodless wilderness, stocked with snakes and inimical birds? He could handle any amount of screaming if the deal included a bath, a fluffy towel, a change of garments and a lot of breakfast. Toast, he thought. Bacon. Eggs. Gallons of tea. In a house, with a nice heavy roof and walls and door, shut away from the beauties of nature.

'I'll come with you,' said Kiwi. His bitten knee had swollen to the size of a tennis ball and burned all the time, so that he had not been able to sleep and had been fully awake to experience the joys of camping *au naturel* in the *joli bois*. French lessons came back to him, and he understood the term *forêt sauvage* for the first time. No wonder everyone was afraid of it. Even now he didn't know if he could walk. But he'd crawl rather than spend any more time in this company and in this horrible landscape, which seemed to hate him and be designed to bite, prick, burn, chill and wound him, personally.

'You can't,' snarled Fraser. There was deep fear in his heart. Product of a broken-spirited mother and a cold, brutal businessman of a father, he had never been able to please his father or rescue his mother and domination over his fellows was the cornerstone of his soul.

'We can,' declared Jolyon, as dusk tinted the sky. He hauled Kiwi to his feet. 'We shall.'

And then they limped off and left him. Without a backward glance. Left him alone. Well, he wasn't going back.

On the other hand, there was no reason why he should stay on Swan Island. There must be better places to sleep than this dreary wilderness. He might find an empty house, or a shop. And if he was to survive, he needed money. He was cavernously hungry. He had never gone without food for so long. What did he have that he could sell?

An idea burst onto his mind like a Guy Fawkes rocket. Of course! All Queenscliff knew of the Ellis brothers and their smuggling of Bundaberg rum. Everyone also knew that the principled Mr. Johnson had denounced them at the Presbyterian Church the Sunday before he and his wife disappeared. And Fraser had a shrewd suspicion that the Ellis brothers might pay for his information that the missing Johnsons were alive and well on Swan Island. They might even take him on as an apprentice smuggler.

His mind buzzing with dreams of criminal glory and his stomach growling, Fraser crossed to the mainland and set out to steal a bike to get him to Point Lonsdale before dark.

◇◇◇

Kiwi and Jolyon arrived at the Mason house and begged penitently for admittance. Instead of screaming, Mrs. Mason ordered, progressively, disinfecting high-temperature baths, a dose of Dr. Pemberton's Tonic, a small tot of restorative brandy, chamomile tea, soup and then dinner, and herself applied arnica to the bullant bite, which subsided directly. Both boys were ordered into fresh pyjamas as soon as their hair was dry and sent to bed with mugs of hot cocoa containing four drops of valerian essence for sleep and two of peppermint essence to cover the taste. Mrs. Mason was so glad to get her son back that she did not even enquire about Fraser, whom she considered a bad influence on her son, and good riddance to bad rubbish was the only thought she spared for the absent boy. She could report him missing tomorrow, when he should be really sorry for leading Jolyon astray.

Kiwi and Jolyon fell asleep almost instantly. In his last thought before falling asleep like a tree falls in the forest, Kiwi hoped that Fraser was all right. Even though he was a blighter.

◇◇◇

Fraser sailed through the deepening darkness on a trike left unattended in the butcher's yard, heading for Point Lonsdale.

As he reached the chained gate and cried, 'Open up!', Phryne was tasting the crayfish chowder and thanking her stars that she had chosen to wear a loose gown of silver and black to Ruth's dinner.

The dogs bayed at him. They sounded hungry. An old man in a grey dustcoat limped to the gate and croaked, 'What d'ya want at this time of night? Go away!'

'I want to see Mr. Ellis,' declared Fraser, his voice reverting to Received Public School. The tone gave the watchman pause.

'Oh, do yer? But does 'e want ter see you?'

'I've got information on the Johnsons,' said Fraser.

'Have yer?' The watchman's toothless mouth grinned. 'Come in, then.'

He unlocked the gate. It swung wide. Fraser pushed the trike inside—he might want it again—and followed the old man to the kitchen door of a substantial house. It was open. Two massive men were sitting at the kitchen table, eating mussels from a huge pot which stood in the middle on a pad of newspaper. Shells littered the table and the floor, dropped among two favoured house dogs. There was a sliced loaf of bread and a pound of butter next to the pot. Fraser salivated.

'Boss?' quavered the watchman. 'Boy ter see yer.'

'Yair?' asked the larger of the two men. 'All right, Harry, get back to the gate.'

'Boss.' The watchman departed rather quickly.

'All right, young feller, what d'ya want?'

'I know that the Johnsons are alive,' said Fraser, more terrified than he had ever been in his life. They were giants, gross and unclean. They ate like pigs. They had hands like hams. They could kill him with a blow.

'Are they?' asked the second man slowly. 'How d'yer know?'

'I'm willing to negotiate a fee,' said Fraser faintly.

'Are yer?' asked the first Ellis. 'Well, I'll tell you what. You stay 'ere. Jim'll go see. If yer right, we might think about givin' yer a job.'

'But...' Fraser backed towards the door.

'And if yer bein' funny with us, you'll be sorry yer was ever born,' added Tom. He rose to his feet and took Fraser by the shoulder. A dog growled from under the table.

'But yer hungry, ain't yer?' asked Jim.

'Yes, very hungry!' said Fraser, his eyes on the ambrosial bread.

'And yer can stay that way,' completed Jim. 'Till I get back.'

Fraser, desperate, made a snatch for the bread. It fell to the floor and was instantly devoured by the under-table dog, who fought off the under-chair dog with much snapping and gulping. Every creature in the Ellis's employ was hungry, except the brothers themselves.

'Yer shouldn' ha' done that,' Jim told Fraser, hitting him across the head with a soggy slap. 'Wastin' good food. I'm gonna lock yer up with the dogs,' he said, hauling the half-conscious boy across the floor and into the yard. 'They won't eat yer if you stay still and don't annoy 'em. Prob'ly. Come on, yer little worm!'

Fraser was flung into the compound where shadowy wolves came and sniffed at him, dismissed him as unimportant for the present, though someone to keep an eye on, and went on with their ravenous pacing. He wept for his aching head and his hunger and his knowledge that he had been cheated and for the unfairness of it all. But quietly, so the dogs should not be annoyed.

◇◇◇

The attack on the Ellis compound began with the stealthy approach of Probationary Constable Basil Worthington, son of a well-respected dingo poisoner, who was required to silence the dogs.

There was something about good old Baz, his colleagues knew, which calmed lunatics, comforted lost children, soothed drunks and subdued angry dogs and runaway horses. He was calm, old Baz, with a broad oceanic stillness which some had mistaken for stupidity. But Basil was not stupid. It was just that he seldom found anything worth getting agitated about.

He was distributing among the guard dogs a recipe of his father's, with some emendation. He did not want to kill the dogs; it was not their fault that their masters were crims. He just wanted to dope them. So to the figgin—a ball made of a mixture of chopped lungs, liver and lights wrapped in caul fat—he had added not the strychnine of the dingo-killer, but chloral hydrate. A sedative, not a stiffener, as his father might have said. Basil Worthington had spent a gory afternoon constructing the figgins and they were going down a treat. He was tossing them over the wire fence and marking down which dog got one as they vanished down gaping maws. Each dog would gulp the figgin and sit down to digest, then, in about five minutes, they just yawned and curled up to sleep. By the speed at which the drug was working Constable Worthington concluded that their poor stomachs had been entirely empty. Those Ellis brothers were real mean bastards.

He had been told that there were ten dogs. He had made twelve figgins, just in case the informant couldn't count. He had distributed eight. There must be more dogs. Perhaps penned?

He sighted a wire cage at the side of the compound. By the sound of it, it contained two dogs. They were the only ones still howling. He was close enough to hear little yips as well; a bitch, perhaps, with puppies. He flung a figgin and the second howl was staunched. Then another, and the last lone barking stopped. There was still something scrabbling in the compound. So he dropped his final figgins over into the enclosure, and listened for further movement.

All was as silent as the grave. But he'd better get into that cage, as soon as they had the Ellis brothers by the heels, and make sure that the bitch hadn't overlaid her young 'uns.

Fraser, next to the silenced mother dog, plunged his face ravenously into raw offal and swallowed, retched, and gulped the rest. Unconsciousness hit him like a wave and he fell with his head on the bitch's flank, cuddled next to her squeaking babies.

Hugh loosed his assault at one o'clock. Constable Worthington crept forward and unlocked the chain on the main gates. He admitted Hugh's army and then closed it again. Harry the watchman was muffled in his own dustcoat and told to stay still and quiet, and he did. The constables swarmed over the yard, unlocking the cargo sheds. Here they found ample evidence of smuggling. A wall of crates contained bottles of overproof rum which had no customs stamp. A pile of malodorous boxes contained cured Queensland tobacco, reeking of tar.

And the Ellis arrest was almost a disappointment. By the time they broke open the kitchen door and crunched over the mussel-shell flooring they found Tom Ellis lying maudlin drunk on the parlour couch, singing along with the gramophone record 'The Sun Has Got His Hat On'. He had been secured with some difficulty, as no available handcuffs would span his mighty wrists. But Hugh had lashed him up with a handy curtain cord, fighting off invitations to sing along. The rest of the household went quietly, including a man with an unhealed slash across his face, apparently made by some sort of teeth. Mrs. Ellis was the only one who showed fight. A straw-headed harridan almost as massive as her husband, she had threatened as they clicked handcuffs on her, 'You wait till my Jim hears about this, you bloody curs, breakin' into a dwelling house at night! You bastards! Jim'll fuckin' settle you, just you bloody wait!'

'Well, where is your Jim, Missus?' demanded Hugh.

But Jim Ellis and his attendant, Bluey, were nowhere to be found.

Chapter Twenty

When this yokel comes maundering
Whetting his hacker,
I shall run before him,
Diffusing the civilest odors
Out of geraniums and unsmelled flowers.
It will check him.

Wallace Stevens
'The Plot Against the Giant'

It had been a lovely night and a strenuous day and Phryne was sleepy. But she was also restless. She had been without male caresses for a week, and that was too long. Her usual remedy had produced a climax, but it was just not the same. She had mosquito bites which she was trying not to scratch and a Dr. Thorndyke book with a few stories left unread, so she sat up and put on her light. On her small table there was a tray bearing a half-bottle of champagne in an ice bucket, a biscuit box containing Waterbury's cream crackers, another containing Ruth's Anzacs, and her ashtray, lighter and a packet of the Balkan cigarettes she favoured.

'Alas, poor deprived Phryne, can't sleep,' she said to herself, as she wrapped her gown around her and sat down to some nibbling and drinking. She was just wondering how Dr. Thorndyke had managed, for such a long career, to avoid assassination for Advanced Smugness when she heard, through the silent house, an odd little click.

Now who would be awake at midnight? She could hear Jane muttering equations in her sleep, as she often did, and Ruth and Dot breathing. Tinker might be slipping out for some night-fishing, of course. But she thought not. That footstep she had just heard was far too heavy to be the lightfooted Tinker.

Then Gaston began to yelp wildly, Phryne heard Tinker yell, 'You let go of me!', and then barking and expostulation were muffled by the slamming of a heavy door. Tinker had been defeated. Housebreakers would, at any moment, be coming up the stairs.

Phryne flitted from room to room, waking the sleepers. Ruth sprang awake, already terrified. Jane came vaguely to consciousness. Dot was awake already, having heard Gaston's protests. Molly was about to add to the general noise when Phryne hushed her.

'Take Molly and go into the secret room and bar the door,' said Phryne to the girls. They collared Molly and obeyed, though Jane had to shove Ruth into the room when she saw what it contained.

'Dot, take my soft soap and go and soap the bottom three stairs,' Phryne ordered, and Dot scuttled down the front stairs and did so, listening to heavy footsteps approaching and cold to her marrow. Then she hurried up again.

'Take the heaviest tray you can find from the housemaid's cupboard,' instructed Phryne, 'and bean anyone who comes up the servants' stair. Don't ask who they are. Just hit them. As hard as you can.'

'Yes, Miss Phryne. Who do you think they are?' asked Dot.

'I suspect something has gone wrong with Hugh's plan. Something unexpected. Could any of us have told any outsider that the Johnsons are alive?'

'Not us, Miss Phryne, we haven't been out of the house since we found out.'

'True. Never mind. We have the girls to defend. And no one,' said Phryne, checking the ammunition of her Beretta, 'is going to get past us.'

Dot traced a cross on her bosom, and went for the tray. On reflection, she decided on a coal scuttle. It was nice and heavy, being made of iron, but not too heavy for her to lift and swing. Dot, in her hair crimpers and candlewick dressing gown, took up her station at the head of the narrow stair, prepared to do or die.

Phryne took her champagne glass and her cigarette and sat down on the top step. There were thumps and crunching noises in the back of the house. Pretty soon the assailant would decide that the Johnsons were not in the servants' quarters. Tinker's voice sounded, yelling, 'Guv! Wake up! We've got company!', accompanied by continuous barking from Gaston, who must have remembered the people who had kicked him and threw him into the sea.

◇◇◇

'Sister Ann, Sister Ann, do you see anyone coming?' asked Jane, hoping to snap Ruth out of her terrified stupor. Ruth was staring out the window at darkened Queenscliff, as the attractive alternative to looking at a row of skulls—actual skulls which had come out of dead people!—on top of the bookcase.

'Only the sun on the road, Sister,' replied Ruth through numb lips. 'And the dust beneath. Though it'd be the moon, if there was a moon. Which there isn't.'

'No, Molly, put that down.' Jane grabbed a long-dried bone from Molly's jaws. Molly was puzzled. It was a bone. Dogs ate bones. She was a dog. What price human logic? Ruth sat down on the floor to hug the dog. If she sat down she could keep her eyes shut. But that was no good. Her imagination was working overtime to scare her to death. She stood up and opened the window so that she could see even better. But the road was quiet. There was nothing to see.

◇◇◇

Jim Ellis was puzzled. He clipped Bluey over the ear, which did nothing to soothe his mind. That sneaking bastard kid had said the Johnsons were alive. Well, they weren't here in their place, only their yappy cur and some noisy boy. He thought he'd killed that dog. But here it was. Still yapping. He would attend to Gaston later.

'What about the rest of the house, Boss?' asked Bluey, unfazed. He was used to the Ellis' agonic dialect, which consisted of curses and blows.

'The dog's 'ere. Maybe they took a bedroom 'cos we pinched their furniture. Someone's livin' 'ere. We better find out who.'

'Right you are,' said Bluey, and ducked the next cuff.

'You go up the back, I'll do the front,' said Jim Ellis.

Bluey assented and slipped away. Apart from Gaston's barking, the house was silent. Except for a delicate clinking noise.

Jim Ellis had always been the biggest dog in any fight. He knew he was strong and had been a dominant, dirty tent boxer who won every bout he had undertaken, in the days before his brother Tom had taken him into the family business. Yair, and every fight since. He came to the foot of the stairs and saw, in the bright light coming from the upper floor, a slim female draped in the sort of gown that Theda Bara used to wear in the pictures. She was pouring the last of the champagne into a tall glass, which explained the tinkling noise.

'I'm not going to offer you a drink,' she told him pleasantly.

Jim stood and gaped. 'Who're you?' he croaked through a suddenly dry throat.

'Oh, I have many names, many names,' said Phryne. 'Nemesis, daughter of Nox, perhaps. The Romans might have called me Adrasta. I could be one of Tisiphone, Megaera or Alecto. But you can call me Phryne Fisher. What are you doing in my house, you vile abomination?'

'I come lookin' fer the Johnsons,' he told her. That smile was beginning to unnerve him. She looked just like a Dutch doll, pink lips, bright eyes, white skin, black shiny hair. But she didn't sound like any doll. Phryne Fisher gave Jim Ellis the willies.

'They're not here,' she told him.

'I'll see for meself,' he said, one foot on the bottom step.

'You won't,' said Phryne. She produced from her silken lap the little gun and pointed it straight at his face. 'Don't come a step nearer.'

'Now look, lady,' Jim Ellis decided to temporise while his offsider, Bluey, crept up the other stairs and could come on this insolent female from behind, 'ya can't shoot me!'

'Oh, I can,' purred Phryne. She was listening for a flurry behind her, as Dot dealt with the intruder.

◇◇◇

'Sister Ann, Sister Ann, do you see the horsemen coming?' asked Jane.

'Only a dark road, Sister, and not a speck of movement. What's happening out there?' asked Ruth in an agony of suspense.

'I can hear Miss Phryne talking,' said Jane, with her ear to the door. 'I can't hear what she's saying. And a man answering. Take that humerus away from Molly, Ruth! Mr. Thomas needs these bones.'

'What on earth for?'

Ruth was a little reconciled to the room of horror, but could not see why anyone would want to construct one.

◇◇◇

Dot heard the burglar coming up the servants' stairs. Bluey had a surprisingly domestic glimpse of a young woman in a beige housegown with curlers in her hair as the scuttle came down and he dropped out of consciousness, sliding bonelessly down the stairs on his front.

Phryne heard the solid clunk of scuttle meeting skull and smiled again on the giant at the foot of the stairs.

'Go away,' she suggested.

'You bitch,' said Jim Ellis, 'I'll have you first, then the others. You'll be real sorry,' and rushed the stairs.

He managed the first soaped step, but the second slid out from under his boots and he stumbled. On the third he fell sprawling, tumbling to the bottom of the stairs and roaring with pain and insult. He was huge, magenta-faced, his mouth gaping, showing rotten teeth, his monstrous hands flexing to grip, tear and rend. He was a creature out of a nightmare, of measureless brutality and animal strength and fury. He gathered himself and rushed again.

Phryne shot him quite clinically in the knee, and Jim Ellis went down for the count. His head impacted the floor. He was beaten.

◇◇◇

'Sister Ann, Sister Ann, do you...'

'Aha,' said Ruth, opening the door a crack. 'We don't need any horsemen to rescue us, Sister. We've got Miss Phryne.'

After which the rescuing mob of policemen who stormed in to confront the evil-doers and deliver the innocent came as a bit of an anticlimax.

Hugh, who had driven like a maniac from Point Lonsdale to Queenscliff, bell clanging all the way, took in the scene which confronted him and his fellows as they pushed inside the brightly lit house on Mercer Street.

His beloved was sitting in a parlour chair. She was wearing a house dress and had curlers in her hair. She was gulping sherry. The two girls were feeding Molly and Gaston with dog biscuits. Gaston, particularly, had the satisfied air of a dog who has given his assailants a really good solid barking. Tinker was slopping water over the first three steps of the main staircase, mopping with a floorcloth and chuckling. Miss Fisher was smoking a gasper, with her unshod feet propped up on a flattened Jim Ellis, who had a tea towel tied tightly around his knee and his hands and feet bound with washing line. Beside him reposed the senseless form of his associate, Bluey, who was being examined by Dr. Green.

'He might have concussion,' the doctor was saying as he thumbed back an eyelid. 'He's had a heavy blow to the head.'

'Yes,' said Dot grimly. 'And he deserved it.'

'Doubtless,' said the doctor smoothly, getting to his feet. 'And as for the other one, Miss Fisher, he'll need to go to hospital to have that bullet extracted. I'll say one thing,' he added. 'This is the sweetest-smelling crime scene I have ever been called to.'

'Floris' Stephanotis soft soap for that perfect complexion,' Phryne told him. 'I order it specially from England. And that was my last bottle, drat all burglars and housebreakers!'

'Are you all right, love?' Hugh asked Dot, taking her hand.

'Miss Phryne had it all under control,' she told him. 'But it wasn't nice for a while there.'

'Well, we've got the rest of them,' Hugh said. 'It was only later that I worked out that someone must have seen the Johnsons and reported them alive, and I rushed back here like fury to find…that Miss Fisher, indeed, had everything under control.'

'As usual,' sighed Dot. Her head ached. She longed to make herself a cuppa, take a Bex and go back to bed. She turned Hugh's wrist to see his watch.

'It's two o'clock in the morning!' she exclaimed.

'Time for you to get some beauty sleep,' said Hugh dotingly. 'Not as if you need it.'

If he could say that, and her in her ratty gown and crimps in her hair, Dot thought, he must really love me. She smiled.

It took considerable time and trouble to get Jim Ellis onto one stretcher and Bluey onto another and cart them off to Geelong hospital, where they would be cared for under guard. Then Hugh took his leave, the Fisher ménage made themselves tea or cocoa or neat cognac as per preference, the dogs were placated with a brief run, and then, at last, the Mercer Street house was silent as everyone went back to sleep.

◇◇◇

Constable Basil Worthington had gently carried all the comatose dogs into their fenced yard and laid out plates of cheap dog biscuits mixed with all the meat in the icebox and bowls of water

for their awakening, which might be cranky. He jemmied the
lock on the cage and attended to the two others and the bitch
and her three squeaking offspring, who were as fat and healthy as
their mother was rib-exhibitingly starved to the bone. He made
up a mash of bread, cooked chicken and milk for her, using the
Ellis brothers' stores lavishly. They weren't going to need them
where they were going. The mother dog was beginning to stir,
and he leaned down to pat her head, when another head was
lifted and a boy's voice whispered, 'Water?'

Basil had never been afraid of an animal in his life, though
this one's advent had given him a bit of a start. This ragged
blood-smeared creature needed help, and he should have it.
He gently assisted Fraser to his uncertain feet and guided him
into the house. There he provided water and then a strong cup
of the Ellis brothers' coffee, spiked with uncustomed rum. The
boy drank water, vomited, then drank more water and then the
coffee. Basil wondered how long he had been caged with the
hounds. He stank of dog muck and blood and fear, but he did
not seem to be wounded.

'Come along, son,' said the constable in his soothing voice.
'We've no need to stay here. The dogs will be all right now.
Come back with me, and tell you what, you can wash yourself
off in the sea on the way.'

'Thank you, sir,' said Fraser.

A great change had come over him. He now knew what
crime was like: brutal, unfair, cruel, disgusting. He had no more
taste for felony. But he felt much stronger in himself. He had
been tortured, mistreated, starved, flung among wolves. He had
survived. Nothing his father could do to him would be worse
than the Ellis brothers' dog kennel. He had nothing to be afraid
of any more.

He washed ferociously in the cold surf, scrubbing off the
blood from the offal he had eaten and the filth from the floor
of the kennel. Thus soaking wet, but not actively noxious, he
was delivered to an unimpressed Mrs. Mason at dawn for her
routine of a scalding bath, medicines, treatment for his various

scrapes and bruises, and forcible soup, breakfast and cocoa with valerian. He complied so humbly and gratefully with this regime that his hostess thought that she might have been wrong about him. He had not even winced when she had practically poured iodine into all those cuts and scratches. Maybe he was a good boy, after all.

As he fell asleep in a clean bed, tended and nourished and scrubbed and in fresh pyjamas, Fraser thought that he might, indeed, be beginning a new career. He had to do something worthwhile with his new-given life. Being alive was so very much better than the alternative.

He resolved to offer the Ellis brothers' heirs for one of the puppies. It had nestled close to his cheek and tried to lick the blood off his face. He fell asleep smiling.

◇◇◇

It was Thursday at last and the Fisher household slept disgracefully late. Máire arrived at eight as usual and found the back door locked, went next door to find out if Miss Fisher was away, and received all the news from the kitchen.

Mrs. Cook had sent the gardener's assistant to supervise the boy Fraser's bath, he having returned a night after the other two, wet as a herring and strangely subdued. Breakfast was imminent and Mrs. Cook was delighted to have some help, since Lily had not been replaced, poor Lily, and Mrs. Mason was always grumpy at breakfast.

'If I drank that much the night before I'd be cross as well,' Mrs. Cook told Máire. 'Sit down, Máire, and shell these eggs for me for the kedgeree. But before you do that, watch the frying pan, will you? That bacon's cut so thin it'll catch. Such doings!'

'What doings?' asked Máire, sliding the big pan off the heat and forking the crispy slices into a dish shaped to go into the bain-marie. Then she expertly rolled the hard-boiled eggs on the table, peeling off the shells in one piece. She passed the eggs to the cook, who cut them up and sprinkled them over the top of her fish and rice.

'Good, now toast for your life, and I'll tell you all,' said Mrs. Cook, who had caught Tinker on an early-morning cadge and at the expense of a bite of this and a munch of that, and that leftover chicken stew for Gaston, had heard the whole story.

And she regaled the attentive Máire with every detail as she toasted bread in the flat-sided temperamental toasting machine, from the discovery of the Johnsons—somewhere unspecified—to the raid on the Ellis brothers' yard, the arrest of Tom Ellis and his workers, and the attack by Jim Ellis and his offsider Bluey on the house next door.

'I heard a shot,' she told Máire, 'past midnight, but it could have been anyone out hunting rabbits. I never thought it would be next door! In Mercer Street! And that Miss Fisher shot him neat as neat, clean through the knee. He's given his wretched boys their last kicking, that's plain. Mind you, it should properly have been through the heart,' said Mrs. Cook, taking up the mound of toast. 'Carry in the bacon for me, there's a dear. There.' She surveyed the table. The bain-marie was alight, the scrambled eggs, the bacon, the mushrooms, the grilled tomatoes and the kedgeree were perfect, and Mrs. Mason's pot of coffee was stewing gently. Excellent. Tea could be had from the urn at any time. Breakfast was now served.

'Now, my dear, time for a little refreshment of our own,' said Mrs. Cook cosily. The kitchen maid looked rather pale, she thought, in need of some hot tea and a good meal.

'So it's quite caught, the Ellis brothers are?' asked Máire, sinking down into a chair.

'One in hospital and one in jail,' said Mrs. Cook cheerfully. 'And good riddance, I say. Don't you worry,' she said, for she too had suspicions about the role of certain fishermen in the shifting of the Ellis brothers' illegal cargos. 'The man in charge's young lady is Miss Williams next door. He isn't going to cause a fuss for anyone here. He's got the criminals. That's all he wants, I expect. Now have some of my scrambled eggs, my dear, and don't be troubled.'

Máire obediently ate the scrambled eggs, which were very good. It does not do to offend a cook, and she would need a new job when Miss Fisher went back to St Kilda. Máire would not mind working for Mrs. Cook. And by the generosity with which she was being plied with dainties, she suspected that Mrs. Cook might like to employ her.

If only the dad hadn't done something rash…

Chapter Twenty-One

Journeys end in lovers' meeting
Every wise man's son doth know.

William Shakespeare
Twelfth Night

After spending the remains of the night doing the paperwork involved in accounting for a housebreaking, a shooting, and a huge quantity of impounded uncustomed goods—not to mention the attempted murder of the Johnsons, foiled by the anonymous boatman (about whose actions the hungover Tom Ellis was quite vehement)—Hugh Collins went back to Home by the Sea for a bath and a few hours' sleep. He woke slowly at noon. The sun had penetrated a hole in his blind. He stretched. Everything had worked out well. Robinson would be pleased with him. Dot was all right. The world was relieved of a pair of scoundrels. Some lunch, perhaps, and then off to rescue the marooned.

◇◇◇

By arrangement, he brought them to Miss Fisher's house at three, just in time for tea. Gaston, who had been sitting under the table awaiting provisions, sniffed suddenly. He had caught a familiar scent. His small nose shot up and his ears pricked. Yes! That was it! It was her! He galloped to the front hall and barked and yelped and bounced as Dot struggled to open the door and Gaston leapt like a salmon.

As soon as she had managed to get the door ajar, Gaston jumped through the gap and into the arms of a woman who wept unashamedly as he whined and wriggled and licked her face in an ecstasy of love and regret. 'I lost you, I couldn't find you!' Gaston tried to convey as his whole body attempted to wag like his tail. 'I looked for you and I couldn't find you!'

Dot blinked back her own tears, and invited Mr. and Mrs. Johnson back into their own house. Mrs. Johnson tried to put Gaston down to greet her hostess but Gaston was having nothing of that. As soon as his paws hit the floor he jumped back into her embrace. Gaston had found his people and he did not intend to lose them again. Mrs. Johnson sat down at the tea table and sat him on her lap, where he stayed, ready to pursue her if she made a sudden move or showed signs of leaving him again.

Mrs. Johnson returned Dot's cardigan, apologising for its bedraggled state after being used as a blanket. Dot told her not to mention it; it would doubtless wash up well in soft soap and eucalyptus oil. Gaston gave a companionable bark.

'He's such a good doggie,' said Ruth, breaking a somewhat strained silence. The Johnsons were uncomfortable. They were not used to taking tea in the parlour, like guests.

'He is a good doggie,' agreed Mrs. Johnson. She inspected the tea table, with its pound cake, fruit scones and cucumber sandwiches. 'Where did you find another cook so far into the season, Miss Fisher?' she asked.

'I brought one with me,' said Phryne. 'My daughter Ruth, who wants to be a cook, nobly took on the challenge of an empty larder and a lot of hearty appetites. I have a telegram from Mr. Thomas here asking what is going on, and I am so glad that I can wire back that all is well. Is that true?'

'You did beautifully,' Mrs. Johnson told Ruth, who blushed. 'I couldn't make a better pound cake myself, my dear. Oh, I did miss bread and cake! Cut me another slice, Miss Ruth, if you please.'

'Ahem. Miss Fisher, we have been thinking,' said Mr. Johnson. 'If you could manage without us for the rest of your visit, we would have time to get our furniture back from the police pound and arrange ourselves again. We haven't had a long holiday for a long time. We could go and stay with my sister in Point, if that would suit, for the next three weeks. We'd stay near enough for Mrs. Johnson to come in and cook, but none of the boarding houses would let us keep Gaston with us, and he's been through enough, the poor little fellow.'

Gaston heard his name and wagged his tail. Phryne looked at Ruth. She grinned. She had more recipes from the inexhaustible Mrs. Leyel to concoct and the household had now arranged itself so that she didn't end up doing all the work. And Tinker was getting expert at washing dishes without those distressing crashes which had marked his early apprenticeship.

'Very well,' Phryne told Mrs. Johnson. 'Please accept a few pounds for expenses. Gaston will need dog food and a new collar. No, no, please take it. It's just an advance—I shall claim it back from Mr. Thomas. You'll need to buy some clothes and so on.'

Mrs. Johnson accepted the money, and shortly after Hugh took them away, to Point Lonsdale to Mr. Johnson's sister's house, where Gaston also had his admirers. The Mercer Street inhabitants settled down to eat some more tea. Molly saw Gaston off with a farewell barking, then pranced back into the parlour, delighted to be relieved of her small noisy rival for titbits and affection. When Hugh came back, he was taking the whole family out to dine at the Esplanade Hotel, a rough but cheerful hostelry, renowned for its fish. Dot went upstairs to prepare. He might think her beautiful in house gown and crimps; he would find her magnificent in her starfish dress.

Hugh, leaving with the Johnsons, caught Máire in the street, and took her arm to gently draw her aside.

'Your dad did nothing wrong,' he told her. 'Well, not a lot wrong, and he saved the Johnsons, so don't worry. His name isn't going to be mentioned. The house won't be searched. Miss Phryne told me that you and your sister took the flour and stuff.'

'But how by all the saints did she know?' cried Máire.

'You knew your way around the kitchen the first time, and you had supposedly never been there before,' said Hugh. 'She's a noticing sort of lady, Miss Fisher is. I just thought I'd tell you so you wouldn't be worried. You're fine, your dad's in the clear, and your sister too.'

Máire promptly did something scandalous, for which her father would rightly have reproved her. But he wasn't there, so she kissed Hugh Collins—an English polisman!—on the cheek, and went home much eased in her mind.

Ruth ate one of her sandwiches, dreaming of future menus. Phryne telephoned her placatory telegram to Mr. Thomas in Katherine. On her return she ate a fruit scone, considering that she had—for once—got through an imbroglio without anyone dying, and she deserved it. Jane sneaked her book out from under the table and sat openly reading while Tinker fed Molly bits of cake. The doorbell rang and Miss Fisher admitted a long line of undress surrealists—in their mundane clothes. They bore offerings.

To the tune of 'The Dead March' from *Saul*, played by the child Laszlo on a penny whistle, they deposited objects on the tea table, while Ruth hastily moved the cakes out of the way. Two RMs, bearing between them a garlic press on a cushion. Sylvia, laying down a twined jelly baby and jelly bean necklace. Pete, handing over a sculpture made out of a ruptured cricket ball with a bail stuck through it. T Superbus, a mourning brooch made of plaited hair. Lucius Brazenose, a specially written poem. Thaddeus Trove, a tangle of string and coins labelled *Capitalism*. Julian Strange, a windbitten piece of salty wood in the shape of a snake. Magdalen Morse giggled as she laid down a perfect copper cast of a dead fish, and Mr. Wellbeloved, looking incomplete without Cyril, silently contributed an eighteenth-century etching of a hyena. And finally Dr. Green, relieved of his household cares, put down a standard chemist's bottle of pink pills marked *To Induce Melancholy*.

They paraded around the room until Madame Sélavy called them to a halt. She was wearing a gown of bright green silk and a turban of silver brocade. Pussykins the parrot stood on her shoulder, shedding the occasional feather. Phryne stood as Madame unstrung one of the gold chains from her own neck and dropped it over Phryne's head.

'For the treasure hunt,' said Madame in her gravelly voice. 'The best surrealist joke in the history of Queenscliff.'

'Canned chance!' remarked Pussykins.

Then they paraded out again, Laszlo, still tootling, following behind like a small and not very attick shepherd.

They had barely time to exclaim before they had more visitors. This time it was Miss Lavinia and Bridget.

They accepted tea and scones.

'Such good news,' said Miss Lavinia. 'I have had a letter from the lawyer who is handling Mrs. McNaster's estate. He has advanced me quite a lot of money, and we are going to Melbourne tomorrow to find me a nice little house. With a large garden. And trees in the street,' she added. 'And Bridget is going with me as my maid and companion. She likes dogs, too,' Miss Lavinia told Ruth. 'And we shall visit the pound and find one who really needs us.'

'I can think of several in Queenscliff,' said Ruth, remembering Hugh Collins' description of the starved guard dogs at the Ellis's yard. She told Miss Lavinia about them.

'I probably want a little dog, like that darling Gaston,' said Miss Lavinia. 'But I'll go down and see them tomorrow—no, the next day. Poor creatures! How glad I am that you shot that monster Jim Ellis.'

'Me too,' said Phryne. She was feeling fine. Lin Chung, he of the gentle, clever hands and astounding, skilled passion, would be here in her actual grasp tomorrow. She could wait. Just. And she had such a lot to tell him. In only a week she had acquired a new attendant, shot a monster and listened to a lot of fairy tales. It had been exciting, but it was other forms of excitement which Miss Fisher had in prospect. She had made plans; she had given instructions which she was sure would be carried out. As soon as he walked in the door, Lin Chung was Phryne's property.

The bed was made with her favourite green sheets. The window was properly curtained so that the early sun should not wake the sleepers. The refreshments were ordered and the beverages already cooling in the icebox. The inhabitants had been admonished that to interrupt Miss Phryne's idyll for anything short of fire would be punishable by her extreme displeasure.

As they were leaving, Phryne congratulated Bridget on her change of employment.

'Oh, it was nothing to rid the world of that oul' witch,' said Bridget affably.

Phryne shook her hand with as much animation as she could muster. Had this plump, red-cheeked, charming girl really meant what Phryne thought she had meant?

Phryne went upstairs and looked in vain in her room. She called to Dot in the shower, 'Dot, what became of that pillowcase I left on my table?'

From the steam Dot replied, 'Oh, it wasn't ours, Miss Phryne, it was the doctor's. I washed it out and dried it and gave it back yesterday.'

Phryne was silent.

Dot, hearing no reply, called anxiously over the roar of the shower, 'Was that all right, Miss?'

'Quite all right,' said Phryne. Well, it was gone. Evidence, perhaps, of an old woman being smothered—the staining of saliva and the marks of her teeth in the pillowcase. There was now no proof at all, and Mrs. McNaster was both unmissed and decently buried.

And I thought I had got through the week without a murder. Heigh-ho.

Phryne shrugged and let the matter go. Bridget was happy with Miss Lavinia, Miss Lavinia was happy with Bridget. Tomorrow, there would be Lin Chung.

Events would have to look after themselves, which, mostly, they did. She went downstairs for another drink.

Recipes

Impossible Pie

This an old *Woman's Weekly* recipe, and I always wonder if it was discovered by a very bored kitchen maid who wanted to see her boyfriend so, instead of performing all that stuff about 'creaming the butter and sugar', she just threw all the ingredients into a pie dish and—miraculously—it worked. Or maybe it was the work of a woman of enquiring mind who had time on her hands to experiment. And lots of hens.

> 1/2 cup plain flour
> 1 cup caster sugar
> 3/4 cup desiccated coconut
> 4 eggs
> vanilla
> 125 g butter, melted
> 1/2 cup flaked almonds
> 1 cup milk

Grease a deep pie dish and preheat the oven to 180 degrees.

Put all the ingredients except half the almonds and the milk in a bowl and mix well, then add the milk slowly and beat until you get a cake batter. Pour it into the pie dish, top with the with rest of the almonds. Bake for about 35 minutes. It miraculously turns itself into a spongy sort of layered coconut cake, lovely with stewed fruit and cream.

Potato Scones

> 1 cup self-raising flour
> pinch salt
> 1 tbsp butter or lard
> 1 cup mashed potatoes
> 1/2 cup milk

Rub flour, salt and butter together. Add potato and mix with milk to a soft dough. Cut into rounds and bake in a hot oven for 7 to 10 minutes.

Noyau Cocktail

Mix one jigger of noyau with one jigger of white rum. Fill up with pineapple juice and mint sprigs. Serve over ice.

Bibliography

Surrealism

Bohn, Willard, *The Rose of Surrealism*, State University of New York Press, Albany, 2002.

Brandon, Ruth, *Surreal Lives,* Macmillan, London, 1999.

Passeron, René, *Surrealism*, Terrail, Paris, 2001.

Tomkins, Calvin, *The World of Marcel Duchamp, 1887–1968*, Time-Life, Nederlands, 1973.

Waldberg, Patrick, *Surrealism*, Thames & Hudson, New York, 1985.

Queenscliff

Pamphlets and brochures produced by the Queenscliff Historical Society and Museum of Queenscliff, and especially the excellent and informative booklets, maps and DVDs of the Queenscliff Maritime Museum, whose timely aid, comprehensive knowledge and cups of coffee were much appreciated. A must if you are visiting Queenscliff. *The Enduring Rip* by Barry Hill, Melbourne University Press, Melbourne, 2004 was also useful.

Cinema

Blum, Daniel, *A Pictorial History of the Silver Screen*, Wattle Books, Feltham, Middlesex, 1982.

Cunningham, Stuart, *Featuring Australia: The Cinema of Charles Chauvel*, Allen & Unwin, Sydney, 1991.

Other

Fitzherbert, Margaret, *Liberal Women*, Federation Press, Sydney, 2004.

Fort, Charles, *Wild Talents*, Henry Holt & Co., New York, 1932.

Frazer, JG, *The Golden Bough*, Papermac, London, 1987.

Freeman, R Austin, *The Famous Cases of Dr. Thorndyke*, Hodder & Stoughton, London, 1929.

Hassell, Alan, *The Lure of Pirate Treasure* and Smith, Reagen, *A History of Buried Treasure* on www.pirates.com.

Hoare, Phillip, *Wilde's Last Stand*, Duckworth, London, 2000.

Kerr, Gary, *Of Men, Boats and Crayfish*, Mains'l Books, Portland, 2000.

Leyel, Mrs. CF and Hartley, Miss Olga, *The Gentle Art of Cookery*, Hogarth Press, London, 1925.

Martin, Thomas, *An Event Called Murder* (The Sexton Blake Library), Howard Baker, London, 1967.

Nichols, Beverley, *The Sweet and Twenties*, Weidenfeld & Nicolson, London,1958.

Nichols, Beverley, *Down the Kitchen Sink*, WH Allen, London, 1974.

Park, Ruth, *Pink Flannel*, Angus & Robertson, Sydney, 1955.

Pike, Andrew and Cooper, Ross, *Australian Film 1900–1977*, Oxford University Press, Melbourne, 1980.

Sabine, James (ed.), *A Century of Australian Cinema*, Heinemann, Melbourne, 1995.

Tatar, Maria (ed.), *The Annotated Classic Fairy Tales*, WW Norton, London, 2002.

Toklas, Alice B, *The Alice B Toklas Cookbook*, Wakefield Press, South Australia, 1995.

Yapp, Nick, *The 1920s (Getty Images)*, Konemann, Germany, 1998.

There are some lovely film websites. Google 'Australian film' and have fun! *Our Painted Daughters,* unfortunately, is lost. Only a few stills remain to remind us of a thoroughly vile and degenerate movie which, regrettably, we didn't get to see...The Miniaturist Meredith Phillips designed Phryne's new bathroom.